SORCERY AND SANDSTORMS

BOOK THREE

SORCERY AND STARDUST

SAMANTHA STORMFURY

Sorcery and Sandstorms

A slave.
A fire sorcerer.
A grumpy cyborg.

Book Three of the Weaver's War

Samantha Marshall

GLOSSARY OF TERMS

Want to know more about a specific character? You've come to the right place!

I keep a working Character Glossary for each of my worlds on my website.

Check it out here:

www.sliceofsammy.com/character-glossary/

For all those who have ever hit rock bottom ...
and climbed back out again.

ONE
FLARE

FLARE STARED AT THE KALEIDOSCOPE OF COLOURS SWIRLING IN THE BOTTOM OF his glass. Red, gold, amber; all flickering with hidden rainbows as the fire sputtered in the hearth. Beautiful and... empty. Already? He tipped the glass upside down to make sure and it slipped through nerveless fingers, bounced off the arm of his favourite chair and smashed on the floor at his feet.

Shit.

Flare rubbed his face and blinked bleary eyes at the dimly lit room. There were other glasses... somewhere. Or maybe it was time to stop pretending to be civilized and just swig straight from the bottle. He tilted his head and stared into the fireplace, contemplating the idea. Yeah, straight from the bottle would do just fine, as long as he could get to it.

Flare rolled to his feet, maintaining an upright position with willpower alone. His latest batch of firewhiskey, no more than a day old, stood in neat glass bottles along the liquor cabinet. Measuring the distance, he took a cautious step. Two. Now three... Ooh. Why was the room tilting like that? Flare threw out a hand and managed to catch hold of the back of a stool, gripping with white knuckled fingers.

Maybe some breathing exercises would help. He just had to stand still for a minute, close his eyes, cycle air in through his nose and out through his mouth. Repeat. Feeling hopeful, Flare cracked an eyelid and peered blearily around him. Nope, the wallpaper was still crawling. Damn. Since when was it so bright in his sitting room, anyway? Hadn't he turned off all the lights? Flare checked his hands in case he'd accidentally cast another drunken spell, but his fingers swam in and out of focus so quickly it was impossible to tell what they'd been doing while he was distracted. Still, the light was blue, and his fire magic was orange, which meant it had to be coming from somewhere else… and it was getting brighter. Careful not to disturb his fragile balance, Flare splayed one hand across the back of the stool and turned to look.

The room exploded.

Fire – *blue* fire – filled the room, washing over Flare's skin and wrapping him in unnatural warmth. The shockwave picked him up like a ragdoll, slamming him against the back wall and pinning his body in place. Flare choked for breath as the intense heat scoured his flesh, boiling the alcohol straight out of his blood. A furnace's roar filled his ears, building ever higher - until it disappeared, leaving him alone in sudden darkness.

Flare slid down the wall and puked right there on the singed floor. His heart raced fit to burst, adrenaline and magic flooding his veins so that he trembled like a newborn. He retched again, and again, and *again*, until his stomach was empty and his throat burned. When at last it was over, he rolled to his back and stared into the inky blackness, gulping great mouthfuls of smoky air into his lungs and trying to make sense of what he'd just experienced.

When nobody leapt out to yell 'surprise!' - or to stab him - and a quick pinch of his forearm revealed that this was not, in fact, a dream, Flare dragged himself into a sitting position and set his back against the wall. The nausea had passed, leaving him with an acidic taste in his mouth, a pounding headache and disturbingly clear thought processes.

"That's one hell of a way to sober up," he muttered, rubbing both hands over his face. Stubble tickled his palms and Flare frowned. When had he last shaved? Gods knew. Taking a deep, ash-filled breath, he muttered a spell and a ball of fire flared to life in his palm.

The room was totally ruined; furniture incinerated and the floor and walls both fractured and scorched. Flare looked down at himself to check for injury, and – naked. Right. Naked and sober, but otherwise unharmed. He rubbed his face again. Considering the explosion had seen fit to burn his clothes right off his body and cremate his furniture, he could only imagine what would've happened had he not been a Class One fire sorcerer of unparalleled strength and skill and, by grace of that fact, fireproof.

But… what *had* happened?

His answer lay in the exact centre of the room, the origin of that initial blue spark which had so quickly become a blaze. Flare took one look and was instantly on his feet, careening down the stairs to the kitchen counter as fast as his wobbly legs would take him. He snatched up his personal communicator and tapped out a call sequence that after last week, he'd sworn never to use again.

Famous last words, apparently.

"What?" Lesce was pissed as hell, but at least she'd answered. "This better be good."

"Get here now."

There must've been something in his tone, because for once in her life, his youngest sister didn't argue. "Five minutes."

Five minutes. Enough time to grab a robe from the downstairs bedroom, flick on the artificial lights and rinse his mouth out with water before the inevitable knock on the townhouse's front door.

"That was four minutes," Flare said as he yanked the door open. Lesce swept inside in the same formal robes she'd worn earlier that day, though the tight knot of her plum coloured hair had lost several pins and now listed sideways. Flare frowned down at his diminutive sister, noting the shadows under her eyes. "You look like shit."

Lesce raised a brow at that, giving Flare a pointed once over. "You've seen better days yourself. Sober for once?"

Biting back his pithy retort, Flare grabbed her wrist and tugged Lesce up the stairs. "I need to show you something."

"The last thing I need is a tour of your den of debauchery at this time of -" Lesce gasped as he dragged her into the scorched, almost empty sitting room. "Great Gods of Sorcen, is that what I think it is?"

"Yeah." Flare stared at the star shape permanently burnt into his floorboards, then at the object in the centre. "Arcana's leather satchel."

Lesce stood in silence for a long minute, then crossed the room to scoop the bag up in both hands. She stroked short, capable fingers over the worn surface and sighed. "Is she dead, then?"

Flare thought back to the last holovid he'd received, the plans Arcana had detailed. He should have shared the holos – he knew he should – but they were his only moments of escape from the maelstrom of official torture his life had become and he coveted them like diamonds. "The mission was dangerous, but… no. She's alive."

"You seem certain."

"I am. If Arcana were dead, my oath would've gone dark, and if Fenris were dead, Taelon would be parading the victory around for all to see. If he's quiet, they're alive, but I don't think things went to plan." Flare chewed on the inside of his cheek, eyes on the leather satchel. "In fact, I think they need our help."

"And you deduced that from the arrival of a bag?"

"The arrival of that bag blew up my sitting room," he pointed out, ignoring her increasing temper. "And why else send it, if not as a message? Arcana needs us. I know it and despite that permanent frown, you know it too."

"Suppose for a moment I'm inclined to agree - what can we do?" Lesce whirled on Flare with eyes like gimlets. "We don't even know where they are."

"Then we look. We turn every stone in the gods-damned universe until we find them." Flare took a deep, shuddering breath and grabbed at the sudden ache in his chest. "Please, Lesce. I can't do this alone."

His sister's eyes unfocussed and Flare knew she was peering inside him with that invisible, unfathomable healing power. "Breogh above, what have you been *doing* to yourself? When did you last eat a proper meal?"

"I don't remember."

"Firewhiskey?"

"Too much."

"Fighting? Sparring," Lesce corrected, waving a hand that showed an innate contempt for the military which Flare had once been solely responsible for. "And using your magic to avoid overload?"

"Not enough. Not nearly enough." Maybe some time in the ring with a few of his generals would've helped, but that privilege had been given to another, along with his old title, when Flare had been shoved permanently into the Fire Elder position.

Lesce hesitated. "What of your... other pastime?"

Flare wasn't so far gone that he'd let her escape easily. He raised an eyebrow. "Wood whittling?"

"Mature as always." Lesce rolled her eyes. "When was the last time you achieved physical completion with a sexual partner?"

"Before Gravella died," he growled. That was the defining line; before and after the betrayal which had shredded what remained of his lonely soul. "And before you ask, no, I haven't been taking care of things myself. I've had no interest."

"I see." Lesce's eyes narrowed as they travelled the length of his body and back again. "All right, Flare. But this is for Arcana."

"Your sisterly affection is scintillating." He allowed Lesce to usher him back down the stairs to the spare bedroom he kept for his visitors. Rule one: never let anyone into your actual bedroom. Too intimate, too binding.

"There will be conditions," Lesce announced, waving him onto the bed.

"I'm listening." Flare shucked his robe and tried not to notice the sharp intake of breath as she appraised him with her external eyes as well as her internal ones. Maybe he should've showered and made an attempt to eat before she'd arrived – but then, it would have done little to hide the wastage of more than a month's worth of poor self-care.

Lesce shoved him onto the mattress and splayed one hand over his heart and the other over his navel. "The only way to find Arcana will be to get you offplanet, but there's no use sending a starved, depressed alcoholic off in a spaceship and hoping for the best. We need a plan."

Flare clenched his teeth as healing magic poured through his body like molten honey. "I'm not an alcoholic."

"The way I see it," Lesce continued as though he'd never spoken, "our best chance will be to get you onto Galactic Alliance Station as Sorcen's official ambassador. That way you'll have access to the entire Alliance's network of information – provided you're stealthy enough to utilise it without getting caught."

"Sorcen's already assigned an ambassador to the Alliance." He should know - he'd spent the last week listening to his fellow Elders bluster endlessly about it.

Lesce clicked her tongue at him. "I was there, remember? However, considering we've only just signed the paperwork and are yet to present our ambassador, it seems an opportune time to get you aboard without raising suspicion."

"Oh? Because I'm sure Liatris will love having her position swapped out for -"

"Quiet." Lesce's healing power rushed even faster through his veins, negating the ability to speak. "I seem to have a sudden recollection that Liatris' intergalactic vaccinations may not be up to date. If that's the case, she'll be detained for several weeks in order to have them updated and the new paperwork officiated, making her application obsolete. A different ambassador will need to go in her stead."

Flare fought the magic's cloying sweetness and glared up at her. "And?"

"In return for getting your worthless backside offplanet and dealing with the Council fallout, I want weekly updates and your promise to consider any suggestions I might have. This is Arcana's life, not a game."

Lesce paused for effect, her stare drilling into him even harder than her magic. "When you find her, I want to be the first to know."

"Done," Flare croaked. The flow of healing magic cut off and he gasped, his body arching off the bed. Energy flooded his cells as he settled, and he knew without looking that Lesce had erased all physical evidence of his self-neglect. "Thank you."

"I already told you; I'm not doing this for you," she snapped. "I don't want your thanks, Flare. I want results. You're a weapon, and I expect you to use any and every tool in your considerable arsenal to complete this mission."

Flare flinched – not from the intensity in Lesce's expression, but from what she was asking him to do. To become. His eyes skittered away, down the length of his healthy, tanned body to his left hand. Energised by the healing magic, the bright orange runes of his oath of allegiance burned with accusing brilliance. The oath of allegiance he had made, not to Sorcen but to Arcana, to the one and only being he knew without doubt he loved more than his own life. His hand curled into a fist and Flare felt his resolve harden along with it. He looked up to meet Lesce's steely gaze, managed to do so without flinching. They didn't agree on much – but in this, yes. In this he would yield. "On my honour, I swear I'll do whatever it takes."

It might have been his imagination, but he swore he saw Lesce's face soften for a fraction of a second. "Find our sister, Flare. You're the only one who can."

Flare curled his hand around her wrist and squeezed. "I will."

TWO
FENRIS

Cold. Blessed, blessed cold, at long last. Fenris filled his lungs to capacity, eyes wide and head tipped back as far as it would go, baring his throat in a moment of vulnerability his father would have scoffed at. It was worth it for the invigorating shivers that overtook his body as true night cloaked the desert and the temperature dropped.

Fenris stared at the sky as the stars appeared - not one at a time as in a conventional nightfall but all at once, as though a great hand had whisked away the curtain which separated the great dark from the world beneath. It was the one moment of the day that he truly looked forward to, and he understood the desperation of the heavens above. With night time lasting a mere two hours, the stars needed every moment they could get to shine.

It had taken only one night to realise the harpies – Hirapthans, they called themselves – feared the dark above all else. On the second night of captivity, he'd tested that theory by picking a fight with one of the guards. He'd allowed her to win, taken a solid blow to the head with the butt of a spear, and woken up tied to a thick wooden pole outside in the darkness as punishment.

Those first few moments of cool, soothing night had been the closest thing to paradise he'd achieved since the day Arcana had first smiled at him.

The third night, Fenris had repeated his actions, earnt a repeat punishment and discovered that nobody, no guard or slave or noble, dared so much as peek outside their shuttered windows during those two hours of darkness. Making them his, and his alone. He'd been prepared to receive a daily blow to the head just to earn his place on the stake, but the guards seemed to think he needed a prolonged lesson and in the weeks since, he'd been chained outside an hour before sunset and left until sometime after dawn.

Safe beneath the cloak of complete darkness, Fenris reached up to the metal collar at his neck. It was finger-thick, would have been heavy if he was as scrawny as the harpy males were, and had a groove running the circumference where the colours of his mistress were meant to be displayed. Given Arcana's unconfirmed status, that groove was currently empty and if the Empress kept her word, would remain so. All males wore a collar just like it, even those down here in the Pit, for a male without a collar was a dead one in Hiraptha.

Fenris wrapped his fingers around the chain connecting his collar to the stake and pulled. He flipped up and backwards, slithering out of the chest deep hole in which he was expected to stand, and landed in a crouch on top of the thick wood. His body protested the movement and he clenched his teeth as he waited for the sensation to pass. The meagre slave rations were beginning to take their toll, but there was little to be done - even if he was comfortable drinking the Hirapthans' blood, he'd had his teeth checked by enough prospective buyers in the last three weeks to know it was impossible they'd missed his elongated canines. He'd be the first and only suspect, and as a male, they wouldn't bother blinking twice before sentencing him to death.

Not that he was worried about that so much as whether he could nurse Arcana back to health after he razed the city to the ground. Physically, the wounds he'd sustained during his battle with Taelon had healed - yet another thing which had sapped his energy - but trapped in the Pit as a slave, he'd had little to no chance to learn anything about the world they were trapped upon, much less it's threats or medicines. Fenris sighed. Better to stay put for now, unless there was absolutely no other option.

The chain slid through his fingers like water, and he counted links until he reached the one he'd carefully split and bent back into shape that third night; a slice of time that seemed an eternity ago now. With little more effort than it took to untie a bow, he prised open the link and slipped free.

Free. Fenris considered the word as he tucked the short length of hanging chain back into the edge of his collar. He'd spent time as a prisoner in many a cell, but never had he been reduced to slavery before. Accepted it voluntarily, no less. He flexed his muscles, carefully testing each one, the cool night air a soothing balm to skin overloaded by sunshine. It had been a fool's bargain he'd struck in that paltry excuse for a desert oasis; his freedom for Arcana's life. Still, for all their barbaric behaviour towards the menfolk, the harpy women had accepted Arcana without question, ensconcing her in a luxurious rehabilitation facility and lavishing her with the attention of the so-called wise women who passed as physicians here.

Once she woke, they could formulate a plan, figure out where they were and how to escape this pitted, blistering pustule of a desertoid. Until then, Fenris was both literally and figuratively chained, slave to these Hirapthans as surely as he was slave to the knowledge that he couldn't leave Arcana, even if he had wanted to - the fledgling bond he'd unwittingly created when he'd taken blood from her wrist had seen to that. Even now, the physical distance between them was a constant, clawing ache in the depths of his gut, blending with the hunger pangs that had become his constant companion and reminding him with every passing moment of his own pigheaded stupidity. Left with no other option, he waited; enduring the endless streams of curious harpy females who came to stare, to check his teeth and run their hands over his body, snatching aside his loincloth as they willed it, sniffing his sweat and arguing over the curls in his hair.

Fenris hopped off the stake and adjusted said loincloth, long immune to the immodesty of such a garment - though he'd have given plenty for something to protect his backside from the endless, scouring sands. Sampling the air, he confirmed his solitude and strode to the edge of the Pit, fitting long fingers into minuscule crevices and beginning to climb.

Keeping male harpies in line was a simple thing. Without their wings, they were hobbled, and untold generations of ferocious behaviour and brainwashing meant they didn't even question when the women came to pluck their feathers. Coupled with malnourishment and hollow, delicate avian bones, it was nothing to keep them quiet. The new, the sick, the unwanted and the temporarily unclaimed came to the Pit and the questionable mercy of the Slave Matron, whose will was exerted through her handlers and guards and their ever-present spears. None ever tried to escape, which made the females arrogant and gave Fenris the perfect opportunity to move at will when the dark of night kept them quivering and praying in their homes. After all, when you assumed the only way in or out of the Pit was by air, nobody thought to watch the walls themselves.

Fenris' keen eyes picked out handholds that were otherwise imperceptible and he scaled the wall with a mixture of skill and preternatural speed, making up for his lack of flight with sheer muscle and determination. Voices floated down to him from the halfway house; no more than a hut built on a small ledge halfway up the side of the Pit. Fenris hauled himself onto that ledge and lay panting – silently, lest the harpies inside were listening to the night as he was listening to them in turn. He'd already begun to form a basic understanding of the Hirapthan language, using his knowledge of other tongues to search for patterns and match them to actions or items, but his grasp was loose at best.

From what he could make out, the two guards inside were discussing their mysterious new guest and whether she would ever wake. Her exotic slave was beautiful, and the Empress grew tired of waiting for the curious woman to heal. One theorised that their ruler would wait, the other believed the Empress should simply take the male for herself. After all, what was the point of being the top of the ladder if you did not simply take that which you fancied? Fenris stiffened as raucous female laughter broke out and was quickly smothered. As the guards began to utter quick prayers they believed would save them from the living beast that was the night, he gathered his hands and knees beneath him, lips pressed into a thin line. So far, Arcana had piqued the Empress' interest enough that she'd been willing to keep Fenris on hold. Now, it seemed, they were running out of time. If Arcana did not wake to explain their situation and make a claim on him soon, then - no. Best not to think of it.

Fenris rolled to his feet, stole past the hut's shuttered window and began the second half of his marathon climb, ignoring the way his body protested each movement. Arcana would claim his ownership; of that he had no doubt. She was strong, brave, intelligent and kind; everything a male could ask for in his mate. But whether she *wanted* to claim him? Well, that was another matter entirely. Fenris' chest contracted, the spike of pain so sharp that he paused, leaning his forehead against the almost sheer rock face until it eased. Pure, undiluted emotion burned inside him, mocking every moment he'd wasted, too caught up in his oath to tell her the truth.

Oh, he'd let her in, to a point. He'd kissed her and he'd wanted her, even if he didn't trust himself to have her. He'd bitten her, though not where custom demanded she deserved. He'd held her close and revelled in her heat, whilst keeping her just far enough away. Offended by her pain and the icy armour she'd encased herself in, he'd battered at those defences until they collapsed. When her personal demons had reared their ugly heads, he'd fought them by her side, and in return Arcana had graced him with the full breadth of her trust.

Even then, he hadn't told her what she was to him, what she meant for his parched heart. Hadn't even dared admit it to himself until the furious energy of the portal was tearing her apart before his very eyes. He should have tried harder, given more, been better. Now she slept, as she had for weeks, and if she never woke... *no.* Fenris bared his teeth in the pitch dark and slowly began to climb again.

Arcana would wake. She had to.

The top of the Pit was a crisp, clear right angle and Fenris winced as he dragged his wasting limbs over the lip, resting on the ground for a moment before he raised his head. Four neat, tiny cloven hooves drifted into view, stepping gracefully without ever touching the sandy earth.

"You look like shit," Caelum announced.

Fenris snorted softly, eyes still on the inch of clear space between the deerken's hooves and the sandy earth. "I feel it, brother." He gathered his legs beneath him and pushed upright, wincing at the twinge in both knees. "How is she?"

"Whoa, big guy, take it easy." Caelum shot forward as he toppled, and Fenris did something rare - he collapsed across the deerken and surrendered his full weight. They stood like that for some minutes, until he gathered the stamina to straighten his legs again. At full height, he was a fraction over seven feet tall and Caelum, who was big even amongst his own kind, stood with the top of his head on a level with Fenris' nose. The deerken's immense antler rack spread out above and beside him and was currently dusted with a sun-kissed golden tint and a handful of spiny succulent leaves. Black eyes that glittered with a whole galaxy's worth of stars watched Fenris with concern as Caelum said, "You're really not okay, are you?"

"Forget it," he grunted, allowing himself a final, comforting rub of the soft silver fur along Caelum's jaw. "Tell me about Arcana."

Caelum sighed and rolled both shoulders in a shrug. "The burns have faded for the most part, and her skin's lost that awful translucency it had. Whatever herbal brews they're managing to slide down her throat appear to be working."

"And still she sleeps."

"Yup. I'm betting that whatever the portal did to her insides was far worse than the outsides."

Fenris tilted his head to one side, considering. "Physical or magical damage?"

"Magical." The answer was swift and sure, no doubt provided through the incomplete soulmerge that allowed Caelum to gain a glimmer of insight into Arcana's inner workings. "There's something else, too. As she heals, she feels... different."

"Different?"

"Yeah, like her body is changing. Or her energy is changing. Maybe both. She feels less what she was and more what she's becoming." A black tipped ear flickered with frustration. "That sounded ridiculous even before it came out of my mouth."

"There is no telling what the wild portal energy did." Fenris growled low in his throat, hands clenching to fists that trembled from the strain of his climb. "I need to see her."

"I know." Caelum's voice was as gentle as the nose he rubbed on Fenris' cheek. "But there are harpies everywhere in there. I can't find a way for you to get in and out unseen. And if they catch you..."

"I have not forgotten." He ran both hands through sweat damp hair and tamped his desperation for perhaps the millionth time. As it was, meeting Caelum here, at the very outside edge of his thirty-pace radius from Arcana, was a risk. Necessary for their sanity, but a risk nonetheless. "Do not fear, brother; I will not jeopardise her safety. I assume you're still trying to reach her through the soulmerge?"

"Yeah. I can feel her stirring sometimes," Caelum admitted, his voice turning distant. "As though she's trying to wake but can't. It's happening more often now, which I like to think is a good sign."

"Indeed." Fenris looked over Caelum's shoulder, where the multi-level building assigned to the wise women hulked in the dark, and then down at the multicoloured bracelet around his wrist. The harpies had tried several times to cut it free, but whether by virtue of the weave or Arcana's magic, the simple, braided strands remained undamaged. "If she's well, that is all that matters."

"There's something else, isn't there? I can hear it in your voice."

"Yes." He nodded once. "My strength is failing. Between the sun, the distance from Arcana, the lack of food and the energy I expended to heal, my body is beginning to turn upon itself. I doubt I'll be able to scale the walls of the Pit tomorrow."

Caelum leant back to assess him with those ever-whirling eyes. "Can't you use the glamour to get extra food?"

"I almost wish I could." Fenris bared his teeth in a rictus grin. "But I need to maintain the eye contact and as soon as it is broken, they will know what I've done - and that is assuming I can catch a singular guard alone. The risk far outweighs the possible reward when you consider that being caught would ensure Arcana's swift death."

"Yeah, okay, maybe not." Again that ear flickered in frustration. "I hate being at a disadvantage."

Fenris snorted. "*You* are not at a disadvantage."

Contrary to how they treated their males, to the Hirapthans, animals were sacred. The desert-hardy jinra, an intriguing creature somewhere between a goat and a pony, were allowed to wander through towns and properties at will. It was forbidden to own, restrain, hurt or even ride one. Some mistresses beat their slaves for so little as daring to look in a jinra's direction. As a beast himself, and a talking one no less, Caelum was given a freedom that bordered on worshipful. Though part of Fenris chafed at the hypocrisy, the majority of him was grateful - Caelum's obvious attachment to Arcana was one of the main reasons the Empress had ordered no expense be spared on her treatment, and her slave placed in holding until she awoke.

Caelum dipped his head in sorrow, nudging Fenris' ribcage. "I'm sorry. These women are barbaric."

"You do not know the half of it – and neither, I fear, do I," Fenris murmured. "Today alone I had four separate nobles come to inspect me. I can still feel the shadow of their fingers on my flesh."

"Still?" Caelum bristled. "I thought it was clear that you're taken."

"Not if Arcana dies," Fenris replied grimly. "I also heard mention that there are other ways I may be procured. If Arcana is not accepted into Hirapthan society, her rights to me are forfeited."

"And if she is, they can still issue a formal challenge for you." Caelum grimaced. "I heard that myself."

"Your understanding of the language continues to grow?"

"Yeah, it gets better every day. I don't know where the skill came from but I'm willing to bet it's something to do with Arcana and the soul-merge." Caelum tilted his head to one side. "Not gonna lie; the ability to jump would've been better."

"Agreed." Fenris looked up at the stars and sighed. They had tried, in the early weeks, to master that skill, but Caelum had made exactly zero progress and finally they'd given up, focussing instead on the more immediate goal of survival. "I must go, brother. It will begin to lighten soon."

"All right. I'll be back tomorrow night but if you don't show I'll know it's because you're not up to it." Caelum paused, the starlight shimmering across his silver-grey fur. "When she wakes... this is only going to get worse. You know that, right?"

"Yes," Fenris whispered, "I know. I only pray that between us, we have the strength to survive."

"I believe we do." The deerken was silent a moment, then he butted at Fenris with his nose. "Go, before they miss you. Someone will want to weigh your balls before too long."

Fenris winced, the joke too accurate to earn a laugh. "I hope to see you tomorrow."

"Me too." Caelum nudged him a final time and faded backwards into the darkness.

Fenris watched the deerken disappear around the curve of a building, then slithered back over the edge of the Pit and half climbed, half slid to the bottom. His very bones ached by the time it was done but he dared not rest; every minute counted now, for dawn came as quickly as the night. He limped back to his stake, fishing the free length of chain out of his collar as he went. Fenris had barely reattached himself when the sky began to lighten, and he slipped into the hollow at the base of the pillar as the stars faded into the bright light of morning, illuminating the environment which had been his home for the last few weeks.

The Pit was a combination of natural formation and slave labour. Roughly teardrop in shape, the deepest section housed the thick stakes where Fenris was chained, and in front of that the ramshackle wooden sheds where the rest of the slaves were chained after curfew. A sturdier stone building squatted at the narrow end of the compound and housed the Slave Matron's facilities, off the side of which were a trio of holding pens and the sort of high-railed yard one might use to break a wild animal for riding.

Fenris yawned, the familiar lethargy that always accompanied daytime stealing over his body. How wonderful it would be to close his eyes and rest, even if only for an hour. He cut a glance in the direction of the nearest guard hut and tried to estimate how long it would take before they finished their morning prayers and ventured outside. It would be foolish to let the harpies catch him unaware, but his eyelids were insufferably heavy. Perhaps, if he simply rested against the stake and let them drift closed, just for a moment?

Yes, he told himself, his body sagging. Just for a moment.

THREE
ARCANA

Blue energy stretched endlessly in every direction. Arcana floated without anchor, her essence swirling and dipping amongst roiling clouds of cerulean without ever truly being part of it. There was no sound, no temperature, no up and no down; simply the eternal brilliance of the portal dimension.

My child, are you well?

The Weaver's voice that was not a voice thrummed through Arcana's spirit, filling her mind with an awareness of words having been spoken without the inconvenience of needing ears to hear them.

Well? If Arcana could have laughed, she would have. *I don't have a body. How could I be sick?*

The energy around her shifted and one of the myriad clouds pressed closer.

You are sad.

Of course I'm sad. She longed to feel the wind on her face, longed to flex her fingers and blink her eyes, the craving so strong as to be almost overwhelming. *I'm a prisoner.*

Your body was scorched from the inside out, child. You could not possibly inhabit it while it heals; your mind would not survive the agony intact. I do not seek to imprison you, only to help you.

I can hear Caelum calling. It was the same argument they'd been having for what seemed an eternity now. *He and Fenris need me.*

Your body needs more time. It has suffered too great a trauma.

Oh really? Arcana swept restlessly from side to side. *What traumas are they suffering while I'm in here waiting, blind and deaf and ignorant?*

Nothing that cannot be endured now and repaired later.

You don't sound certain. What have you done to them?

You attribute me with more influence than I am capable of in this state. I have done nothing, but likewise, I can prevent nothing. Healing you, hiding you from Taelon, has stretched my meagre energy to the limit.

Whilst I'm grateful for the physical healing, I'm tired of moving through my life feeling like a meat puppet tied to your celestial strings. Frustration coursed through Arcana's spirit and the nearby clouds sparked in response. *You've isolated me from my companions - who were injured in your name, I might add - and now you demand my trust without giving anything in return. Why should I listen, when you can't do so much as answer a few measly questions?*

The clouds rolled and roiled, the energy rippling from bright azure through deep indigo and back again.

Very well. I cannot guarantee answers, but you may ask.

Arcana was so astonished at the sudden change that it was a full minute before she could gather her wits, spitting out the first question that came to mind. *How long have I been here?*

In your time? A little over four weeks.

Four weeks?!

Your body suffered catastrophic damage. Not only must it be rebuilt, but altered to accept the changes I have wrought.

Changes? Arcana's temper sputtered, replaced by a curl of fear. *What changes?*

Be calm, my child. I -

I'm not your child!

The clouds froze, their edges turning jagged as shards of crystal before smoothing out one by one.

You are more my child than anyone else's. That has been the case since your soul was bound to Caelum's and your veins woven directly into the weave. You may have been birthed biologically to one mother and tied in soul to another, but the very essence of your makeup is mine.

Are you… Arcana paused, caught between losing the momentum of her argument and ensuring her assumptions were accurate. *Are you saying my magic is born directly of the weave? That's how I absorb different elements?*

Yes.

Arcana's thoughts stalled, her spirit frozen by that single, simple admission. Breogh above, she wasn't even really a sorceress of Sorcen anymore - hadn't been for fifty-two years. Surely, with such an admission, she should feel something? Rage, grief, hysteria? Instead, she merely sighed. *Great.*

No answer came, the clouds settling into what amounted to motionlessness in this liquid, not-quite place.

After what seemed an interminable wait, Arcana pushed her essence at the nearest cloud. *If I draw directly from the weave, why does the magic still follow the basic principles of sorcery I learnt as a child?* More silence, the clouds soft and still. *Are you still there?*

A tendril of cloud twitched, brushing over where Arcana imagined her cheek would be, if she had one.

Taelon visits me.

Arcana flinched from the agony in those words. *He's hurting you again, isn't he?*

It is necessary, if he wishes to keep me weak enough to prevent escape.

Necessary? Anger surged as memories of torn tapestry and Fenris' anguished expression filled Arcana's mind. *It's cruel and deranged.*

… Such has he become.

Arcana shivered. *Are we in danger?*

Not yet, but I must concentrate.

The Weaver's presence faded to almost nothing, and Arcana could only wait anxiously until she felt the other woman's weary, pained return. *He's gone?*

For now.

And you?

I do what I can.

Did he learn anything?

No.

Pride shimmered through the cloudscape, but alongside it, a dreadful weariness. In spite of the tension between them, Arcana ached at the Weaver's suffering. *I'm sorry we couldn't defeat Taelon when we faced him.*

There is no need for sorrow. Taelon is a formidable opponent, and what appears to be a defeat on the surface can be weighed against other, more subtle successes. Even the most carefully laid plans must bow before chance in the end.

Chance! So you're not all powerful after all, huh?

Far from it. I am certain Fenris has said as much.

He has, but he still thinks the sun shines out your ass. The barest flicker of humour made Arcana wish she could smile in return - at least, until she tried to move her facial muscles and was reminded all over again of her helplessness. *I'm not going to be crippled by these changes you're making, am I?*

I hope not.

Wait, what? Horror twisted her in knots. *Are you telling me that you've altered my body based on a guess?*

There was little choice. Your body was ill-equipped for the strain under which it was placed - a mistake which had to be rectified above all else.

Fury blasted through Arcana and for a moment, the blue energy around her wavered. *How dare you!*

Please. What I wrought was done in ignorance, that is true, but I cannot willingly consign the myriad layers of reality to death by warg. Would you have done otherwise, in my position?

Yeah. I'd have asked, Arcana muttered, but the words felt petty even as she spoke them. *How in the name of magic did you manage to alter my body without actually knowing what was happening?*

I had some of my consort's energy, hidden deep within. Were he here, Auron would know how to direct it, how to mould you appropriately, but such is not my talent. I could only gather his energy, wish upon it, and spend it on you.

A fool's chance, Arcana whispered. *A final act of desperation.*

Yes. And now, for better or worse, you carry within you the last of the other half of me.

I'm sorry for your loss. Truly, I am.

Thank you. Taelon believes he can replace the Keeper of Life, but my heart will always belong to Auron. No injury inflicted upon my body can ever exceed the agony of having my mate severed from me.

Something tells me Taelon's not likely to understand that.

He is beyond accepting and understanding many things. Whatever plagues the warg also plagues him, and it has stolen his ability to reason. The man you fought is not the same man who once laid his blade at my feet and swore fealty forevermore.

Arcana thought of Fenris, and felt a sharp pain where her chest should have been. *I have to go back.*

I know.

So you'll let me -

Not yet.

Not yet? Arcana's anger shuddered through the nearby clouds, so that they darkened as if to storm. She knew it was unfair, frustration born of fear and the inability to make her own decisions, and yet she couldn't quash the feelings. *When? When will you set me free?*

Soon.

FOUR
FLARE

TWIN METAL DOORS WHOOSHED OPEN, REVEALING A POLISHED BLACK FLOOR that sparkled with hundreds of tiny, hidden lights. Enormous, full-length windows displayed an equally impressive spacescape, giving Flare the impression of floating amongst the stars as he stepped through the doors and into the official council chambers for the Galactic Alliance.

A woman in a sun-gold mermaid gown turned from the window at his approach. Flare's initial perception of her being tall was punctured by the slit in her golden gown, revealing shapely calves and matching golden shoes whose platforms were at least a foot high. She was stick thin, with pale grey skin and an enormous beehive of amber hair atop her head which added an extra foot to her scant four feet of natural height. The Pscryllax met his gaze from all four of her golden eyes, which were tilted in towards each other at the innermost corners like the petals of a flower. "You must be Ambassador Flare Veritax. Welcome aboard Galactic Station."

"Chancellor Kaiora." Flare swept a flourishing bow that took his nose almost to his knees. "I am humbled to be in your presence."

"No comments on my unsurpassed beauty, Ambassador? I rather thought, from your reputation, you'd have led – how do you say – from the hip." Kaiora sashayed forwards, the corners of her lips curling in a way that said she was very much aware of the alluring swing of her backside.

Flare offered a simmering smile. "I would never seek to cheapen your intelligence nor tarnish the high honour of your esteemed position with such unimaginative comments, Chancellor."

"Oh ho." All four of Kaiora's eyes flicked upward at the corners as a smile blossomed across her face. "As dangerous as you are handsome. Very good, Ambassador."

"Thank you." Flare crossed to the window, deliberately shortening his stride to allow the Chancellor to keep up. His formal robes spread out behind him, black and gold and burgundy brocade that caught the shimmer of the fairy lights so that he seemed clothed in banked embers. A deeper red underrobe peeked out of dripping sleeves and a crossover neckline that displayed a fair amount of muscular chest, enhanced the natural bronze of his skin and provided an impressive backdrop for his thick, rose gold chain of office. The cavernous room in which he stood was a far cry from the sparring ring or the battlefield, but as Flare stared out at the blinking stars, he felt a whisper of anticipation in his gut. Arcana was out there somewhere and he was going to find her. The thought made his smile genuine as he said, "I'm looking forward to seeing what Sorcen can offer the Alliance – and what the Alliance can offer to us."

"Safety in numbers, certainly. Though you may find some traditionalists wary of your particular brand of warrior, I'm afraid." Chancellor Kaiora curled dainty fingers around the thin, almost invisible railing ringing the inner window. "There are many who wonder what your planet has to offer that we do not already claim."

"The glass cannon effect." He nodded, clasping his hands in front of him. "I'm not surprised."

Kaiora raised an eyebrow so thin Flare wondered if it were pencilled on. "Nor do you mince words, it seems."

"I'm a warrior myself, Chancellor. Flowery language has never been a skill in my repertoire." He turned to survey the empty room behind them. "In fact, I'm surprised there wasn't a bigger interrogation committee present for my arrival."

"Oh?" Kaiora remained facing the window. "I don't recall scheduling an interrogation today."

"I see." His robes swished over the floor and Flare knew – *knew* – that the Chancellor turned to watch him move, searching for answers to whatever questions burned inside her elaborately styled head. He reached the centre of the room and glanced over one shoulder, arching a brow as he met the woman's gaze. "Tomorrow, then?"

A sharp laugh startled out of the Chancellor, her face crinkling before she schooled her features into the picture of calm collectedness. "It is rather late, for the station, but I felt it necessary to welcome you properly. As for an interrogation, that will be at the discretion of the Ambassadorial Council meeting in the morning."

"What time in the morning?" Flare had known his arrival, nigh on midnight station time, would be a quiet one. He'd timed the shuttle trip for just that reason, to allow him some time to feel out the facility before being dropped feet first into political warfare.

"Four hours after official station-rise." Kaiora paused as though waiting for a protest, and Flare was gratified to see a pursing of the Chancellor's lips when he simply inclined his head in acknowledgment.

"I haven't been fortunate enough to see my quarters yet. I trust there will be some sort of alarm clock?"

Kaiora offered a thin smile. "Of course, but I'll send someone to fetch you for the first day. I wouldn't want you to get lost."

Indeed. Galactic Station was composed of a multitude of levels that were each as large as Sorca City and featured extensive training facilities, a shopping complex, an organic garden and several high brow bars and clubs in addition to the more practical features a space station of its size required. Flare had spent several hours familiarising himself with the station's blueprints to avoid the very disorientation that the Chancellor was no doubt relying upon.

He pasted a smile on his face that promised wicked things in the dark, and said, "Oh, I don't know, Chancellor. Some of the best discoveries happen when you get lost."

To her credit, the Chancellor only blinked once. "I look forward to seeing you in the council meeting, Ambassador. I truly do."

Flare bowed low and swept out. A robed and hooded servant waited at the door, turning to lead the way through corridors lit dimly to signify the 'night' – a necessity considering the station wasn't positioned near any one singular star but rather floated through a section of dead space in the exact centre of Alliance territory. Flare's quarters on the residential level were, as he'd predicted, towards the outer edges; a sign of Sorcen's current position within the Alliance's political hierarchy. Whilst his primary objective was to locate and rescue Arcana, both he and Lesce had readily agreed – for once – that the better Sorcen's standing within the Alliance, the easier it would be to find and retrieve their sister when the time came. Meaning that, for now and the foreseeable future, Flare had to play the game.

After demonstrating how to use the biological scanner outside his door, Flare's silent guide bowed and departed, leaving him alone in front of his quarters. With a glance up and down the empty corridor that was more habit than suspicion, he ducked inside. As soon as the door closed, Flare tugged off the velvet sash around his waist and shucked the heavy brocade outer robe, letting both puddle at his feet as he looked around. His rooms were well appointed, with the functional air of an up-market inn. Decorated in shades of beige and burgundy with splashes of cream, a cursory inspection revealed a bathroom off to one side, a bedroom more like a closet, of which the bed took up all but a few inches of floor space, and a rudimentary reception room with a tiny kitchenette and two stiff leather chaise lounges.

Flare's clothes had already been hung in the wardrobe and his other various belongings installed around the room – a courtesy which doubled as an opportunity to search his things and one Lesce had warned him about. He'd deliberately packed a random assortment of blush-inducing items from his house for just such a purpose, and chuckled when he found his pair of eight-inch black stilettos parked in the shoe rack next to sturdy combat boots and a loose-lidded box containing a collection of glittery cock rings. He hadn't used them in years, having discovered far more creative ways to amuse himself and his partners, but they'd function well for the rumour mill. Not even Lesce, for all her grimacing and eye rolling, had been able to protest that.

The question was, what now? Flare looked down at his red satin underrobe, tapped a foot in thought and then yanked a sleek, black velvet overrobe from the wardrobe and shrugged it on over the top. It secured at his waist with a thin red sash that tumbled down the front of one thigh and matched perfectly with the glimpses of red satin underneath. The robes swished and whispered across the floor as Flare stumped into the bathroom, snatched up a black eyeliner and swept thick lines across both bottom and top lids, followed by a smudge of charcoal shadowing for a smokier effect. It was a simple routine that made his carnelian eyes glitter with their own inner light and emphasised the smattering of bronze freckles across the bridge of his nose and his cheekbones. His hair was notoriously unruly and Flare allowed it to do as it wished, sticking up off his head in an asymmetrical arrangement of bright orange spikes and tufts.

Now, the only decision he had to make was which of the bars and clubs he'd visit to take the station's pulse. Flare considered his mental map as he strode out of his quarters and down the hall. The clubs and bars were all located in the market area, alongside a smattering of restaurants, cafes and specialty stores. Five minutes' worth of wandering and a short elevator ride later, he stepped onto a tiled concourse lined with potted shrubs and towering, well-lit facades. Affecting a casual, irreverent air, Flare examined the closed shopfronts and bustling late-night cafes in the immediate vicinity. No, not coffee at this time of night. He needed something stronger – though he'd promised to keep his wits about him, and he would. A bar, then? Flare eyed one such establishment as he passed it by and crinkled his nose. A good place to relax and chat with friends, but given he didn't have any, perhaps not.

Heavy, thumping drums trickled out of a violet-lit doorway a little further along, followed by strains of insistent music which all but begged to be danced to. Flare glanced up at the sign – Macadre – and ducked through the doorway. A black-clad mountain troll with skin in grey and brown shale stopped him with an upraised finger and a bio scanner. Flare waited while the device read his palm and the troll patted him down for weapons, then proceeded through the anteroom and into the club proper. Frosted glass doors slid wide to reveal a two-story building filled with sparkling lights, artificial smoke and that alluring music which had called him through the doorway. People of all shapes, sizes and species thronged on the dance floor and mingled on the mezzanine, where a well-appointed bar served colourful drinks in tall glasses.

After a longing look at the heavy, crushing mass of dancing bodies, Flare ascended the wide, shallow stairs that embraced the dance floor like a lover's arms and crossed the mezzanine to the bar. The multi-armed bartender waved one of his six appendages at the shelf behind him. "What'll it be?"

"What's good?" Flare asked.

"New here?" The male squinted at him in the half light and nodded. "Yeah, ain't seen your face before. Sweet or sour?"

"Sweet," Flare answered, watching as his glass was promptly filled with several layers of different coloured liquid. He scanned his palm to have the cost sent to his room and sauntered off to lean against the banister, sipping tentatively while he surveyed the dance floor below. *Faugh.* Sweet, indeed! Flare wrinkled his nose and swallowed what tasted suspiciously like liquid fairy floss. Too bad his latest batch of firewhiskey was to be saved as a gift for the welcoming banquet tomorrow night - it'd be far better than whatever made up the confection in his glass. Just as well he hadn't come to drown his sorrows; he'd likely die of sugar poisoning first.

"Awful, isn't it?" Said a voice near his left ear. Flare looked up, and up, and up – into the face of an absurdly tall woman who appeared to be made entirely of branches. She spread full lips in a smile that showed neat rows of stumpy, bark coloured teeth. "They gave me one on my first day, too."

"Is it that obvious?" Flare dredged up a disarming grin just this side of bitter and offered his hand in the warrior's way. "Flare."

The tall woman raised a mossy brow at his arm before stroking her long, twiggy fingers gently along the inside of his wrist. "Just Flare?"

"It's done me well enough so far." He shrugged a casual shoulder as the woman offered her own wrist. He repeated the gesture she'd demonstrated, marvelling at the smooth warmth to her woodgrain flesh. "And you are?"

"Priestess Alyssenia Lessietta Cavarronne, Ambassador for Karrjhan." Eyelashes dotted with miniscule white flowers lowered coquettishly. "You may call me Lysse."

"Lysse," Flare repeated. Once upon a time he'd have already been salivating, eager to explore the possibilities of this intriguing woman - but with Gravella's betrayal, that spark of curiosity had been extinguished. He looked back down at his fairy floss drink, where layers of pink and purple and blue mixed gelatinously together. All the tools, Lesce had said. Whatever it took – not just for Sorcen, but for his sister. Right. Flare allowed the corner of his lip to quirk; a tad bitter, but he knew his own body well enough to make it work. He lowered his lashes slightly, giving the other woman a smouldering look made more intense by the smudged makeup, and said, "It suits you better than all those fancy titles."

Lysse smiled and leant on the balcony beside him, a calculatedly casual gesture that was given away by the way her fingers wound together. She wore a flowing mint gown composed of many light layers, secured in place by a jewelled brooch at one shoulder. The artificial smoke curled through the fern fronds of her hair and hugged her lithe figure, giving her an ethereal air that was both compelling and fascinating. Deliberately dropping his guard, Flare drew a deep breath of her floral perfume and waited. Nausea curled in the pit of his stomach, strong enough he had to clench his teeth to keep the bile down.

Damn. Bad boy it was, then.

"So how long are you here on Alliance Station?" Lysse asked, her eyes on the dancers below.

"As long as it takes." Rule two: honesty. Making up weird shit was not only too hard, but almost impossible to remember later. "I love my people, but damn if I didn't need a break."

"You may not find it here." Lysse fluttered her eyelashes again, setting the tiny blossoms waving. "The station is a veritable smorgasbord of kindling. It takes little to ignite a blaze."

Flare smirked. Of course, for a creature made of wood, what could be worse than an open flame? "Lucky I'm fireproof."

"There you are, Priestess." An ebony skinned man with astonishing muscle tone and yellow snake eyes draped an arm around Lysse's shoulders. If the gesture alone wasn't possessive enough, the look he shot Flare certainly was. "Drakkone's getting into trouble again. You know how she only listens to you."

Lysse sighed with genuine frustration and turned to Flare. "It's been a pleasure," she murmured, tucking a folded piece of paper into his hand. "I hope we meet again soon."

She straightened and stalked away, her diaphanous gown billowing around her. Flare saluted her male companion with the paper clearly visible between his fingers, grinning viciously as the other frowned and turned away. When they were both out of sight, he had a brief look at the note – a room number – and slipped it inside his robe. Barely had he finished the motion when a pair of identical women in shimmering white fairy wings and far too much glitter appeared either side of him, smiling wide enough to display pointed teeth.

And so it began. For the next few hours Flare flirted his way across the mezzanine, a brooding mystery in black who drew both male and female characters - and a few in between - with his intense expression and bitter-edged smile. At four in the morning, the bar closed, and he made his way slowly down the stairs with a veritable goldmine of gossip and sixteen written offers of company tucked into his robes. It was an unusual feeling, to have mingled and smiled and traded steamy glances without any intention of following through. He felt... dirty somehow, dishonest in a way that had never happened before. Flare frowned as he stepped onto the concourse, quiet but for the few other patrons who'd taken their time leaving. Apart from the lurid cocktail with which he'd started, he'd had only water to drink - and while his body appreciated the deviation from his usual firewhiskey diet, walking back to his quarters sober meant the ghosts of his past shoved from the shadows to occupy prime thinking space inside his brain.

Gravella. What a mess. Every time he closed his eyes, he saw the moment she turned on his sister with words of hatred that had been brewing for decades. That moment had been like having an adhesive bandage torn from raw skin; the woman he'd believed had changed, whose intentions in securing his assistance had been honourable and professional, exposed as no more than a jealous bitch willing to use any means necessary to trample Arcana into the dirt. Including, but not limited to: luring Flare to her house, pumping him for information in the name of intellectual research, taking advantage of his generosity and, yes, his loneliness. Like a trusting idiot, he'd fallen for it, not bothering to look beneath the surface and believing his 'I don't do relationships' speech would keep him safe, the way it had always kept him safe. In a way, it *had* kept him safe - but not Arcana. Great gods of Sorcen, he'd never forget the look on his sister's face when Gravella's venomous personality had surfaced, leaving Flare with the sudden and horrific realisation that he'd been neatly manipulated onto Gravella's side of the fence as nothing more than a tool for revenge. It was that betrayal which had not only caused him to swear an oath of allegiance to Arcana, but had ignited the flame of self-loathing which barrel-loads of firewhiskey and endless sleepless nights had been unable to extinguish.

Flare's feet carried him blindly through the corridor, with no other desire than to get away from his rooms and the empty bed which would only make the nightmares worse. He clenched his fists, wishing in vain that he could dismiss both the nightmares and the endless gossip surrounding him. The short but decisive display of public affection Gravella had indulged in right before her death had led the general public to believe they'd been legitimately involved, and had resulted in both pity and an extraordinarily large amount of comfort offers which made him feel sick to his soul. Hard on the heels of that had been Lesce and - no. Best not to think about *that* particular sister right now. Flare pressed a hand to his hollow gut and swallowed a bitter laugh. Ironic, really; the sister he craved, lost, while the sister who hated him beyond all measure breathed down his neck like a hungry dragon.

A wide glass door slid aside and Flare stepped into a humid wonderland. Greenery everywhere – to call it a garden would have been a gross injustice. It was a lagoon, a jungle, a greenhouse, an oasis created purely to provide Galactic Station with oxygen. He moved forward wide-eyed, head craned back to take in the sheer enormity of the undergrowth. How his legs had known to wander here Flare had no idea, but he knew better than to look a gift horse in the mouth, allowing ferns and foliage to swallow him whole. Steam curled between the branches, greenery caressed his skin and clothes and condensation stuck to every available surface. His velvet robes were sodden within minutes and his dark makeup streamed down his face but there was a lightness in his heart; not a true alleviation of despair but rather a smooth surface upon which to lay that burden temporarily and simply exist in the moment.

Flare dropped down in the shadow of a broad-leafed bush and tucked his arms behind his head, staring up at the veined greenery above. There were no councils here, no servants or well-wishers or greedy, reaching creatures who saw his body as a treat they could taste at will. No angry, accusing faces, no bottles of firewhiskey, and no judgement when he looked in the mirror. In fact, with the thick, warm air and blessed silence, it was the most peaceful he'd felt since Arcana had left Sorcen - and himself - far behind her. With that thought lingering in his mind, Flare fell instantly and totally asleep.

FIVE
FENRIS

Fenris woke as the butt of a spear slammed into his jaw, forcing his head backwards into the wooden pillar. He raised both hands to clutch at his face, then froze as sharp metal pricked his throat.

"Still," the guard holding the weapon commanded.

Fenris complied, and after a few heartbeats the spear retracted. He lowered his hands and lifted his lashes to discover the sun was well up, the promise of another excruciatingly hot day heavy in the air around him. How long had he slept?

A second guard unlatched his chain from the pillar, tugging imperiously on the end. "Come."

If Fenris were any other slave, he'd be dragged out by the collar, but the harpies had discovered early on they didn't have the strength for such a feat; at least not without several more pairs of hands and a fair amount of effort that made them sweat and swear profusely. Refusing to admit their own weaknesses, they instead resorted to tugging his chain and, if he were too slow, jabbing with the tips of their spears until he either bled or obeyed.

Gathering his strength, Fenris crawled out of the hollow and allowed himself to be led across the compound to the holding pen. The first guard swung the wooden gate wide, the tip of her spear flickering in the bright sunlight as she gestured inside. "In."

He went, dropping onto a crude wooden bench as the second guard latched his chain to the stone wall of the building behind him. For now, he was in the shade, a blessing Fenris savoured from behind his carefully calm facade. It would have been nice to close his eyes a little longer but he didn't dare, knowing it would earn him yet more discipline from the butt of a nearby spear. If he got out of this hellish nightmare with his head in the same shape it started, he'd be very lucky indeed.

"Eat." A new female – shorter, younger – slid a bowl of boiled greens beneath the fence.

Fenris cupped the bowl in both hands, careful not to spill the tepid broth lurking at the bottom. The meal was barely a third of what he'd usually consume in a single sitting, let alone once a day, but there was nothing else but to make do. Keeping his movements slow and easy, he emptied it in two swallows and set the crude bowl aside. Yet another harpy arrived, clicking and twittering under her breath as she stepped close to fuss with his hair. It was too long by far, hanging in front of his eyes and brushing the base of his neck, but the harpies were fascinated by the colour and texture, and most particularly by the way it hung in soft curls. Every single female who'd come to appraise him so far had spent many minutes comparing the silky softness with their own hair, which was comprised of long, wispy strands with a featherlike vein in the centre.

In another situation Fenris may have returned the curiosity, admiring their delicate, avian bodies, or the way their feet were replaced by sure-footed talons that enabled superior balance and doubled as excellent weapons. It was too bad the women's faces were often pinched by cruelty and greed, their hands reaching or slapping or simply taking what they wanted with no thought for others involved. In contrast, the males stooped in hopeless submission, downy hair lank and skin drawn tight over too-frail bones.

"Up." A spear poked his leg in emphasis, and Fenris stood as the wooden gate to his pen once again swung open. Four additional guards strolled into the enclosure, armoured in heavy leather and carrying spears far more ornate than any he'd seen thus far. One of the slave handlers followed along behind, a sharp faced woman in a no-nonsense leather skirt and bustier which was the basis for all the women's clothing. Her downy mane was drawn back from her face by a strip of leather and she had a string of black and white beads braided into the fronds at one temple which, so far as Fenris had been able to determine, marked her status in society.

The handler gave Fenris a cursory glance and then tweeted something over her shoulder. Another female entered; reasonably young, with black-speckled grey feathers and enough strands of brightly coloured beads woven into her mane and looped around her neck that he knew immediately she was wealthy. She walked right up to Fenris, uncaring that he was head, shoulders and chest taller, and leant in close to sniff his skin. After a moment's thoughtful introspection, she stepped back and twittered at the handler.

Every single spear turned in his direction, one of them poking his ribs in warning as the handler yanked on his chain until he bent, putting their faces on a level. A slender finger tapped his chin. "Open."

Fenris opened his mouth, standing perfectly still as the handler pointed out his teeth, paying particular attention to the elongated canines which had become almost as big a fascination as his hair. The noblewoman blinked at the inside of his mouth for some moments, then the two harpies swapped some quick, terse banter which Fenris tried to follow to the best of his limited ability. Questions regarding his teeth, the fangs in particular... Oh. Poison. She was asking if he was venomous, like a snake.

Really?

"More." The handler tapped his top lip imperiously and Fenris curled it back to bare his fangs – a little too convincingly, for she dealt him a swift, backhanded blow which would likely have put a smaller male on the ground. Imagining what it might be like to tear the handler's throat out with the very teeth they were arguing over, Fenris forced himself to remain still as his fangs were prodded and poked at gum level. Neither woman was game to lay a finger over the pointed ends, which he found simultaneously amusing and frustrating. Even a drop of harpy blood, however unpalatable, would be sustenance of a kind... though, if these women were foolish enough to prick themselves on his fangs, it would be deemed his fault and punishment would be meted out accordingly.

The noblewoman at last twittered satisfaction, and the slave handler leant back. "Spread."

The amount of spears poking his flesh increased from one to four. After a heartbeat to ensure he wasn't stabbed by mistake, Fenris slid his legs further apart and raised both arms to shoulder height. Several pairs of raptor eyes glittered as he moved, and more than one female let out an appreciative whistle.

Maybe it wouldn't be so bad to kill them. Even weakened as he was, it would be less than a moment's effort to take a spear in each hand and return them, point first, to their owners. At least one of the other guards would have time to strike him, but if the spear burrowed deep enough, the harpy would have to let it go. And once they were disarmed, it would be only a short, bloodied minute before he could finish the lot of them and drink his fill.

The thought of warm blood trickling down his throat slapped Fenris back to reality - although harpy fingers trailing down his stomach might've also had something to do with it. He clenched his teeth as the noblewoman flipped his loincloth aside and took a long look at his genitals.

No matter the indignity, he had to restrain himself, at least until Arcana was awake. Caelum had informed him early on that there were armed guards around Arcana's bed night and day, waiting on the Empress' command. At the slightest misstep from Fenris, the sleeping sorceress' throat would be slit, the sheer number of harpies at her bedside negating Caelum's strength and skill.

So while he wanted nothing more than to slap the noblewoman's hand away, Fenris remained motionless while she stroked her fingers down his shaft and cupped both testicles as if weighing sacks of coins. It was a relief when the loincloth slipped back into place and she straightened with a soft clacking of beads.

The slave handler waved an imperious hand at the gate. "Out."

Fenris blinked. The command was such a deviation from the norm that at first he wasn't sure he'd heard correctly, but the spears pricking his lower back did not lie. The guard behind him unlatched his chain and let it run to full length, allowing him a foolish five pace leeway and a deadly amount of slack. Reminding himself of the spears prodding him from the rear, Fenris lowered his arms and ventured out into the blistering sunlight.

The high-railed corral they took him to had been set with a heaped pile of stone blocks. The noblewoman twittered at him, a detailed speech about strength and impression and... Fenris squinted at her in the heat. The Empress? His gaze raked the woman from head to toe, safe in the knowledge that nobody save Arcana could detect where his featureless eyes were actually looking. The harpy was dressed well, but not excessively so. She moved with authority and had the manner of someone used to being obeyed, but... no. She was nowhere near impressive enough to be the Empress. A handmaiden, perhaps?

"Lift." The handler pointed at the stone blocks and Fenris moved mechanically to obey.

Perhaps the noblewoman was not inspecting him for herself, but on behalf of her Empress? If the rumours he'd heard in the guard hut last night were correct, then it was more than possible. Fenris barely caught the grimace about to steal across his face, willing his brow back into an expression of calm.

If the Empress truly had grown tired of waiting for Arcana to wake, he'd have no choice but to fight. He wished, not for the first time, that he could speak with Caelum, or call his fellow Guardians to him through their blood bond. Having a sympathetic ear would go a long way to solidifying his thought processes, but the space inside him where his people rested was quiet, and Caelum was beyond his reach at the top of the Pit. For now, he was alone.

Fenris finished stacking the blocks and turned to see his audience gaping, realising too late this was the first time he'd hinted at being stronger than the average Hirapthan male. Again he fought the urge to grimace; his wits were well and truly addled if he was making mistakes of this magnitude. Still, it was too late now. He waited while the Empress' handmaiden blinked twice, regained her composure and squawked a demand.

The handler pointed at Fenris and then at the ground. "Drop."

He sank immediately to his knees, waiting with senses now sharpened by the adrenaline roaring through his veins, but no blows came. Instead, the handler made a frustrated sound in the back of her throat and turned to the nearest guard, snatching the woman's spear and twittering rapidly at her. The harpy moved a few paces closer, dropped to the ground and did several push ups.

Swallowing a sigh, Fenris began to copy the guard's demonstrations, allowing her to lead him through increasingly difficult exercises. He was careful not to move too fast, or to act with excessive surety, particularly now they'd seen a fraction of his strength. Once, keeping a lid on himself had been second nature, but time with Arcana had made him comfortable, wearing away at his rigid self-control - and Weaver damn him if he hadn't begun to enjoy it.

The slave handler tweeted a stop and the harpy guard struggled upright. Fenris rose slowly, keeping his movements as non-threatening as possible and his eyes downcast. The Empress' handmaiden eyed him critically, her golden eyes tracing the path of his sweat as it ran over his chest. He made no effort to control his laboured breathing, allowing the signs of his failing body to help spin the illusion of limits where usually there would be none. After a long, considering moment, the handmaiden spoke, her voice so low the syllables of her words ran together and made them impossible to understand.

The handler placed one clenched fist inside her opposite palm and accorded the handmaiden a short bow. "As it pleases."

A superior smile touched the handmaiden's lips, and then she removed a stoppered water skin from her belt and held it out in blatant offer. Fenris raised a questioning brow – a whippable offence - but the handmaiden simply nodded and mimed drinking. "For you."

He accepted the skin with trembling hands, popped the cork and sniffed. Water, clearer and purer than anything he'd yet been allowed, with strong herbal undertones. Another test? A trap? Or simply how the wealthier harpies chose to take their refreshments? After a long moment, Fenris set the skin to his lips and sipped. Bitter but not unpalatable, with distinct minty overtones. Conscious he walked a fine line between appeasing his audience or angering her, Fenris took three large swallows and then paused for breath.

"More," the handmaiden said. "All."

His hesitation must have been obvious because, once again, those spears pricked warningly against his flesh. Disliking the anticipatory expression on the handmaiden's pointed face, Fenris forced the skin back to his lips. The water was cool and his body was glad of it, but the handmaiden's smile became more predatory with every swallow, and he knew he'd been right. A test or a trap. The question was, which?

His knees wobbled on that thought and Fenris slithered bonelessly to the ground, hot sand scraping mercilessly over his naked flesh. One of the guards supported his head and a second caught the water skin as it slipped from his hands.

"Good," the handmaiden announced, her voice filled with satisfaction. The handler twittered a question which he loosely translated to 'what now' and the other female shrugged. "Wait and see." She turned to the guard with the water skin. "All gone?"

"No."

The handmaiden eyed him for a long moment, then nodded and waved an imperious hand in his direction. "He must have all of it."

The water skin pressed against his lower lip and Fenris tried to struggle, but his body was no longer his own. Cool liquid swirled down his throat and he swallowed instinctively, unable to protest as the remaining guards spreadeagled his body in the sand.

It should have been an awkward position but Fenris could feel nothing beyond the swift, all-encompassing lethargy of the herbs. Why put him through all those tests, then drug him? The tonic was so strong he couldn't so much as – oh. Now what was *that*? A faint sheen of sweat broke out across Fenris' brow. The tingling wave of heat which accompanied that sweat swept downward, causing his spine to jerk and his heart to lurch before pooling in his gut, churning and gathering until, beneath the laughable modesty of the loincloth, his body twitched.

All rational thought fled at the sensation, and horror curdled in Fenris' veins as the handmaiden crouched beside him. Her smile was coldly triumphant as she switched his loincloth out of the way to reveal a swiftly lengthening erection.

No.

Sweat trickled into Fenris' eyes but he lacked the facility to blink it away. His blood was burning, flooding downstairs in a frenzy that made him so hard it hurt. The handmaiden reached out a finger and stroked the length of his shaft from base to head, then spread one hand in blatant measure of his flesh. Fire scorched beneath her touch, a pain so intense tears blurred Fenris' vision and trickled down the side of his face.

Panic began to set in but even that was silent, his body completely and utterly beyond his control for the first time in over a century. The erection was a drug-induced falsehood but Fenris knew that wouldn't matter; any one of these females - perhaps all of them - could hop on board and ride themselves into oblivion, and there'd be nothing, *nothing*, that he could do to stop them.

He should have killed them when he had the chance. He should have gone for Arcana and taken her out of this place or died trying. He should have trusted himself to tell her the truth -

The handmaiden took hold of his testicles, her fingers sharp as knives against his overly sensitive skin. While Fenris screamed inside his head, she set about weighing and measuring each, no doubt to compare to her earlier impressions. Every touch flooded his veins with an agony so heavy it stole his breath and dragged him down, down, down into the vast well of unconsciousness.

The last thought Fenris had before he succumbed was that he would make sure to enjoy tearing their filthy throats out with his bare hands.

SIX

ARCANA

Arcana!

The Weaver's scream reverberated through the endless blue nothing, shaking Arcana's spirit like a doll.

What's going on?

Taelon is here. He knows that I severed Fenris' bond.

A chill pervaded Arcana's essence. *How?*

He used our blood oath to access my memories during a moment of fatigue. Jumbled images of your flight through the portal dimension surfaced before I was able to repel him.

So, first you can't cut Taelon off and now he's using your own blood link against you? Just what we need. Arcana swirled restlessly, trying to get her thoughts in order. *Does he know where we are?*

No, I managed to keep that from him, but he is now endeavouring to discover that information via other avenues.

Torture, you mean. The blue clouds contracted and Arcana retreated into the centre of what was fast becoming a suffocating space. *Take my strength. Push him back!*

I cannot.

Didn't you say I was made from the weave? You are the weave!

I create the weave and it is part of me, but I do not control the life upon it. I cannot broach the space between us in the way you demand, not even if we were blood linked. I must release you.

Arcana hesitated. Right up until a moment ago, she'd have given almost anything to be set free - but she couldn't ignore the other woman's pain. *What will become of you?*

Taelon cannot kill me, not if he wishes to achieve his true goal, but he is determined to break my soul open. I stand a better chance of resisting if I am not also -

She cut off, and the space around Arcana shrank alarmingly. *Is my body ready?*

Ready enough. Be warned, however, that I had to bury your power, lest the full force of your magic tear your freshly hewn form to pieces. It will return over time, but until then, you'll have access to merely a trickle.

Great Gods of Sorcen. If she'd had a stomach, it would have lurched. *How long?*

I cannot say... it was hastily done.

Of course it was. Arcana hissed a frustrated breath. *All this secrecy, and for what? For weeks you've avoided my questions and now it's too late, and I'm leaving with no more information than I had when I arrived.*

Forgive me... I thought… we had… more time.

Not like I have a choice, do I? Arcana made a conscious effort to steady her temper, and in response, the blue clouds surrounding her settled somewhat. *You've sent us where we need to be, and we'll solve whatever cryptic puzzle you've no doubt left for us to find.*

… I had to… if he guesses...

I know, I know. Arcana drew herself up as best she could, imbued her words with a confidence she didn't feel. *We'll come for you. I promise.*

… Tell Fenris…

Yes?

That I... am sorry.

I will. The clouds slipped and slithered, shrinking dramatically. Arcana shifted back from the void, fighting to keep her voice even. *Let me go, now. Focus on yourself.*

The clouds seized and for a moment she feared it was too late, but then the Weaver's voice whispered through her, so faint as to almost be imagined.

… Arcana… you have… all the tools... already...

Reality jerked, and with a curious whistling Arcana was flying, clouds and screams and wisps of darkness lashing at her spirit. A bright light loomed ahead and she slammed into it with enough force to shatter bones, if she'd had any.

Silence.

Arcana came to with a snap, filling her lungs with warm air and relishing the soft, silken sheets across her body. Her eyes flew open to see a many layered gauze canopy above, the long, draping strips wafting in a gentle breeze. She knew without looking that Caelum was nearby, his presence a comforting warmth on an internal radar she had never possessed before.

Unsure if her voice would work after so long silent, Arcana turned her head to see a broad, double arched doorway leading out onto a sandstone balcony. The sky was a piercing cobalt without so much as a hint of cloud, twin suns beating down on yellow bricks dotted with deep green plants and brightly coloured shade cloths. A soft smile creased her cheeks as she spotted the tip of Caelum's tail flickering back and forth, the rest of him hidden behind the wall.

Arcana raised trembling hands to her face, memories of blistered, blackened flesh crowding the surface of her thoughts. The Weaver had promised her body was healed but until she saw the proof herself, it was almost impossible to believe. Fear frissoned down her spine at the thought of whatever changes had been wrought, but a thorough examination of her person revealed a soft nightgown and a strange, pearlescent sheen that seemed to float just below the surface of her skin. Arcana grimaced, turning a hand back and forth. Just what she needed - to look even more different than before. Still, it was better than horns or a tail or an extra set of arms. Perhaps, if she was really lucky, the sheen was an after-effect of her healing and would fade as time went by.

Setting her hands behind her, Arcana dismissed the changes from her mind and pushed slowly into a sitting position. Her hair swung forward and she blinked to note it had been cut, and instead of brushing the base of her spine now barely reached past the line of her shoulders. She took a tangled hank in one hand and caught the scratchy evidence of melted hair, yet another reminder of her body burning up in the portal. Reminding herself firmly that it would grow back, Arcana let the knotted locks fall where they would and turned her attention outward.

The bed she reclined upon was vast, soft and decadent, carved from a mottled cream and brown wood. It sat in the exact centre of a room built from soft cream sandstone, each roughly hewn block separated by a darker mortar. The floor was also sandstone, though these blocks had been carefully smoothed and polished with barely a hair's breadth between them. Directly opposite the foot of the bed was a wooden door and to the left, the double archway that led towards the balcony, and Caelum.

Confident there were no surprises lurking in her sparse surrounds, Arcana flipped back the light blanket and set her feet on the floor. Her legs wobbled but held, her muscles burning in protest at the sudden use. After a moment to become accustomed to being upright, Arcana smoothed both hands down her borrowed nightgown and frowned. The soft, suedelike fabric clung to her curves and revealed more décolletage than she would normally be comfortable with. The skirts fell in waves from her hips, layers of thin suede that draped across the bed like sea foam at the shore. When she took a few tentative steps forward, the long train swished and dragged across the floor, making her feel like a fairytale virgin waiting to be ravaged by some hungry beast.

What in the name of boiling water *was* this place?

Only one way to find out. After several failed attempts to correct the neckline of the gown, Arcana gathered the skirts in her fist and made slow, careful progress towards the balcony.

"I thought I asked for - Arcana?" Caelum's head, followed quickly by his body, rushed into the chamber and within moments he barrelled into her, forcing Arcana to either throw her arms around his great neck or be knocked flat.

She chose his neck, wrapping him tight and burrowing her face into his fur. "Caelum," she whispered, uncaring that her voice was hoarse. Tears slid down her cheeks, glittering like diamonds where they landed on his short coat. "Great Gods of Sorcen, I've missed you."

"You have?" He pulled back far enough to give her a quizzical look, his black eyes swirling with a multitude of stars. "You've been asleep."

"I… well, yes and no."

"I think you should sit down." Black and silver lids lowered, then raised. "You feel all right, but you were asleep a long time. You might be delirious."

"What?" Arcana gave him an indignant shove that sent her toppling backwards onto the bed. "No, you furry goat! I'm fine."

"Furry *goat*?" He repeated, dropping to his knees so they were eye to eye. "Sounds like you. Looks like you. Must be you."

Choking out a half sob, half laugh, she hugged him again. With their faces pressed together and her fingers stroking his neck, Arcana recounted everything she could remember since falling through the portal.

"I know I've said this before, but Taelon's an asshole," Caelum muttered. "How much magic have you got?"

Worrying her lower lip between her teeth, Arcana closed her eyes and spread her senses out. She could feel the immense heat of the air, the steady pulse of the stone building. With concentration, she could pick up smaller signatures - the plants on the balcony, the leathery fabric of her nightgown. "It feels okay so far, but… we should probably test it."

"Try something simple," Caelum suggested.

Arcana opened her eyes and scooped up a potted succulent from the bedside table. Curling her fingers around the pot, she sent her magic into the leaves and pushed. Nothing happened. Frowning, she burrowed deeper, soaked up the soft rush of life inside the plant, and tried to bend it. Again, nothing. "Uh oh."

Caelum's black tipped ears flickered. "Try an actual spell?"

"I don't need to - okay, okay." Arcana made a face at his raised brows, then searched through her memory for something simple. "Rietta's Bloom, tenth level."

Caelum watched in silence as she transferred the pot to a one-handed grip and began drawing runes in the air. For a moment nothing seemed to happen but as Arcana muttered the spell under her breath, a faint green shimmer grew in the wake of her dancing finger. After a frozen moment in time, the plant's leaves twitched, curled in, and then opened again, revealing a singular flower bud on the tip of one spiny leaf.

"Great Gods of Sorcen," Caelum breathed. "You're almost completely useless."

Staring at her spectacular failure, Arcana swallowed heavily. "What are we going to do?"

"Well," Caelum drawled, "We could always tickle Taelon to death."

"Riiiight. I'm sure Fenris would love that idea."

The deerken's ears flickered. "Drown him in your cleavage?"

"Caelum!" She tried in vain to cover what could only be described as a heaving bosom. Considering she was in no way generously endowed, the designers of the nightgown needed either an award, or a strong lecture. "I wish I had my own clothes."

"They were burnt," Caelum returned, his tone causing goose bumps to raise long tracks across her skin. "Trust me when I say that was the most modest clothing option on offer."

"I don't think I want to know." Taking a long, steadying breath much the way she'd wished to for weeks, Arcana set down the pot and glanced around. "The Weaver said my magic would return in time, so I guess we just have to wait. Where's Fenris?"

Caelum's tail switched back and forth. "He's not here."

"I can see that." She waited, but the deerken said no more, his eyes shifting over her shoulder. Arcana's heart lurched. "What is it?"

"The portal spat us out in a desert," Caelum said at last. "You were unconscious and we could barely walk. We didn't get far before a raiding party found us."

"A raiding party?" She looked around with a frown. "We don't look like prisoners."

"I'm not. Your status is uncertain, but Fenris…"

Feeling her stomach knot, Arcana took firm hold of his jaw. "Tell me everything."

"This planet is ruled by harpies. More specifically, female harpies. There are males here but they are property only. Trophies, bought and sold and bartered for by the women who own them," Caelum said quietly. "In order to get you the medical treatment and shelter you needed, Fenris had to become a slave."

A slave.

The words were like hammers on her heart, and before Arcana realised what she was doing, she was on her feet, tripping over the long, ridiculous skirts of her nightgown as she headed for the door.

"No!" Caelum shoved in front of her, his face frantic. "You can't."

"What? Why not? He's a *slave*, Caelum!"

"Yes, and he's given up almost everything to keep you safe. Craddagh's Cauldron, up until yesterday you had armed guards around the bed."

Arcana paused. "Why did they leave?"

"They didn't." Caelum's ears flickered, and he lowered his voice. "They pulled back to the hallway yesterday afternoon, after saying Fenris was being relocated for further training."

"Relocated to where?" She couldn't stand it. Every cell in her body screamed for Fenris, for the sound of his voice and the comfort of his implacable strength. Firming her jaw, Arcana gripped her skirts in trembling fists and started forward again. "I have to find him."

"If you storm out there right now, without bothering to get the lay of the land and without your magic, you spit on his sacrifice," Caelum snapped, pushing against her with his broad chest. "For Sorcen's sake, you can barely stand! You'll get us all killed."

Bullied by his larger frame, Arcana stumbled back to the bed for the second time. Her knees shook treacherously as she lowered herself onto it, staring up at Caelum with a thundering heart. "But -"

"No buts. Will you shut up and listen, or not? We don't have long before -" He cut off and took a half step back as a sharp knock sounded on the chamber door. "Here they are."

There was the deep scraping of wood on wood, then the door swung open and a wizened old woman stumped through. Her skin was the colour of terracotta, her hair a fine white down that floated around her face like a mane. She was draped in ropes of woven gold and wore an embroidered leather skirt that fell to her knees. Her breasts were bared, painted with a bright gold and turquoise geometric design that extended up her neck and across part of her face. Her legs ended in bird's talons and feathers sprouted down the outside of her arms, also painted with turquoise and gold.

"You're awake," the harpy said, her voice buttery smooth in comparison to her weathered appearance. Several younger female harpies filed through the door, each wearing a simpler, two-piece leather outfit. Two carried long spears, fletched with feathers similar to the ones down their arms, and took up positions either side of the door. The third carried a large woven basket brimming with tools and brightly coloured glass bottles.

"Greetings." Arcana offered a tentative smile. "Thank you for looking after me. My name is Arcana."

"So, the male spoke truth. I am Beera'ketheen, wisest of the women. You may call me Beera," the harpy said, moving to the side of the bed and taking Arcana's wrist in her reedy fingers. "You healed faster than I thought for a wingless wonder."

"Thank you." Arcana winced as Beera pinched at her skin, looked over at her assistant and spoke rapidly in a language composed of squawks, tweets and clicks.

"Mirran'iketra will be in charge of your rehabilitation now the immediate threat is gone. Mirran for short," Beera said, gripping Arcana's chin and twisting her head to and fro. "I will arrange for food to arrive soon. What is the diet of your species? Meat, vegetable, grains?"

"Yes to all of those," Arcana replied.

"Good. Eat, for you will need your strength." Beera clapped her hands and the two guards by the door thudded the butts of their spears into the ground, turned and preceded her out.

"Beera," Arcana called as the wise woman reached the doorway.

The harpy flicked a glance back over her shoulder. "Yes?"

"Am I a prisoner?"

"No woman is ever a prisoner here." Beera's eyes narrowed. "You are a guest, but you will need to prove your worth to attain a position. Particularly if you want the male who claims to belong to you - many have already got their eyes on him."

Crushing the nausea in her gut, Arcana forced her expression into a quizzical frown. "When can I see him?"

"When you prove your worth," Beera repeated.

"Prove my worth?"

"Mirran will explain; I have better things to do." The wise woman nodded sharply and left, slamming the door closed behind her.

"Right," Arcana muttered, then glanced over her shoulder at Caelum. "Friendly."

"You haven't seen the half of it," he returned, then sighed and rolled his eyes as the remaining harpy in the room gasped and prostrated herself before his hooves. "You really don't have to do that."

"Most holiest of beasts, I am honoured -"

"Caelum," he snapped, "and get up. Now."

The harpy pushed upright, raptor eyes wide and face flushed. "Of course."

"Don't worry about Caelum, he's often grumpy." Arcana offered her gentlest smile and said, "Mirran, right?"

"Yes." Mirran spoke in a heavily accented voice, her face earnest. "Please excuse the wise woman, my lady. She is rude."

"She is rude," Arcana agreed dryly, and the other woman gasped and blushed.

"I have said wrong. I am still learning the speak. Beera *seem* rude, but is not..." Mirran waved a fine boned hand, the feathers on her arms fanning out to reveal a beautiful black and grey mottling across the surface.

"She's not intentionally rude? I find that hard to believe," Arcana snorted. When Mirran flinched away, she sighed. "I'm sorry. I've been sleeping a long time and I'm not entirely myself. May we start over?"

"As your wishes." Mirran tilted her head to one side, examining Arcana's face. "I am Mirran, wise woman beginning."

"I must admit that I know nothing of your customs. I don't understand what a wise woman is."

"I am here to treat you," Mirran said, flipping her feathery mane away from her face. Arcana admired the delicate strands, white tinged with grey and black to match her feathers. The colour contrasted beautifully with her peach coloured skin and golden eyes. "For the wounds."

"What of teaching?" Arcana asked. "Beera said you were in charge of my rehabilitation, and would explain how to prove my worth. I'd appreciate some other lessons on the nature of your society, too, if I'm to function here."

Mirran fell silent, digging through the large basket until she produced a blue bottle with a cork stopper. She procured a glass from the bedside table and decanted a small amount of amber liquid into it.

"Schooling better after healing," she said, offering the glass to Arcana. "Drink."

"No, thank you." Arcana leant back against the cushions with her arms crossed. "I'm grateful for your hospitality, but I'm not in the habit of consuming unknown drinks handed to me by someone I don't know or trust."

The harpy boggled. "Mirran is wise woman beginning! Always to trust wise woman."

"Do all wise women visit their patients in the company of armed guards?" When the harpy remained silent, Arcana set her hands beside her and made to push upright. "As I thought. If you can't even answer a question as simple as that, then there's no reason for me to waste my breath asking anything more. If you'll excuse me, I have a male to collect."

"No!" Mirran squawked, holding the glass closer with hands that suddenly trembled. "Not strong enough. Must wait, rest, drink."

"Really?" Arcana raised a brow, leaning further away from the glass. "I've woken in a strange place, separated from my companion, and now you think to command my behaviour? Beera said I wasn't a prisoner but I don't think I agree."

Mirran lowered the glass, shifting restlessly from one talon to the other. "Not prisoner, not free. Outsider." She hesitated, then lifted her chin. "Once entered the Citadel, there are only two choices: become Hiraptha or take the longsleep."

"I see. And the drink?"

"In glass is herbal extract to give strength and energy back." She held it out once more. "Mixed with ferment to taste better."

"Thank you." Arcana accepted the glass and drained it in one swift mouthful, the heat of the liquor warming her throat and stomach. "Now, why don't you start at the beginning?"

Mirran glanced at Caelum, and he nodded. She cleared her throat. "To become Hiraptha, must face the Gauntlet. Walk from one end to other. Simple seeming, but can be challenged by all comers. No rules. No limits. If reach other end, gain blessing of Goddess and can own males."

"I already have one."

"Forbidden," Mirran returned simply. "He is in Pit on Empress' mercy. Chance to walk Gauntlet and reclaim male will be given, but should you fail…"

"And if I prove my worth?" Arcana asked. "What then?"

"Status given, according to result. Becoming Hiraptha allows amount of males, amount of males kept defines permanent status." Mirran waved her hands vaguely, as though to shape her words better. "More males, more respect. More powerful."

"So… with only one male I'm seen as lower class?"

"Yes." Mirran nodded. "One male is low. No males is lowest."

"Do you have a male?"

"No. I am wise woman beginning. I have walked Gauntlet but may not choose males until finished." Mirran shrugged. "Wise women are different rules."

"Right." Arcana rubbed at her forehead. "To clarify, once I walk the Gauntlet, I'm safe?"

"Safe enough," Mirran replied. "Any can challenge but must be done formally. Before Gauntlet, may murder in sleep and nobody blinks."

Arcana stared at her, aghast. "Murdered in my sleep?"

"Not while ill. That brings dishonour," Mirran reassured her.

"How comforting." Arcana flicked Caelum a glance, but his expression was carefully blank.

A soft knock at the door preceded a harpy wheeling a laden food trolley. She accorded Mirran a short bow and they exchanged a quick series of squawks, clicks and gestures, then the serving woman left, closing the door behind her.

"Eat and grow strong." Mirran took a bowl from the tray and handed it to Arcana, along with a crude wooden fork. "Sorry. Spoons are all missing."

"I beg your pardon?"

"Someone has stolen all spoons," Mirran reiterated. "Kitchen vexed."

"Someone stole the *spoons*?" Arcana stared for a long moment, then turned to Caelum. "Really?"

"This is the first I've heard of it," he admitted. "I don't use spoons."

Mirran immediately prostrated herself. "Oh great and holiest of beasts -"

"Get up, Mirran."

Arcana choked back a laugh as the flushed harpy returned to her feet. "You really don't have to do that every time Caelum opens his mouth."

"He is sacred," Mirran replied, her voice hushed with awe. "Sacred beast who speaks sacred language of Goddess."

"He's just Caelum to me," Arcana answered, smiling. When Mirran boggled in astonishment, she sighed. "Never mind. I can handle soup with a fork - I think."

The soup contained floating chunks of meat and vegetable in a clear broth. It had been spiced so heavily that Arcana choked on the first mouthful, gladly accepting the glass of water Mirran offered.

"No good?" The harpy asked, her brow creased with concern.

Arcana fanned her mouth. "It's fine, just a little hot."

"Ah." Mirran rummaged in the basket and drew out a red glass bottle. "To fix?"

"Please." Arcana held the bowl out and the harpy droppered the tiniest amount of clear liquid into her soup. "Thank you."

"Stir first," Mirran warned.

Arcana did as she was told before taking a tentative mouthful. "Much better. What did you put in it?"

"Herbal extract." Mirran screwed up her face. "Add to elderly food as strong spices make them plik'thal."

"Plik'thal?"

"Shit themselves," the wise woman said.

Arcana choked on her soup a second time. "Okay, I'm going to let that one go. Thank you for easing the burden on my delicate taste buds, even if it's usually for the old people."

"Welcome." Mirran gave her an enquiring look. "Soon I will go."

"Before you leave, will you tell me about males?"

Mirran frowned in confusion. "What about males? You have one. He does not undress and perform as directed?"

"No! No, that's not what I meant. Tell me the rules regarding males," Arcana clarified.

"Ah. Not sure to answer." Mirran shrugged. "Mistresses choose rules for males."

"Surely there are some general guidelines," Arcana insisted. "Things I - or he - can and cannot do."

The harpy hesitated, biting her lip as she considered. "Males must always be collared. Unbound males shot on sight. Males always wear identification markings of mistress, or shot on sight. All wings must be clipped, or male shot. Mating males permitted certain exception, but if unaccompanied at any time, shot on sight. Non mating males return to pens by nightfall, or shot." Mirran spoke slowly, as though her words were the most basic of knowledge.

"What exception is granted to mating males? Why are they different?"

"Singular male of owner's choice may accompany Hiraptha by her will. Must wear collar but not always chained." Mirran gestured at the low neckline of Arcana's gown. "Also permitted chamber access for the releasing."

"Oh." Arcana fought a blush and failed miserably. "If I only have one male, is he a mating male by default?"

"No. He claimed your ownership as guardian. Term unfamiliar but exception was accorded until your vouching. Once have walked Gauntlet, you decide if he is mating male." Mirran tilted her head to one side. "Provided he is equipped."

Caelum snorted. "He's well and truly equipped, don't worry." Both women turned to stare at the deerken and he shrugged. "What? They put him in a loincloth, for Sorcen's sake."

Blinking rapidly at that mental image, Arcana turned back to Mirran. "Anything else?"

"Males not permitted to speak without invitation. Males has no names of own. To accord own name accords status as Hiraptha. Sometimes callings are given by mistresses, if more than one male to be told apart, but rare."

Arcana fought the urge to punch the smaller female, race from the room and go hunting for Fenris. "What happens to those who declare a male independent?"

"Highest sacrilege." Mirran's eyes turned down, as though she could stare into the centre of the planet. "Condemned by Goddess then sacrificed to the Brokkarra."

"You knew someone?"

"I am orphan. I know no-one. Declare love for males is foolish. Declare males equal is death." Mirran's fine downy hair stood up on end. "You rest. I return."

"If I offended you, I'm sorry," Arcana said gently.

The younger woman twittered under her breath as she jammed bottles and tools back in her basket. "You outsider. You no understand."

"That doesn't give me the right to hurt your feelings, even by accident."

Mirran grunted, hefted the basket and strutted to the door, where she used her curled talon to knock sharply. "I return two meals from now. Rest."

The door opened, giving Arcana a glimpse of two armed guards outside. Mirran swept through without so much as a backwards glance, squawking at the other women as she went. The door slammed shut and there was a dull thud as a bar fell into place.

Arcana shook her head, then glanced sideways at Caelum. "Not a prisoner, huh?"

SEVEN
FLARE

HE WOKE WHAT FELT LIKE AN INSTANT LATER, SITTING BOLT UPRIGHT IN THE damp grass. Humidity pasted his sodden robes to his skin and had his hair in matted clumps, but none of it mattered. Flare stretched and grinned at the green wonderland around him. For the first time in weeks, he'd slept without nightmares or the need for firewhiskey induced unconsciousness. Except... what time was it?

"Damn." Flare rolled to his feet and hurried through the enormous greenhouse, breathing a sigh of relief to discover the outer corridor was still dimmed for night. He hadn't slept overlong, then - just enough to put a spring in his step as he returned to his rooms.

The bio-scanner beeped him inside and Flare wasted no time shucking his wet clothes, kicking them into a pile with the formal robes he'd dropped before his trip to the club. The clock announced two hours before he was due at the meeting, which turned out to be the perfect amount of time to shower, dress in a black linen under-robe and a burgundy outer robe, and sit down to the breakfast tray which had appeared on his kitch-enette bench as if by magic. A little investigation revealed a hidden hatch in the wall and a discreet console that allowed him to order the next weeks' worth of meals, to be delivered at an allotted time or the touch of a button. Nice.

Flare prodded his fruit speckled porridge with a spoon, added a little honey and scooped some into his mouth. It was warm and soft, pleasant on his tongue, but his stomach was already protesting the idea of having to house something solid. Flare winced as he chewed, taking extra time on the fruit pieces before he swallowed, holding his food down with a combination of willpower and prayer. Healing magic might have repaired the immediate damage malnutrition and too much liquor had done to his body, but true recovery would take time.

Eyeballing the porridge as though it were a mortal enemy, Flare forced himself to take another tiny spoonful. Great Gods of Sorcen, he had an eating disorder! Add that to the list of his other instabilities and it was no wonder Lesce had gone easy on him. Flare swallowed, choked until the porridge went down his throat, and allowed himself a derisive snort. Who was he kidding? His youngest sister had an extra special stash of scorn just for him. She'd have found something to curl her lip at even if he'd answered the door in his finest clothing with a choir of angels to serenade her during the visit. Although if he was honest, now that he was sober, he had little respect for how badly he'd allowed his life to derail.

Whatever. No use sulking about it now; fractured or otherwise, he had a job to do. Several, really, and damn if that sweet burn of purpose didn't feel good. Flare straightened his spine and set his shoulders. He was the Fire Elder, representative for the Great God of the Flame, Firius the Everburning. He was a Class One fire sorcerer of unparalleled strength and skill, a prodigy among his generation who had come from nothing to lead Sorcen's armies as their First Flame. He was fireproof. Charming. Young. Strong - or at least, once he got his godsbedamned muscles back, he would be. There was no-one more ideally suited to strengthening Sorcen's position within the Galactic Alliance, nobody better to search for Arcana. Lesce, for all her expostulating, clearly agreed or she'd never have pulled the strings to get Flare offplanet in the first place.

No pressure, then.

Not that it mattered what his youngest sister thought. Flare snarled into his porridge. Lesce had made her opinions more than clear enough, and she carried her fair share of responsibility when it came to the firewhiskey lake in which he'd attempted to drown himself the last few months. Dim memories of screaming, smashing and burning rose in Flare's mind and he swallowed them with the same amount of determination as his breakfast. He wasn't ready to think about that argument, may never be ready to think about it. Better to concentrate on his immediate concerns - finding Arcana, wooing the Alliance, smashing Taelon's face in and protecting innocent lives from the warg.

Flare turned his military mind to Taelon's warg army and considered what he knew. So far, they'd gone out of their way to avoid the combined might of the Alliance, which meant one of two things: either Taelon was waiting for the appropriate time and battlefield to present itself, or he was going to try infiltrating the Alliance from the inside. Official banter – no doubt encouraged by the Alliance propaganda campaign – suggested that sheer numbers made the warg reluctant to attack, but after fighting them on Sorcen, Flare didn't believe that for a moment. No, Taelon was staying his hand on purpose and he was determined to find out why. Even if the knowledge didn't lead him directly to Arcana, it'd make the job of stopping Taelon that much easier when they did finally reconnect.

Which they would.

Something hadn't gone to plan, but Flare's active oath of loyalty was proof his middle sister was alive. Flare clenched his left hand into a fist and watched the bright orange runes of said oath flare to life. Making that vow to Arcana had been an impulsive decision that had quickly become the defining moment of his withered existence; without the twirling runes around his forearm and wrist to remind him there was something worth living for, he might not have bothered. Again the recollection of his fight with Lesce - *the* fight with Lesce - rose, and again he quashed them. He would never be anything but proud of Arcana, never regret the choice he'd made to put her above all else in his life... and he'd tear apart the universe to find her.

If he could manage to get through breakfast without vomiting, that is. Flare screwed up his face and swallowed another leaden mouthful. He could do this. He needed the energy, needed to prove to both Lesce and himself that he wasn't the complete and utter wreck of a man he appeared. He *would not* give in.

When a polite knock sounded at the door, Flare had managed most of the bowl of porridge and half a glass of fruit juice. His stomach rolled in protest at the sheer volume but he stoically ignored it, running a final eye over his reflection as he went to open the door. No makeup this time, no fancy brocade. He was going to this meeting as a warrior - and although his burgundy robe was made of fine fabric, it was also the colour of dried blood and would never be mistaken for overtly ostentatious.

Flare slapped his palm to the door panel and it swished aside, revealing the same guide who'd ferried him to his rooms the night before. The man's face was barely visible within his deep hood as he dipped his head politely and gestured along the hall. "Good morning, Ambassador. This way, if you please."

The corridors were lit for daytime now, a pleasant yellow-tinted glow that reminded Flare of lazy spring afternoons. He followed obediently behind his guide, comparing their path with his mental map of the station and using the steady pace to help settle his stomach. By the time they arrived in a round anteroom dominated by two enormous black doors, he felt almost normal.

"Ah, Ambassador. Welcome to Galactic Station." A short, rotund official bustled forward, smiling beneath a neatly trimmed beard. He proffered a datapad and bowed. "If you would?"

"Of course." Flare flattened his palm on the screen, waited for the bioscanner to beep a cheerful affirmative. As he lifted his hand, he caught a fleeting glimpse of a long list of names highlighted in green. "I appear to be running late."

"Oh no, Ambassador." The bearded man smiled. "You're right on time."

"I see," said Flare, and he did. "Thank you, mister...?"

"Harthax. Olivie Harthax."

"Pleased to meet you." Flare offered his arm. "I'm Flare."

Olivie stared down at his arm with a faintly mystified expression. "You do realise I'm just an administrative assistant, Ambassador?"

"I'm just a sorcerer," Flare shrugged. "And it's just Flare."

"Flare," Olivie repeated faintly, accepting the forearm grip with the same pressure one might apply to a severe burn. The round little man straightened his Alliance uniform, cleared his throat and gestured to the formidable black doors behind him. "Welcome to the Galactic Alliance."

Flare grinned and received the tiniest flicker of emotion in return. "Thanks. Wish me luck."

"Good luck," Olivie said, and palmed the door open.

The room was as he'd last seen it – black, lit by fairy lights and wholly open to the spacescape beyond the windows – only this time, the floor was stepped to create an amphitheatre. Flare entered at the ground level, with the talking space on his right and the stands on his left. Chancellor Kaiora stood in the centre of the room, her four eyes sharp and her auburn hair in the same beehive style as the night before. Instead of the gold mermaid gown, she wore a severe black powersuit with platformed heels that Flare estimated gave her an extra ten inches of height. The hum of conversation which had pervaded the room cut short and a sea of faces turned in his direction.

"Ambassador Veritax, how delightful to see you." The Chancellor extended a delicate hand. "Welcome."

"Flare," he corrected, offering a professional smile. "Veritax is my second name, but it's not a surname, and it's rather odious to boot." He took Kaiora's hand and bowed over the top of it, a sweeping motion he'd unashamedly stolen from Fenris. "I hope I'm not interrupting your speech, Chancellor."

"Not at all." Kaiora's smile was tight lipped. She turned to face the room and said, "Ambassador Flare from the planet Sorcen is new to our esteemed Alliance. I trust you will all bid him welcome."

Flare bowed again, earning a smattering of murmured greetings. He raked his eyes over the crowd, spotting several familiar faces from Macadre the night before, some of whom blushed beneath his brief regard. "I thank you for your hospitality. Sorcen is looking forward to becoming an active part of the Alliance."

"Perhaps you might elaborate on that whilst you have the floor," Kaiora invited. "Sorcen has remained staunchly autonomous for many years. There are a number of Ambassadors who are curious about your reasons for ending this solitary existence after such a long time."

"Because of the warg," Flare replied.

An uneasy murmur ran through the room, but the Chancellor merely raised a brow. "The warg?"

"Correct." Flare crossed both arms over his chest. "Sorcen recently repelled a full-scale invasion of our capital city which resulted in a tragic loss of life and the destruction of one of our five Towers. Once the initial chaos passed and our dead were buried, it was decided that if the warg are to be truly defeated, it would be best done with allies."

"So you lost a few dozen citizens and decided we'd be better cannon fodder instead?" A female voice called from up the back. Murmurs of agreement rolled across the room, though nobody else was game to speak up.

Flare eyeballed the approximate location of the speaker and gave a short, stiff bow. "The death toll from that invasion stands at two thousand, nine hundred and sixty-two, including two of our Elders. Far from a few dozen, my lady." When murmurs subsided into shocked silence, he cocked his head and smiled a predator's smile. "We estimate a similar amount of deceased warg."

The Chancellor frowned. "Only an estimate?"

"I'm afraid so. My younger sister dropped our Healing Tower on the bulk of the warg forces, so we've been unable to form an exact head count." He paused to let that sink in. "I may stand before you as the Fire Elder, but I am no bureaucrat. I commanded Sorcen's military for over fifty years and still maintain an active interest in the way it operates. Sorcen is asking for your assistance, yes, but we've also come to offer our own. Our sorcerers are a force to be reckoned with on any battlefield and we boast a sizable space fleet."

"A force to be reckoned with, you say?" A woman halfway up the stands got to her feet and Flare recognised Lysse, with her fronded hair and woodgrain skin. "How can that be, with such a catastrophic loss of life?"

Flare allowed his brows to shoot towards his hairline. "Large as the numbers may seem, Sorcen is currently one of only six planets in the last twenty years to survive a warg invasion, and one of only two who managed to repel said invasion without external aid. While I believe every life is precious, just shy of three thousand deaths is negligible when compared to the slaughter of billions."

"So many," Lysse murmured, her bark coloured skin blanching. "Surely those figures cannot be correct."

"They are," called a hard, male voice from the shadows. "The warg are not to be trifled with. If Sorcen was able to defend itself, it's warriors are of consummate skill."

"Of course." Lysse's blossom-framed eyes narrowed, but she gave a short nod. "There are those of us here who know little of sorcery. Perhaps a demonstration of your abilities might be in order?"

"I would love nothing more than to demonstrate my abilities for you, Priestess." Flare bowed in her direction and smiled, giving the expression a subtle bedroom edge. "I pray you find them to your satisfaction."

Lysse's gaze narrowed further, until she watched him from beneath the veil of her lashes. "Chancellor? Would such a display be permitted?"

"Within reason." Chancellor Kaiora took several steps backwards, waving Flare into the centre of the room. "Nothing that will endanger lives, Ambassador."

"Of course not." Flare spread his legs and sank into his knees, murmuring a quick mantra for calm as he visualised the spell to be cast. Hands to base chakra. Clasp fingers, raise to heart. Draw magic on the inhale, release one hand to trace the rune. Twist the hip, drop one knee, leading hand goes to ground whilst expelling energy on the exhale and... Flare slapped his palm against the floor with a loud crack. Fire burst from his hand, radiating outwards in a spherical shield which encased his entire body. He held it for a moment, then released the magic on a wave of crackling flames that spread outward from the leading edge of the shield as he straightened to full height.

All the lights went out.

Smirking in the whispering dark, Flare rolled his wrist and traced another rune in the air. He snapped his fingers to cue the spell and uttered a single, potent word of power. Orbs of flame flickered to life around the room, drifting through the air like fist sized fireflies and bringing the assembled faces of the Galactic Council back into view.

"I am a fire sorcerer," he announced, lifting both hands to make the floating fire dip and spin. "The first spell you saw was Flame Shield, sixth level. This is one of my own, far more complex and as yet unnamed." It was also a solid drain on his magic - particularly on such a large scale - but worthwhile for the effect. Flare clenched his fists and fire roared to life around his hands, trailing sparks as he pivoted through some basic punches and strikes. "Fire magic has a variety of applications. It is ideally suited to both defence and attack, can be used close or long range and has other, more practical applications as well." The fairy lights in the room began to wink back on and Flare let his floating flames die. "Sorcen boasts five general schools of magic: Fire, Earth, Water, Nature and Healing. Our sorcerers range in strength and some also boast interesting micro talents. We have a vast array of skills to contribute to the Alliance which I know is all in the information that was submitted upon our acceptance, but I am open to fielding any questions you may have."

The man who'd been seated beside Lysse stood, and Flare recognised the ebony skinned warrior who'd accompanied her at Macadre. He wore an animal skin toga that displayed impressive musculature and slammed the butt of a ceremonial spear on the ground, acid-yellow snake eyes fixed on Flare. "I want to see how you fight without the fancy smoke and mirrors."

"Ambassador Krowley, that is an entirely unorthodox suggestion," Chancellor Kaiora snapped.

Krowley shrugged. "Put it to vote. Show of hands by those in favour of seeing the pretty boy move."

An older man in a slick set of blue leathers stood with a growl. "You'd really sully the peaceful intent of this Alliance council by fostering violence? The man's offering his aid - surely even you can see that."

"It would be like you to run from a fight, Eyrton." Krowley grunted a laugh. "All bark and no bite."

"Chancellor, permission to escort Ambassador Krowley outside and pummel him senseless?" Eyrton crossed leanly muscled arms over a wiry chest.

"Absolutely not." Kaiora made a cutting motion with one hand, all four of her eyes narrowed to slits. "Sit down, both of you." Once the two men grudgingly complied, she turned to Flare. "My apologies, Ambassador."

"Don't worry about it." Flare shrugged and dug out an easygoing grin. "I can understand why Sorcen's past reluctance to join the Alliance would lead to suspicion. Shaking up our leadership has also led to a change in ideology and the Council of Elders now believe we stand a better chance of victory by sharing our resources with others, rather than hoarding them. As a gesture of our goodwill, I'd like to offer a contingent of both healers and warriors for Alliance starships."

The Chancellor's brows winged skyward. "So quickly?"

"The warg struck a fearsome blow to my people, Chancellor. We are eager to return the favour."

"Understandably so." Chancellor Kaiora's beehive bobbed as she nodded. "I shall have Mister Harthax garner some data for us to discuss at the next meeting." She looked into the stands. "If anyone wishes to object to the proposal, now is the time." Silence. Kaiora offered Flare a faint smile. "Very well, Ambassador, we will discuss this further next session. Until then, if you'd like to take a seat, we'll progress with the other matters on our schedule. Welcome to the Galactic Alliance."

Flare swept another low, flourishing bow. "Thank you, Chancellor and esteemed Ambassadors."

Kaiora ushered him to the nearest empty seat, then took the floor once more. She ran a tight ship, progressing through the meeting with little tolerance for deviation and stomping on several disagreements that could easily have evolved into full disputes. Flare learnt that many planets had two or even three Ambassadors who worked as a team and that, unlikely as it was, Lysse and Krowley were one such pairing. It helped to explain the sheer number of people packed into the room when there were only twenty-six systems in the Alliance – twenty-seven with the addition of Sorcen. Strength in numbers sounded appealing, but the amount of planets wielding warriors who'd be useful against the warg were slim enough to count on one hand.

The meeting progressed into a mind-numbing debate about trade and coin, complete with visual charts that popped up as holos in the middle of the floor. Though finances and logistics were nowhere near his area of expertise, Flare paid close attention and did some quick mental calcula-tions. The majority of the Galactic Alliance might be little more than cannon fodder, but they had enough collective financial influence to pay the small group of warlike planets to fight on their behalf. It was no wonder that Sorcen, rich in knowledge, supplies *and* warriors, had been welcomed with little protest.

As Chancellor Kaiora wrapped up the meeting with a particularly drool-worthy pie chart detailing grain stores lost in a flash flood on the verdant planet Xurdak, Flare decided he'd add a third option to Taelon's potential reasons not to attack the Alliance: they were literally no threat. Unless they were planning to bore the warg to death with graphs, of course.

Flare managed to conceal a yawn as the Ambassadors around him gained their feet and left. When he was no longer in danger of being trod on, he rolled upright and stretched. Chancellor Kaiora sashayed to his side, lips curved in a faint smile. "Well, Ambassador? What did you think?"

What did he *think*? That this whole farce was a gargantuan waste of time and money, with rich people pontificating pointlessly while out there in the greater galaxy, people were dying at the hands of the warg. Rather than say that out loud, however, Flare fixed a smile of about thirty percent strength on his face and inclined his head. "I think that the current Potentate of Pscryllax was very intelligent to let you head this eclectic organisation of planets."

"Flattery, at last?" Kaiora's head tilted to the one side. "Or a perceptive remark cloaked in charm?"

"Take your pick," Flare shrugged, amped his smile another ten percent. "What did you do to piss the Potentate off, anyway?"

The Chancellor barked a sharp laugh, her eyes tilting towards each other in the inner corners. "If you read your dossier - and I have no doubt you did - then you'd know I am his eldest cousin."

"And, therefore, the biggest threat to his throne."

"Perhaps." Kaiora inclined her head.

"The Potentate is nothing if not diplomatic. Perhaps he made you a different kind of throne, to keep you distracted?"

The Chancellor's face shuttered. "Whilst Pscryllax is one of the founding systems of the Galactic Alliance and contributes much to its financial might, to assume I have been placed here with impunity would be arrogant and foolish, Ambassador Flare."

"I meant no offence, Chancellor Kaiora," he returned, lifting her hand to brush his lips across her knuckles. "I'm merely attempting to ascertain the lay of the land, and how Sorcen might fit into such an eclectic landscape."

"Sorcen's ability to meld, fade, or rise depends entirely upon the finesse of its representative," Kaiora said, her voice chill as she retracted her hand. After sweeping a long, assessing glance over his body, she turned and strode away.

Flare watched her go, her gait graceful in spite of the enormous platforms of her shoes. He had, as she'd intimated, read the extensive dossier that all new planets received upon being granted entrance to the Galactic Alliance but he wasn't interested in prettily worded factoids or transcripts of sleek speeches. Truth wasn't found in the council chambers in the same way battles weren't won by kings or queens - it was the things unsaid, the people behind the scenes, who were key.

The council chamber had been empty for some minutes before Flare strode out through the enormous double doors and went looking for Olivie. After a swift lap of the room, he discovered a solid oak desk hidden behind a hefty potted plant.

"Olivie! There you are."

The administrator glanced up in surprise. "Ambassador Flare?"

"Must be some interesting data on that holo screen if you didn't see me coming," Flare said with forced cheer. "Doing well, I trust?"

"Nothing to complain about." Olivie removed wire-rimmed glasses from where they rested low on his nose and rubbed them on the breast of his jacket. "How can I be of service to you?"

"As interesting as today's session was, I find I'm at a disadvantage regarding the inner functionings of the Alliance on a day to day basis." Flare dredged a blazing smile from the depths of his soul and pasted it on his face. "Is there a way to access previous meeting minutes so I can catch up? I'd hate to waste everyone's time with useless questions."

"Of course, Ambassador." Olivie pursed his lips and tapped a few keys on his holoboard. "I shall have the information delivered to the console in your quarters."

Flare accorded the official a short bow. "Thank you, Olivie."

"Most welcome, Ambassador."

He waved away the title with an impatience that wasn't entirely feigned. "Please, call me Flare. The welcome banquet is tonight, am I correct?"

"You are indeed correct, Ambassador." Another few swift taps. "At precisely seven hours past the midday mark."

Flare raised an eyebrow. "Is that everyone's time, or just mine?"

"I'm certain I don't know what you mean, Ambassador, but the official time upon my console is a seventh hour commencement," Olivie said, folding his hands across his substantial girth. "Though perhaps you may like to know that the dress code is noted as formal."

"Formal," Flare echoed, then tossed a glance down at his robes. "Have I underdressed today?"

"What an Ambassador chooses to wear is at their own discretion," Olivie replied, his tone flat. "I wouldn't presume to comment."

"Right." Shaking his head, Flare flicked out a lazy salute and turned away. "Thanks, Olivie. Until next time."

"Ambassador." Olivie's voice stopped him half a step from the corridor.

"Yes?"

"Impressions mean a great deal here." The round man's eyes narrowed, as though Flare's blood coloured robe offended his gaze. "They may make or break your planet's reputation."

Ah. Flare tossed a grin over his shoulder. "Noted. Will you be at the banquet?"

"I will be at the door attending the guest list," Olivie nodded.

"You can tell me how well I've scrubbed up, then." He winked and strode off down the corridor while the official coughed and choked behind him.

Appearances, as always. Flare had the wild urge to kick the corridor wall, reined it in at the last moment. Damn this whole situation, right into Craddagh's Cauldron! He wanted to find Arcana, not dance to the tune of the Alliance's reedy pipe. Flare sighed. It would almost be worth the pain to have Lesce here with him. She was far better at politics and had the seemingly inexhaustible patience many healers tended to exhibit - at least, when it came to anyone who wasn't her older brother.

No. That line of thinking helped no-one, would only end in firewhiskey. Then who'd rescue Arcana? Certainly not Lesce, with her diplomatic expression and capable, healer's hands. Flare's lips creased into a razor-edged grin. Fractured and bitter he might be, but there was something to be said for the determination of a starving wolf - particularly when he walked unnoticed through a flock of blindfolded sheep.

If it was a show they wanted, who was he to argue?

EIGHT
FENRIS

Fenris woke to the sound of curtains crinkling in the breeze, the cool damp of a cloth on his forehead, a deep ache in his bones and the chafe of manacles at ankle and wrist. Someone with a scent like old paper lingered nearby, humming tunelessly over the top of an insistent grinding noise. Fenris cracked an eye and was greeted by the gritty interior of a basic stone room with shoddily shuttered windows and a thin coating of sand on the hard-packed floor. A glance to the side revealed the naked, gleaming back of an older male harpy, his mane braided in a long tail down his spine. He bore significantly fewer whipping marks than other males Fenris had seen so far, and wore a neat linen loincloth rather than the customary ragged scrap. His arms still bore the deep, crater-like scarring which characterised Hirapthan men but there was a sophisticated grace in his movements that seemed almost at peace.

Something about the serene atmosphere of the room felt distinctly off, so much so that Fenris chanced opening the other eye, staring at the polished grey collar visible around the harpy's throat. It was set with stones of turquoise and gold, and was superior quality to the one Fenris himself wore. The other slave was also clean and though he was slender, it was not the pinched shape of starvation, but the lithe build of fitness. Fenris tried to sit up to get a better view of his surroundings and was rewarded with a sluggish flopping of his arms on – not a bed. A pallet, whose rough surface itched at his bare skin.

Recollection flooded back in an unwelcome rush and Fenris rolled anxious eyes down the length of his body. He was totally naked, had been scrubbed and oiled until his skin gleamed in the dim light - but his penis was gloriously flaccid.

Thank the Weaver for that.

The tuneless humming beside him changed tempo and Fenris turned his head to the side, meeting the sharp yellow eyes of the male who was either his keeper or fellow inmate. He was by far the most handsome male harpy Fenris had yet come into contact with, his features smooth and aristocratic. He held a mortar and pestle in calloused hands, continuing to grind the contents even as he regarded Fenris with raptorlike intensity.

After a long, brooding silence, he set aside the mortar and pestle and patted his chest. "Gryde."

"Fenris." It came out a wheeze, his throat raw as though he'd been screaming.

"Fenris," Gryde repeated, twisting his tongue around the unfamiliar syllables. His eyes were standard harpy gold, his skin a dark terracotta, his mane a soft tawny brown flecked with black and grey. The turquoise and gold stones in his collar glittered in the dim light, and directly beneath them was a sturdy ring through which a chain could easily be threaded. The fact that Gryde was not chained – the only male Fenris had met thus far who wasn't – said he was either no threat, or wherever they were had a far better security system than the simple room suggested.

He became aware the other male was speaking, a quick tumble of words that had the lilt of a question. Fenris licked chafed lips with a dry tongue and scraped together what he knew of the harpy's language so far. "Still learning to speak."

Gryde paused, considering, then nodded. His next sentence was slow and clearly enunciated. "No names here. Slaves only. Names are secret."

"Secret?" Fenris concentrated on the patterns and cadences of Gryde's voice, gleaning new words even as they were spoken. "What do I call you, then?"

"Here, to men, Gryde. Out there, to them, nothing. Slaves have no names unless mistresses give them."

Fenris tried to clear his throat, was appalled at the mewling noise he produced. "I didn't think any of the males were brave enough to defy the women like that."

"Defy?" Gryde made an odd, trilling sound that Fenris realised was laughter. "There's no defiance, but we can't all go around calling each other 'you.' Too awkward." The harpy shrugged his muscular shoulders, sunlight glinting off his oiled skin. "Here, among only males, private names are safe enough."

Fenris' eyes narrowed, nostrils curling as he weighed Gryde's scent for lies. "Still seems risky to me."

"It is," Gryde inclined his head. "But we are male. Being born is a risk, breathing is a risk. Sleeping is a risk, waking is a risk. Looking too often, not enough. Moving, eating, thinking -"

"I understand." Fenris squeezed his eyes shut against the peculiar fluttering in his chest. When it subsided, he fixed Gryde with the impassive expression he used most often at court. "Where am I?"

Gryde gestured at the featureless walls. "A place to prepare mating males."

"For what?" Fenris demanded. Gryde said nothing, but his eyes travelled the length of Fenris' body, coming to rest on his genitals. "*No.*"

"You don't know how?" An assessing head tilt, a man considering what tools he had at his disposal and how best to employ them. "We can teach."

"I know how." Fenris fought the urge to flush. "On my own terms."

Gryde laughed, the sound completely without humour. "Good. If you can perform on demand, you won't need the meetha." A narrowing of eyes, an amber gaze critiquing Fenris' male equipment with the eye of a professional. "No wonder the flightless one requisitioned you for her own. It is a rare male who can respond reliably without assistance."

"Without -" Fenris broke off, retreating behind yet another layer of court calm. Was it possible that Gryde – and every other male in Hiraptha – had no concept of consensual sex? An image of Arcana wearing flimsy pyjamas and arching against him from the softness of her bed rose behind Fenris' eyes and he blinked back sudden moisture. To never understand the emotive connection behind the physical, to be raised believing it was something done *to* you rather than something you participated in... "Is there no love here, in this place?"

"Love?" Gryde rolled the word across his tongue, his expression guarded. "Love is a word punishable by death."

Weaver's grace. Fenris' hand twitched as though to reach for the greatsword, but the harpies had abandoned it in the desert after discovering they couldn't lift the enormous blade. Fenris swallowed, the movement uncomfortable beneath the crude metal collar. He lifted his hand to rub, realised the collar's loop was empty. "No chain?"

"Not here." Gryde waved a vague hand. "This facility is in the deepest, most protected part of the Pit, locked and walled and heavily guarded.

Chains make our training more difficult, although there are some lessons where they become necessary. As long as you stay within the walls, all will be well. Attempt to step outside, however, and..."

"I understand." Fenris drew a breath so deep his lungs ached, let it out slowly. "You speak often of meetha. What is it?"

"What they made you drink." Gryde waved a hand at Fenris' flaccid shaft. "A herb mixed with water that makes your body work while your veins burn. It enables us to perform our services as soon as they are required."

"I passed out."

"They gave you too much – not that it matters. Some of the mistresses prefer it that way." A fleeting frown. "The dose was a guess based upon your size but if you have not taken meetha before, it's no wonder you were overwhelmed." Gryde picked up the mortar and pestle, angled it to display a mostly pulverised plant whose thin fronds were a dark green that bordered on black. "Preparing it is one of our duties."

Some of the mistresses prefer us that way. Fenris forced his sluggish body into a sitting position so he could pat himself down. "Did they -"

"No." Gryde's voice was gentle. "Until the Empress has spoken with your mistress, you remain her property and will not be sullied by another."

Refusing to even think about the hidden meanings in that announcement, Fenris concentrated instead on swinging his legs over the side of the pallet. "Then why the inspections, the water, the meetha?"

"To make sure your body works as intended. You are a fine specimen, the only one of your kind. If your mistress lives, she may yet claim you. If she doesn't, the Empress will take you for herself. Either way, you must be properly prepared for your duties." Gryde strode to Fenris' side and took hold of one arm, turning it this way and that with a curious expression. "You truly grow no feathers."

"No. I do not."

Gryde ran his fingers down the edge of a smooth bicep, a myriad of emotions chasing their way across his mobile face. "Would that were the case for all of us. Plucking only becomes more unpleasant as the years go on."

Fenris eyed the craterlike scarring down the outer edge of the male's arms and made an educated guess. "You're an older slave."

A sharp nod. "Middling. The Empress still calls upon me now and then, to ensure I haven't lost my edge, but most of my duties are here, preparing the next generation."

"I see." And he did – a great many terrible things. "Do you not resent the lot you have been given?"

"Resent?" Gryde barked an incredulous laugh. "I have serviced the Empress. Eaten for many seasons without the pang of hunger. Tasted pure, fresh water. Why would I resent a life so few males attain?"

"Of course." Fenris ducked his head until he was certain his face conveyed none of the horror he felt deep inside. "Well, you have nothing to fear from me. I wish only to return to my mistress."

"It may not be that simple." Gryde sighed, a tired, aging sound. "You don't comprehend how well coveted you are, with your exotic colouring and features." A flicker of a glance towards his groin. "That, too, is the talk of the city."

Fenris felt his cheeks heat. "It is nothing special."

"Tell that to females used to squabbling over males half your size," Gryde answered dryly. "I was assigned as your tutor in part because of my experience, but in part because of my unnatural prowess." He patted his loincloth the same way one might pet a dog. "Most males who come through here follow a set program, but our Empress has higher standards."

Fenris twisted his hands in the sheets. "I mean no offence, but I do not belong to your Empress."

"No?" The other male's fingers played across the collar at his throat. "Your mistress is not of Hiraptha. Unless she can prove her worth, everything she owns will be forfeited to the Empress."

"Including me?"

"Especially you." Gryde smiled and this time, it had a cold edge. "Why else do you think you've been handed over to the Empress' favourite concubine?"

Blood filled Fenris' mouth as he bit his own tongue in an effort to keep from answering. His hand once again twitched for the greatsword, but even if he'd had it, the blade would be of little use. He was so weak from the meetha that he could barely remain sitting, let alone fight. Before he could do anything, he needed to regain his strength - and if he were to survive until then, he was going to need Gryde's guidance. "How long have you been the Empress' favourite?"

"Since she came to her throne." The harpy shifted from one talon to the other, then shrugged. "Many have tried to take the position from me, and all have failed."

"I assure you, I do not covet your place at her side. This city is strange to me and you are one of the first who has been willing to talk." Fenris offered Gryde the ghost of a smile, hoped it appeared sincere. "What now?"

"You must eat and drink and rest," the male answered, "and we must work at getting your meetha dosage right."

"I thought you said -"

"Perform for me," Gryde interjected smoothly.

Fenris blinked. "What?"

"Perform for me, right now, and I will be convinced you do not need it."

"… Perform?"

Making an impatient noise in the base of his throat, Gryde twitched his linen loincloth aside to reveal a penis that was, indeed, far larger than the proportions of his body would at first suggest. The thing twitched once and then rose smoothly, thickening and stretching until it was fully erect in the space of less than three heartbeats. Gryde stroked a hand down his own shaft and back up again, coming away with a few beads of moisture which he proffered like coins. "Like this."

"Weaver's grace," Fenris muttered, leaning backward. Dizziness took hold and after a prolonged moment of vertigo, he groaned and toppled.

Gryde was kneeling on the bed beside him a second later, his loincloth back in place and his hands - one distastefully sticky - firm on Fenris' shoulders. "You speak the language of the Goddess?"

Biting back his pithy retort and wishing he had the energy to flick Gryde's hands away, Fenris took a long moment to realise that not only had he cursed in Universal Galactic, but Gryde had answered in kind.

"Yes," he said slowly, noting the odd intensity on the older male's face. "I do. I'm surprised that you do, too. I was under the impression it was for the women only."

After a moment to ensure Fenris wasn't going to outright faint, Gryde released him and sat back on his talons. "Mostly." He hesitated, eyes narrowed as though trying to sense a trap. "Some of us still know and keep the old ways, such as they are."

"I'm unfamiliar with your ways, but Hirapthan is not my native language," Fenris confessed. "Nor Arcana's. I'm learning as I go."

"It's not wise to speak her name aloud," Gryde cautioned, wiping his hand on his loincloth. "If you're overheard, there will be trouble."

"It may prove a hard habit to break." Fenris pressed his lips together in a thin line. "Where we come from... things are different."

"That much is obvious from your appearance." The harpy offered a far more genuine smile than Fenris had yet seen. "Still, if you know the language of the Goddess, then we are as family. Now it's not only my duty to help you as the Empress' concubine, but a calling of honour among brothers."

"If you want to help me, I need to get back to Arcana," Fenris returned flatly. "She is my sunrise."

Gryde hissed between his teeth. "Don't say that, either. It's forbidden for slaves and mistresses to share a heart."

"Somehow, I'm not surprised," Fenris returned. "When I said before that I perform on my own terms, I meant it - but my desires are only for her."

The harpy rolled off the pallet and began pacing the room, hands clasped at the small of his back and a frown marring his brow. "The meetha will be vital to your survival, then. I am the highest ranking male here, but my influence only goes so far - should any of the other males get wind of your feelings for your mistress, they will sell that information to better their positions as surely as the suns beat down from the endless sky."

"But not you?"

"Of course not." Gryde stiffened, his scent carrying the hard edge of offense. "Those of the mat'ichka would never forsake one of their own."

"Mat'ichka?"

"Those like me, who keep ancient secrets and speak the language of the Goddess." He waved the explanation away as though it were an irritating insect. "We are few, however. Pitifully few."

Unhelpfully few, Fenris translated. He pushed carefully upright and was pleased when the dizziness didn't return. "What do you suggest, then?"

"For now? There are few choices." Gryde scooped up his mortar and pestle and began grinding, switching back to Hirapthan as he did so. "You must learn your place here. Even if it is only show, it will keep you alive. I will teach you everything I can, but... you will have to take the meetha. It is part of a concubine's life and I cannot teach you without it."

"It has stolen my strength," Fenris muttered, returning to Hirapthan himself. "I'm not sure the plant agrees with my constitution."

"You simply had too much." Gryde set out a cup and added some of the freshly crushed leaves to it. He poured water over the top from a jug nearby, then set it aside to steep. "Once we perfect the balance, the fainting will stop."

"And what is the perfect balance?"

"A level at which you can be mostly comfortable, but able to respond immediately upon request." Golden eyes flicked in his direction. "Do you need another demonstration?"

"No." Fenris held up both hands in placation. "No, no, no."

The corner of Gryde's lip twitched. "You will have to get used to thinking of your little friend as a tool. It is one of the first lessons we teach here."

"My tool, as you put it, is attached to me," Fenris groused, "and it does not take artificial orders well."

"Not yet," Gryde said, sipping from the cup with a contemplative expression. With a short nod, he held it out to Fenris. "Here."

"Now?"

"The Empress does not like to wait," the male returned, shrugging. "There is no telling how long we have before your mistress wakes, or the Empress takes matters into her own hands."

Fenris accepted the crude wooden cup with trembling hands. "I am far from recovered from the first bout."

"I have made this less than half the strength of what went before to allow for that," Gryde promised. "Just take a few sips. If the meetha disappears completely from your system, we will have to start over and that will be even more unpleasant."

Every instinct screamed that drinking of the cup was a terrible idea, but in his current condition it would be the work of moments for Gryde to force the doctored water down his throat. Clinging to the illusion of control, Fenris raised the cup and sipped cautiously. The bitterness he recalled from his previous encounter with meetha was gone, and the mint overtones were so slight that he had to strain to catch them. His body cried out for the water, tired of being so thoroughly abused, but Fenris forced himself to go slow, taking no more than a quarter of the cup before he paused.

"How do you feel?" Gryde asked.

"So far, so good. It took only a minute to set in the last time, but I assume that was due to the strength of the dosage."

The harpy nodded. "Yes. It was four times that of a normal male, but you are easily four times a normal male."

"This will not be the first occasion that I have wished to be average," Fenris sighed, his breath rippling the surface of the water. "How long should we -"

Gryde darted forward, catching the cup as it slipped from his fingers. Some of the tonic sloshed over the side and landed on Fenris' thighs, each droplet a shard of ice against his skin. His body stiffened, convulsed, and then slithered down the wall into an awkward, quivering heap.

"Well," said Gryde, rearranging tangled limbs until Fenris was once again stretched out on his back. "I suppose that means the dosage is still too strong, brother."

Fenris' penis twitched in response, the only part of him that seemed able to move. Both he and Gryde watched as that traitorous part of his body hardened and rose, the movement sending licks of agony through Fenris' nerves. He was aware his companion was speaking, but couldn't make out the words through the screaming inside his own head. When the warm arms of unconsciousness stole around Fenris and dragged his eyelids shut, he went without a fight.

NINE
ARCANA

Arcana stood on her balcony, head tipped back to appreciate the
sparkling curtain of night. Though she wasn't at home in the dark like
Fenris or even Caelum, she savoured the chill which rode in the air, and
wondered if her Guardian looked up at the same stars from wherever
he was.

"Brooding?" Caelum's soft whisper preceded his equally soft nose
against her cheek.

"Yes."

"Is it a private session, or can anyone join?"

In spite of her mood, Arcana smiled. "When have you ever cared about
my privacy?"

"It's not that I don't care," he responded easily, "so much as I believe
that your privacy is also my privacy."

"Explain that to Fenris," she muttered, leaning against his shoulder.

"Wouldn't you prefer to tell him yourself?"

"That you're irritatingly determined to stick your nose in at every
possible opportunity? I think he's noticed." Arcana gave a dry chuckle.
"Your timing is impeccable."

"For the record, I didn't intend to waltz in while you were playing hide
the salami," Caelum grumbled. "It just kind of happened."

She blushed, glad the Hirapthans had their windows shuttered so
tightly that not even a speck of light filtered out. "There was no hiding of
any salami, thank you very much. It's too dangerous."

"Because you might find yourself in over your head?"

Too late, she thought, but said instead, "Because Fenris thinks he might bite me and ingest enough magic to kill all of us."

"Do you think he would?"

"No, but it's not up to me to make that decision, is it?" Arcana sighed, long and deep. "Fenris has to come to me on his own terms."

"You mean he has to come *in* -"

"*Caelum.*"

"Sorry, couldn't help it." Caelum fell silent and Arcana sensed that he, too, was staring up at the sparkling carpet of stars. "He wasn't at the meeting place tonight."

"I figured."

"I'm worried." The deerken shifted his weight restlessly. "I'd like to look further afield, make sure he's well, but I'm hampered by the elastic band effect. As long as those guards are in the hallway, we're stuck with blind hope."

"Mirran assured me he's being taken care of. We have to take her at her word for now." Arcana shrugged. "With any luck, they'll ask me to walk the Gauntlet soon."

Caelum shivered. "Be careful what you wish for. These women are brutal and without your magic…"

"Have a little faith, won't you? My senses are getting sharper every minute and I feel a lot stronger."

"Oh yeah? How many flowers did you bloom on the cactus today? Two?"

"Two and a half," she muttered, clenching her hands into fists.

He snorted, creating enough wind to ruffle her hair. "Oh, wow, I'm terrified. At this rate, you can brain them with a bonsai sometime next week."

"This place has made you cranky." Arcana wove her fingers through the precious few inches of fur which only appeared at night, when it was cooler. "Why shouldn't I be impatient? The sooner we can get Fenris, the sooner we can get off this miserable hunk of rock."

Caelum fell silent for so long she wondered if he'd fallen asleep. Then, "We can't leave. There's no way offplanet."

"What?"

"I've spent the better part of your convalescence eavesdropping shamelessly, and calling these harpies technologically inferior is as big an understatement as calling Flare pretty. There's no spaceport - gods above, there's not even running water. I've scanned with my senses and there's no portal here, either. Mirokke's tooth is gone, so we can't jump out, and there's no holo console to call for help." Caelum paused, allowing the weight of his words to sink in. "We can't leave."

"Great Gods of Sorcen," Arcana whispered. "Does Fenris know?"

"Some," Caelum allowed, "but not all. I didn't want to make his life harder than it already is."

Rubbing a hand over her face, she forced her racing heart to calm. "Okay… what else can you tell me about this place? It sounds like you've had the best chance to gather information out of all of us."

"Considering you were in a magical coma and Fenris is a slave, I'm not sure that's much of a compliment," he grumbled.

"So grouchy," Arcana chuckled, kissing the tip of his nose. "I'm sorry for leaving you alone in a strange place. Please?"

Caelum lipped at her hair for a moment, then snorted hard enough to send it into complete disarray. "Fine. The planet is, as far as I've been able to work out, completely shrouded in desert. Water is so precious it's used as currency - something which will come in handy when your magic returns - but for all the vast desert you see, there's no other sentient life." He paused, ears flickering. "Unless you count the weird horse-goats they call jinra, of course, and probably a bunch of bugs and other gross creepies, but there's been no mention of any other creature with more than two brain cells and I've certainly not been able to sense anything."

"I must be missing something," Arcana muttered. "The Weaver wouldn't have sent us here if there wasn't a way out."

The deerken's body undulated beneath her as he shrugged. "She was desperate."

"Yeah, but she's not stupid." Arcana frowned, tapping a finger against her chin. "Maybe Fenris can teach you to jump once we rescue him."

"As much as I'd like to put my eggs in that basket, he hasn't had much luck with it so far." Caelum's voice was softly resigned. "We have to face the possibility that this is it."

"No." Arcana dug her fingers mercilessly into the side of his jaw. "No, Caelum. We don't give up. Ever."

He sighed, long and breathy and slow. "I'm just so tired. We've been dragged from pillar to post without any real guidance or answers. Maybe we're better off leaving this entire mess for someone else to handle."

"Who?" Arcana demanded. "There's nobody else - you know there isn't. Are you really just going to languish here while Taelon sets the warg to tearing the universe apart? Think of what they'll do to Lesce, or Flare. Think of the mothers and fathers and brothers and sisters and babies who'll die because we gave up. Do you really want that on your conscience?"

Again, a long silence and a gentle, drawn out sigh. "No."

"Then pull yourself together," she snapped. "At the moment, we're on the outside of society but once I walk the Gauntlet, I'll be accepted as Hirapthan and with any luck, it will gain us not only some privacy, but we'll get Fenris back. Once we have Fenris, we can plan. Do they know about my magic?"

"No."

"Right, let's keep it that way. The longer they think we're weak, the better."

"And Taelon?"

"Forget Taelon for now." Arcana made a cutting motion with one hand. "He can't find us here, not after the Weaver severed Fenris' blood bond. Right now, all that matters is surviving the Gauntlet and rescuing Fenris."

"All right," Caelum murmured. "I'm sorry, Arcana. I just... while you were sick, I..."

"Shhh." She wrapped her arms around his neck and pressed a kiss to his jaw. "It's going to be okay, I promise."

Rather than pick on her cliché - and possibly empty - vow, Caelum curled around her in the deerken equivalent of a hug. They stood like that until the sky began to lighten, the stars disappearing with a singular, gut wrenching whoosh. As shutters began to slam open and the trilling of harpy voices filtered through the dawn, Caelum stepped back. "Someone's coming."

Arcana kissed him on the nose and headed inside, the relative cool of the brief night already fading as the sun's first rays dug into the sandstone walls. She'd just stepped through the archway when the door to her chamber swung open, admitting a flustered looking Mirran carrying her heavy basket and a frowning, older female wheeling a food trolley.

"You awake! Good." Mirran hurried to her side and, after a peremptory prod and poke, gestured to the food trolley. "Come, eat."

Arcana allowed the younger harpy to usher her towards the end of the bed. "You look flustered. What's the matter?"

"Change plan." Mirran twittered and clicked at the woman with the food trolley, who bowed low and then left, closing the door behind her. "Eat, eat."

Arcana held up both hands to ward off the thick slice of bread and jam that came sailing towards her. "Mirran! Stop, just for a second, and talk to me. What's going on?"

"Already said, change plan." Mirran shoved the bread impatiently into Arcana's hands and turned to rummage through her basket. "Are well enough walk?"

"Yes, I can walk - but I'm not going anywhere until you explain yourself."

Mirran paced a short circle on the chamber floor, tugging at a lock of downy hair and cheeping mournfully under her breath. Just when Arcana thought she couldn't take another moment, the petite harpy stopped and announced, "Empress call to see you."

"The Empress?" Arcana shot a glance at Caelum. "The Empress is coming to visit?"

"No!" Mirran mimed walking with two of her fingers. "You visit."

"The Empress has summoned me?"

"Yes! Must hurry," Mirran urged, indicating the bread and jam again. "She no like wait."

Arcana raised the bread and took a mouthful, chewing thoughtfully. "If I'm going to visit the Empress, I should know something about her. How is she crowned?"

"When old Empress dies, new applicants present to Goddess. Goddess decide who is worthy. Once Empress, always Empress." Mirran wrung her hands together as she watched Arcana eat. "Word is law. Can challenge Empress, if dislike, but to succeed does not make Empress - only Goddess can. Death only forces new choose."

"If you can challenge the Empress, that means you can disagree with her?"

Mirran raised both her hands in a warding off gesture. "Not advised."

"I'm not saying I want to disagree, Mirran." Arcana smiled to take the sting from her words. "I'm trying to understand how everything works before I have to meet the woman. I wouldn't like to embarrass you, or myself."

The harpy relaxed considerably, tilting her head in thought as Arcana continued to eat. "Empress job to protect Hiraptha, not to be nice. Empress hand of Goddess. Has much responsible."

Caelum took a step forward. "Is she a warrior?"

"All Hiraptha warriors," Mirran replied, thumping a clenched fist to her chest. She looked like she wanted to prostrate herself in front of the deerken, but noted his narrowed gaze and straightened her spine. "Strength is life."

Arcana finished her bread as Mirran dug through her basket and produced the same blue bottle as the day before. "Strength is life, huh? I guess you're right."

"Is only way. Now drink." Mirran poured a few drops into the crude wooden mug on the tray, swirled it about and offered it to Arcana. "Must dress."

Downing the contents in a few quick swallows, Arcana shovelled a lump of hard, bitey cheese into her mouth and then shifted sideways as Mirran pulled a leather bundle from her basket and dumped it on the bed. The harpy picked the ties and rolled it out, revealing a short leather skirt and strapless crop.

"You want me to wear this?" Arcana asked, her breath catching.

"All Hiraptha wear." Mirran looked up at her curiously. "Why?"

Arcana swallowed. "I'm just used to a little more... uh... coverage, that's all."

"Underthings to cover," Mirran said, handing Arcana a pair of suede underpants. "See?"

Feeling distinctly lightheaded, Arcana tugged at the nightgown which barely covered her breasts. They were on the smaller side of average, but compared to the almost flat harpies she'd seen thus far, she was well and truly over endowed. "I'm not sure that strip will cover my front."

"Hmm." Mirran pursed her lips, gazing first at Arcana's bust and then down at her own. "Have less, for flying."

"I suppose they would get in the way, even ones as average as mine," Arcana muttered.

"*Average*?" Mirran squawked, reaching out to prod at the fleshy mound of Arcana's left breast. "Large! Soft."

"Er," Arcana managed, taking a step backward and covering her cleavage. "Trust me, where I come from, they're not that impressive."

"Believe when see. Still, not other choice of dressing." Mirran paused, eyed Arcana's half-covered bosom and then frowned down at the little crop. "We will try."

"I can't just wear this?" She waved a hand at the nightgown.

Mirran looked instantly scandalised. "To see *Empress*?"

"All right, all right." Resigning herself to her fate, Arcana slipped the nightgown off and allowed Mirran to help her into the underwear and the leather crop. The strip laced up at either side, and with Mirran's help they managed to get Arcana's breasts contained, if not entirely comfortable.

Mirran stepped back to inspect her handiwork and then shrugged. "Nipples in. Will do."

Caelum snorted loudly but, seeing the fierce look on Arcana's face, subsided. Mirran held out the leather skirt and clicked her tongue until Arcana stepped into it, then showed her how to fit it properly using the laces. By the time they were done, the skirt rode low on her hips and barely covered her buttocks, which were by no means abnormally large, but certainly larger than the average harpy's. Arcana's heart hammered in her chest and she fought the urge to cover her exposed ribs and belly. "I've never felt so naked in all my life."

"It's… an interesting look for you," Caelum said slowly. "I'm not sure if you're here to rescue me or whip me into submission."

Arcana groaned. "I'm so glad I don't have a mirror right now."

"What is mirror?" Mirran asked.

"Something you use to see your own face." She frowned in thought. "Like… like when you look into a still pool of water."

"Oh," Mirran brightened. "To check for poison sheen?"

"Er... yeah, sure. Do you have a brush? For my hair?" Arcana tugged at one of the matted black locks tumbling over her shoulder, and caught her lower lip between her teeth. "Was it really necessary to cut it so short?"

"Was much melted. No choices." Mirran dug in the basket and produced a wide toothed comb, watching closely as Arcana combed her hair. "Look different with no feathers."

"Think how you look to me, then."

Mirran blinked. "Never thought."

"Will Fen - will my male be present at the audience?" Arcana asked, setting the comb back on the bed with a deliberately casual air.

"No." Mirran shook her head. "Not allowed until claiming completed. But, not so bad a thing. The more to see, the more will wish to steal."

"You said nobody would attempt to steal him while I was ill," Arcana returned, her stomach flipping.

"Never - bring dishonour. But once better, yes. More to see him, more to make Gauntlet harder."

Arcana smoothed her hair into place, watching Mirran repack her things into the basket. "I'm surprised you're concerned about his safety."

"Am not. Beera task your recovery." Mirran shrugged. "You fail, I fail. You succeed and become Hiraptha, Mirran become full wise woman. Interest in man only to make the success for you."

"I see." Arcana sucked on her teeth a momfent, then said, "Beera doesn't seem the sort to hand out praise on a whim."

"No. Beera skeptical of wingless wonder. Think too soft," Mirran admitted.

"So... she set you a task she expects you to fail?"

The younger female looked suddenly uncomfortable. "Made angry last week. To look after you probably to punish me."

"Ah. Well, perhaps we can turn this whole situation around and surprise her." Arcana offered a smile, but the harpy remained melancholy. "Don't worry about it now, Mirran. Like you said, the Empress is waiting."

"Yes. To stand half chance of living, must be quick." Mirran took a deep breath, as though preparing herself. "Empress less forgiving than Beera."

"Any final pointers before we go, then?" Caelum asked, drifting closer to Arcana.

Mirran hesitated, playing with the strings on her basket, then finally shook her head. "Only to say, not catch other male's eyes. Females possessive and jealous, may make Gauntlet harder."

"I don't think you have to worry about anyone looking my way," Arcana murmured. "I don't have a drop of water to my name."

Mirran sighed and shook her head sadly. "True said, but males stupid. Many nice looking, but all heads of air. Cannot trust to listen."

"Oh." Arcana choked back the sudden laugh threatening to emerge and glanced at Caelum, who looked suitably indignant at having his gender so summarily maligned. "I'll keep that in mind."

"We go?" Mirran was already at the door, fingers drumming impatiently on her arm.

"Yes." Arcana followed Mirran into a wide corridor lit with torches, where a contingent of four female harpies awaited them. Each wore leather armour and headdresses decorated with an array of dyed feathers, and carried carved spears wrapped in thread and beads.

"These are Hira'tatheen, Spears of the Empress." Mirran waved a hand at the guards. "Come to summon, to wait, to bring."

Arcana smiled and inclined her head. "Hello."

The females remained silent, their yellow raptor's eyes eerily intent. Mirran made an impatient noise in her throat. "Cannot understand language of Goddess."

"Oh. Will I need to learn your language, then?" Arcana followed the young wise woman along the corridor to a staircase which wound back and forth down the side of the building and spilled them out into a featureless lobby.

"Depends if wish to speak to anyone. Hiraptha all speak Hiraptha. Only wise women and Empress speak language of Goddess." Mirran paused at the foot of the stairs. "Could change, learn, become. Or, could stay as are and be rude."

"Which would offend people, making them likely to challenge me," Arcana mused. "Better to try and learn the local language."

"Yes." The young wise woman beamed as though Arcana had performed a difficult and unexpected trick. "Now come."

Mirran crossed the lobby and Arcana followed. The guards flowed into formation around them, using the butts of their spears to push open the reed door leading outside. Arcana gasped as she stepped through, taken aback by the sheer weight of the heat and the blistering feel of the sun across her skin. Sand stretched off to her left, endless rolling dunes that dwindled into a shimmering haze. Mirran led her down a paved pathway that curved to the right, where curious fern-like trees had been planted to provide a measure of shade. They walked between a haphazard collection of properties, some fenced and others open, some large and built from sandstone and others no more than reed huts.

No matter their size or quality, each house had a heavy wooden post driven into the ground by the front door, from which several large iron rings were suspended. Many of the hovel-style huts had a glassy-eyed slave, sometimes two, chained to their posts. The better built homes showed evidence of more males, and those chained to the posts out front sat attentively, as might a well behaved animal waiting for their master to return.

It was impossible to be certain in their half-starved, dirty states but for the most part Hirapthan men seemed as reedy and delicate as their female counterparts. Each one wore little more than a scrap of fabric that was far too scant to be a proper loincloth, held in place by a combination of thin cord and sheer luck. Their skin ranged from shades of peach and apricot to a deep, heavy terracotta, with downy manes in white, grey and black. Unlike the women, the feathers down the outsides of their arms were missing, replaced by a mess of pocked and scarred flesh. Many were malnourished enough that bones jutted and cheeks were gaunt, their gazes sunken and shuttered. Scars, cuts and bruises marred their bodies and each one was weighed down by the heavy metal collar and chain at their necks.

Unable to quiet her horror, Arcana turned her face away from Mirran and met Caelum's grim gaze, his starry eyes swirling with what she recognised as barely concealed temper. "Great Gods of Sorcen," she whispered, tightening her fingers in his fur. "Is it all like this?"

Caelum nodded.

"Are you well?" Mirran asked, proving her hearing was sharp as any bird's. "Sound like struggle for breath."

Arcana forced herself to clear her throat, offering the harpy the best smile she could muster under the circumstances. "I'm all right. It's just the farthest I've walked since I woke."

"We rest moment." Mirran paused beneath the shade of a tree and gestured ahead, where the pathway forked in two different directions. "Soon we come to Pit. Stay close, steep edge."

Arcana took a few long, deep breaths, trying to order her thoughts. "The Pit?"

"Yes. Where slaves not claimed wait mistresses."

Something clenched in her gut. "Is… that where my male is?"

"Was," Mirran agreed. "Not sure if still. Empress will tell."

"Of course." Arcana forced herself to remain still, though her spirit screamed to go searching for Fenris. "Is this the whole community, then?"

"Only some. Land ranges further back." Mirran waved a vague hand off into the distance. "Soon will see Palace, and know full extent. Can walk?"

"Yes, I can still walk. The ground is a little hot underfoot, though." In truth, if Arcana were anyone else her skin would be blistered and peeling, but thanks to her slowly returning magic, her body absorbed the heat.

"No talons," Mirran noted, frowning down at Arcana's feet. "Keep to shade. Not so hot for un-talons."

"Feet," Arcana corrected, wiggling her toes for emphasis.

"Feet," Mirran repeated, testing the unfamiliar word. She nodded and set off along the path that branched to the right. "This way."

They turned the corner and the ground beside the path simply dropped away, revealing a vast hole. The walls were sheer and at least four stories deep, reinforced in places by a mixture of sandstone brick and wooden scaffolding. The Pit was several hundred meters wide and roughly teardrop in shape, with no obvious way up or down save a harpy's wings. A variety of hellish looking buildings, corrals and thick wooden pillars were arranged across the stone floor and both male and female harpies were scattered throughout.

"Pit," Mirran said unnecessarily, waving a hand at the depths. "For unclaimed males, young males, and sometimes other reason males." She turned and pointed where the enormous hole came to a point. "Deepest section for mating males. Through pass, mines and repurposing camp."

Arcana slowed as they neared the edge, frantically searching for a hint of teal skin. "Which building is F - is my male in?"

"Hard to say." Mirran drew to a halt and they stared into the Pit together. Finally, she shrugged. "Been while since Pit work, and Empress impatient."

"Impatient?" Arcana repeated. Caelum stiffened in silent warning beside her, but she couldn't quite get her voice under control. "Impatient for what?"

The female harpy drew under the shade of a nearby tree and lowered her voice to a hiss. "Watch to speak! Guards right there and cannot make words, but will understand tone. Empress can have killed on whim."

"She can try," Arcana growled, her heart stuttering as she recalled the starving, bruised males they'd already passed. "And unless you can give me some reassurance, I might get it in my head to ask her some of these questions myself. I'm sure it wouldn't reflect well on your training if I brawl with the Empress at our first meeting."

Mirran crossed her arms over her chest, her raptor's eyes sharp - but after a moment, she sighed and twittered under her breath. "Empress like his look. Different." She paused, then patted her crotch. "Big."

"Big?" Arcana repeated, eyes wide. "She has no right to look at that!"

"She's the Empress. She can look at whatever she likes," Caelum said quietly, his tone thick with warning.

Arcana strove for calm. "If she's hurt him -"

"No, no." Mirran shook her head. "Would not make outright move without your death."

"Not very reassuring."

Mirran clicked her tongue between her teeth. "Males. Always males. Filthy, airheaded creatures - why to war over them? Useless. Even once to wise woman, not sure I want one."

In spite of the panic clamouring in her blood, Arcana managed a small smile. "If they're so terrible, why keep them around?"

"Have uses." Mirran shrugged. "Feathers for spears and clothing. To work, to buy favour or product. For reproduce, or for relief. Many things for man to do - just not see why fight when there are plenty."

"For relief?" Arcana echoed. "Relief of what?"

"Scratch inner itch with equipment. Fix tension." Mirran's brow creased. "You have mating male, you know how works."

Caelum turned his laugh into a snort, and Arcana flashed him a warning glare. "I know how it works. I just wasn't sure of your meaning."

"Sorry. Goddess tongue hard."

Arcana stared at the lip of the Pit, her chest aching. What had Fenris suffered so that she could recover? What did he continue to suffer? Did he even know she was awake - or that she lived at all? She longed to charge into the depths of the hole and find him, set him free, but her magic was in no shape to terraform the cliffside and without harpy assistance, it would be a battle she had no hope of winning. If she had allies - Arcana blinked. Composing her face into a mask of serenity, she turned to Mirran with a smile. "The Goddess tongue is hard, but perhaps I can help you get better. In return, you could teach me the Hirapthan language."

"Really?" Mirran's eyes widened. "You would?"

"I would."

"Very good to get better. Will accept!" Mirran smiled, her downy mane flattening in pleasure.

"Excellent." Arcana smiled back, then gestured towards the path. "Shall we keep going?"

"Yes. Empress waiting," Mirran agreed, hurrying onward.

Though she longed to slip away, Arcana followed. They began to pass more elaborate looking properties, some several stories high. A group of Hirapthan women lounging on an upper balcony tweeted and whistled at Mirran, whose tart answer rendered them silent for a long moment before they fell about the balcony, laughing hysterically.

Arcana fought the urge to glare up at the women, instead following Mirran further down the sandy pathway. "What did they ask you?"

"Ask if your male good at scratching itch, can they have when you fail Gauntlet," the apprentice wise woman said. She smiled, showing all her teeth. "Remind them you might succeed and become Hiraptha."

"I gather they found the idea of my success amusing?"

"Give no mind," Mirran answered, waving a hand in disgust. "Too much sun, too much ferment."

They continued on in silence, passing more and more Hirapthan women whose reactions were of a similar nature. A couple even sashayed closer as if to confront Arcana directly, dodging away when the guards brandished their spears.

"They're like vultures," Arcana muttered, dodging a half-eaten piece of fruit that came flying her way. "Circling vulnerable prey, waiting for an opportunity."

"Not know vulture, but you different, look squishy. Male looks virile. Good prize." Mirran frowned, her yellow eyes shimmering with concern. "Many go to see. Many want."

Arcana shivered at the thought of Fenris being leered at by a group of lecherous harpies. "You sound worried."

"Yes. More to see, more to challenge at Gauntlet, or after. Much danger-ous. Your job harder, my job harder," Mirran grumbled. She glanced at the guards and lowered her voice. "Empress curious to your male. Likely plan to meet when others can see and decide to challenge, then take male for self when all over."

"You don't think I can complete the Gauntlet?" Arcana demanded, bristling in spite of herself.

Mirran lifted one shoulder. "How? No talons, no wings, no claws - just squashy. Impossible."

"I have learnt," Arcana said quietly, "That nothing is impossible."

"Oh?"

"Yes." She offered a small smile, then feigned a yawn and a stretch. "Is it much further? I need to rest."

"Almost. Can recover inside palace for short before see Empress." Mirran gestured as the path took another sharp turn to the right, around the back of a walled property. "See? Palace."

The sandstone pathway tripled in width and was bordered either side with long lines of tall, fernlike trees. The impressive drive stretched a hundred meters to a set of large wooden gates which stood open, revealing a domed palace beyond. The walls were the same yellow sandstone Arcana had seen thus far, the roof painted in turquoise and gold. Inside the palace walls, paved pathways wound through a lush oasis of greenery and several pony-sized creatures grazed on the vegetation.

"Is that a jinra?" Arcana asked, waving to the closest almost-goat. When Mirran blinked in surprise, she added, "Caelum told me about them."

"Yes, is jinra. Empress' favourite," the harpy said. The four guards who had accompanied them fanned out and hurried ahead, using the butts of their spears to push the palace door open. Mirran smiled and held out a slender hand. "Come. Cooler inside."

TEN
FLARE

Olivie was, as promised, manning the enormous double doors to the official banquet hall. His jaw dropped when Flare drew up outside, opening both arms as though for a hug. "Well, Olivie?"

The administrative assistant snapped his jaw shut with a click and fumbled hastily for his bio scanner. "Very... impressionable, Ambassador."

Flare grinned. He'd dragged his formal robes back on – after a quick shake to get rid of the wrinkles – polished his chain of office and then replicated his makeup from the night before, with further emphasis on smoky eyes and thick eyeliner. The effect was formal, mysterious and, most importantly, striking when paired with his bright hair. He gathered the long, draping folds of his robes in one hand and bowed. "I'm glad you approve, Olivie. Any tips for the evening?"

"No, Ambassador. I think you'll do just fine." Olivie Harthax adjusted his glasses and for a fraction of a second, Flare was certain the little man smiled. "A waiter will show you to your seat. Enjoy the feast."

As promised, a waiter in an immaculate Alliance uniform appeared in the doorway. After a moment in which he fought valiantly not to gape at Flare's long, trailing robes, the other man pressed his palms together and beckoned his charge to follow. The banquet hall was every bit as opulent as Flare had anticipated, with a large central dance floor in pale wood surrounded by sumptuous furniture in dark upholstery and crisp, white linens on every table. Giant chandeliers hung from the ceiling, dripping tiers of crystal which refracted the light into glittering prisms.

Wait staff threaded between the guests who had already arrived, bearing trays with flutes of what turned out to be a tangy fruit punch when Flare swiped one. The table he was shown to was partway around the room and contained half of the guests it had been allotted, a vase of blooming lunar lilies in soft mauve and a daunting display of silver cutlery.

Flare's seat was marked by a place card which declared his name in carefully inked scrollwork. He slid in beside a man in navy leathers with a curling wirework design over his chest in shimmering silver. Long, silky blue-black hair hung over the other male's shoulders and hid his face from view, leaving only the impression of slim, wiry strength and a pair of slender hands calloused from the use of weaponry.

"I've read that book," Flare said, catching a flash of the title as the man turned a page.

His tablemate didn't even bother to look up. "Fuck off."

Flare blinked. The other guests at the table were beyond the lunar lilies, leaving him alone with his determinedly antisocial companion. He clicked his tongue between his teeth. "My favourite chapter is the one where the damsel ends up rescuing the hero after he accidentally floods the palace."

The man beside him stiffened, then slowly raised his head. His skin was pale, with a soft dusting of glacier blue near the temples that flowed seamlessly into his blue-black hair. His eyes were a deep indigo and long, sweeping cheekbones tapered into an elegant jaw. Full lips were pressed into a thin line somewhere between pain and disapproval, long fingers tight around the edges of the book. "You really have read this."

Grudgingly admitted, but in a voice smooth as silk and just as soft. Banishing the bad boy retort he'd been planning, Flare smiled gently. "Yeah. Sorry if I took you by surprise - I'm new."

"Obviously," the other replied, "or you'd not be sitting here talking to me."

"I appear to be cursed by a place card." Flare cast a look around and then lowered his voice to a stage whisper. "Am I likely to combust for being seen in your presence?"

The man blinked, a slow lowering of dark lashes far too luxuriant for the hard expression on his face. "Perhaps."

"Hah!" He grinned and offered his arm. "I'm Flare."

"Congratulations." The man didn't so much as glance at the proffered greeting, turning back to his book instead.

"Zaire, are you being a bastard again?" A man in similar blue leathers slid into the seat on the other side of his companion. He gave Flare an apologetic smile. "Don't mind Z, he's contrary at the best of times. I'm Eyrton." He reached across to grip the arm Flare still had extended.

"I saw you at the council meeting earlier," Flare recalled. "Arguing with tall, dark and frowny."

Eyrton laughed. "Krowley, yeah. He's been a real pain in my ass these last few weeks. Thanks for the opportunity to give him a prodding."

"The enemy of my enemy?" Flare grinned in return, squeezing the leather clad arm once before withdrawing to his own place setting.

"Something like that. I must say, regardless of Krowley, I enjoyed your magic show. If all your people are that good, the Alliance will be licking your boots in no time." Eyrton tipped his glass in Flare's direction and took a long drink.

Zaire snorted softly. "Subtle as a sledgehammer, as usual."

"Oh, I'm sorry, were you taking part in the conversation?" Eyrton fiddled with the leather thong securing his hair – also black, though not quite as long or strokable as Zaire's, with hints of silver at the temples rather than blue – and then prodded his surly companion in the shoulder.

"Wrong arm," Zaire said absently, turning the page in his novel and continuing to read.

Flare met Eyrton's gaze over the other man's head and offered a lopsided smile. "You two have got to be related."

"Cousins," Eyrton confirmed and though he smiled in return, the gaze he turned on Zaire was equal parts frustration and concern. "Not that we look all that much alike."

Considering both men had similar skin tones, builds and even eye colour Flare begged to differ, but kept that thought to himself. "So... Ryllin?"

"I see you've read your notes," Eyrton inclined his head. "Most only bother with the top tier systems."

Flare shrugged. "I like to be thorough, particularly when I'm walking on eggshells."

"You're taller than you should be," Zaire said, flipping another page. Eyrton winced and gave his cousin a firm elbow, causing Zaire to sigh and clap the book shut. The Ryllin turned sharp indigo eyes on Flare and raised a questioning brow. "Am I wrong?"

"No." Flare yanked up the edge of his robe to reveal the patent black stilettos underneath. "I'm rocking an extra eight inches. Helps keep me from tripping on all this extra fabric." Zaire stared as though he'd never seen feet before and Flare wiggled his toes for emphasis. "Want a pair? I can hook you up."

"I'm tall enough." And with that, Zaire pulled his book open again and went back to reading.

Flare shrugged. "Suit yourself. I need all the help I can get."

"I seriously doubt that." Eyrton snorted and when Flare raised a brow in question, the other man shrugged. "I saw you at Macadre the other night. You drew quite the crowd."

"No accounting for taste, is there?" Flare winked, all the while filing that titbit of information away in the back of his mind. "I'm still trying to get the lay of the land, and it seemed as good a place as any to start."

"You could've had more than the lay of the land," Eyrton said tartly, then softened the words with a self-deprecating smile. "I've been here for months and I've barely managed to keep my edge off."

What would the other male say if he knew Flare hadn't had an edge in need of softening for the better part of two months now? He opened his mouth to say something scathing, but was saved from his own bitterness by the arrival of the entrees – and with them, the rest of the guests. Thankful for the reprieve, Flare ate in silence, answering the occasional question and sticking firmly to the bad boy persona he'd adopted in the club the night before. It didn't take long to discern that he'd been seated the same way he'd been quartered – with the planets who were less important on the Alliance's political scale. Flare stifled a smile. If only they knew how little he cared for such manoeuvring, perhaps they'd not bother. Then again, he reflected, poking at the unfamiliar greens on his plate, if the Galactic Alliance was so consumed with petty machinations that it made a statement out of where guests sat at a banquet of supposed equals, perhaps it was time to issue a wakeup call - before the warg did.

"Scheming already?"

Flare looked up from beneath his lashes to find a woman with wood-grain skin and fern frond hair silhouetted in the glittering light of the chandelier. "Lysse. To what do I owe such an honour?"

The priestess gestured with one willowy arm towards the dance floor, where several people swished and swayed in time to an elegant string arrangement. "I thought perhaps you might be convinced to dance with me."

"No grumpy guts tonight?" Flare peered around her too-slender form for the unmistakable ebony bulk of Krowley, but he was nowhere to be seen.

Lysse lowered her blossom tipped lashes coquettishly – a move so similar to the one she'd performed in the club the night before that Flare knew it was calculated for effect. "He's currently indisposed."

"Well, in that case, what are we waiting for?" Flare pushed back his chair and rose, offering an arm. "It will be my pleasure to stomp on your feet until he returns."

Lysse laughed delicately and tucked her fingers into the crook of his elbow, leading the way to the dance floor. Flare's formal robes trailed along behind him, the intricately detailed brocade flickering like embers in the fractured light as he swung Lysse into his arms. She wore a multi-layered gown in shades of mauve that offset her rich brown skin and had tucked a matching sprig of flowers amongst the ferny fronds of her hair. The effect was elegant and ethereal, but as Flare spun and dipped across the pale parquetry floor he felt only an echoing loneliness.

"You dance exceptionally well." Lysse clutched convulsively at Flare's shoulders as he swooshed them backwards in a series of quick, elegant movements for no other reason than he could.

He glanced up – not all that far, thanks to his shoes – and gave her a coolly assured look. "You sound surprised."

"I am." The honesty appeared to startle her and Lysse lowered trembling lashes while her cheeks darkened with a blush. "It seems I have underestimated you."

The music faded to a close and Flare glided to a stop. Though it had been far from an exacting score, he'd intentionally overcomplicated his movements and the priestess was flushed and panting with effort, clinging to his chest for support. Very deliberately making eye contact, Flare raised Lysse's knuckles to his lips. "I look forward to exceeding your expectations again in the future." And then he released her, watching with a quirked lip as she wobbled slightly. With a sharp nod, Flare stalked back across the dance floor to his seat in a swirl of dark brocade.

Yeah, he was an asshole.

Eyrton's deep blue eyes shimmered with laughter as he reached the table. "You're a dangerous man," he said as Flare sat down. "Every eye in the room was trained on you then – and the priestess, too, no less."

Flare let his gaze drop to Zaire, still buried in his book. "Every eye?"

"Do you fuck as well as you dance?" Zaire asked without looking up.

Flare bent down and put his lips against that silky, shimmering hair, in the approximate location of the other man's ear. "Would you like to find out?" He'd aimed to mimic Fenris' court calm, but the words came out husky and aggressive. Zaire flinched away, flicking him an astonished look which Flare returned evenly. "Don't throw around heavyweight words if you're not prepared to follow them through, cupcake."

Eyrton laughed in delight, clapping Flare on the shoulder and snatching him a drink off a passing waiter's tray. "Look, you've sealed his sour lips shut. Cheers to that!"

The rest of the meal passed slowly, with several other females accosting him for dances and leaving the floor as breathless and flushed as Lysse had done. Though Flare did his best to pay attention, their faces blurred together and it took every scrap of his considerable determination to avoid being outright rude. The entire gathering was a ridiculous, overwrought confection populated by tittering nitwits, and as time wore on Flare began to envy Zaire his jerkish attitude, his book and, more particularly, the solitude it afforded him. When Chancellor Kaiora stood just before the dessert course and called for silence, Flare gritted his teeth against what he instinctively knew was coming.

"Honoured guests," the Chancellor intoned, spreading both arms to encompass the room. Her gown was of glittering silver, turning her grey skin into a living, cold flame crowned by the rich amber beehive of her hair. All four of her slanted eyes turned to Flare. "Tonight we welcome the planet Sorcen and her esteemed Ambassador Flare to our number. He has brought you all a gift and, I hope, will be convinced to offer us a toast with that gift. Ambassador?"

Flare shoved back his chair and stood, regarding the crowd with a haughtily chill expression as waiters passed around tumblers of firewhiskey. Gods knew, he wasn't up to this, but he wasn't a coward, either. When every guest – including himself – held a glass, he drew a deep breath and squared his shoulders.

"I made this," he announced, angling his drink so the firewhiskey caught the light. A few surprised murmurs greeted the statement and his lip twitched. "Convenient, isn't it, the ability to make your own hard liquor? One of the many hidden talents of a fire sorcerer." He flicked the rim of the tumbler, setting it on fire for a flickering moment. "I made this particular batch shortly after the warg invaded Sorca City and claimed thousands of innocent lives. I made this thinking about all the brothers, mothers, children and cousins who weren't going home – among them, people I knew and cared for. I brewed it thinking about how hard we fought and how, regardless of that determination, it wasn't enough for those sorcerers who lost their lives. Not enough for the leaders who sought to protect their people, and for the innocents who sheltered underground in the desperate hope that someone would save them. The hope that I, and warriors like me, would be competent enough to stem the tide of bloodshed." Flare caught his lip between his teeth and stared down into the glass. "I was hailed a hero but in actual fact, I let my people down - because for all our efforts, I couldn't save every life. As I crafted this fine liquor you now hold in your hands, I thought how very different the result might have been if, for a moment, my government had put aside pride and posturing and connected with others. If we'd reached out, how many Sorcen lives could have been saved – and how many innocents on other planets, too?" Flare raised his glass and raked a scathing look across the assembly of upturned faces. "And now, after months of hard work, here I am. Here *we* are, part of the great and powerful Galactic Alliance. Imagine my surprise when I discovered that rather than rallying against the warg who've slaughtered so many, you're all sitting around on your fat backsides debating the best paint colour for grain silos and whether or not canapés taste better on a Thursday." He chuckled, a dry sound that echoed through the room. "So, a toast. A toast to new beginnings, and to change. A toast to the warg, for bringing us together, and a toast to the room full of snivelling toads intent on ignoring them. Drink, and know the bitter taste of sorrow which comes from the death of good, hardworking people. I hope it makes you all choke."

A collective gasp swept the banquet as Flare knocked the firewhiskey back in one swift movement and stared out at the crowd in blatant challenge. After a long, drawn out silence, a chair scraped beside him and Zaire unfolded to his full height. Taller than Flare, perhaps six foot six - though Flare's shoes made them a similar height - wiry with a good layer of musculature over the top. Blue-black hair shimmered in the light as he raised his glass and clinked it against Flare's empty one with the sharp, true peal of which only crystal was capable. "Rylle welcomes Sorcen to the Galactic Alliance," he said, and threw back his firewhiskey.

Flare bit back a grin as one by one, the other Ambassadors were forced to do the same or risk shame from their peers. He had no doubt Zaire had stepped in only to see the rest of the guests squirm, but he was pleased all the same. Chancellor Kaiora stood with both arms crossed and Flare favoured her with his best bedroom smile, dialled up to full wattage. She simply shook her head and drained her glass alongside the rest of the Council, wheezing as the full impact of the liquor hit her stomach.

Waiters began to appear and Flare sank gratefully back into his seat. Zaire plopped down beside him looking amused. "No effervescent words of thanks?"

"For what?" Flare growled. "Providing you with an evening's entertainment?"

Zaire's cocky expression faltered. "You're not the only one who's suffered because of the warg. I'll back anybody willing to fry those things."

Flare reclined into his seat as a multi-tiered chocolate creation landed in front of him, along with another glass of punch and a folded slip of paper. He snatched it up, scanned the room number and the raunchy invitation scrawled beneath, then slid it safely into his robes. The waitress remained hovering by his side, and Flare glanced up to see the woman's face lit with curiosity. "From the Ambassador over at -"

"Thank you," Flare murmured, not quite able to bring warmth into his voice. "I'll handle it."

"Of course." The waitress bowed and whisked away.

Flare turned back to the table to see Zaire bent to his food, hair falling forward to block his face from view - but Eyrton was watching over his cousin's head, as were several other people at the table. So rather than slam both fists against the wood as he wanted, Flare winked at a primly dressed woman on his right, picked up his spoon and dug it into his dessert.

Progress was slow, but he managed to get three quarters of the way through before his stomach protested. After a moment's queasy indecision Flare surged upright, crossing the room as swiftly as he dared and slipping into the communal bathroom beyond. He barely made it to the privacy of a cubicle before emptying the contents of his three course meal into the toilet bowl, retching over and over until his abs ached and his nostrils burned from the overflow.

Great. He bared his teeth at the cistern and struggled upright, grateful the bathroom was empty as he moved to the sink to wash his face and rinse his mouth. Slow. He had to go slow. He'd be no use to anyone if he couldn't keep his head on straight, food in his belly and his tongue coated in proverbial silver. Then again, he'd gotten this far in life by being unashamedly himself, so why stop now, even if his unashamed self was a wreck?

Flare grabbed a paper towel and patted his face dry, examining his complexion in the mirror. Pale, but not too sickly. Makeup miraculously still in place. Broad shoulders, muscular chest – although he could do with building up his strength again – narrow hips. Height on the shorter side of average, bronze skin offset by astoundingly bright orange hair and a smattering of darker bronze freckles across his cheeks and nose. Lesce's magic had erased the outward physical evidence of too little sleep and too much drink, but they persisted in the shadows behind his eyes. Flare grimaced. He almost hated that off-kilter smile and the bitter humour which accompanied it, but it seemed to be working for him, so who was he to argue?

From the moment he'd been shoved permanently into the Fire Elder position, something inside him had shattered irrevocably and no matter what the future held, there'd be no going back. He wrapped one fist around his thick, rose gold chain of office and squeezed, letting the palm-sized links dig painfully into his hand. He'd never wanted to be an Elder but he was, and his people depended on him whether he liked it or not. Drawing focus from the pain, Flare forced oxygen down his throat and straightened his spine. Time to stop drowning beneath the weight of that chain and stand for those who couldn't stand for themselves. Or, at the very least, track down his sister and that crazy sexy Guardian so that he could help *them* stand for those who needed it.

Flare binned his paper towel, fixed his robes and slid back out into the banquet hall. With the formal part of the evening over, the musicians had struck up something a little more lively and many of the guests were taking to the dance floor. Just as many were choosing to leave and after a moment's smiling indecision, he decided to follow suit. Instinct said that after a quick shower and change, he'd learn far more at one of the station's clubs than he would here.

The halls were well and truly dimmed for night but Flare barely noticed, trusting his feet to take him where needed. At first the winding ways were crowded with servants and officials alike, each going about their own business, but they dropped off one by one until his only company was the soft swish of formal brocade and the rhythmic clicking of his heels.

And... he stopped.

Almost lost beneath the rustle of fabric... what was that? The soft whirring of machinery? Flare frowned, peering back the way he'd come, spotting only softly illuminated walls and polite, boring art. The sound had ceased almost immediately and whilst it could have been a figment of his imagination, Flare always trusted his instincts - and in this instance they insisted he was being followed. Except that the more he strained his ears, the more empty the corridor seemed.

Hitching the leading edge of his robes in one hand, Flare tiptoed back to the juncture he'd passed only moments before and peeped around the corner. Nothing. He rolled his eyes up to the roof – no, nothing there either - and down to the floor, where he at last spotted a droplet of dark liquid.

Flare crouched down for a better look, bracing one hand on the cool metal and squinting in the half light. Blood? Or oil? Hard to tell without touching and if there was one thing he'd learnt, it was to never dip your fingers into an unknown substance unless you were prepared for the consequences. Barthax had tried that once on a mission and was now missing his favourite finger courtesy of the high acid content in Malrino ichor.

Flare scanned the floor of the corridor and found another droplet ten paces further along, as wet and fresh as the first. Whatever the liquid was, it was leaking from someone or something who'd gone in the other direction. He pushed upright and crept down the corridor, skirting drops of darkness until he heard the unmistakable sounds of a scuffle. Picking up speed, Flare came abreast of an intersection in time to see a figure in a servant's uniform crumple to the floor. Another three servants crowded someone Flare recognised with a start as Zaire; though this whirling dervish with two short, wicked looking daggers was a far cry from the aloof, bookish Zaire he'd built in his mind. As Flare watched, the Ryllin dipped and spun and stabbed until he was in a position to defend the fallen servant, neatly beheading one of his assailants with a stealthy back-handed slash that made Flare simultaneously envious and impressed. Rude the man might be, but he was talented, no doubt about it. The question was, why was he being set upon by servants?

In a move so terrifically obvious that Flare grimaced, one of the remaining assailants feinted left. Zaire shunted right in anticipation of the real strike - and froze, his face twisting in pain. Flare heard a sound like shrieking metal, then the servant's chain-wrapped fist connected heavily with Zaire's jaw and the Ryllin crashed to the ground, his limbs still stuck in the positions they'd been while he was standing. The second servant immediately straddled his chest, tugging at the neck of Zaire's leathers with one hand while the other drew a wicked looking syringe from inside the jacket of his uniform.

Flare surged from the shadows and twisted the syringe from the servant's fingers, tossing it across the hall where it embedded hilt-deep in the wood panelling. He dropped his shoulder, bent one knee and flipped the servant onto the floor before the man even realised he was disarmed. "Where I come from, it's rude to stab someone on the first date," Flare said, ducking a wildly swinging arm to render the man unconscious with a sharp blow to the temple. "Sleep tight."

"You! Don't move."

Flare glanced up to see the remaining servant had looped the thick links of his chain around Zaire's straining throat. He frowned. "Don't move?"

"Yeah, you heard me," the servant sneered. "Stay right there, or he gets it."

"Are you sure about that?" Flare buffed his nails on his robe, checked their sheen, then snapped his fingers. "Because your ass is on fire."

"What?" The man twisted as flames burst to life across the seat of his pants, crawling hungrily up the back of his jacket. He loosened his hold on the chain with a shriek, and Flare yanked the weapon out of the way, twisting in place to land a solid kick to the side of the man's head. He dropped like a stone.

Flare crouched beside Zaire, bending to peer into his sweat-sheened face. "You okay?"

"Fine," Zaire's voice was hoarse. "I always get mugged after dark by the hired help. It's part of the service they offer here."

Flare quirked an eyebrow. "Your rousing gratitude has moved me to the core, brother. If you've got the situation in hand, I'll just move along." He snapped his fingers again and the flames that had eagerly devoured most of the mugger's uniform went out. "See you at the next meeting."

"Sure." Zaire's face went, if possible, even paler. His skin stretched taut over his bones, his spine arched with agony and his next words – probably curse words – came out as little more than a strangled gargle.

Dropping all pretence, Flare scooped the lankier man into his arms. "Tell me what you need."

Zaire's face contorted with effort. "Eyrton... wait," he gasped as Flare shoved upright. "No blood. Destroy... all of it."

"Destroy the blood?" Flare noted that the same, almost black fluid that had been in the hallway now leaked from Zaire's nose. His eyes tracked up to the empty syringe and realisation dawned. "They were after your blood?" A nod. "But why-"

"Hurry," Zaire squeaked and then his eyes rolled back in his head and he fainted.

"Great." Flare cradled the Ryllin against his chest with one arm – great gods, the man was heavier than he looked – and traced a rune in the air with his free hand. The tip of his index finger caught alight and he laid the flame ever so carefully against the blood oozing from Zaire's nose, uttering a word of power as he did so. Puffs of smoke went up all around him, continuing on up the hall as Zaire's blood incinerated, leaving behind a dark smoke that smelt oddly like bacon. Wrinkling his nose, Flare quashed the sudden urge for breakfast and headed off in the opposite direction, where his memorised blueprint of the station insisted the Ambassadors of Rylle had their rooms.

Unconsciousness had stolen the stiffness from Zaire's limbs and he hung like a ten-tonne rag in Flare's arms, luxuriant blue-black hair spreading like silk across his shoulder. With his face relaxed, he was startlingly beautiful, like a precious museum exhibit one dared not breathe on lest it crack.

By the time Flare reached the right apartment, his arms were trembling with strain and he resolved to fit in some extra training sessions as soon as possible. With both hands full he had no option but to kick the door and was relieved when Eyrton opened it almost instantly.

"I believe this is yours." Flare made to transfer Zaire to the other man and was surprised when Eyrton stepped back to allow him inside instead.

"On the bed," Eyrton instructed, sticking his head out into the corridor for a moment before palming the door closed and locking it. "Were you followed?"

"Of course not, or I'd never have come." After a cursory glance around quarters that, albeit larger, were not dissimilar to his own, Flare tottered into the nearest bedroom and dropped Zaire on the bed. "He got jumped by some people in servant's outfits, fought well and then froze. Post-traumatic stress?"

Eyrton clicked his teeth noncommittally, leaning against the doorjamb. "Something like that."

"One of them had a syringe," Flare added, stepping back so he could watch the other's reaction.

Eyrton's jaw hardened, but he did a respectable job of remaining otherwise unaffected. "Did they get anything?"

"No. I stepped in." Unabashedly examining the relief on Eyrton's mobile face, Flare added, "Zaire also asked me to take care of the blood before he passed out."

"He's bleeding? Shit a brick." Eyrton leapt to his cousin's side, casual air gone as he yanked at the lacings on Zaire's leather armour. "Bathroom cupboard, second shelf. Blue medkit. Go!"

Intrigued, Flare did as he was told, returning with the medkit in question - which had been stuffed so full that bandages and steristrips exploded out of it when Eyrton yanked the zip free. Zaire's torso was already exposed, his skin a sickly pale shade even beneath the hints of icy blue that were a characteristic of the Ryllin people. The same dark, thick blood Flare had seen in the hallway smeared one side of Zaire's chest but there was no sign of a wound. "On the back?"

"Maybe." Eyrton prodded and poked his cousin's inert body, checking reflexes and lifting limbs until Zaire's right arm refused to bend. "Elbow," Eyrton muttered, lifting the entire arm and revealing, as predicted, a slash in the skin just above the joint. The Ambassador moved with the quick assurance of a man familiar with his task, instructing Flare to hold Zaire's arm aloft while he cleaned, stitched and bandaged the wound, then shoved a couple of pills down his cousin's throat and massaged until they were swallowed. "You said you cleaned up his blood?"

"Yeah," Flare snapped his fingers and flame sprang to life in their cradle. "With this."

Eyrton eyed the tiny flame and then looked down at the blood coating Zaire's arm and shoulder. "Maybe not."

"Not unless you want his skin burnt clean off his bones," Flare agreed, banishing the fire with another snap. "But I can heat him one hell of a bath."

"He'd drown," Eyrton laughed, shaking his head. "You've done more than enough already. Zaire won't say it, but I will – thank you."

"For the rescue, or for not asking sticky questions?"

"Both." Eyrton's eyes twinkled with mischief and Flare snorted a laugh of his own in response. "I wish I'd been there to see you fight in that monstrous dress, though."

"It's a robe," Flare replied, waving an admonishing finger, "but I look just as fabulous in a dress."

Eyrton blinked at that, then laughed. "I have the strangest feeling you're right. Do you not take women to bed, then?"

"Where else would I get their dresses?" Flare waited until Eyrton blushed uncertainly and then winked. "Well, I guess if cranky pants is safe, I'll be on my way."

"Yeah." Eyrton looked back at Zaire and sighed. "I guess I'll stay here and keep an eye on this cretin. Shame - I had a lovely little barmaid lined up at Macadre."

"She'll be there tomorrow." Flare clapped the other man on the shoulder and sauntered to the door. "Take her a gift with your apology. It helps."

"Hmmmm." Eyrton frowned off into the middle distance, then shrugged. "I suppose it can't hurt. Shall I pass on your regards to Zaire when he wakes?"

Flare paused with his hand over the door plate. "Not unless you want to tell him that if he's not battle ready, he shouldn't be wandering the halls alone; especially if he's got secrets to keep."

Eyrton pursed his lips. "Maybe I'll tell him that just to see what he does to you."

Flare slapped the door panel and offered Eyrton one of his most wicked bedtime grins. "After the speech I gave tonight, he'll have to get in line."

ELEVEN
FENRIS

Leaning heavily against the sandstone wall to rest his trembling legs, Fenris passed weary eyes over the crowded eating hall and swallowed around the lump in his throat.

"Come," Gryde encouraged, his shoulder a steady support and his arm strong around Fenris' waist. "You need to eat."

"No." Fenris shook his head, closing his eyes against the waves of dizziness it caused. "I cannot."

"Come with me," Gryde insisted, tugging until Fenris lurched off the wall and staggered into the room, the other male all-but carrying him to a shadowy back corner and rolling him onto a bench.

For two days now, everything Fenris had eaten or drunk had been laced with varying degrees of the damnable herb the harpies favoured, and for two days he'd been constantly sporting an unwelcome erection whilst also being violently ill. Every nerve ending burned, every sensation against his skin felt like hot knives and the strength and speed which had been his since birth had fled like mist in the sun. Fenris' gut clenched as Gryde set a plate of crusty bread on the table between them, a mixture of clawing nausea and debilitating hunger causing sweat to bead across his forehead. "No."

"Brother." Gryde sat beside him, hands and voice patient as he tore a hunk of bread free. "Trust me."

Fenris accepted the morsel with shaking hands, holding it to his nose and taking several long, deep breaths. Once, he'd have known every ingredient in the loaf in a matter of moments, but now, it was all he could do to ascertain that the minty tang of meetha was conspicuously absent. Slipping the warm bread between his lips, Fenris began to chew with single-minded intensity - with his cheeks so hollow, he had to be careful not to slash the inside of his mouth with his fangs. The effort to swallow was more than he'd dare admit, but when Gryde held out a second piece of bread, Fenris took it. "How?"

"I have ways," Gryde murmured, his voice so low Fenris barely caught it, "but it will not be easy to uphold without your assistance."

"I am useless to you like this."

"Nothing lasts forever." Gryde reached out an elegant hand and nudged the bread closer. "Whether you like it or not, you have caught the Empress' attention. No other of our brotherhood can say the same."

"You can."

"Perhaps, but I age." Gryde shrugged easily. "It will not last forever. Whether your mistress survives the Gauntlet and claims you or not, the Empress will come knocking. It's my duty to prepare you, if you're willing to learn."

In ordinary circumstances, Fenris was sure he'd have no trouble grasping what the harpy was trying to tell him, but in his current state he could understand little more than that the bread he was eating was easing the cramped ache in his stomach. "Speak plainly, Gryde."

The harpy drew in a long breath, his yellow eyes scanning the other males who ate nearby. "If you die, my life also becomes forfeit," he whispered at last. "And if you succeed, you will do so with a knowledge few males ever attain."

"Meaning I'm dangerous no matter what?"

Gryde's nod was slow, his expression serious. "Yes."

"I mean no harm to you," Fenris murmured, finishing the last of the bread with a soft sigh. "I wish only to be back with Arc - my mistress."

"And when the Empress sends for you?"

He blinked. "I just said -"

"Come with me," Gryde interrupted, rising from the bench and offering a well-muscled arm.

Resigned to the continuing weakness of his body, Fenris placed his hand in the other male's and allowed himself to be dragged upright. Together they left the hall, traversing corridors that switched back upon themselves without warning, as though each new extension to the building had been slapped on without any care or forethought. The small meal had given him a measure of energy but was by no means a cure-all, and Fenris was panting heavily by the time Gryde ushered him into an elaborate room decorated in layers of hanging gauze and a foolish multitude of soft cushions.

"What is this?" Fenris asked, battling to keep his voice steady.

"A room, one of many, where concubines are brought for testing before purchase." Gryde barred the door behind them, his well-oiled muscles bulging in the light filtering in through the room's high windows. "It is also a doorway."

No longer as disturbed as he should be by phrases like 'testing before purchase,' Fenris sagged against the wall as Gryde crossed to the pile of cushions and began to kick them aside with his strong talons. In a matter of moments he'd revealed the woven rug underneath, which then rolled aside to display the paved stone floor.

"Do you need my assistance?" Fenris asked, brow furrowing as the harpy slid his fingers down the crack between two cobbles and began to tug.

Gryde flicked him an amused glance from beneath his lashes. "I thought you were useless to me in your current condition."

Before Fenris had a chance to respond, the palm-sized stone came free and Gryde set it aside with a grunt of satisfaction. He plunged his hand into the loose earth beneath, brows set with concentration as he rummaged almost elbow deep. A sharp click sounded in the back corner of the room, and the harpy drew back with a smile.

Fenris turned to eye the brickwork. "A false wall?"

"Yes." Gryde replaced the stone, rug, and cushions, then moved to the back corner and laid his palms flat against the stone. "This way."

Fenris staggered across the room as the section of wall slid sideways with a faint grinding sound, revealing a dark stairway leading downwards. He took Gryde's offered arm and wobbled down the first few steps, waiting while the harpy closed the door - cleverly mounted on a system of pulleys - and locked it in place.

"Incredible," Fenris murmured, leaning heavily on his guide as they descended. Fifty-two steps later, the crudely carved staircase emptied into a tunnel whose floor was worn smooth with the passage of many talons. The walls bore flickering torches set in iron brackets and there was barely room to walk side by side, the low roof forcing Fenris to bend almost double. "This place feels older than the building above us."

"Yes," Gryde agreed. "It's part of an ancient tunnel network which once stretched a great distance, but is now isolated after a cave-in. Such solitude suits our purposes."

After a short walk which left Fenris gasping and sweating, they emerged into a round cavern large enough to comfortably house twenty people. The floor was covered with an ancient, much-repaired rug that had a hole in the centre to accommodate a merrily burning brazier. Cushions in varying degrees of bad repair were strewn in groups across the rug, and a single crooked bookshelf slouched against one wall. Three other tunnels besides the one Fenris had entered through were spaced evenly around the walls, with torches burning in brackets either side of their openings.

Two other male harpies rose as Gryde and Fenris approached; one young, covered in whipping scars so severe that he only sported a single eye and seemed fortunate to be able to move at all, and the other so old and wizened that his facial features were almost impossible to make out beneath a veritable legion of wrinkles. And… he had feathers. Only a few straggly feathers barely the length of Fenris' pinky finger, but feathers nonetheless.

"Father." Gryde spoke in Universal Galactic, releasing Fenris so he could drop to his knees and clasp the ancient male's hands in his own. "I have returned."

"Gryde, my son." The older harpy's voice was strong and filled with an unwavering affection, his Universal Galactic impeccable. His raptor's eyes, bright in his wrinkled face, settled curiously on Fenris. "Who have you brought to me?"

Unable to remain standing without Gryde's support, Fenris also fell to his knees. He held out his arm in the warrior's way and said, "I am Fenris, Guardian to the Weaver, Warden to the Deerken and Overlord of the Timeless Kingdom."

Why he felt the need to pontificate the full breadth - or at least, the most relevant - of his titles, he couldn't say, but the Father smiled as though he'd been anticipating it all along. Clasping Fenris' extended hand in both of his, the harpy kissed his upturned palm. "Welcome, son. You may call me Juno."

"Juno is our Father," Gryde explained, his reverence making clear differentiation between title and biology. "He keeps the forbidden history of males, guards our spirits and is our beating heart in the desert. This," and he waved a hand at the younger male, "is his apprentice, Clecke."

"Hello," said Clecke, his musical lilt at odds with the barbaric nature of his scars. "I am pleased to be meeting you."

"Pleased to meet you," Juno corrected smoothly, his smile indulgent. He offered Fenris a conspiratorial wink. "Our Clecke's grasp of the Goddess' tongue is not yet perfect."

"So I see." Fenris sat back on his heels and waved a hand at their surroundings. "What is this place?"

"A closely guarded secret," Gryde said heavily, his eyes glittering as they locked onto Fenris' face. "And entirely forbidden."

Clecke shifted his feet further apart, muscles tensing. Turning his head in the direction of the young apprentice-come-bodyguard, Fenris raised a trembling hand. "Peace, little brother. I will keep your secrets."

"And share your own, perhaps?" Juno asked.

Before Fenris had a chance to formulate an intelligent response, there was an odd, almost-there popping noise and something warm and very much alive dropped directly onto the top of his head. The three harpies jerked back in shock as Fenris raised both hands on instinct, plucking the furry bundle off his sweat-stiffened curls.

Huge blue eyes stared out of a ginger-furred face framed by ears big enough to catch a wayward holo signal. The interloper had a disproportionately small body in comparison to her head, a ridiculously long tail and whiskers which would, given the opportunity, wave mischievously in the wind. Most importantly, she clutched a crude wooden spoon between two adorably tiny paws.

"Mrow," the spoon kitten announced, her expression settling into one of deliberate innocence.

Weaver's grace, how had the creature come to be *here*? Fenris had last seen her in the Timeless Kingdom, before they'd fought Taelon, and assumed she'd remained behind. Giant eyelashes fluttered winsomely and a moment later the kitten disappeared, popping back into existence on top of Fenris' head again. He immediately snatched her off, his fingers trembling as he held her at eye level and growled, "No."

This time when she disappeared, she was gone a heartbeat longer - only to re-materialise on Fenris' shoulder, where she wrapped her tail several times around the column of his throat and settled her body across the back of his shoulders with a satisfied purr.

"What... is that?" Gryde asked, his jaw slack as he regarded the kitten.

Not in the least certain how to explain a being he didn't understand himself, Fenris grunted. "Someone who thinks I'm her personal ride."

There was a long silence and then Juno laughed, the echoing sound causing the other two harpies to jump. "She seems rather fond of you, my son. I think you've got yourself a partner."

"Just don't let her see your spoons," Fenris muttered, trying to ignore the way his heart softened as the kitten purred and rubbed her head against his jaw. It proved impossible; moisture gathered in the corners of his eyes and escaped to trickle down his cheeks.

"My son." Juno waved a hand and Clecke obediently produced one of the better looking cushions, helping Fenris settle onto it. No sooner had the young harpy stepped aside than Gryde offered a wooden tumbler of cool, blessedly meetha-free water, steadying Fenris' hands when their shaking would have caused a mess. Juno nodded in approval as the cup was emptied and set aside. "Better?"

"Thank you," Fenris managed, inclining his head. The spoon kitten took immediate advantage of the opportunity, purring even louder as she rubbed against his jaw.

Juno watched the encounter with a knowing look. "Well, now. Why don't you start at the beginning?"

To Fenris' surprise, words began to tumble from his lips. Haltingly at first, then with greater precision, he recounted the events which had led him to escape the Timeless Kingdom by leaping into a destabilised portal, and waking in a frozen ruin with Arcana staring down at him. That moment was branded into his memory for all eternity, a slap in the face which he'd assumed was due to shock but now knew was something entirely different. He continued speaking, describing his visit to Sorcen, his battle with the warg, the trip to Corrin's Run and the ensuing rescue of Burke. Finally he told of his parents, of his return to the Timeless King-dom, and the fierce, foolish battle with Taelon which had led to yet another leap of faith into an unstable portal.

A portal which had torn Arcana apart.

Editing out his feelings had been easy enough until that point, but Fenris couldn't control the way his voice cracked when he came upon the telling of her injuries; of realising they were stranded in a desert whilst she clung to life by the merest thread. To his surprise, Juno reached out a wrin-kled hand and gave his shoulder a firm squeeze.

"Our women are nothing like yours, but they will care for her - if for no other reason than they share a gender," the elderly harpy reassured him. "If she lives and breathes, I have no doubt she will come for you."

"If I live that long."

"You will," Juno assured him, then flicked Gryde a sharp look. "He must."

"I agree more than ever before, Father - but how can I make a warrior, a leader, into a slave and concubine? His life has not been like ours." Gryde shook his head, eyes shining with a newfound respect and awe that made

Fenris shift uncomfortably. "At least now I understand the reason behind your upset with the meetha and your c-"

"Yes," Fenris cut him off, covering his loincloth with a trembling hand.

"What name do you give your creature?" Juno asked.

Fenris blinked rapidly. "My... what?"

"Your creature." The Father waved a hand at the spoon kitten. "It is magnificent."

"Oh," said Fenris, sagging with relief. "For a moment I thought - never mind. I have given her no name, not yet."

Clecke looked horrified. "Didn't your mistress - my apologies, your... woman - say you should?"

"I suppose she did." Fenris reached up with one trembling hand and stroked the spoon kitten's head, feeling another treacherous tug in his chest as she nuzzled into the caress. After a moment's consideration, he said, "Lyra."

"Lyra," Gryde repeated, testing the unfamiliar syllables and doing a fair affectation of Fenris' rolling pronunciation. "What does it mean?"

"It is a derivative of the fey term for freedom of heart." Fenris paused and then, clearing his throat, spouted the first line of an ancient fey song about a queen and king who'd found their freedom of heart in one another. Though he knew the three harpies would have no understanding of the language, hearing the tongue upon which he was raised helped to soothe his nerves. He stroked the kitten's head again. "If she is to be named, I think it should be for freedom."

Lyra mewed in agreement and the three harpy males beamed in delight. "Lyra it is, then." Juno's smile abruptly faded. "You must not let her be seen upstairs."

"I think, considering this is the first time I have seen her at all since my arrival, that she knows," Fenris returned, then shrugged. "Either way, I have no method to force her compliance. You've seen how wilful she is - and truthfully, we barely know each other."

Gryde's lips tightened, and he sighed. "We will have to hope, then."

"Hope," Juno agreed, his hands pressed together as if in prayer. "Now that you've shared something of yourself with us, I think it's fair to say we do the same. Clecke?"

"Yes, Father." The younger harpy immediately stood and moved to the bookshelf, rummaging through the piles of scrolls.

"While he looks, I'll begin," Gryde said, settling more comfortably on his cushion. "First and foremost is that we were not always slaves. The first

Empress' reasons for casting us down are unknown, but the first Father was chosen shortly after the enslavement of our gender, in the hope that there may be some of us, however few, who remembered the truth. Back then we had names, and rights, and laws beyond the word of our mistresses. We speak the language of the Goddess to remind ourselves that once, things were different."

Clecke returned with a scroll, which he reverently laid into the Father's hands. Juno smoothed it out, revealing a partly burnt hide depicting a male and female harpy hand in hand. Each had a full set of wings, and a string of beads and feathers was woven into their downy manes. Clecke's voice was thick with longing as he said, "Once, we all flew."

Fenris eyed the pockmark scarring on the younger harpy's arms and noted it was far less than that of his counterparts. "You're young yet. It may still happen, brother."

"Unlikely," Juno said softly, though not without kindness. "As far as the females are concerned, both Clecke and I are dead. We may be safe here, but we are also entombed. Even should his feathers breach the scarring, we will never see the sky."

Struck with equal parts pity and rage, Fenris reached out a trembling finger and traced the delicate illustration. "They wear matching beads, and each other's feathers."

"A ceremony in which two equals chose to bind their lives together. The beads signify the colours of their house - a custom which continues amongst the women today - and the feathers are from each other's wings as a symbol of undying loyalty."

"And love," Fenris murmured, noting the way the two figures stared at each other. "This is a marriage vow."

"Marriage," Gryde tasted the unfamiliar word, then looked at Juno with a furrowed brow. "What is a marriage, Father?"

Juno gave Fenris a look of respect before turning to answer. "Exactly what you heard; a choice to join lives and hearts for a shared future."

"To love a slave?" Clecke's nose wrinkled. "Such a thing is forbidden. Instant death."

"That was not always the case." Juno's voice was soft and sad. "As we were not always slaves, so too was it not always forbidden to care."

"You say the circumstances are unknown," Fenris said slowly, "but you must have some details, surely."

Juno ran a reverent hand over the scroll and then allowed it to close, returning it to Clecke's care. "Not many. One day, the Empress rose up in a great rage and declared all those with phalluses to be evil. Our gender was imprisoned in one foul, sweeping gesture. Those who fought were executed, male and female alike, and the rest beaten to submission. Children were stolen, locked away, and trained in the new ideology until they were strong enough to take over the duties of elders they never saw. Once that happened, the older generation were slaughtered and burnt, that the past may never be discovered. Only the Father and his few chosen sons, safely hidden here below ground, escaped the carnage."

"Eliminating the history of an entire civilisation in a matter of years," Fenris murmured, shaking his head.

"Yes." Gryde nodded. "Now we all live our lives in chains, one way or another."

Juno reached out a soothing hand, brushing it over Gryde's oiled forearm. "You do well for us, my son. Do not allow bitterness to overcome your generous heart."

"Have you ever thought of fighting back?" Fenris asked, eyeing each of them in turn. "Regaining what was lost?"

Clecke laughed. "How? We have no weapons, no knowledge, and apart from the few males who came down here as brothers, no inclination. It is suicide."

"Did you try?" Fenris asked, eyeing the young male's horrific scarring. "Is that why you were beaten and thrown out for dead?"

Clecke's single eye narrowed. "I dared to help a fallen slave when weakness overtook him. When a guard came to separate us, I slapped her spear away."

"Brave."

"Stupid," Clecke snorted. "The fallen male was immediately run through and I was whipped almost to death. If not for a brother in the Pit, who sensed the spark of life inside my broken body, I would have long been food for the Brokkarra."

"Brokkarra?" Fenris looked up at Juno, whose face was sad as he regarded his scarred apprentice.

"The monster in the catacombs beneath the palace," Gryde answered instead, his tone sombre. "Once, these tunnels joined them, but as I said earlier, a cave-in keeps us separate and the Brokkarra itself prevents the blockage being discovered by our mistresses. The bodies of deceased jinra are gifted to the Brokkarra, as well as any live harpy sacrifice the Empress deems worthy."

"Worthy?" Clecke's lip twisted. "Anyone who displeases her, you mean."

Gryde's lips tightened. "I have seen worse mistresses than our Empress, young one. She treats those who please her well."

Clecke waved a hand down his length. "*I am clearly not to her taste.*"

"No," Juno murmured when Gryde made to rise. "I know you care for your Empress, my son; as her head concubine, it is part of your position. But you must see the flaws to truly appreciate the diamond."

After a long, tense moment, Gryde subsided back onto the cushion with a jerky nod. "Fine."

"So tell me," Fenris said, more to break the tension than anything else, "What, exactly, is your brotherhood's purpose?"

Juno interlinked his fingers and laid them in his lap. "It was the hope of the first Father that, one day, we can return to the surface and help our brothers re-integrate into society as equals. My sons keep an eye out for those we think may be willing to look beyond the veil which darkens their vision. When our society decides to suture her wounds, we will be ready with needle and thread."

Struck by the metaphor, Fenris' gaze dropped to the woven bracelet around his wrist - a simple, multicoloured adornment made from lost threads of the weave which Arcana had braided and fused in place with magic. He'd taken to toying with it when he needed reassurance, a dangerous tell for anyone paying attention but a compulsion he couldn't deny. Even now, his fingers spun the braided length in place, his eyes drawn to the many different colours that shimmered in the torchlight. Duty demanded the sight evoke thoughts of the Weaver and his home, but his heart offered only the image of Arcana's face, creased with a tender smile as she'd magicked the strands into permanency.

"Hope," Fenris said finally, "Is as essential as it is dangerous." When nobody answered, he raised his eyes not to Gryde, but Juno. "What is it you wish of me? Speak true and succinct, for I am weakening and will soon be in need of rest."

"Ah, yes, the meetha." Juno nodded slowly. "Gryde said it did not agree with you."

"It is killing me," said Fenris, his voice so blunt they flinched. "With every dose, as my - how do you put it? - male equipment hardens, the rest of my body weakens further than before. Whatever you wish of me, consider that my response will be limited by the noxious weed that your mistresses continue to shove down my throat, and the fact that should it continue, I will be dead within days."

"I said before that you will live, and I mean it," Juno returned. He took a deep breath, then turned to Gryde. "Why did you continue to offer meetha when it was obviously making him ill?"

"A standard over indulgence can cause fainting, so I assumed the problem was simply acclimatisation." Gryde bowed so low his forehead almost brushed the floor. "Please accept my apologies, brother. I should have listened to you."

"Apology accepted." Though it sent a shaft of agony up through his fingers, Fenris patted Gryde's shoulder. "I am unique; there was no way to guess what the herbs would do."

Gryde nodded and sat back again, his handsome face relaxing some-what - though his yellow eyes flickered with concern as they looked Fenris up and down. "We will have to work twice as hard to conceal your true nature from the women. If they realise you're not taking the meetha, there will be trouble."

"True." Juno frowned, then shrugged. "There is nothing for it but to take the risk; we cannot toy with Fenris' life more than has already been done."

Fenris rubbed both hands over his face, biting back the groan which threatened to escape. "I do not think you can make things any worse."

"Perhaps not, but with work, we might make things better."

Something in the old harpy's words had Fenris lowering his hands. "Work, indeed. What is it you wish of me, Father?"

"Don't look so worried, my son. All I ask is that should your mistress return, you plead our cause to her. Together, you have the means to show our people another way." Juno smiled, but his eyes were sad. "Conversely, should your mistress die and you fall into the hands of the Empress, I would ask you to assist Gryde in protecting as many of my sons as possible, that the memories of a better time might survive for younger generations."

Fenris' eyes drifted south, where the tiny, etched tattoo that had been necessary as part of his participation in the emancipation of Bel Itan stood out in stark relief against his grimy skin. Cradled by his hipbones, no less, as his naturally lithe frame ate itself from the inside in a desperate attempt to fuel his body. What he had suffered - what he would suffer - for Arcana, for the Weaver, for his cause, seemed as nothing in comparison to the generations of abhorrent slavery and torture the male harpies had endured. Fenris shook his head. "I have had people in far less desperate situations than yours asking me to overthrow governments for far lesser crimes, yet you ask only for words? For talk?"

"I ask for nothing I would not be willing to do myself," Juno said firmly. His wrinkled face swept into a brief, bright smile and he held out his knobbly arms, their few feathers silvered with age. "I cannot carry a spear, nor move in combat. To ask it of you would be unfair."

Clecke made a noise of protest in the base of his throat, turning his scarred face away to hide his expression. Fenris didn't need his heightened senses to see the tension in the young harpy's shoulders, or the way his hands balled into fists.

"I was once taught that a truly wise leader knows when to do things himself, and when to reach for the assistance of others." Fenris curled back his top lip, revealing his fangs. "My body may not be much now, but when I am stronger, I will do everything I can to aid your people."

Juno looked startled. "You will?"

"Yes." Fenris squared his shoulders and offered his arm in the warrior's way. "Without you, I die. Without me, you continue to rot in secrecy and stagnation. It is not so badly weighted a bargain as you think."

"Be certain," Juno warned. "We are asking for -"

"Life," Fenris interrupted. "You are asking for life." He offered them a smile, thin but real. "As am I."

The Father's fingers twitched, and then he laid them in Fenris' palm. "The bargain is sealed."

"No," Fenris shook his head. "Like this." He gripped the male's forearm and waited patiently until it was reciprocated in kind. "Greeting, farewell, binding. A warrior's oath."

"A warrior's oath," Juno repeated, staring down at their clasped arms for a long moment. "The women have a saying up above, you know - strength is life."

"They are right." Fenris retracted his hand before his body began to shake from the strain of extending his arm so long. "I once believed strength came from within, but since meeting Arcana I discovered there is more strength to be gained together than we could ever have accessed apart. Strength *is* life, but it comes from the heart and is best shared."

"Heart strength," Gryde murmured. "I like it."

"Me, too," Clecke agreed, his single eye shining as he looked up at Fenris. "We are all warriors, then, with strong hearts."

"Yes," Fenris agreed. "And one day, you will be free."

He had no business making such a promise but he made it anyway. All three men brightened at his words, and Gryde clapped him enthusiastically on the shoulder. The force of the blow toppled Fenris backwards, his body so weak he could do no more than flop helplessly across the cushions. Lyra, unseated by the movement, gave a furious yowl and disappeared. Feeling the kitten's loss more than he dared admit, Fenris squeezed his eyes shut against crashing waves of dizziness and the enormity of trying to stage a revolution when he couldn't even remain upright.

When at last he dared to lift his lashes, it was to see three concerned faces staring down at him.

"You didn't pass out." Gryde's surprise turned swiftly to a grin. "Looks like that loaf of bread did more good than I thought. We'll have you back to normal before you know it."

Accepting the proffered hand, Fenris allowed Gryde to tug him upright. "I fear we have different concepts of normal, but it will be better than death."

Clecke grinned, the movement making his scarred face all the more contorted. "On that, brother, we are agreed."

TWELVE
ARCANA

The interior of the palace was a welcome change from the heat of the desert, and Arcana sighed in relief as Mirran indicated a stone bench just inside the door. She dropped down, leaning back against the wall as Caelum drifted around the large foyer, sniffing at potted plants and poking his nose behind tapestries and hangings.

Mirran gestured at an enormous set of gilded doors opposite. "Throne room just through there."

"All right." Arcana eyed the wooden doors, noting the plants and animals carved into each. "Give me a minute."

"Yes. Smart to catch breath." The apprentice wise woman slid onto the stone bench at Arcana's side, her eyes tracking Caelum's exploration. "What called?"

"He's a deerken."

"Deerken," Mirran repeated, her tongue thick around the unfamiliar word. "You know well?"

"I was born into Arcana's arms," Caelum announced, crossing to stand beside the bench. "I've never been anywhere else than by her side."

Arcana smiled at Mirran's astonishment. "I was young when Caelum crashed into my life, but I've never regretted having him around."

"Good to have loyal." Mirran nodded. "Empress have many Jinra companion. Much favour for Jinra."

"A favour which has passed to Caelum." Arcana hesitated, biting her lip a moment. "Will he be in any danger before I walk the Gauntlet?"

"Never danger, before or after." Mirran's eyes rounded and her downy hair stood straight on end. "Never harm companion. Never harm Jinra, deerken, other creature. Caelum not property, cannot be taken. Belongs only to self."

Squashing the urge to snort, Arcana forced her smile to remain in place. "I'm relieved to hear that."

"So am I," Caelum added, bending to lip at her hair. He lowered his voice to little more than a suggestion of sound. "Too bad they kill me if they kill you."

Arcana leant into his strength. There was nothing to say to that, so why bother? The harpies were highly unlikely to believe in the soulmerge, and even less likely to grant concessions because of it. If anything, it would paint an even larger target on their backs, something Arcana was determined to avoid at all costs.

"Can walk now?" Mirran tilted her head, gaze assessing. "Empress waits."

"Yes, I think so." Arcana curled her fingers around one of Caelum's antlers and let him haul her upright. "Any last advice before we go in?"

Mirran was silent for a moment, her eyes roving the empty foyer. "All court inside to see. Much spectacle. Be brave, be strong. Strength is life."

"So you keep reminding me." Arcana slid her fingers down to Caelum's shoulder and straightened her spine. "All right. Let's go."

Mirran strode to the doors and loosed a shrill whistle. Barely a heartbeat passed and they swung wide to reveal a pair of guards in ceremonial leather, who waved them through with their spears. Mirran turned to Arcana and held out a hand. "With me."

The throne room of Hiraptha was much like any other great hall; long and cavernous, with a dais at the far end. Upon the dais knelt an enormous statue of a female harpy, her face chiselled into a serene expression and her cupped hands forming the throne. The Empress of Hiraptha sat straight backed and solemn in her sculpted chair, her skin a deep apricot and her feathery mane pure white. She wore the same leather crop and skirt as the other women, only hers was bleached white and decorated with rows of gold and turquoise beading. A long, thick golden cord hung around her neck and the crown upon her head was a circlet of woven gold feathers.

Beera stood by the Empress' left hand, watching with sharp eyes as Caelum advanced down the aisle that had been left in the centre of the room. Mirran's fingers tightened on Arcana's as they followed, a subtle warning to keep pace beside her. The room was filled with silent

Hirapthan women, each bedecked in copious amounts of jewellery and holding at least one slave's chain in her hand. The collared men stood in stark contrast to those Arcana had seen so far; each one washed and oiled to show off muscular physiques, their loose gauze loincloths so transparent that nothing was left to the imagination. Many bore stylised paintings over the scarring on their arms and some even had beads and feathers hanging from their slave collars.

Caelum sidestepped as he reached the foot of the dais, allowing plenty of room for Arcana to draw up beside him. Mirran dropped to her knees on the lowest of the stairs and spoke rapidly in Hirapthan, her twitters and clicks echoing in the vast, silent room.

The Empress stood amongst a clatter of beads, slowly descending the stairs and extending a hand to Arcana before speaking in perfect Universal Galactic. "Welcome, outsider. I am Empress Hisha'maniketh, Protector of all Hiraptha."

"Thank you for your hospitality, your Imperial grace." Arcana accepted the proffered hand and inclined her head respectfully. "My name is Arcana, and I am indebted to your healers for their impeccable care."

"Indeed." The Empress' inflection was unusual, her accent otherworldly in comparison to those wielded by Beera and Mirran. Her golden gaze slid over Caelum before returning to Arcana and making a thorough examination. "I would know from where you come and what business you have here, outsider."

Arcana gestured off into the distance. "I'm from far away. I was stranded here by accident, your Imperial grace."

"Oh?" The Empress arched a fine eyebrow. "My scouts didn't see your method of transportation."

"It caught fire, your Imperial Grace, and was destroyed." Arcana sighed and shook her head regretfully. "I was grievously wounded in the process, as I'm sure you're aware."

The Empress' eyes narrowed. "Unfortunate."

"It was indeed." Unsure of the proper etiquette, Arcana dared a small smile. "You can imagine my surprise to awaken here."

"Most certainly. Has it been explained that once you enter the protection of the citadel, you must face the Gauntlet and become Hirapthan?" The Empress tilted her head with avian precision. "Unless you choose death, of course."

"Mirran's explanation was most thorough, your Imperial Grace. I'm grateful to have a second chance at life."

"Delightful." The Empress inspected her nails, her tone clear that it was anything but. "And with that response, I take it you intend to collect the male who claims to be yours, should you succeed?"

"I do, your Imperial Grace."

"Hmm." The Empress clasped both hands in front of her. "He called himself Guardian. That is a term unfamiliar to Hiraptha."

"It is a name for the mating males where I come from," Arcana answered smoothly. "A Guardian is responsible for the care of his mistress above all else."

"A curious term. He is an exceptional specimen, to say the least. I found his colouring rather… intriguing."

Arcana tried not to look too eager. "Is he well?"

"As well as can be expected. I had him moved to better quarters to prepare for your ascension." The Empress paused, her gaze flitting over the assembled courtiers. "You may find it hard to keep him once you walk the Gauntlet. If you make it to the other side, of course."

"He is *mine*."

The Empress gave her a sharp look, the feathers on her arms fanning in spectacular display. "Will you fight for your rights to own him, outsider? For your place within Hiraptha?"

"Yes, your Imperial Grace."

"Excellent." The Empress smiled, showing two even rows of white teeth. "You will walk the Gauntlet tomorrow."

Arcana blinked, her hands balling into fists with the effort not to scream. A trap, and she'd walked right into it. Logic demanded she protest, but knowing the harpies would see that as a sign of weakness, Arcana lifted her chin. "I look forward to the opportunity to prove myself, your Imperial Grace."

"Good." The Empress hooked a finger and Beera hurried to her side. "Arcana will walk the Gauntlet after first meal. Will you announce it to the court?"

"Yes, Empress." Beera curtsied and hurried away, raising her voice to twitter and squawk at the gathered Hirapthans.

The Empress watched her courtiers' reactions for a few moments, a distinctly smug expression wreathing her sharp features. When she turned to Arcana, her smile carried a haughty edge. "Mirran will continue to assist with your preparations, but be warned - if you are successful in walking the Gauntlet, you will have to pay for her services."

"Of course, your Imperial Grace," Arcana returned, inclining her head. "I wouldn't dream of assuming she worked on charity."

"Hah! I will watch your progress tomorrow with interest, outsider." The Empress jerked her chin towards the door. "You are dismissed."

Arcana accorded the Empress a short curtsy, then turned and stalked away, Caelum hard on her heels. Rage propelled her through the streets of Hiraptha, her longer legs forcing Mirran to jog to keep up. For all her fury, her body wasn't used to the exercise and she was panting by the time they arrived back in her chamber - a fact that only served to make her angrier than before.

"A trap," Arcana hissed, throwing herself onto the bed. "The whole audience was nothing but a trap, and I fell for it."

"Spectacularly," Caelum drawled, kicking the door shut. "Still, if it makes you feel better, I think she'd have ordered you to walk the Gauntlet whether you fell for the trap or not."

Arcana growled low in her throat. "Mirran?"

"Honoured Caelum is right." The young wise woman pressed her lips into a thin line. "Empress has seen male. Wants."

"Well, she can't have him," Arcana muttered, raising both hands to scrub at her face. "If the Empress thinks she's got the better of me, she needs to think again."

Mirran looked at Arcana as though she thought there might be a screw loose, then dug through her basket and pulled out the now familiar blue bottle. "One measure every meal. Help to fix," she said, pressing the bottle into Arcana's hands. "Will return two meals to check, then third meal to go. Try sleep. More sleep, more energy."

"All right," Arcana set the bottle beside her bed. "I'll do my best."

"Is all can ask." Mirran shouldered her basket, bowed to Caelum and left.

Arcana waited until the bar thumped into place on the other side of the door before she rolled to her feet and wrapped her arms around Caelum, burying her face in the comforting warmth of his shoulder. "I'm not thinking straight, am I? I walked right into the Empress' trap."

"You did, but we both knew this was coming," he replied, nudging her back to the mattress and dropping to his knees so they were eye height. "How much magic have you got?"

Turning towards the partially bloomed succulent that had been her bane the last few days, Arcana summoned her magic and gave a shove. The little cactus stiffened, and a moment later sprouted a multitude of sharp spines.

Caelum blinked. "I take it we're going with strategy over strength, then."

"Thanks for that, Captain Obvious."

The deerken narrowed his eyes. "Oh, I'm sorry. Would you prefer to discuss the extraordinary amount of penises on display in that room instead?"

"Great Gods of Sorcen, no," Arcana shuddered. "Those transparent loincloths were horrible."

"Weren't they just?" Caelum levered upright and drifted towards the table, bending to inspect the little plant. "How much magic did you pump into this thing?"

"Everything I had." Arcana squinted in the succulent's direction. "Why?"

"It's just… shit!" Caelum jerked backwards, several sharp spines lodged in the end of his soft nose. "It's defending itself."

Arcana stared at the spines in silence, then at the cactus, which was already regrowing what it had shed. "Well… okay."

Caelum's eyes crossed as he examined his besmirched nose. "A little help, please."

With careful fingers, Arcana removed the trio of spines and held them up for inspection. "At least we can say for sure my magic's getting stronger."

"Did you cast a spell?" Caelum asked, his eyes once again on the cactus. "Set an intent?"

"No. Why?"

He hesitated. "I felt your anger when you reached for the plant, and then… I felt an echo from the plant itself. When I bent to check more closely, it attacked. Now the echo is gone."

Arcana stared down at her hands. "Are you saying I infected the plant somehow?"

"Infected is the wrong word. I think you magically imprinted your emotions on the cactus, which I was able to sense because I can sense all your emotions." Caelum directed a scathing look at the blood-tipped spines in Arcana's palm. "When I leant close, I triggered a proximity alarm and the plant attacked."

Tossing the spines across the room, Arcana slumped backwards onto the bed with a groan. "What has the Weaver done? What have I become?"

"We'll worry about that later. For now, let's focus on freeing Fenris."

"The Empress said he'd been moved to better quarters." Arcana twisted to watch him pace across the floor and back. "You don't believe her?"

"The men here are all slaves. On a scale of deep hell to glorious paradise, how good a place do you think it's going to be?"

"You're right." Arcana closed her eyes, her mind filled with an image of Fenris' soft smile. "We have to get him back."

Caelum's head settled onto her abdomen, his voice vibrating deep in her bones. "We will. Whatever it takes, we will."

THIRTEEN
FLARE

Flare wasted no time returning to the scene of the attack to see what else he could learn. He wasn't particularly surprised to discover the halls were sparkling and clean, all three bodies missing. Propping both hands on his hips, he stared down at the polished floor and tried to think. Two of the servants had clearly been cretins in disguise, but what of the one Zaire had tried to defend? Had Zaire been with one of them, or on his own? Had he followed Flare, or the servants? Or had the servants lured the Ryllin Ambassador out into the middle of nowhere, only to attack him?

Whatever the answers were, he wasn't going to find them here, with the smell of bleach singeing the inside of his nostrils. With a final look over the corridor, Flare returned to his rooms and stripped off his formal robes, heading for the shower. As the scalding water cascaded over his skin, Flare replayed the night over and over in his mind. Whilst he had no proof, he was certain Zaire had been following him - which led to the ludicrous assumption that the servants had been following Zaire in turn, waiting for an opportunity to bop him over the head and steal his blood. The entire situation didn't make a lick of sense, but the more Flare thought it over, the more his gut insisted he was right. But... why? Whilst there was clearly more to Zaire than met the eye, his indifference to Flare at the banquet had been genuine, so it seemed unlikely the man had wanted to continue their less than scintillating conversation.

Grumbling under his breath, Flare stepped out of the shower, towelled off and wandered naked to his bedroom, where he threw himself onto the immaculately made but incredibly uncomfortable bed. The room was so small the mattress touched the walls on all sides and the only way he could stretch out fully was to stick his legs into the open wardrobe. Flare snorted, propping his heels on a pile of clean towels. He didn't even top six feet; how did the taller Ambassadors handle it? Gods knew that Fenris, at seven feet, would be almost folded in half.

Thoughts of the softly spoken Guardian led inevitably to thoughts of Arcana. Flare longed to watch the holo she'd sent him of herself mucking about in bed – in *bed* – with Fenris, but didn't dare access his personal channel on the station's consoles. He sighed. She'd sent that holo to tease him, but he loved it because, for the first time since her bonding with Caelum, she'd looked happy. Flare had noticed the pull between Arcana and Fenris from the moment they'd arrived on Sorcen and though he'd done his older-brother best to test the other male's resolve, he'd been thrilled when Fenris had gone after Arcana anyway. If anyone could charm his younger sister out of her self-imposed emotional stagnation, it was Fenris. Wherever they were, Flare hoped they were together and that Caelum was giving them hell in his absence.

He hooked a toe through the strap of Arcana's leather satchel and flicked it upward, snatching it out of the air with one hand. Battered from use but otherwise unharmed after the magical explosion that had melted Flare's sitting room, it had been the first thing he'd packed for his trip. Without Arcana to activate the bottomless pit spell it was nothing more than a normal bag, but Flare needed the reminder of her existence the same way he needed air. When Lesce had given him her patented stink-eye, he'd justified the satchel's inclusion by throwing some of his own things inside and boarding the Alliance transport with it over his shoulder. Settling the bag comfortably against his naked chest, Flare wrapped both his arms around it and closed his eyes.

He didn't remember falling asleep, but nonetheless woke several hours later in a clammy sweat, the nightmare so familiar by now he couldn't remember what it was like to sleep without it. Somewhere during the course of his restless dreaming he'd ended up on his stomach, the buckles on the satchel digging painfully into his ribs. Groaning and scrubbing his face, Flare struggled upright and padded into the main room, locating a clock and blinking muzzily at it until the numbers came into focus. 4am. Right. Shuddering at the thought of attempting more sleep, he threw himself into a rigorous full body workout. It was, like everything else, too much too soon but he stoically refused to quit, continuing until he collapsed from exhaustion.

After an hour to collect himself and another hot shower, Flare regarded his quarters with a frown. The moment the janitors entered, they'd see that he'd slept on the bed rather than in it, then puked and sweated everywhere – valuable information in what he was certain was about to become a political battlefield. His speech at the banquet made his position on the warg painfully clear and just as Zaire had been quick to support him, Flare had no doubt there'd be others who stood in opposition, which meant leaving evidence of weakness lying about was a terrible idea.

Raising his hands, Flare drew a quick set of runes in the air, spoke a word of power, and incinerated his vomit. That left an odd scorch mark on the carpet in his rooms, but he was a fire sorcerer, right? Who was to say he hadn't eaten a bad batch of beans and farted himself stupid? Nobody, that's who. Tugging the covers on his bed straight, Flare drew on another set of comfortable, functional robes, forced a nutrition bar down his throat and made his way to the Council chambers. The moment he stepped into the foyer, Olivie appeared with a soft clearing of his throat.

"Hello, Olivie." Flare offered the portly man a smile. "What can I do for you?"

"Ambassador Flare." Olivie flicked a glance at the other ambassadors filing past and swept a courteous half bow. "I have those files you requested for your report, and took the liberty of booking you a presentation slot in this morning's session."

Flare blinked down at the datapad in Olivie's neatly manicured hand and then back up at the man's glittering black gaze. "This morning?"

"Yes, Ambassador. I thought you might wish to strike while the iron is hot, as they say."

"Right." Flare coughed delicately and received the slightest quirk of a brow in return. "Sure. Always been one of my favourite sayings, that. Thank you, Olivie."

"You are most welcome, Ambassador. I look forward to seeing the presentation." Olivie bowed again and turned away.

Grinding his teeth, Flare stomped into the Council chamber and sank onto one of the chairs, setting his back to a side wall and angling his body so that the datapad was shielded from curious passers-by. He studied the information Olivie had gathered as the room began to fill, looking up only when Eyrton slid into the chair beside him. "Z sleep in?"

"Something like that," Eyrton said, his voice carefully diplomatic. "Though he promised to thump your useless hide later on."

Flare snorted. "Does he normally sleep so late after a big night?"

The Ryllin considered, reaching back to play with the pewter clasp that kept his silvering hair off his face. "Sometimes. He's not lazy by nature."

"I see." Flare sucked on his teeth a moment, then shrugged. "Let him know that I look forward to my attempted pummelling."

Chancellor Kaiora clapped her hands then, forestalling Eyrton's reply. "Thank you, everyone. If you'll kindly take your seats, we'll begin." There was a rumbling of voices and a whispering of fabric as the last few Ambassadors sat, and then the Chancellor began to work through the long, tedious list of chores on her schedule. After what seemed like forever, she turned to Flare. "And now, we will hear from Ambassador Flare, on behalf of the planet Sorcen."

"Thank you, Chancellor." Flare stood, smoothing down his robes more for effect than necessity. He glanced at his datapad and cleared his throat. "As I said in the last meeting, Sorcen is willing to provide soldiers and healers to the Galactic Alliance post haste, but that's not all we have to offer."

"More of that liquor?" Someone called. The interruption was met by a smattering of laughter and a few grunts of approval.

Flare inclined his head in the voice's direction. "I can brew that myself at any time, friend. Simply knock upon my door and we can make arrangements."

"I thought you were too busy lusting after warg blood," another voice called.

"Ah, Ambassador Krowley. How good of you to make yourself known." Flare's lip quirked, his gaze settling on the sour faced warrior who wore an animal-skin cloak and a bandolier of knives. "My primary concern is indeed the warg, but I'm not without bartering chips when it comes to achieving that end. To begin with, Sorcen is willing to offer the use of our crystal array technology in Alliance starships." He tapped his datapad, causing the holo display in the centre of the room to show an image of a crystal cruiser heart wrenchingly similar to the one Arcana owned. "In addition to the engines in these ships - which are a quarter of the size of your current engines, can handle twice the strain and require no fuel other than sunlight - we will provide the services of the earth sorcerers who create and tune them. With the artisans on hand, crystal engines can be made to suit any kind of mechanical device from your largest starship to your mechanised toothbrush."

"According to this data, we could considerably expand the storage capacity on both haulers and troop transport," buzzed an insectoid looking alien. "Our fleets will be faster, too."

A low murmur went through the room and Flare waited for silence before he continued. "We also have an extensive range of specialist sorcerers at our disposal. Artisan spellwork can be used for a variety of applications from strengthening steel and enchanting arrows, to water-proofing fabric, making medicines and preserving foodstuffs. A more detailed list is available for you here." Again he tapped the datapad, sending the relevant files into the Council's public directory. "I can arrange any and all of these services upon request."

"For a price, no doubt," Krowley snarled.

Flare offered his best boy-next-door smile. "I believe the correct term is an exchange of service and goodwill, Ambassador. That is the tenet of the Galactic Alliance, is it not?"

"It depends on what you want in return." A thin woman of middling height with violet skin, two slender tentacles instead of arms and a nest of thicker tentacles in place of legs, stood and focussed silver eyes in his direction. "Your speech last night left nothing to the imagination where your motivations are concerned, Ambassador."

"Indeed, Miss…?"

"Vashkeena," she supplied, "Ykkron Nine."

Flare let his face turn contemplative. "Ah, Ykkron Nine. Tell me, is Dhorkanna doing well?"

Vashkeena blinked, her tentacles curling in surprise. "The crown princess is doing very well, thank you."

"Wonderful. I was worried after that unfortunate accident with the alduccia tree, despite her assurances." Flare pondered a little longer, then shrugged. "In any case, my motives are what I feel to be delightfully trans-parent, Ambassador. The warg are a plague upon life which, if not addressed, will consume each and every last one of us. I'm not afraid to admit that thwarting the plans of the madman driving them is of utmost importance to me."

"I see." Vashkeena attempted to remain expressionless and failed spec-tacularly. "A mighty goal for one man to undertake."

Flare lowered his lashes to half-mast and allowed a sinful smile to curve his lips. His body softened, his posture became inviting and he purred, "I can be very convincing, Ambassador. Have no doubt."

The Ykkroni's silver eyes flashed pink and she sat abruptly, one curled tentacle held to her mouth. "I will pass your regards to the crown princess, Ambassador."

"Thank you." Flare inclined his head, sloughing off his bedroom air with a quick roll of his shoulders. He turned to Chancellor Kaiora, whose four eyes were narrowed in contemplation, and said, "If it pleases the Council, I'd like to open the topic of the warg for debate."

She flicked a glance at her timepiece. "It's never truly closed, but we haven't time for a lengthy discussion now. Say your piece quickly."

"In exchange for full access to Sorcen's services - which, as I've extolled, are many - I ask only that the Alliance bend a portion of their attentions to finding and repelling the warg." Flare gestured at the room full of Ambassadors. "Until now, you've kept your cards close and only reacted when necessary, but that time has passed. If we do not make a stand soon, we will be overrun."

"Separating our military might is a big risk," a nervous looking male demurred.

"Hiding is a bigger one," Flare countered. "Particularly when I'm offering soldiers to bolster your ranks."

"Untested soldiers," Krowley spat, thumping a fist against his chest. "In *dresses*."

Flare raised an eyebrow. "Would a test of our enrobed mettle please you, Ambassador?"

"It would." Krowley rose to his feet, hooking one thumb in his thick belt. "Two weeks ago, several Alliance ships went missing in the twelfth quadrant. A search has been launched, with no real results. I propose Sorcen's Ambassador take over the investigation and either recover our missing ships and personnel, or present a satisfactory explanation as to their fate."

"And if we succeed?" Flare asked.

"Then I'll be willing to back your proposal, and those allied with me will do so too." Krowley paused, his ebony lips curving into a cold smile. "Should you fail, however…"

Flare simply turned towards the Chancellor and waited. Kaiora frowned at Krowley. "You're willing to relinquish control of the investigation to Ambassador Flare, that he may act on Sorcen's behalf?"

"I am."

"Any objections from the Council?" Kaiora stared around the silent room, then nodded. "It is done, then. Have Olivie forward the relevant information to Ambassador Flare's console."

"Yes, Chancellor." Krowley bowed, then flicked Flare a smile that was all teeth. "Good luck."

Flare returned to his seat, suffering through the last few items on the agenda before the Chancellor finally called an end to the meeting. Flare muttered a hasty goodbye to Eyrton and shot out into the foyer, using his new assignment as an excuse to track down Olivie as fast as was decorously possible.

"We meet again, Ambassador." Olivie took the datapad from Flare's hand and swapped it with another. "This is a more secure pad than the previous and contains all of Lord Krowley's notes upon the missing ships, as well as any other relevant data. I've scheduled a meeting for you after lunch, so that you can touch base with the other Ambassador assigned to the case."

"Another Ambassador?"

"Yes, yes, we rarely do these things on our own." Olivie smiled, then tapped the datapad to show the time. "You have an hour before you're expected in the meeting room. Co-ordinates are on the datapad."

An hour? Gods above. Bowing in thanks, Flare hurried back to his rooms and ordered a thick toasted sandwich for lunch. He'd barely taken a bite when his room console chimed with a familiar call code. Grimacing, he answered with the tap of a finger. "Sister dear, how lovely to hear from you."

Lesce's face appeared on the screen conveniently placed above Flare's tiny table. She was dressed in casual robes, with strands of plum hair escaping her bun, a steaming mug in hand and heavy shadows under her eyes. None of it lessened the sharp look she gave him before she said, "You still look awful. Are you eating?"

He hefted his sandwich and took a deliberately large bite. "Yup."

"Craddagh's cauldron, how much cheese and bacon is in that thing?"

Flare chewed as slowly as possible, then swallowed and turned the sandwich for her viewing pleasure. "There's no such thing as too much cheese, or bacon, dearest sibling."

"If you weren't sorely malnourished, I might lecture you on the dangers of heart disease," Lesce muttered, adopting the pained expression with which he was so familiar.

"You're a heart disease."

"Mature." She rolled her eyes. "How secure is this channel?"

Flare took another bite of his cholesterol sandwich. "As iron clad as my underwear."

"You don't wear -" Lesce cut off and pinched the bridge of her nose. "Right."

He smiled around his bacon. "Salve there?"

"Hello, Flare." Lesce's husband appeared in the frame, his iron grey hair glinting in the firelight. "You're looking better."

"He is not," Lesce scoffed.

Salve shook his head. "I didn't say he was looking well, heart of my heart, simply better."

"It's seeing your handsome face that does it," Flare returned with a wink.

Salve snorted. "If you say so. Well, come on, give it up."

Flare provided an edited version of his adventures thus far, keeping purely to the official events so that whoever was spying on the call - and he wasn't foolish enough to believe there wasn't someone - would hear nothing more than dreary grain reports, a bitter sorcerer delivering a scathing speech at a banquet, and the deal he'd just brokered with Krowley. Salve and Lesce nodded as he spoke, his sister crinkling her nose every time he took a bite of his sandwich and deliberately spoke with his mouth full.

"It's progress," said Salve, squeezing his wife's shoulders.

"Yes." Lesce nodded, her face tight. "No other news, then?"

Flare raised an eyebrow. "I've barely unpacked, sister dear. There's been time for nothing else, though I've had no lack of invitations."

It wasn't what she'd been asking and they all knew it, but Flare would be damned if he was discussing Arcana aloud on an insecure connection. Lesce's face darkened at mention of possible bedroom exploits, and she snapped, "Try not to contract some sort of hideous, sexually transmitted disease, won't you? I'm not there to hand out cures and kiss boo boos."

"Such faith from the Healing Elder." Flare waved a lazy hand. "I've had my shots and my protection spells are all active. There will be no diseases, surprise conceptions, or accidental soiling of familial honour."

Her eyes narrowed. "Reassuring."

"Have I let you down thus far?"

Lesce's jaw tightened and he knew she longed to say yes, but Salve deliberately bent closer to the camera, obscuring her from view. "We best not keep you, brother. I'd hate you to be late for your meeting."

"Indeed." Flare offered Salve a genuine smile. "Don't be afraid to call without your piranha next time. If I want my toes nibbled, I've got plenty of options."

There was a shriek behind Salve. The stocky sorcerer's eyes widened at the sound of smashing crockery and, a moment later, a slamming door. "Did you have to?"

"She makes it so easy."

The healer shook his head. "I don't understand you two, I really don't. Are you going to fight forever?"

"Did she tell you -"

"She won't talk about it."

"Well then," Flare drawled, "I'd say you have your answer."

Salve's eyes narrowed. "You're not innocent in this, Flare."

"Nor am I the aggressor," he reminded, shrugging. "I will die for my family, Salve, but that doesn't mean I have to accept how they treat me."

The other man sighed. "Fair enough. Take care of yourself."

"You too." Flare shut off the call and shoved the last bite of sandwich in his mouth, chewing out his frustration. A quick glass of water later, he slid his datapad into Arcana's satchel along with an old-fashioned notepad and pencil, and went to meet his new comrade.

The door to the meeting room slid soundlessly open when he arrived, revealing a small bar with an assortment of carafes and glasses, a long, polished wooden table surrounded by twelve richly upholstered chairs, and a floor to ceiling screen on the far wall which currently displayed a faux space-scape. Flare stepped inside, already shaking his head at the single occupant who sat at the far end of the table. "Well, toss me in Craddagh's cauldron and start me over."

"Belief in deities is often misplaced and distracting," Zaire replied, not bothering to look up from his datapad. "Besides, I don't think starting over would fix things."

"Probably not." Flare sauntered around the table, hanging Arcana's satchel on the back of the chair opposite Zaire's. "I see your sparkling personality survived your recent adventure."

The Ryllin's lips tightened, indigo eyes flashing beneath gorgeously luxuriant lashes. "Are you always so… you?"

"Unapologetically."

"Shame," Zaire sighed. "You'd be much prettier if you didn't open your mouth all the time."

"All the best things happen with my mouth open - keeping it shut would be a crime against pleasure." When Zaire jerked in surprise, Flare clicked his tongue between his teeth. "I warned you not to lay down the gauntlet unless you were prepared for me to pick it up."

"Hmm." The faint hints of blue at Zaire's temples darkened ever so slightly and Flare realised the Ryllin was blushing. "So, you're taking over from Krowley. Here I thought it couldn't get any worse than that overbearing, stuffed-up peacock."

"I think Krowley and his spear might have something to say about that comparison," Flare returned, amused in spite of himself. "He's wasted no time painting himself as a warrior."

Zaire snorted. "He's a show pony. Too busy waving his animal skins and banging tribal drums when, on my planet, he'd already be dead."

Setting one forearm on the table, Flare leant over until they were almost nose to nose. Zaire smelt of impending rain with a faintly metallic edge, a refreshing and surprisingly pleasant scent that matched his pale, blue-tinted skin and perfect dark hair. "Is that a threat?"

"A statement of fact." Indigo eyes flashed and Zaire's voice lowered. "My people are assassins and rogues. We fight in the dark and it's quick, dirty, and effective."

Flare lowered his lashes, tilting his head so that several stray locks of orange hair flopped down on his forehead. "Again with the challenges."

"Is everything sexual to you?" Zaire sat back with a frown. "People have gone missing - this isn't a game."

"Life is sex and sex is life," Flare replied, studying his companion's expression. "You know someone who's missing."

Zaire sighed, looking suddenly weary. "Have you looked over the files yet?"

"Haven't had a chance."

"The ships which disappeared were a Ryllin medical frigate and her Alliance escort. They were delivering much needed supplies and personnel from Rylle to Galactic Station." His jaw tightened briefly. "I know a few of the staff on board the ship, but there's nobody I'd call friend. That doesn't change the fact that they're gone, however."

Flare leant back, tapping his datapad to bring up the relevant files. "The medical frigate was from Rylle, and the escort made up of Killkarro reavers from Karrjhan. That's why Krowley was involved?"

"Yes." Zaire reached over to tap Flare's screen, displaying a list of cargo and supplies on board. "Once every two months, Ryllin personnel are cycled between Alliance Station and our home planet. It helps avoid stagnation."

"And provides an opportunity to pay homage to your Oracle," Flare added. When Zaire blinked, he offered a razor's smile. "Well, those of you foolish enough to believe in deities, anyway."

"Yes." Zaire's head tipped forward, his waterfall of silky black hair sliding forward to hide his face. "Many feel the absence of the Oracle's presence and require regular trips home to worship in person."

"But not you?"

"I have no need of any religion bar that of my blades," Zaire said softly, his voice as slick as the blue sheen on his hair. On impulse, Flare reached out to run his fingers through it, savouring the cool, almost liquid feeling of the strands brushing over his skin. The tip of a dagger was at his throat before he'd blinked, Zaire's blazing eyes filling his vision. "Don't. Touch. Me."

"Sorry."

Flare's quick and ready apology had the other man shifting back, confusion marring his brow. "I -"

"No need to explain. I wasn't thinking, and it was inappropriate to touch you without invitation." Flare lowered his eyes to the dagger, now wavering towards the table. "Nice."

Zaire's knuckles whitened, then he flicked his wrist and offered the dagger's hilt. Flare accepted the weapon graciously, turning it over in his hands. It was surprisingly light, with a balance point perfect for both slashing and throwing. He twirled the blade back and forth in his fingers before returning it to Zaire, whose indigo eyes shimmered with grudging respect. "You know what you're doing."

"So do you." Flare tilted his head. "You move well."

The Ryllin's face pinched and he flicked a glance around the room. "When the occasion calls for it."

"Of course." Taking the warning for what it was, Flare spent the next few minutes looking through the files in greater detail. "The place the ships disappeared was nothing special. Were they pulled out of jump space?"

"Krowley thought so, but I disagree." Zaire shoved to his feet, stomped to the bar and poured himself a measure of water. "The amount of effort required to pull a ship out of jump space is phenomenal."

"Not to mention, you'd have to know exactly where they were going to be, and when." Flare pursed his lips. "Something must have happened to make them drop jump space, upon which they were ambushed."

Zaire's nod was crisp. "That's what I said."

Flare looked back down at the datapad, then up at Zaire, who was watching him intently over the lip of his glass. "The ambush was in the middle of nowhere."

"You already said that."

"Perhaps I enjoy repeating myself." Flare's jaw flexed, and he wondered how to word his question without alerting any potential listeners to the suspicion forming in his gut. It seemed impossible, so he said it straight. "Sounds like sabotage."

"One of many possibilities Krowley and I discussed," Zaire responded, his tone so breezy Flare immediately knew it was fake. "The most agree-able theory is that some sort of mechanical fault caused them to pop back to real space, and a group of pirates stumbled upon the convoy by accident."

Pirates. A chill rolled down Flare's spine and his mouth turned dry. Getting to his feet, he uttered a low string of ancient Sorcen under his breath, his hands flowing through the air in a series of quick, precise movements that left a trail of orange sparks in their wake. He pressed both palms together to activate the magic and a shimmering bubble spread out from his hands, ensconcing himself and Zaire inside. "I can't hold this forever, but it's soundproof. You know there's more to this, don't you?"

To his credit, the Ryllin only glanced at the bubble before his indigo eyes settled back on Flare. "Yes. Krowley didn't want to listen, but there's more."

"Does it have to do with the attack the other night?"

"Yes and no." Zaire sucked his teeth, his expression curious as he swept his gaze up and down Flare's length.

"Whatever you're looking for, make it quick," Flare grunted, sweat forming across his brow. "I've got another thirty seconds on this."

"I've got more information," Zaire answered promptly, "but becoming involved is not a decision you can retract."

"I'm in."

"You don't want to think about it?"

Flare shook his head. "I'm more a jump first kind of guy."

"Somehow I'm not surprised." Zaire pressed his lips together in a thin line and then nodded. "All right. Drop the shield and follow my lead."

The magic dissipated with a soft hiss and Flare sagged against the table, his heart hammering. "Gods above, I hate that spell."

"A personal nemesis?"

"I'm a fire sorcerer," he snapped. "Did you see any fire then?"

Zaire's brow furrowed ever so slightly. "No."

"Right. The particulars are complicated, but basically the spell uses fire to heat the air and forge it hard, like an actual shield. The magic particles are not only microscopic but must burn at incredible intensity to maintain their shape." He hesitated, conscious of revealing a limit to any listening ears. "It's hard."

Zaire accepted the explanation with a nod, face smooth. "I suppose such an effort must make you hungry."

"It can."

"Shall we adjourn for a meal, then?" Zaire smiled, the expression so forced his face looked as if it might crack. "I make a mean casserole."

Flare smoothed his robes and slid his datapad back into his bag. "Are you asking me on a date?"

Indigo eyes narrowed for a fraction of a second. "Eyrton will be there."

"You know what they say - two's company, three's a teenage boy's fantasy."

Scooping up his own things, Zaire crinkled his nose. "Nobody says that about dates."

"I do."

"Are you coming or not?"

Flare waggled his eyebrows. "If we're both very, very lucky."

"Oracle save us." Zaire blew out between clenched teeth, then turned and made for the door. "I'm going to regret this."

Knowing he should stop and horribly aware he couldn't, Flare paused in the taller man's shadow, staring guilelessly up into those fathomless indigo eyes. His heart kicked up a notch as their gazes locked and the scent of metallic rain teased his nostrils. "Not if I can help it."

FOURTEEN
FENRIS

"AGAIN."

Fenris looked up and then swiftly back down again, narrowly avoiding the cardinal sin of raising his head in front of a mistress. Or in this case, Gryde, who was standing in for the exercise. His heart beat like a drum and his limbs trembled but he remained upright, determined not to faint in front of the other young males in the room. "A moment."

Gryde offered a cup of water and after a habitual sniff, Fenris took a sip. He'd never savoured water so well in his entire life as he did now, his body soaking up every single cell of goodness and turning it into energy. With Gryde's help, Fenris had managed to go a full day without ingesting any meetha and, in addition to no longer sporting an uncomfortable erection, was able to walk without pain and could hold his own weight for over an hour. It wasn't much, but even that tiny improvement was enough to give him hope for the future.

He sipped again, buying time by flicking his gaze around a room that, like so many others in the compound, was strung with gauze hangings and scattered with cushions. Gryde had paired the other males off with each other and remained with Fenris, demonstrating how to correctly apply scented oil to their skins, both efficiently when alone and sensuously if a female was watching. As a result, his dusky teal skin now glistened with the same sheen Gryde wore on a daily basis, and he'd learnt some demonstrative poses that would likely make Flare jealous - or proud.

"Brother, we cannot delay forever," Gryde's voice was as gentle as the hand which prised the cup from Fenris' fingers. "It is time."

Fenris let the cup go, biting his tongue to keep from protesting as Gryde set it aside. Keeping his head down as he'd been taught, he grit his teeth as the other male's warm, smooth hands slid over his skin, beginning - again - the nauseatingly intimate check a potential mating male was required to endure.

"Steady," Gryde murmured, his fingers rounding the curve of Fenris' thigh.

"Stop." He took a swift step back, before those fingers could slide beneath his loincloth. "I cannot."

"You can." Gryde's hand clenched to a fist, his raptor's eyes flicking over the younger males, who'd progressed beyond the initial check and were now laying each other down on the cushions to test flexibility and body positioning. "You must."

Fenris closed his eyes to block out the sight - if not the sound - of loincloths being swept aside, cushions rearranged and hands sliding over oiled flesh. "This is…"

"What?" Gryde's fingers curled around his chin and tugged it up. "What is it?"

"Where I come from, these acts are sacred. Private."

"Here, it's what we do for food and water," Gryde murmured, his fingers tightening until Fenris lifted his lashes and approximated eye contact. "It's not so much, is it, really? Only your body."

"So they cannot have my heart, my mind, or my soul, but my flesh is fair game?" The corner of Fenris' mouth crooked ever so slightly. "I've endured many a torture in my life, brother, but nothing like this."

"I'd spare you if I could, but there's no other way." Rather than looking sympathetic, Gryde's face hardened. "If you cannot master this, you will die."

"I -" Fenris cut off with a grunt as the harpy's other hand grabbed his genitalia in a punishing grip.

"I told you before, this is a tool," Gryde continued, "and it is my job to teach you to use it. Both our lives depend on it." He whistled softly, and the six other males in the room came immediately to their teacher's side. "This is the way of Hiraptha, my brother, and whether you like it or not I must help you accept it."

Fenris' lungs seized as the younger concubines surrounded him, their hands insistent as they caressed his skin, their bodies hot as they lowered him onto the cushions. Fenris tried to backpedal but there was nowhere to go; Gryde and the other males pinned him to the soft surface, their seemingly endless supply of hands and lips tracking across his body with terrifying intent.

"Pay attention," Gryde murmured, yanking Fenris' loincloth clean away. "Put your emotions aside and learn how to survive."

"I don't -" Fenris jerked as several hands stroked over his flaccid penis, but his body was too weak to escape. "They're not even - they don't have a -"

Gryde's eyes flickered with something that may have been regret. "Anything a female can accomplish with her body, a male can replicate with his mouth."

Fenris' eyes widened in fearful comprehension as one of the men took a commanding grip on his testicles and began nibbling across the curve of his hip. "No."

"The first time is always the hardest," Gryde reassured, his tone soothing. "I am here with you, brother. We will do this together."

"*No*," Fenris gave a wild heave and succeeded in freeing one arm. It shot down, twisting in the hair of the harpy whose face was horrifically close to its goal. "Gryde, please."

The other males twittered gentle encouragements, likely scenting his fear. Gryde pressed a trembling kiss to Fenris' jaw, reaching down to disentangle his fingers and leave his comrade a clear path. Just as Fenris realised this was a battle he could not win, a female harpy swept into the room amidst a clacking of beads, several guards in feathered livery hard on her tail.

"Stop," she announced, and the room froze.

"Mistress." Gryde rose from the cushions and bowed low. "What can I do for the hand of the Empress?"

The female took her time replying, drinking in the sight of Fenris naked and spreadeagled on the floor with a gaggle of other naked men lounging over the top of him. For a horrifying moment Fenris thought she was going to instruct them to continue, but then she sighed and waved a hand in his direction. "I need this one."

Gryde blinked. "Now, mistress?"

"Now," she confirmed. "His female walks the Gauntlet in less than an hour, and the Empress wants him present and ready."

"I shall have him cleaned and -"

"No." The handmaiden shook her head. "There's no time. Put his cloth back on and I'll give him the sacred water."

The male harpies released Fenris, pulling back so that he could catch the loincloth Gryde tossed his way. Though he tried to rise, his legs didn't work and several of the concubines who'd been holding him down only a moment before helped him upright.

"Here." Gryde took the loincloth back and slung it around Fenris' hips, tying it in place. "Mistress, if it pleases you, I will prepare the sacred water."

"No need," the female announced, snapping her fingers. One of the guards pulled a waterskin from her belt and stepped forward, holding it out. "I had it prepared before we came."

Fenris stared down at Gryde with wide eyes, his heart thumping erratically. The other male's expression tightened, but he schooled his face almost immediately, turning towards the handmaiden with a respectful air. "Mistress, I beg you. Our guest is unique, and I haven't discovered the proper dosage of sacred water yet."

The sound of a slap rang out and Gryde dropped to the floor. The handmaiden followed him down, catching a handful of downy mane and yanking his head back at a painful angle. "You seek to question me?"

"No, mistress," Gryde managed. "I don't want to disappoint the Empress should he die from too much meetha."

"Too much meetha," the female scoffed. She flicked a glance Fenris' way. "I've seen his assets. The bigger they are, the more is needed."

Gryde swallowed heavily. "I'd normally agree, but his body is different from ours. The herbs make him ill."

The handmaiden tightened her grip and shook, rattling Gryde's head like a dog with a bone. When she finished, she leant close enough for her breath to stir his hair. "If you are lying, it will be your life."

"As it should be," Gryde managed.

"Very well." The handmaiden threw the head concubine down and Fenris suppressed a wince as Gryde's head bounced off the stone floor, his body collapsing into unconsciousness. With little more than a sneer for her handiwork, the female stood and snatched the skin from her guard, closing the distance to Fenris in a few strides. "Hold him still."

The males who supported his weight stepped closer, their grip tightening. Fenris kept his head down but the handmaiden gripped his chin and forced it upward, leaning in close to examine his face.

Too close.

Fenris' eyes shot to hers, their gazes locking. He might abhor his glamour and the free will it stole, but it was far preferable than another moment of this torment. If he could control the female, maybe implant a suggestion that he'd drunk the water - his thoughts derailed as she slapped his face, hard enough that he saw stars. "Open your mouth."

It didn't work. Disbelief, followed quickly by horror, turned his legs to jelly and if not for the slaves on either side, Fenris would have fallen. Beyond Arcana, never had someone within arm's reach escaped the hungry grip of his glamour - but it seemed the meetha had rendered even his cursed eyes impotent. Once he would have cheered, but now Fenris only felt empty as the female's fingers dug into his jaw, her other fist slamming into his gut hard enough that his mouth flew open.

Then the water skin was in, and minty, meetha-laden water slid across his tongue. Fenris choked, trying to spit it out. The handmaiden merely angled his head differently, whistling for her guards to massage his throat until he had no choice but to swallow, again and again.

"Stop," the handmaiden announced, leaning back. "Wait and see what happens before I give him the other half, in case the concubine was right."

"Males," one of the guards snorted in derision. "Stupid."

"Agreed, but if this male dies it will be our hides tanning in the sun, not theirs." The handmaiden stoppered the skin and gave Fenris an assessing once over. "A minute won't hurt."

Maybe not her, Fenris thought, but a minute was more than enough for him to feel the meetha racing through his body, stealing what little strength he'd regained even as it heated his blood to boiling point. His loincloth twitched and he groaned as his body began to ache, waves of tingling pain sweeping from head to toe and back again.

One of the guards pointed at his groin. "It's starting to take effect."

Fenris gagged, his body turning boneless. Agony snapped his teeth together and made his skin crawl, and all the while his treacherous erection thickened and grew.

"Lie him down on the cushions," the handmaiden snapped. "He looks like he's going to pass out."

Yes. The black cloak with which Fenris had become all too familiar this past week was already stealing over his limbs, turning them blessedly numb. He barely registered the cushions forming to his body, nor the rapid-fire questions that came in his direction - questions he couldn't understand, much less answer. Fenris' eyes slid closed, his breathing becoming laboured in a way that would have alarmed him if he wasn't already too far gone to care. With a rattling sigh, he blocked out the alarmed shrieks of the women and the frantic hands slapping his face, and let go of the waking world for the soothing arms of the dark.

FIFTEEN
ARCANA

Hɪʀᴀᴘᴛʜᴀ's sᴛʀᴇᴇᴛs ᴡᴇʀᴇ ᴅᴇsᴇʀᴛᴇᴅ, sᴀᴠᴇ ғᴏʀ ᴀ ғᴇᴡ ᴡᴀɴᴅᴇʀɪɴɢ ᴊɪɴʀᴀ. Arcana sat easily on Caelum's back, shading her eyes with one hand while Mirran walked ahead, flanked by a pair of female guards who glared regularly at everything. They moved in silent formation to the far side of the city, threading between a selection of squat buildings and lean-tos until Caelum stepped out into the desert beyond. Mirran stopped at the end of the road, looking up at Arcana through squinted eyes. "Tradition say walk in alone."

"I understand," Arcana nodded. "Tradition is important."

Mirran pointed into the distance, where great stone pillars jutted out from the sand. "Marks Gauntlet."

"Thank you. And my male?"

"Likely waits at end. Empress to know for sure." Mirran hesitated. "If make it, will still teach the speak?"

"I will if you will."

"Deal. No charge," Mirran replied. Arcana was shocked to see the harpy wink at her. "Be safe. Strength is life."

"Strength is life."

Mirran spread her wings and leapt into the air, beating hard for height and then catching an updraft, soaring away into the sky. The two guards followed suit, circling above Arcana with their spears gripped tightly in their talons.

"Woah," Caelum murmured.

"So they *can* fly." Arcana followed the harpies' progress, unable to stop herself admiring how graceful they were in flight. "How can something so lovely be so awful at the same time?"

Caelum shrugged, his shoulders rippling beneath Arcana's knees. "You going to tell me you've never seen a poison plant that's hypnotically lovely? Or a cute animal with sharp teeth? Or a sweet, lovable space deer who can gore you with his nasty-ass antlers? Or a pastry that will make you -"

"I get it, I get it." Arcana eyed the stone pillars in the distance. "I guess it's time to find out if my magic works."

"Grumpy cactus says it does."

"Okay, this is where we find out if it works enough," she clarified, squinting further into the desert. "Do you really think he's out there?"

"Yeah, I do." Caelum's ears flickered. "Just try not to get us both killed in the effort to get him back."

Arcana knew that was her cue to say something comforting, but the words wouldn't come, so she settled for rubbing a soothing hand over the back of his neck instead. Caelum sighed and, after a cursory glance at their airborne escort, began to pick his way across the desert towards the Gauntlet. At first Arcana thought the journey would be hours long, but after barely twenty minutes Caelum crested a dune to reveal a long, jagged fissure in the earth ahead. The stone pillars Mirran had indicated earlier rose on either side of the Gauntlet, hung with coloured flags and brightly painted wooden scaffolding. Harpies lined the canyon and hung from the scaffolding above, the air around them thick with the clank of chains and the twittering, clicking language of the avian people.

The Empress stood waiting at the entrance, with Beera and Mirran on one side and two richly decorated women on the other. Arcana's escort landed in a spectacular flurry of feathers and sand, crossing their spears to prevent Caelum moving any closer. Arcana slid off his back, making her way down the dune's shallow face until she stood before the Empress, where she accorded the other woman a short bow. "Good morning, your Imperial Grace."

"Outsider." The Empress gave the barest nod of acknowledgement. "You make a grand entrance on the back of your companion. That is not how things are traditionally done here."

"I volunteered, your Imperial Grace." Caelum shouldered past the spear-toting guards and bowed his head, his antler rack passing bare inches from the Empress' nose. "It is my honour to assist."

The Empress' face creased with wonder as he straightened. "In that case, I will allow it."

"I'm most grateful, your Imperial Grace." Arcana gestured at the fissure in the earth. "I presume this is the Gauntlet through which I must walk?"

"It is."

Arcana considered the long, shadowy canyon with narrowed eyes. "And what are the rules?"

"You must walk alone to the other end, where I will be waiting. If you survive, you will be granted status as Hirapthan. There are no rules for those wishing to oppose you - women may attack directly, or send men in their stead. They may be already lying in wait, or lurking undecided within the crowds." The faintest smile twitched her lips. "Until such time as you reach the other end, you will be considered fair game."

"All right." Arcana bit her lip and turned to face the Empress. "And my male?"

"He waits at the far end, where you will be able to claim him - if you succeed." She waved an elegant hand towards the far end of the Gauntlet. "If you die, he will be offered to the people. Anyone interested will endure trial by combat and the victor takes the spoils."

"I look forward to disappointing them," Arcana said softly.

The Empress blinked, her face smoothing. "You are a brave woman, outsider."

"Thank you, your Imperial Grace."

The Empress sniffed and turned away, clicking her fingers at her escort. They thumped their spears on the ground in response and the Empress spread her wings, launching into the air with the wise women and her handmaidens close behind.

"Bitch," Caelum muttered, drifting closer to nuzzle Arcana's hair.

"Agreed, but until I'm stronger, we have to play by her rules."

The deerken sighed in reluctant agreement. "I take it you have a plan?"

"Besides staying alive?" Arcana rolled her shoulders uneasily. "Not really."

The Empress' entourage reached the far end of the Gauntlet and Beera began to speak, her raised voice carrying easily across the desert. Caelum's ears flickered as he listened. "They're introducing you. The guards are going to signal when to start."

"Okay." She went on tiptoe to kiss his nose. "I'll see you at the other end?"

"I still think I should come with you, but let's not have that five-hour argument all over again." Caelum watched Beera shout and gesticulate a little longer, then huffed a snort through his nose. "I'll follow your progress through the canyon, keeping to the outer edge of our thirty pace limit. If the shit hits the proverbial fan, the elastic band effect will have me by your side in an instant."

"All right, but don't interfere unless there's absolutely no other option." When Caelum frowned, she wrapped her arms around his neck and squeezed. "Magic or no magic, I'm not going to make this easy on them. Trust me, please."

"I do trust you, I just have a bad feeling about all this." Caelum curled his head around her shoulders and held her close. "Be safe, okay? Here they come."

Arcana drew back as the guards high-stepped up the dune, gesturing with their spears. She nodded once in their direction, gave Caelum a final pat and began to slither through the loose sand towards the Gauntlet. Two more guards waited in front of the shadowy fissure with lit torches in either hand, watching in cold silence as she staggered onto more solid ground.

Beera shouted a command and one of the guards stepped forward, offering Arcana her torch and a short dagger. After a cursory inspection, Arcana took the torch and ignored the blade, stepping between the guards and into the Gauntlet. The Hirapthan crowd fell silent and then someone laughed, rousing a chorus of jeers and titters from the rest of the onlookers.

"Nice," Arcana muttered, dodging a blob of something sloppy and brown. "So civilised."

She dodged a second missile and rounded a bend in the rocks, stopping short as a pair of men slunk out from behind a boulder. Their bodies were hollow with hunger and their chains trailed behind them but they moved in practised unison, blocking the path with matched sneers and outstretched arms.

"I don't want to hurt you," Arcana murmured, holding both hands up in a gesture of peace. The males didn't budge, their faces set. "All right, then."

She lifted her free hand and plunged it into the naked flame of her torch, drawing the fierce energy into her body. The shouting crowd quieted as the fire flickered and died, a thin plume of smoke spiralling up into the cobalt sky. Weighing the magic now running through her veins, Arcana dropped the torch, raised her hand and began to draw runes in the air. They crackled and spat with life, leaving a trail of orange sparks in the wake of her finger as she used the spell to focus her meagre strength.

One of the men darted forward, shoulder down and head tucked in. Arcana sidestepped, flames bursting to life around her hands as she shoved the harpy aside. Her opponent howled and staggered as the fire licked over his skin, leaving a trail of blistering burns wherever it touched. The second male lurched forward to pick up the torch, snapping it over his knee to make two jagged stakes. Arcana clapped her hands and uttered a word of power, transferring the flames from her hands to the broken pieces of torch. The male shrieked and dropped his impromptu weaponry, tucking singed hands into his armpits as the torch became no more than smoke and ash. After a terrified look in Arcana's direction, he turned and fled.

Arcana sidled further down the Gauntlet as the first man stepped around his companion. The skin of his shoulder had blistered but his face was set with determination, his hands bunched into fists. Arcana flicked a finger in his direction, spoke another word and his ragged loincloth caught fire, the flames licking their way up his ribs. He shrilled a protest, dropping to the ground and rolling wildly.

A battle cry rang out from above and Arcana flung herself into the lee of a rock. Several arrows thudded into the ground where she'd been standing, closely followed by a second volley that pierced the fleeing male through the shoulder and back, and a final one into the head of the man who'd been on fire. Arcana stared in horror as the crowd roared in approval, their voices echoing off the walls of the canyon until the very ground vibrated.

A quick glance upwards revealed the silhouette of a harpy circling in the sky, dipping her wings in acknowledgment of the crowd's appreciation. Keeping as much of her body beneath the overhang as possible, Arcana began building a fireball in the palm of her hand. It grew to the size of her fist before warning prickles tracked up and down her spine, forcing her to stop. She took a moment to breathe and focus inward, noting that whilst her magic might not be strong, it was already refilling. Bolstered by that thought, Arcana took aim and flung the fireball into the air. The crowd shrieked in warning and the harpy banked sharply to one side, getting her feathers singed rather than her face.

"Damn it!" Arcana pressed harder against the rock as another trio of arrows thumped the ground at her feet. Fire magic wasn't going to cut it; not if the crowd were going to give her away. Setting her jaw, Arcana took a deep breath and extended her senses, feeling out the solid, beating heart of the desert and then stretching up into the air itself.

The magic came in fits and starts but it came, and Arcana breathed a sigh of relief. She chanced a quick glance out from under the overhang, spinning her finger in small circles and chanting under her breath. The wind picked up in response, building swiftly into a tall, narrow twister. Sweat broke out on her forehead as she stretched the twister upwards, flinging it at her aerial attacker. As far as offensive spells went it was pathetic but it was also invisible, catching the harpy by surprise and twisting her feathers unmercifully. She tried to right herself and failed, spiralling out of sight with a mournful wail that cut eerily short a few moments later. Arcana waited a full minute to be sure the woman was truly gone, then staggered over to check the slaves on the ground.

Both were dead.

Blinking back tears, Arcana slithered around an outcropping in the rocks and up a small rise to see a short, deep crevasse separating her from the rest of the Gauntlet. A female harpy stood on the other side with a whip in hand, flanked by two lanky, unwashed men with heavy scarring on their arms and shoulders. The crowd jeered as Arcana clung to a boulder for support, taking advantage of the position to judge the width of the crevasse. For a winged Hirapthan it would be no problem, but it was far too wide for her to jump, particularly in her current state.

For the first time in her life, Arcana was glad of those long months she'd been locked beneath the Healing Tower, with only Flare and an endless supply of spell books for company. Dredging an earth spell from the depths of her memory, she released the air energy swirling through her veins and dropped to one knee to absorb the solid strength of the canyon. With her meagre magic tank already back to full, Arcana closed her eyes, whispering the spell aloud as she drew runes in the fine coating of sand at her feet. For a long moment nothing happened; then the tongue of rock beneath her rumbled and began to move, thinning and stretching until it connected her to the other side of the crevasse with an echoing slam.

A low whistle was all the warning Arcana had and she threw herself forwards, narrowly avoiding the metal-tipped edge of a whip as she sprawled in the loose sand. Spitting out what felt like half a desert, Arcana scrambled upright whilst the woman coiled her whip for another strike.

Hand to hand combat might not have been her skill, but Arcana had worked with more than enough warriors and sorcerers to recognise that when the harpy's shoulders bunched, the whip was coming her way. Arcana lunged aside, kicking a cloud of sand in the female's direction that swirled around her face like a cloud of gnats. The spell only lasted a moment before Arcana's strength petered out but the harpy squawked and backed away, motioning for her slaves to take her place.

One of the men edged forward, the other balking with a shake of his head. His mistress' eyes narrowed and a moment later, her whip cracked across the male's shoulders, the cruel metal tip cutting deep into his already scarred flesh. The slave dropped to his knees with a cry that had his companion glancing over one shoulder, but the female only brandished the whip anew and jerked her chin in Arcana's direction.

The slave closed his eyes a second, then darted forward with deceptive speed, shoving Arcana into the dirt and burying a fist in her gut. She curled inwards, wrapping her arms around the harpy's wrist and dragging him down with her by luck more than skill. Though the male's body was broader, his avian bones made him light and he slammed onto the rocky ground with enough force to leave him dazed and wheezing for breath.

Arcana rolled to her feet in time to see the female harpy's whip come down hard enough on the second male that he collapsed. She squawked at him, kicking him in the gut with one talon and gesturing with her free hand for the slave to stand. When he made no move to comply, her jaw set in fury and she began to whip him in earnest. Forgetting all about the man on the ground, Arcana darted inside the whip's arc in a move that would have made Fenris proud. She caught the whip as it descended, allowing the thick tail to wrap around her wrist like a coiled snake. The metal tip bit deeply into her forearm but Arcana held her ground, gripping the leather as tightly as it gripped her.

"No," she growled as the woman shrieked in rage and pointed imperiously at her slave. "*No.*"

The harpy yanked on her whip and Arcana followed the momentum forward, dropping her shoulder and ramming the other woman with all her weight. The Hirapthan's slender arm broke with a loud snap and she screamed, releasing her whip as the force of Arcana's blow sent her body flying backwards into a boulder. The woman's head collided with unyielding rock and she slumped to the ground, eyes closed.

Arcana didn't bother checking if the harpy was alive. Instead, she unwrapped the whip and yanked the metal tip free of her skin. The sharp end tore her flesh even further on the way out, sending a splatter of black blood across the sandy ground and causing spots to dance in front of her eyes. She waited for the pain to pass, then wriggled her fingers to confirm her arm still worked as it should. The wound was deep enough that it'd leave a hell of scar, but as long as nothing major was damaged, Arcana didn't care.

Tossing the whip into the crevasse with a snarl of disgust, she knelt beside the bloodied slave. Whether by habit or fear he held still, allowing her to assess the nasty gashes streaking his flesh. In Arcana's limited experience, none of them were severe enough to kill him - but like her, he'd bear the whip's scars for the rest of his life. As though sharing her thoughts, the male spotted the trail of black blood oozing down Arcana's arm and babbled incoherently, his terracotta skin blanching to a shade of peach.

"Yeah," she muttered, offering what she hoped was a reassuring smile. "I know."

He opened his mouth to reply and then froze, eyes going over her shoulder. Arcana began to turn, the movement arrested as pain sliced through her calf. The crowd shrieked in approval as she toppled sideways, a curved dagger buried in the back of her leg. Clenching her teeth, Arcana yanked the dagger free and straightened to see the harpy female was awake. She twittered furiously as she sought to drag herself upright, raptor's eyes focussed on her two slaves. If the hatred twisting her avian features was anything to judge by, nothing short of death would satisfy her.

So be it.

Threading her magic through the blade in her hand, Arcana took a deep breath and threw. She didn't have much of an arm but magic kept her aim true, the dagger embedded itself in the female's forehead with a decisive thunk. The harpy's eyes had glazed even before she toppled backwards, disappearing into the crevasse in a limp tangle of limbs.

A shadow fell across Arcana and she looked up to see the male she'd winded earlier, his face shadowed as he looked from her to his comrade. For a moment she thought he was going to hit her, then he held out a hand and tugged her upright. When Arcana smiled and immediately returned to his friend, the male followed and knelt beside her.

"We need to stop the bleeding," Arcana said, motioning to his loincloth and then making a tearing motion. He frowned in confusion, so she reached to the injured male, tore a strip off the bottom of the rag and pressed it over one of the wounds. "See?"

The harpy nodded and immediately tore into his own cloth, padding the worst of his companion's wounds. When there was no more they could do, the male took up the remaining strips and, without meeting Arcana's eyes, began to bandage the wounds on her arm and leg.

"Thank you," she murmured, smiling as he tied the ends of the fabric in a firm knot. The male nodded and though he still wouldn't look at her, his lips twitched ever so slightly in return.

Arcana scanned the skies as he scuttled back to his companion, ensuring the two men were safe before she limped further down the Gauntlet on her own. No sooner had she rounded a bend in the pathway when small rocks began to fall like rain, peppering her head and shoulders until she found shelter in a hollow between two boulders. Reluctant to poke her head out in case larger missiles came her way, Arcana spread her senses wide, moving between earth and air until she was able to track the stones to an outcropping just over the crest of the next rise.

Keeping her body as low as she could, Arcana ducked around the corner and limped over the crest. A tumble of rocks partially concealed a kneeling harpy, a collection of roundish stones on the ground at her side. She leapt to her feet with a squawk, grabbing at her stones as they floated into the air of their own accord. Arcana almost felt sorry for the harpy as magic turned the stones jagged, the bladed projectiles piercing the woman's leather clothing and slamming her into the earth.

Snatching a stone from the ground, Arcana fashioned it into a dagger and nudged the tip against the harpy's throat. They stared at each other for long moments before the woman lowered her eyes, hands open in placation. Arcana nodded and shoved the stone dagger into her waistband, limping along the Gauntlet until she stood before a shallow slope. The Empress waited at the top, with Beera on one side and Mirran on the other. The younger wise woman's face twitched and Arcana hesitated, remembering all the warnings she'd received about the vicious women who'd seek to kill her.

Arcana eyed the sandy slope in front of her. Injured as she was, it would be an awkward climb to the top, making the slippery incline the perfect place for a last-ditch ambush. As though to lend credence to her theory, the bloodthirsty harpies in the stands had ceased their shouting, their raptor's eyes trained on the end of the Gauntlet with an intensity that raised the hairs on her arms.

Something nudged at the back of Arcana's mind and she reached for it on instinct, acknowledging the presence as Caelum's even though she'd never felt anything of the like before. No sooner had she brushed against the deerken's essence than Arcana's stomach flip-flopped and her vision wavered. When it cleared, she was viewing the Gauntlet from Caelum's perspective. Shock stormed through her but Caelum held them firm, his solid presence soothing her jagged nerves and urging her to pay attention. The deerken was standing outside her direct line of sight, but in a perfect position to see the end of the canyon - where a heap of rocks to the side of the final slope concealed a harpy with a short spear clutched to her chest.

Arcana blinked and was abruptly back in her own body, her heart racing and her world spinning. What she and Caelum had just done should have been impossible, but there was no time to linger on the implications of their new skill when there was a harpy lying in wait barely five paces away.

Lifting her chin, Arcana did her best to stride up the slope as though she didn't have a care in the world, all the while spreading her senses into the ground. The crowd erupted in a roar that shook the earth but it wasn't enough to mask the thud of taloned feet, or the vibration of a spear used like a walking stick to help increase speed.

When Arcana judged her attacker close, she spun in place, catching the spear as the woman lunged towards her. They fell together, rolling and wrestling for the weapon, but Arcana used her superior weight to land on top, jamming the long handle of the spear hard against the other woman's throat.

"Enough," Arcana gasped, pressing down until the harpy wheezed for breath. After a final, useless struggle, the female went limp.

Arcana eased off slowly, but when her opponent remained quiescent, she got to her feet and limped up the slope, using the spear to help navigate the loose sand. The watching crowd quieted with every step and by the time she stopped before the exit, silence once again blanketed the area. Arcana held the spear out before her, tunnelling her magic into the shaft and twisting until it disintegrated, the remains scattering on the wind. When the final speck disappeared, she met the Empress' gaze and flourished a bow. "Your Imperial Grace."

The Empress stared at Arcana for several long moments, her face inscrutable. "So, it appears you have some secrets after all."

"Everyone has secrets, your Imperial Grace."

"I suppose that's true." The Empress tilted her head to one side. "I didn't expect you to make it here, even with the powers of a witch to aid you."

"And yet here I am, your Imperial Grace."

"So it would seem." The Empress stepped forward, taking Arcana's hand in her own. She raised their joined arms into the air, looked out at the people and squawked loudly. The crowd erupted, a mixture of cheering and jeering that echoed across the landscape. Beera stepped forward and scooped a handful of sand from the desert floor. She strutted a circle around Arcana and the Empress, chanting loudly and scattering the sand in her wake.

"Welcome to Hiraptha," Beera said, taking Arcana's free hand and depositing the last of the sand into her palm. "Breathe deep and be well, sister."

Arcana inclined her head. "Thank you."

"Now that you are part of our society, it is time for you to understand your responsibilities," the Empress announced, releasing Arcana's arm. She clicked her fingers and a group of guards staggered out from behind a covered litter, carrying a long bundle between them.

Caelum drifted to Arcana's side as the cloth-wrapped bundle was dumped at her feet - and it was just as well, because when the top layers were whipped aside she sagged against the deerken for support.

Cocooned inside the dirty lengths of gauze was Fenris. At least, he had Fenris' pale teal skin and darker teal hair, but the Guardian Arcana remembered was a far cry from the man unconscious on the ground in front of her. His cheekbones stood out in sharp relief, his closed eyes sunken and bruised. The lean muscle which had cloaked his body was gone, revealing every bone and joint with a nightmarish clarity made even more dramatic by the laughable modesty of his loincloth. Dark teal curls were plastered to his head by sweat and even unconscious Fenris shivered, as though there was no escaping the nightmares his fading bruises and scabbed cuts attested to.

Arcana stared at the Empress, her heart in her throat. "What have you done to him?"

"*I* have done nothing," the Empress returned primly. "I was informed only upon his arrival that the meetha had an unforeseen effect."

"Meetha?" Arcana stumbled over the unfamiliar word, looking to Mirran for clarification.

Beera stepped forward, neatly cutting in front of her apprentice. "A plant which we grind into the mating males' water to assist their function."

The explanation made little sense, but Arcana was of no mind to comprehend it anyway. She dropped to her knees in the sand, probing for a pulse beneath Fenris' angular jaw. Every moment that passed felt like a lifetime, and her eyes were blurred with tears before she finally located the thready rhythm. "He lives."

"I smell sickness all over him," Caelum murmured, snuffling at Fenris' shoulder. "Whatever he drank... it was a close call. By all rights, he should be dead."

"Do you wish to renege your claim?" The Empress asked, her tone waspish.

Fury boiled through Arcana and she spoke through clenched teeth. *"Never."*

"Very well." The Empress motioned to Beera, who caught up Fenris' chain and handed it to Arcana with a flourish. "You will have five sunrises to select a plot of land and establish a holding. When the sun births on the final day, I will arrive to assess your efforts. If you do well, you will earn a social standing and be able to keep your slaves. If not, they will be taken from you."

Arcana's eyes narrowed and she motioned to Fenris. "I only have the one."

"Not so. Two Hiraptha died in the Gauntlet, and two were defeated," Beera replied, gesturing to one side. "You inherit their males as the spoils of victory."

Arcana turned and gasped. A group of seven men stood several paces to the left, among them the two who had survived facing her inside the Gauntlet. The man who'd been whipped hung across the shoulder of his comrade, his breathing shallow and his eyes closed. She swallowed heavily and pushed to her feet. "What happens if I don't accept them?"

The so-called protector of Hiraptha shrugged. "Rejected slaves have no use. They will be slaughtered and their bodies repurposed."

"And if I accept them, but cannot provide for them?"

"Then, because the fault is yours, they will be returned to the market and sold to the highest bidder." The Empress pursed her lips and then shrugged again. "If they fail to impress, they will be slaughtered and repurposed."

Arcana frowned. "Repurposed?"

"It is a standard service for a male who has no further use," Beera explained. "Feathers for spears and down for yarn. Bones for jewellery, skin tanned to hide for furniture and clothing, such as you wear now. Nothing is wasted."

Arcana's jaw dropped and her stomach rebelled, robbing her of the power of speech. The Empress smirked and raised a hand. "Would you like me to have the males escorted away?"

"No," Arcana said, her voice trembling as she looked over the dejected, dirty group. "No. I'll take them."

"Then they are yours - provided you can keep them," the Empress answered, her smile widening to show teeth. "I'll see you in five sunrises."

"Five sunrises," Arcana echoed.

The Empress nodded once and leapt into the air, Beera close behind her. They winged back towards the city, the rest of Hiraptha's citizens turning to follow. For a few minutes, the air was filled with the rushing of wings, the clank of chains and the relentless slough of sand - then Arcana stood alone in the desert, her eyes on the group of slaves that had been thrust into her care.

"Glad to see still alive."

Arcana jumped, spinning around to find Mirran crouched beside Fenris. "I didn't realise you were still here."

"Must go soon." Mirran leant forward, her ear close to Fenris' mouth and her brow furrowed as she listened to his breathing. "Stay to advise a moment."

"A little something extra to add to your bill?" Arcana asked, not bothering to hide the bitterness in her voice.

The younger harpy flinched, then sighed and sat back. "Is custom here. No rude intended."

"I don't care about manners," Arcana snapped, returning to crouch at Fenris' side. "I care whether he lives or dies."

Mirran checked Fenris' pulse, then looked up into the cloudless sky. "Meetha will start to leave body by dark. If to die, would die already. Will sleep, will wake. Will live."

"So Caelum said." Spreading one hand across her Guardian's thin chest, Arcana worked to swallow bitter tears. "What is meetha, so I know to avoid it?"

"Hard to explain." Mirran looked at the group of slaves and issued a long string of tweets and whistles. After a pause, one of them answered. "That male know. He show later, if ask."

"Thank you." Reassured by the wise woman's assessment - and the constant, if unsteady, thump of Fenris' heart beneath her palm - Arcana forced her sluggish brain into motion. "What now?"

Mirran rolled her shoulders uneasily, looking from Fenris to the group of slaves and back again. "Can choose anywhere to establish holding, as long as not belong to other Hiraptha already. Ability to provide for males based on water."

"Water?"

"Yes." She nodded. "To own males is sign of skill in find water. Water give life. Not enough water, cannot keep males. Cannot keep males, lowest on... ladder?"

"Yes, ladder," Arcana murmured, nodding. "So as long as I can provide water and shelter, I'll be left alone?"

"In essence. Must be good water," Mirran added, "and may to defend challenge, when harpies gather courage to test."

"That makes sense, I guess." Arcana rubbed at her face, suddenly and completely exhausted. Caelum's foreleg nudged her spine and she rested against him, drawing comfort from the simple touch. "Thank you for your help these last few days, Mirran."

"No need." Mirran grinned. "You win, I win. To be made real wise woman now."

"Yes, I remember." Arcana offered a weak smile in response. "When will you be officiated?"

"Feast for third meal. When see next, will be wise woman completed," Mirran answered. She frowned down at Arcana's bloodstained calf, then prodded the bandage on her arm. "Show the hurts."

Arcana eyed the small pouch of medicinal supplies around Mirran's waist, then shrugged and extended her leg for the younger woman's ministrations. Mirran unwrapped the bandage and poured a bitter-smelling liquid on the gash, cleaning it with a cloth before packing salve into the cut and wrapping a fresh bandage over the top. Arcana curled her hand into Fenris' while the wise woman worked, moisture streaking her cheeks.

"He'll be fine, you know." Caelum brushed his soft nose against Arcana's cheek, snuffling at her tears. "He's strong."

"Did you know he was in this condition?"

"No." The deerken's face pinched with sadness. "He wasn't great when I last saw him, but he definitely wasn't this bad."

"Heart still beats, lungs still work, bones still straight," Mirran said, her voice quiet as she finished tying off the fresh bandage on Arcana's arm. "In time, male will be useful again."

As far as comforting words went, they sucked, but Arcana forced herself to smile nonetheless. "Thank you."

"Wounds to heal quick. Not too bad," Mirran continued, packing her salve into the small pouch hanging from her belt. "Must go now for prepare."

"All right. I'll see you soon?"

"Soon enough." Mirran patted Arcana on the shoulder. "Good luck."

"You too."

The harpy waved as she launched into the air, wheeling back towards the Palace. Arcana watched until Mirran was out of sight, then dropped her head into her hands. "Great Gods of Sorcen."

"Breathe," Caelum murmured, nuzzling at her hair. "We'll find a way out of this."

"How?" Arcana demanded. "Not only am I in charge of a half-dead

Guardian, but a bunch of harpies who I can't communicate with and are probably terrified of me."

"You were right to take them in."

"I couldn't leave them to die." Arcana shivered as she recalled the explanation of how a male was 'repurposed'. "That said, I have no idea what to do next - which I'm sure the Empress was counting on."

"The way I see it, we need a supply of water and some distance from the city so that you and Fenris can recover in privacy." Caelum's ears flickered. "I know you're tired, but do you think you could sense water if you tried?"

"I might, if it's close enough to the surface." Finding strength in his calm, Arcana got to her feet and tried to follow Caelum's gaze. "Why?"

"I think - and I could be wrong - but I think the oasis where we were captured is that way." The deerken rolled his shoulders and looked back at Arcana. "There wasn't much there, but there *was* a soak of water, and a couple of scraggly trees."

"And?"

"The greatsword." When Arcana started in surprise, he snorted. "The harpies couldn't carry it after they knocked Fenris out, so they left it behind. I think he'd like it back, don't you?"

Arcana flicked a look back at her Guardian, heart aching at the thought of what he must have endured. She wanted nothing more than to drop in the sand beside him and close her eyes, but if there was even a chance they could find the greatsword, she'd take it. "How far from the city?"

"For me? Couple hours. Half a day's walk for the harpies." Caelum paused, then shrugged. "Not sure how fast they fly, but I guess a couple of hours there, too."

"Perfect."

"As long as we can find it," Caelum replied, lips twitching in the deerken approximation of a smile.

"True. All right, let's go meet our new family." Arcana smoothed her hair out of her face, squared her shoulders and limped across the sand towards the group of slaves. They watched her approach with various degrees of uncertainty, some with bodies slumped and others stiff like statues. Arcana stopped in front of the two males she'd defended from the whip, offering what she hoped was a reassuring smile. "Caelum, will you translate for me? Ask how our injured friend is doing."

The deerken took a half step forward and spoke, the twittering language of Hiraptha sounding strange on his tongue. The males' mouths dropped open in astonishment but they held still, listening. At the end of his short speech, the man supporting his wounded friend replied in a soft, leathery sounding voice.

"He says his friend will survive for now, but needs shelter and attention," Caelum translated.

"What else did you tell them?"

"That you're not going to hurt them." His ears flickered. "I'm not sure if they believe me."

"Not much we can do about that for now. Is anyone else injured?"

Caelum spoke again to the men, listened to the soft answers. "No, they can walk. I'll carry Fenris and the other guy."

"All right." Arcana left Caelum to twitter and chirp at the group of men, returning to Fenris. She dropped to the sand and lifted his head into her lap, pushing sweat-stiff hair back from his forehead and settling her fingers against the pulse in his throat. He was frightfully thin - fragile, even - but his ethereal beauty was still evident, the resemblance to his fey mother highlighted by the bones pushing at his skin. "If not for my crappy magic, I'd take the Palace apart piece by piece and wring the Empress' neck."

"Believe me, I've fantasised about exactly that on a daily basis since we got here - but for now, it'll have to wait." Caelum's voice preceded him up the dunes, the wounded harpy draped across his back. "You know Fenris sleeps to heal; let his body do what it needs to. He might look terrible, but the scent of sickness is already less than it was a few minutes ago."

Arcana dashed at her tears and sat up, allowing the other slaves to lift Fenris out of her lap and slide him onto Caelum's back beside the other male. "I should have been here. I should have been with him."

"And done what? Languished in your own set of chains? Starved together? Don't be ridiculous." Caelum shifted from hoof to hoof, shoulders rippling as he settled his two charges more comfortably. "Instead of drowning in what you can't change, focus on what you can. Right now, we need water and shelter."

"You're right." Arcana closed her eyes and took a deep breath, forging her melancholy into cool, clear purpose. Her magic gave a warning shudder and her stomach lurched, but after a long moment her senses spread out into the ground. The next few minutes passed in tense silence, the remaining slaves drifting closer until, when Arcana opened her eyes, she was surrounded by a group of concerned male faces. "I can sense water. Let's go."

SIXTEEN
FLARE

Eyrton's eyebrows looked fit to climb into his hairline when he opened the door and found both Zaire and Flare on the threshold. No sooner had they ducked inside, the lock clicking shut behind them, than Zaire yanked his formal bracers from his wrists and threw them on the floor with a clatter.

"Water," he snapped, and stomped off into one of the bedrooms.

"I'll admit," Eyrton murmured as he moved to the chiller and pulled out a bottle of water, "that I expected to see at least one of you bleeding when you walked through that door."

"I'm surprised you expected me to walk through it at all," Flare returned, leaning against the bench while the older Ryllin filled three glasses.

"The moment you stood up in that Council room, I knew it was inevitable." Eyrton sighed, returning the water bottle to the chiller. "You're nothing if not determined."

Zaire prowled back into the room, snatched one of the glasses and drained it in several solid swallows. "It's safe now. Talk."

"So?" Eyrton looked from Flare to his cousin and back again. "What's going on?"

"You already know this idiot's taking over Krowley's role in the search for the missing medical frigate," Zaire returned, jerking his chin in Flare's direction. He reached for the buckles on his leather armour, shucking layers as he spoke. "We want the warg, we need to find the ships. We want the ships, we need to work with Captain Fancy Hair."

Flare raised a hand to his hair - a product of kinetic energy, not enough sleep and his own restless fingers - and ruffled it. "If you think this is fancy, you need glasses, little Ryllin."

"Little?" Zaire shoved into Flare's space, clad only in leather pants and the soft, dark blue thermal that went under his armour. At six foot six he had a good seven inches on Flare, but lacked the edge in breadth and musculature. He stared down out of deep indigo eyes that seemed to ripple in the artificial lighting. "Who are you calling little?"

"Spoken like a man used to compensating." Flare tipped his head back to stare Zaire full in the face and dialled his sharpest smile up to full wattage. "Want to measure and find out who's really the larger?"

"Boys, please," Eyrton drawled, holding a fresh glass of water between them. "Now is not the time or place."

Zaire's spectacular eyes narrowed and he swirled away, opening kitchen cupboards and yanking out pots, pans, spatulas and ingredients without rhyme or reason. "Casserole."

"Come on," Eyrton sighed, pressing the glass into Flare's hands. "You may as well sit down. He won't say a thing until he's done."

With an idle shrug, Flare hung his sister's leather satchel over the back of a chair and sank into it, one leg curled beneath him as he sipped from his glass and chatted idly with Eyrton. The Ryllin was pleasant to talk to, well educated and clearly the political brain of the two Ambassadors, judging by his ability to recall the tedious details of the council meeting without pausing to think about it. Flare filed away each word out of habit, knowing he was learning things about the other Ambassadors and Galactic Station that would be beneficial to him in the long run, but was unable to devote his complete concentration to the conversation.

Instead, he watched the delightful contradiction that was Zaire. With his silken waves of blue-sheened black hair tied back in a leather thong, flour dusting his clothing and a pair of tongs in hand, he was a far cry from the surly creature who'd refused to surface from a book at the banquet; in fact, the odd sounds coming from his throat as he worked might have, on some planets, been referred to as humming. When the meal hit the table it was in the form of steaming meat and vegetables in a rich, brown sauce, home-made crusty rolls that oozed with cheese when torn open, and sparkling lemonade.

"Thank you," Flare said, leaning back to avoid being shoved off his seat as Zaire began ladling the dish into bowls.

The Ryllin grunted, making sure all the glasses were filled before he dropped heavily into a chair and threw a roll at Flare's head. "Just eat it."

Flare snatched the bread out of the air and bit into it, savouring the sharp bite of the cheese. "Were you always such a magnificent asshole, or is this a recent thing?"

"By-product of staring at your face," Zaire growled, his head down as he focussed on his food.

"Z!" Eyrton threw his spoon down with a clatter. "What the fuck is going on? Why is he here?"

Zaire's eyes narrowed in such a way that Flare imagined he was planning the slow and methodical evisceration of his cousin, but when he spoke, his voice was calm and smooth. "Our new Ambassador suspects a link between the missing frigates and the attack the other night."

"And you're going to just trust him?" It was the blatant disbelief in Eyrton's voice, more than anything else, which caused Flare to sit up a little straighter.

Zaire dipped his bread in the thick sauce of his casserole, bit and chewed with agonising slowness. "No."

"Oracle above," Eyrton muttered, rubbing at his temples as though they ached. "I'm too old for this shit."

"You want to test me," Flare guessed. When neither Ryllin spoke, he scooped his bowl up, reclined in his chair, rested the casserole on his chest and began dipping bread in measured motions. "All right. The way I see it, those servants who attacked the other night weren't servants." Flare slid his spoon into the casserole, rescued a sinking piece of bread, and shoved the whole thing in his mouth. As he chewed, he pinned Zaire with a stern look. "Those thugs wanted blood - literally - and there's a medical frigate from your planet missing. You made me destroy all traces of said blood - which, by the way, is the most un-blood-like fluid I've seen in a long time - and something is clearly going on with your body judging by the way you froze and collapsed." Another pause, another spoon of casserole. "I've also begun to wonder whether the servant you tried to protect was also not a servant, which brings to mind the question of why they were in that hallway in the first place. In addition, I haven't ruled out the idea that you were following me that night, because I know *someone* was."

"Well, shit," Eyrton breathed. He flicked a look at Zaire. "You were stalking him?"

Zaire shrugged. "It was the warg speech. I wanted to see if it was all for show, or if he really intended to put his money where his mouth is.

Besides, I was due to meet Beelo anyway." Indigo eyes narrowed slightly. "You're clearly smarter than you look."

Flare donned his sauciest grin, an expression he'd not attempted since before the warg had attacked Sorcen. It felt strange on his face but he managed it, proven by the way Eyrton's breath caught and he leant away from the table. "How do you *do* that?"

"Practice." Flare dropped the smile and turned to Zaire. "A test, then. If I pass, you tell me everything you know."

The Ryllin nodded. "Everything. You'll also have to swear on your life that it stays between us - and believe me, I'm quite capable of collecting."

"Once I make an oath," Flare said quietly, "I don't break it."

Zaire gave him a look so cold and appraising that a thrill of danger tracked down Flare's spine. His heart kicked into gear, his breathing turning shallow as his body tightened. What in the world? Blinking to clear the sensation, he deliberately took another bite of casserole, savouring the tender meat as he waited for the Ryllin to make a decision. Whatever Zaire was looking for he must have found, because he said, "All right. But I'll be demanding a little truth from you, too."

"To be expected." Flare shrugged. "If I deem *you* trustworthy, I might even answer."

Eyrton groaned but Zaire's face split into a wide grin, the expression bringing a feral light to his eyes that had Flare's heart speeding up again. The Ryllin held out a long-fingered hand. "Deal."

When Flare reached to shake, Eyrton caught his wrist and gave his cousin a long look. "Other hand."

"No." Zaire and Flare spoke in unison, exchanging a surprised look which shifted quickly to cool determination.

"Oh, for the love of - fine." Eyrton sat back, crossing his arms over his chest. "You two are as bad as each other."

Flare's lip quirked into a smirk as he caught Zaire's forearm in a traditional warrior's grip. The other male's fingers were cool even through the sleeve of his robe, applying a steady pressure just shy of bruising. Indigo eyes met carnelian and held, the moment gathering a charge between them that seemed to spark in the air. Captivated by the unusual sensation, it wasn't until Eyrton pointedly cleared his throat that Flare let go, his fingers trailing across smooth fabric and brushing Zaire's palm as he sat back.

The dusty blue skin around Zaire's temples darkened and the Ryllin ducked his head, hiding behind the slick waterfall of his hair. "Your skin is hot."

"It's the fire magic; makes me a few degrees short of uncomfortably warm." Flare looked down at his hand. "Did you like it?"

A short, sharp silence, during which Zaire sat perfectly motionless. "I don't have a preference. I only asked because it'd be annoying if you died of a fever."

"Uh huh." Amusement threatened to crack his face but Flare was nothing if not practiced at hiding his feelings. "What sort of hoops do you want me jumping through to prove my worth?"

Zaire eased back in his chair, interlocking both arms behind his head and propping polished black boots on the vacant chair beside him. "The servant I met the other night services our dear Ambassador Krowley's quarters. I have reason to believe that Krowley's got more information on this disappearance than he's sharing, and I was attempting to bribe the servant into getting me a DNA sample from the posturing barbarian so that I could hack his personal files."

"Straight to shady deals and hacking?" Flare asked, raising a brow.

"No," Zaire shook his head, "but it's all I'm giving you until you prove your worth."

"Fair enough. Did the servant agree?"

"I was attacked before I could even ask," Zaire growled, his face tight with frustration. "And I haven't been able to find the useless creature since."

Flare tapped a finger against his chin. "The servant went down during the fight, but I'm pretty sure it wasn't fatal. I went back to the scene after I delivered you to your cousin and there wasn't a soul to be found."

Zaire's eyes turned flinty. "Did you make a report?"

"Don't be ridiculous," Flare snorted. After a moment's shared glaring, he set both elbows on the table and steepled his fingers. "You want me to get that DNA sample from Krowley."

"What?" Eyrton jumped to his feet, his chair crashing to the floor. "You can't be serious, Z!"

"He is," Flare murmured.

Zaire didn't so much as flutter an eyelash. "Deadly serious."

"Oracle's voice." Eyrton pushed both hands into his hair and tugged. "This plan was already borderline, cousin. If you think -"

"I'll do it," Flare cut in, his eyes never leaving Zaire's face. "You can supervise the entire time, so you know I didn't cheat - but if I do this, I'm in neck deep. I don't just want the whole story, I want equal parts in the hacking, planning and execution of everything else moving forward. I'm nobody's lackey, little Ryllin."

"Partners?" Zaire looked startled, boots lifting off the chair to propel him upright. He paced back and forth in the small space, brows heavy and lips pressed into a thin line. Just as Flare opened his mouth to needle a little further, Zaire stopped dead and nodded. "All right."

"Good." Flare grinned, feeling alive for the first time in months. "Let's go, then."

Both men blinked. "Go?"

"Sure." Flare carried his dirty dishes to the wash drawer and arranged them inside. "No time like the present, right? Strike while the iron's hot? Why put off until tomorrow what we can do today? Start grinding before the boner goes sof-"

"I get it," Zaire snapped, making a cutting motion with one hand. "I meant, where do you want to go?"

"Wherever you'll let me," he purred. When the Ryllin looked like he was poised somewhere between tears and homicide, Flare shrugged. "Krowley's a warrior. I'm willing to bet he spends his free time at the gym, in the training ring."

"You want to go there… now?" Zaire's shoulders hunched inward. After a moment's jaw clenching, he bent and snatched his leather armour off the floor. "Okay."

Eyrton's jaw dropped. "Z, are you sure -"

"I have to be there to get the DNA, don't I?" Zaire snapped, shouldering into his sleeveless leather armour and fumbling with the buckles. His hands shook so badly that Eyrton slapped them away and took over the job. While his cousin worked, Zaire flicked out a glance that was surprisingly vulnerable. "I can't get in the ring."

It would've been easy to make a snide comment but the distress in the other man's voice was so deep that Flare gentled his tone. "I'll handle it."

"I..." A multitude of expressions flashed over Zaire's face before it settled into the surliness with which Flare was most familiar. "For their safety, not mine."

"Sure." Flare shrugged easily, but didn't miss the furtive glances passing between the two cousins. He stretched and cracked his knuckles. "I haven't hit the training ring yet anyway."

Eyrton turned to face him, eyes full of doubt. "Take it carefully - they don't muck around. Particularly Krowley."

"Good." Flare's grin was a baring of teeth. "I wouldn't want anyone holding back."

Zaire snorted a laugh that was more breath than humour, patting at his armour to ensure it sat properly before retrieving his bracers and sliding them on for Eyrton to tighten. After a roll of his shoulders and a barely concealed shudder, the Ryllin strode to the door and slapped the pressure plate with an open palm. "Let's go."

The gymnasium took up an entire level of the space station and had an internal map all to itself. Flare allowed Zaire to lead him there, though his memorised blueprint meant he already knew the way. There was an information console just inside the door listing the floor's numerous facilities but they'd walked into the traditional gym section, beyond which Flare could already see a handful of cordoned off sparring rings. Whilst many warriors of different races took their turns it was impossible to miss Krowley, his ebony skin gleaming in the artificial light as he bent over the ropes to talk to a young, coffee-skinned woman who wore a female version of the Ambassador's animal skin clothing.

"They look like cavemen," Flare muttered as he followed Zaire through a maze of silent treadmills.

"They are." Zaire's voice carried back as no more than an exhalation. "Just don't say that to him unless you want a spear in your asshole."

Snorting a laugh, Flare danced around a set of weights that had been left on the ground - did nobody anywhere, in any gym, ever put them back on the rack? - and lifted his robes to step over the ankle high chain that delineated the gym from the sparring area.

"Well, well." Krowley looked up as they approached, crossing both arms over his extraordinarily muscular chest. "If it isn't my favourite Ambassadors."

"Sarcasm will rot your teeth," Flare sang, sliding in front of Zaire. "And then how will you go about slaughtering animals for the spring collection in your wardrobe?"

Krowley laughed the sort of big belly laugh belonging to people who believed they were top of the food chain. "You're good, little mage, I'll give you that."

"Sorcerer."

Yellow eyes rolled inside Krowley's head. "Whatever. Now, what brings my favourite dress-wearing 'sorcerer' to the sparring ring?"

"Exercise, mostly." Flare jerked his chin at the young woman in the ring. She was a similar height to himself, with a svelte physique and a thick tumble of tight black curls. "I thought it might be nice to test my strength against a barbarian or two."

Krowley's eyes narrowed. "That happens to be my daughter."

"Really?" Flare caught the flexible rope of the ring in one hand and swung himself up to look the young woman in the eye. Taking pity on her age - surely this creature was barely out of adolescence - he offered the least sensual smile he owned. "Condolences on your genetic makeup. I'm Flare."

While Krowley spluttered indignantly behind him, she held out a hand. "Kerris."

"Kerris." He took her arm in a warrior's grip, grinning wider at her start of surprise. "Care to dance with a sorcerer?"

She held his gaze for a long moment and then those yellow eyes flicked away, heat staining her cheeks. "Depends how badly you want to lose."

Flare slid between the ropes, nodding at Kerris' previous training partner before smoothing his robes and offering a lopsided smile with the merest hint of heat. "If it's up against you, I'm willing to lose quite badly."

Krowley choked at that, barking something in a language composed entirely of guttural grunts and growls. Flare wasn't surprised in the least when Kerris tugged a pair of short knives from her animal-fur skirt and lunged forward, lips pulled wide in a rictus grin. He sidestepped with smooth grace, then again, then a third time. Kerris, by sharp contrast, slashed with her knives in an increasingly frenzied effort to land a blow.

Flare's lip twitched. She was a rank beginner, no doubt training on the job beneath her father's watchful eye. Being beaten by Kerris would not only be a humiliation for Sorcen, but would make his life difficult in Alliance political circles. Too bad neither of them had any real idea what he was capable of.

Switching tactic, Flare stepped inside Kerris' guard and trapped her left arm against his ribs, the knife swishing harmlessly against the back of his robes. He caught her other hand with a simple block and twist manoeuvre he'd learnt as a trainee soldier and leant in close. "You're telegraphing your movements. Keep calm, look at my face, and make your attacks precise."

Kerris hissed in wordless rage, tugging until Flare released his grip. Over her shoulder, Krowley grunted and growled a series of what could only be interpreted as instructions. His daughter's eyes narrowed a second and then she leapt forward, daggers slashing wildly at chest height. Flare dodged the feint, twisted his foot beneath her wild kick, and had Kerris flat on her face in moments.

Dropping to a crouch, he set one knee against the small of her back and put his lips against her ear. "You're still looking where you're going to strike. You'll never win that way."

"I'm not a *child*."

"Prove it." Rolling back on his heels, Flare inserted a hand beneath her shoulder and flipped her upright.

Kerris stumbled as she landed, Krowley still blathering on behind her. A dagger flew from her hand, parting the fabric at Flare's shoulder before thunking into the mat. The second dagger followed behind the first, catching the sleeve on his opposite side before it, too, thudded into the floor. The girl's eyes widened in horror, her follow up blow faltering. "Why didn't you move?"

Flare tackled her knees, slamming her none too gently to the ground. Pinning Kerris with the lower half of his body, he bared his teeth and hissed, "Because you didn't mean it."

"I could have killed you!"

"Bullshit. You never even aimed at me," he retorted. "You can't play at being a warrior - you either are, or you aren't."

"I am my father's daughter," Kerris snapped, slamming her palms against his shoulders.

Once upon a time, he'd have taken the hint and moved. Now, Flare dropped more of his weight against her slighter frame. His words, low and furious, vibrated through them both. "Your father's a fool if he can't see how much you hate this."

A hand twisted in the back of his robe and yanked. Flare went boneless and twisted, lashing out with his heel and slamming Krowley down on the mat beside his daughter. The movement was accompanied by the sound of tearing fabric and when Flare rolled to his feet, it was to find his robe hanging half off his shoulder.

"You wretch," Krowley roared, struggling upright. "You don't get to touch her."

Flare raised a single brow. "You were the one who put a child in the ring with a wolf, Ambassador. Either face me yourself or shut your mouth."

Kerris flinched, her lower lip trembling for a fraction of a moment before she flipped to her hands and knees and scuttled for the ropes edging the ring. Flare watched her go through narrowed eyes, feeling every inch the asshole she now thought him. Still, he'd achieved his aim - Krowley began peeling off layers of animal skin, tossing them beyond the ropes with single minded intensity.

"I will break you into pieces," the Ambassador growled, "and strangle you with your own skirts."

"Not with all that windbagging, you won't." Flare snatched one of Kerris' daggers from the floor and slashed into his torn robes, removing everything from the waist upwards. As he bunched the fabric in his hands, he heard more than one audible gasp from around the room and looked up to find, among others, his opponent ogling his chest. "What? Never seen a topless fire sorcerer before?"

Krowley blinked, his eyes tracking up to Flare's face. "You're very muscular."

"And you're very surprised." Flare wriggled his sculpted pectorals up and down one at a time. "Wanna feel?"

"What? No!" Giving himself a shake, Krowley - whose musculature was undeniably far more impressive - settled his weight into the balls of his feet and raised both hands like claws. "I'm going to rip your arms off."

"Suit yourself." Drawing the rose gold chain of the Fire Elder off over his head, Flare rolled shorn fabric and metal links into a bundle and threw it at Zaire. "Hold those for me, won't you?"

The Ryllin clenched his hands in the torn robe so hard the knuckles whitened. "Fuck you," he mouthed.

Replying by way of a broad wink, Flare forced his attention back to Krowley as the Ambassador surged forward. The barbarian moved with a litheness belied by his large frame, clawed hands striking swift and sure. When Flare deflected the opening blows with ease, kicks with the weight of tree trunks behind them followed. Two he dodged, the third he stepped inside to catch above the knee, slamming his elbow upwards. Krowley jerked back just in time, Flare's bronze-skinned elbow brushing the hard line of an ebony jaw. The Karrjhani Ambassador answered with a swift kidney punch that Flare bore with a grunt, unwinding his body in the reverse direction. This time, Krowley was too slow and the elbow's return trip threw him to the floor with a noise like a gunshot.

The barbarian didn't miss a beat, rolling over one shoulder and coming upright with a bloodied chin and his nose at a sickening angle. He wrapped his fingers around the cartilage and righted it with a crunch. "You'll pay for that."

"Oh come on, it's not the first time you've had your nose broken," Flare chuckled, jumping up and down on his toes. "Old bastard like you probably doesn't even feel it anymore."

Krowley's eyes narrowed to slits as he slunk closer, fury quivering in every oversized muscle. Blows flew and were blocked, each with increasing speed and strength, until the Karrjhani's fingers slid around Flare's wrist, locked, and twisted. Rather than have his wrist broken, Flare used Krowley's thigh as leverage and cartwheeled with the motion, speaking a single word of power as he whizzed by overhead. Fire wreathed his hands an instant later, causing the barbarian to release his hold with a shout of surprise. Gripping hard at Krowley's shoulders, Flare drove his knee into the other man's groin amidst the hiss of burning flesh.

A howl of agony split the air and Krowley toppled forwards, wrapping both arms around Flare's waist and tackling him backwards onto the mat with his heavier bulk. They hit with such force it drove the air from his lungs, but Flare'd been winded many a time and the awful feeling did nothing to distract from the battle at hand. When Krowley reached for his throat, Flare slapped his hands away with flaming fingers and, quick as flipping a switch, turned his body from hard and aggressive to soft and inviting.

Krowley hesitated, his muscular form instinctively relaxing into Flare's gentler lines. While the Ambassador tried to work out the sudden and confusing influx of sensations his body was now experiencing, Flare wrapped one leg around the other's hips, twisted… and suddenly their positions were reversed, Flare's robe swirling over the other man's bleeding face. "You know, if you really wanted to see what a sorcerer wears under his robe, you only had to ask."

Muscles bunched in warning, and Flare dropped his backside heavily onto Krowley's chest, forcing the breath from his lungs. Before his opponent could recover, Flare leapt up and away, tracing runes and muttering under his breath as he went. By the time Krowley rolled to his feet, there was a shimmering shield of fire between them.

"Stop." The barbarian took a step backwards. "Enough."

Flare released the magic shield, extinguished his flaming hands and took two steps forward, offering his arm. "Good match."

"You surprise me, sorcerer." Krowley accepted the warrior's grip, fingers strong and smile crooked.

"I get that a lot." Flare grinned and ducked back through the rope. "Thanks for the workout."

"And what of my daughter's honour?"

Flare raised a brow. "She's welcome to reclaim it whenever she likes. You know as well as I that a warrior's honour isn't taken, it's given away."

Something flickered in Krowley's eyes but he merely nodded. Flare strode towards the change rooms without looking back, Zaire trailing in his wake. He waited only long enough to ensure they were alone before untying the black sash which served to keep the remains of his robe together, bunching his fist in the fabric when it would have fallen to the floor.

"What are you doing?" Zaire baulked in the entryway, plastering his back to the closed door.

Flare looked over one shoulder, his free hand hovering above the temperature plate for the water. "Showering?"

"But -" Zaire cut off as the topmost layer of Flare's robe, covered in Krowley's blood and sweat, wrapped around his face and shoulders. "Oh."

"Will that give you what you need?"

Zaire made no move to untangle the fabric, his voice cold as a glacier. "Yes."

"Excellent." Flare allowed the remains of his underrobe to fall to the floor and stepped into the scaldingly hot water, his bitter smile hidden by the steam. "I'll be right out."

SEVENTEEN
FENRIS

HEAT. BLAZING, BURNING, BLISTERING HEAT. ALL CONSUMING, SMOTHERING heat from which only death would bring the cool, blessed darkness of surcease. Though he'd sworn to fight, perhaps it wouldn't be so terrible a thing to just let go and drift away? Anything would be better than the agony which coursed through his veins, piercing even the thick veil of unconsciousness - though the thought of leaving Arcana ignited a different kind of pain, one that clenched his chest and stole what little air rattled in his scorched lungs.

Leave Arcana?

Never.

Fenris' eyes flew open and he drew in a sharp breath, withered chest inflating as though surfacing from deep underwater. His body shot upright - or attempted to - but cool hands caught his shoulders and kept him pinned on his back in the sand. He blinked to clear his vision, flinching instinctively as a shadow fell across his face. The shade was welcome, but it meant someone else was in close proximity and after his last encounter with the harpies, the mere thought was more than he could handle.

With a throaty rattle, Fenris squeezed his eyes determinedly tight and then forced them open, taking advantage of the cool shadows above to try and get his bearings. Brilliant azure skies, devoid of any cloud, haloed a feminine silhouette, straight black hair falling around her face in a sheet of liquid silk. Rather than reflect the intense light it seemed to absorb it, a living creature of the darkness. It took Fenris a long moment to register unnaturally white skin the colour of fresh-fallen snow, with a pearlescent sheen that shimmered beneath the sun's punishing rays. No harpy had skin that colour. Driven by instinct - by a desperate, impossible hope - he locked his gaze with the black, bottomless eyes that haunted his heart's dreams and drew in a deep breath. Chocolate, with overtones of burnt sugar. A scent he'd never mistake, a scent impossible to imagine with all its complexities. Which meant...

"Arcana?"

"Fenris." Letting out a choked sob, she knelt and gathered him to her, one arm around his shoulders and the other tucking his head into the crook of her neck, where her pulse beat strong and steady against his face. "Gods above, I was so worried."

Too close. She was too close. Nausea twisted Fenris' gut and his breath hitched in panic as he tried to raise his arms and push her away. "Stop."

She froze, and a moment later carefully laid him back on the ground. "Are you okay? Did I hurt you?"

"No." Fenris stared into her face, heart sundering at the thought that he'd waited so long for this moment - and now wanted to be anywhere else than right in front of her. "I just... I can't."

Agony twisted her features, driving the knife harder into his heart, but Arcana cleared her throat and forced it away behind a shield he hated so much he'd spent weeks consciously attempting to breach it. "I'm sorry."

"I..." A larger silhouette appeared, and Fenris sighed with relief. "Caelum."

"Brother. I have water." The deerken lowered a crude wooden bowl suspended on a plaited rope, which Arcana took with trembling hands.

"No!" He tried to scramble backwards, couldn't.

"It's clean," Caelum assured, dipping his nose into the water and then moving fractionally closer so Fenris could assess it himself. "I drew it from the spring only a minute ago."

Managing at last to raise a shaking hand, Fenris collected a drop of moisture and held it beneath his nose. His senses were damaged, but he recognised the purity in the moisture and relaxed marginally. "All right."

"Here, let me -"

"No!" This time he did manage to move; a bare few inches, but movement nonetheless.

Arcana flinched, retracting the hands she would've used to help him sit. Her face settled into impassivity but there was no disguising the hurt in her voice as she turned her face upwards. "Caelum?"

"Brother, let me help you." The deerken dropped to his knees in the sand, close but not touching. "Lean on me. You can't drink lying down."

After a brief hesitation, Fenris nodded. Caelum inched closer, carefully positioning his body against Fenris' and waiting patiently as he laboured until his head and shoulders rested against the deerken's haunches. His eyes moved to the water bowl, still cupped in Arcana's shimmering white hands. Transferring her grip to the string so there was no chance of physical contact, she held it out like a sacrificial offering. "Here."

"Thank you." His arms shook like leaves in the wind, but Fenris managed to get his fingers around the bowl and raised it to his lips. The water was cool and soothing, pure in a way nothing had been since he'd arrived on Hiraptha. He flicked a look at Arcana as he forced his throat to swallow over and over. When he finished, the empty bowl sliding from his hands to land on his chest, he said, "You purified the water."

Panic flitted across her delicate features but she nodded. "It's a simple enough spell."

Not sure why that mattered, he forced himself to meet her gaze, hating the barriers she strengthened with every passing second, hating even more that he lacked the fortitude to bring them back down - or to lower his own. "The effort is appreciated."

"Are you…" she trailed off, cleared her throat. "We don't have anything to eat yet. Probably not until tomorrow."

"No matter." Rather than stare at her, Fenris allowed his eyes to drift closed. "Water is fine."

"Okay." His ears weren't so far gone that they missed the wobble in her voice. "Do you need more?"

"He should go slowly," Caelum murmured, his voice rumbling against Fenris' shoulders. "Too much will have him hurling everywhere."

"I do not require anything more," he said, his tone clipped. Forcing another deep breath, Fenris opened his eyes, skittering them across her forehead, down one cheek. "My apologies. I am tired of being ordered around by those women." Reminded of the harpies at long last, his brow furrowed and he looked around. They lounged in the meagre shade of two scraggly trees, the hard-wearing kind the desert favoured. He could hear nobody in the immediate vicinity, but caught the clink of chain on the breeze and knew they were not entirely alone. That same breeze tickled the skin at his throat, causing the irritated skin to ache and bringing Fenris' fingers to the emptiness. "My collar is gone."

"I took it off," Arcana announced, her tone thick with rage. "You are no-one's slave."

He gave her a long look. "If you completed the Gauntlet, then I am yours."

"Never." The word hissed out of her, glorious fire and life. She made to lean forward, checked herself and settled instead for slamming a shimmering fist into the sand by her knees. "Voluntarily, or not at all."

He knew she didn't mean the slavery, but it was too hard to address anything other, his edges too jagged. "I hear chains."

"Yes." She sighed, her shoulders hunching. "I killed two women in the Gauntlet, defeated two others. The laws of Hiraptha dictate that I inherit their males as part of my victory." A glance from beneath long, dark lashes. "I couldn't leave them."

"I see." Pride surged through him, followed swiftly by searing relief that this horrid place hadn't sunk its talons into her soul. Hard on the heels of that, crushing guilt as Fenris realised he'd doubted her, lumping his vibrant, vital sorceress into the same category as the other women on this useless excuse for a planet. He forced himself to breathe, closing his eyes for a moment's clarity. "You did the right thing."

The breeze came again, bringing her scent to him on curling tendrils of air which held the faintest hint of a cool change. Even as he dragged the complexities of chocolate and burnt sugar deep into his lungs, Fenris' eyes flew open and he looked skyward. "Sunset."

"Caelum says the harpies are afraid of the dark." Arcana tilted her head back too, staring up at the sky and baring the elegant pillar of her throat. Fenris' eyes locked onto her pulse and his fangs suddenly ached, gut tightening with two very different types of hunger. Unaware of his inspection, she sighed. "I have no way to make fire. Nothing to calm them."

Fenris didn't answer, goose bumps sweeping his body in a tide as he struggled to swallow. The ache of her absence these last weeks had gone, replaced instead by a throbbing need in the base of his fangs. She'd taste good. He already knew she did; better than anything he'd ever had on his tongue. There was no meetha in her blood, nothing to sap his strength - bar her magic, of course, which would slaughter him where he sat the instant the blood hit his veins. It didn't stop the desire to bury his hands in her hair and his teeth in her throat, the compulsion so strong his fingers twitched.

So did his loincloth.

No.

All-too-familiar horror and nausea returned and whilst he should have been relieved that he was capable of functioning of his own accord, between panic, self loathing and the increasingly insane need to bite, Fenris had no room for anything else. He was too weak to fight, nothing but a base creature of pure, primal instinct.

Arcana lowered her head, the movement doing nothing to ease his cravings. Catching his expression, she frowned. "Fenris? Are you all right?"

Darkness fell, night sweeping across the sky with the breathtaking speed he'd witnessed only on Hiraptha. He barely registered the males' panicked whistling, the frantic rattle of their chains - all Fenris knew was that with the dark came a surge in his energy. The desert began to relax, the air carrying the specific kind of chill produced by a night with no clouds. He blinked, and that singular movement was all the time his eyes needed to adjust; the landscape was abruptly silvered, soft and clearer than he saw it during the day.

In spite of his misgivings, Arcana drew him like a moth to a flame. Fenris didn't notice he'd moved at first - not until he was close enough to sense the heat from her body. She was blind in the darkness, muttering curses under her breath while her skin glittered as if coated in crushed diamonds. The scent of chocolate tinted with burnt sugar rose around him, Arcana's body a confection of sweet curves and softness while her eyes promised an eternity of furious passion and sharp wit. The slight frown creasing otherwise smooth features was how he'd first seen her - leaning over him at the base of the portal on a frozen planetoid, huffy and grimy and bursting with life.

Life he ached to taste.

Reality rushed in and he drew a half pace back, covering his mouth with a trembling hand. Two more inches and he'd have been drinking from her throat like a savage.

"Fenris?" As though sensing him nearby, she began to turn.

He took another step back, silent in the sand, buoyed by the night. Caelum watched him, the deerken's expression silent and sad.

"I'm sorry," Fenris whispered. "I can't."

He knew she called out - he heard her heart in her voice - but it was too late. Gathering his second wind around him like a blanket, Fenris fled into the freedom of the desert.

EIGHTEEN
ARCANA

Arcana didn't need the daylight to confirm what her shattered heart knew beyond doubt; Fenris had fled from her as though she bore a virulent disease. His horrified expression and wasted body haunted her mind's eye, his clear terror at the thought of her touch a blade that continued to plunge into her chest until she couldn't breathe, couldn't think, couldn't move.

She had revolted him, and now he was gone.

"It's not your fault." Caelum's nose whispered across her forehead, the darkness no impediment to his superior vision. His voice carried enough pain that she knew he was being assaulted with her emotions, but Arcana couldn't staunch the flow of what felt very much like her heart's blood.

"He ran," she whispered. "He ran from me."

"Fenris isn't in his right mind," Caelum soothed, sand crunching as he shuffled to her side. "He's still got that drug coursing through his veins. When it wears off, he'll come back."

"You don't know that."

"Great Gods of Sorcen." Sharp teeth nipped her ear, the shock of pain cutting the overwhelming tide of emotion threatening to drag Arcana under. Caelum blew a hot breath across her face, his voice a furious whisper in her ear. "Fenris surrendered himself to the harpies of his own free will to save your life. He's been beaten, starved, drugged, tortured, and gods know what else, for *you* - and now, when he needs us more than ever, you're going to sit there and sulk?"

Arcana blinked in the darkness, the words like a bucket of chill water to her seizing heart. "You're right."

"I know," Caelum snapped. "You're still carrying baggage from Algae, I get that. Your instinctive reaction is to feel rejected and abandoned, I get that too. But haven't we established by now that Fenris is very much *not* Algae? The man's so damned pure it makes me want to puke sometimes."

Tears rolled down Arcana's cheeks and she pressed her hands to Caelum's face. "Stop. Stop it."

"Not until you come to your senses," Caelum growled, pushing at her chest. "This place has worn us all down; the only way we survive is together."

"I know. I *know*, Caelum." She took a deep breath, then another, squashing the shrieking demons inside her. "You're right; I'm being self-ish. And petty."

"Yup."

Arcana tightened her fingers in his fur, but took the reprimand and tried to think. "It's dark, but Fenris hasn't washed in a while. Can you track his scent?"

"I'll check," Caelum replied, his tone thick with relief. "Wait here."

His giant head tugged free of her hands and Arcana dropped them into her lap, shame replacing the agony in her heart. Fenris had given up his freedom - almost his life - for her safety. In return, she'd taken the first available opportunity to find fault when there was no fault to be found; not with the Guardian who fought for his people, nor the man who'd laughed and kissed her breathless, stripping her armour away to cup his hands around her heart. Caelum was right. Fenris deserved better, and she would give it to him.

Sand whispered against her skin, Caelum's burnt sugar scent filling her lungs a moment before his nose whispered over her cheek. "Nothing."

"Nothing?" Shock coursed through Arcana's system, followed by the first threads of fear. "What do you mean, nothing?"

"No scent," the deerken clarified, his voice impatient. "It's either too windy, or Fenris is capable of hiding his scent trail."

"Option two," Arcana said, resting her forehead against Caelum's in an effort to absorb his strength. "He was frightened and confused; he's running, and he doesn't want to be followed."

Caelum huffed out a slow breath. "What now?"

"If we can't follow, we have to wait here and hope he comes back." Arcana drew herself up, straightening her shoulders and dragging her tattered courage close. "Fenris needs a place to heal, physically and emotionally; so do the other males we've rescued. We need a place to call home. Shelter, food, water... a refuge."

"And you're going to what, snap your fingers and conjure it up from nowhere?" Caelum's voice was tart, but his body trembled with worry. "Your magic is almost gone."

Arcana stroked his face, willing him to feel her resolve. "It doesn't matter, Caelum. I've already let Fenris down once - I'm not about to do it again. We need shelter, we'll have it."

"And if this breaks you? What do I tell him then?"

"Nothing, because if I die, so do you," Arcana whispered, pressing a kiss to his nose. "But I won't let that happen. Trust me, Caelum. Please."

"All right." A long sigh, his soft lips moving through her hair. "I'll guard the men while you work."

Arcana didn't even register his presence drifting away; she'd already gathered her paltry energy and thrust it into the ground. Whilst Hiraptha's relentless suns baked the desert into a barren mixture of sand and stone, beneath the surface the scenery was vastly different. Enormous underground rivers and oceans moved deep beneath the planet's sandy cloak, a twisting labyrinth of moisture that made a mockery of the desolate landscape above. Hiraptha city stood at the edge of a large subterranean lake, and Arcana would bet everything she owned that the Empress had a personal well dipping directly into that very body of water. Where other lakes or rivers came close to the surface, she knew she'd find more small oases or hidden pools very much like the one they'd chosen for themselves.

Channelling her newfound determination into a blade, Arcana tunnelled downwards until she found the underground river whose tiny soak fed their dubious excuse for an oasis. Pain shot through her veins in a rush as she dragged at the water, pushed at the earth, her body warning her she didn't yet have the reserves for magic of such magnitude. Rather than halt, Arcana screamed out the rage and heartbreak she felt when she thought of all Fenris had endured at the hands of his captors and dredged deep inside herself, shattering layer after layer of barriers the Weaver had erected to protect Arcana from the magic she now sought to command. Lights flickered behind her eyes, agony assaulted her from all angles, then her body shorted out and she knew nothing more.

When Arcana woke, she had a mouthful of sand and it was still dark. Moving only to rearrange her limbs into a more comfortable position, she plunged her senses back into the ground, pouring her soul into the earth. Raw nerve endings shrieked in protest but the magic was there, ready to be used, if she dared defy the shivering weakness in her body and the pain that using too much power caused. Gritting her teeth, Arcana thought of all she wanted to achieve; a sanctuary not just for Fenris but for all those in her care, and dove in. Fire swept her veins and tears streaked her face but she drew the power close, moulding the land with her magic until the agony became unbearable and unconsciousness claimed her once more.

The next time her lashes lifted, dawn had broken and the sky above was clear blue. Battered senses informed Arcana that Caelum was nearby; she didn't need to sit up to know Fenris hadn't returned. Tamping down the flash of concern for his welfare, she dipped sluggish senses beneath the desert's surface. Her body cramped in desperate warning, but Arcana ruthlessly ignored the sensation. Any other sorceress would be well and truly burnt out by now - perhaps even dead - but Arcana was nothing if not unique, her body dutifully refilling the ever-growing magical well inside her even as it protested the use to which it was put.

"You okay?" Caelum's head drifted into view, his face slightly blurry as Arcana's eyes struggled to focus.

"Peachy."

A snort. "Looks like it. You want to stop for a bit?"

"No." Arcana coughed, firmed her voice. "I want this done before Fenris comes home."

"All right." Caelum pressed a deerken kiss to her temple, his tongue rough where it brushed across her skin. "Do what you need to. I'm here."

Arcana smiled and returned to her task, casting spell after spell until she saw only sparkling stars behind her lids and her breathing turned ragged. Day turned to night and back to day, Hiraptha's twin suns relentless. Her body absorbed the heat, then the shade as her faltering fountain of magic nurtured the environment into something other, something new and lush. Caelum brought water at regular intervals, concern tightening his elegant countenance when she wasn't always strong enough to drink.

He wanted her to stop but Arcana knew she couldn't, driven by the desperate hope that if she threw all her love and desperate longing into her task, Fenris would somehow sense it and find his way back to her. She worked until she hallucinated beautiful singing in the stone heart of the rocks, until the trees seemed to smile and she dreamed dragons in the clouds. When the sun set the third night, leaves rustled overhead and nobody cried out in terror. The total darkness was soothing after a day of fantasy and fatigue, the stars' gentle laughter catching at her imagination. Dehydration made Arcana falter, magic slipping through mental fingers in a fountain of rainbows and runes. Rather than fight, she rode the gentle waves and was mostly conscious when the grey light of dawn brought warm hands on her shoulders, long fingers sliding under her body and rolling her onto her back.

"Arcana." His voice was a melody of velvet and feathers, eyes aflame with passion and life. "What have you done?"

"I was building a house," she murmured, tears gathering unbidden in the corners of her eyes. "A safe place. But I'm tired now, and everything is hazy. Is this a dream?"

"No."

"It has to be," she mused, her body light and heavy all at once. "You left; I saw you. You can't be real."

Shame broke his expression, fingertips trembling where they brushed her cheeks. "I'm real."

"I wish that were true." Arcana sighed, relaxing into the hallucination with a soft smile. "I like this dream. I wish it would last. I wish… I wish you were really here."

"I *am* here." Bony arms gathered her against his sunken chest and suddenly she was looking up at the stars as they winked out, swallowed by the greedy jaws of dawn. The sun blazed to life and Arcana turned her face instinctively into the scent of the night-time forest, tinted with the smooth warmth of cinnamon.

"I love your smell."

He startled and she thought the vision would fracture - but those phantom arms held and the sky disappeared as they moved into the shade. "I haven't bathed in weeks."

"I don't care." Sand on her body again as he sat, cradling her against his chest, her legs entwined with his on the ground. Cool wet against her lips, water trickling down her parched throat and threatening to wake her. Panic flared, and she gripped her hallucination with desperate hands. "Don't go. Don't leave me."

His hand trembled on her hair, his lips on her brow. "Never. I will never leave you."

"But you did," she whispered, a shudder wracking her body. "I'm sorry. I tried so hard, but I left you all alone. I wasn't good enough to keep you safe."

Moisture on her face; his tears mingling with her own. "You were the only thing that kept me safe." Gentle fingers pressed against her heart. "Here. I was safe here."

"They hurt you," she recalled with a frown. "They hid you."

"And you found me," he rumbled, midnight velvet stroking her skin and soothing her eyelids closed. "Nothing else matters now that we're together."

Silver tears dropped from her lashes to splash against teal skin. "But you're not real."

"Rest," he murmured, his voice vibrating through her cheek. "When you wake, you can see for yourself."

"I can't."

"You can." Wiry arms tightened, lips returning to her face. "I've got you."

With a sigh, she surrendered to the inevitable and let her mind fade into sleep. "Always."

NINETEEN
FLARE

"Ambassador?"

"Yes?" Flare didn't bother to look up from the datapad in his hand.

The hooded servant cleared her throat. "Refreshments."

"Hmmm?"

"Refreshments," she repeated, her voice notching up in volume. "For you."

"Right." Flare nodded, tapping the datapad and then chewing on his lower lip as he analysed the list he'd revealed. "Thanks."

The servant bowed, slid the tray onto a nearby table, and disappeared. Flare continued working until a broad hand covered the screen. "Don't you think you should take a break?"

"I can't afford to take a break." Sighing, he looked up into the eyes of a fire sorcerer who'd fast become indispensable since Arcana had left Sorcen. "Lesce dumped these poor souls on me without so much as a 'yo, bro, incoming troops as requested' and now the hangar bay is milling with sorcerers who have no purpose, you included."

Pytch grinned. "Well, if you're not going to eat, I am."

"Go for it." Flare waved the solid sorcerer away. "Save some for that lovely wife of yours."

"If she's fast enough." Pytch pushed his mane of pale blond hair off his face and bent over the plate. "Ooh, they're still hot."

"Stop trying to tempt me," Flare muttered. "If I allocate these teams incorrectly, I'll never hear the end of it."

172

"From the Alliance?"

"From Lesce."

Pytch fell silent, and Flare took advantage of the reprieve to finalise his posting choices. Most of the soldiers and healers were being spread amongst the Alliance fleet, while he'd chosen to keep the artisans and crystal engineers closer at hand, with a smaller team of higher ranked soldiers to oversee them and report directly back to Flare - among them, Pytch and his nature sorceress wife, Verdure.

"Teams of eight should keep them satisfied, don't you think? Six soldiers, a leader, a healer?" When his companion didn't immediately answer, Flare raised his head. "Pytch?"

The Class Two fire sorcerer was faced away from him, both hands braced on the table and head bowed. Something about the tense set of his shoulders sent a tremor through Flare and he set his datapad aside, crossing the room to grab Pytch's arm. The other man's teeth were clenched, breathing laboured and face grey. Flare took one look at the half-eaten pastry on the table in front of him, then put his fingers to his lips and let out a shrill whistle. "Healer!"

Within moments, a scrawny young man barely out of his youth rushed over. "Class Two healing sorcerer Mendin, sir!"

"Poison," Flare snapped, wrapping an arm around Pytch's waist and squeezing with all his might. The sorcerer's jaw unlocked and his mouth opened, partly chewed pastry flying out. "He's swallowed some - not much."

"Lay him down, sir." Mendin was already on his knees on the cold metal floor, hands outstretched. "Poison is one of my strengths."

"Thank Firius," Flare muttered, scooping Pytch's shuddering body into his arms and carefully spreading him on the floor. When he looked up, it was to find several unfamiliar sorcerers hovering nearby. "Find his wife!"

Verdure appeared a minute later, a petite nature sorcerer with eyes and a long braid in deep bottle green. She threw herself unabashedly into Flare's open arms, eyes wide as Mendin's hands moved over her husband's body. "What happened?"

"Poison," Flare repeated. He snatched a rag from the hangar bay floor and used it to pick up the half-eaten pastry. "What can you tell me?"

For a moment he thought he'd lost her, then the tiny woman straightened her spine and took the rag, focussing her senses on the food. "A natural substance," she said at last. "Plant based. Heavy enough that I'd say it was cooked in rather than added later."

"Can you isolate the ingredients?" He asked, one eye on the woman in his arms and the other on her husband. A fine sheen of oily sweat began to build on Pytch's skin, bubbling to the surface in response to whatever Mendin was muttering as he passed his hands back and forth. The kid was young, but Flare'd witnessed enough healing magic to recognise real talent when he saw it. Coupled with the knowledge that high Class healers were at a premium on Sorcen had him frowning. Why had Lesce sent the boy his way instead of hoarding him like the precious resource he was? Realising Verdure had yet to answer his question, he lowered his head and nipped the shell of her ear. "Babe."

"Don't call me that." She exhaled the words in a rush, shivering in reluctant delight. "Isolating ingredients isn't my specialty. I'm combat and you know it."

"Oh, I do," he returned, putting every ounce of dark seduction he possessed into the sentence. "I also know you've got hidden depths, lovely. Pytch may have eaten that pastry, but it was intended for me. For all our sakes, concentrate."

She rallied with visible effort. "I don't know the name but I'd recognise the energy signature in a heartbeat."

"Good." Flare glanced up from under his lashes, noted the healer watching them. "Report, Mendin."

"The poison is gone." The young man sat back on his heels, face grey with effort. "He'll live."

Verdure slid from Flare's grasp and dropped to the ground beside her husband, laying her head on Pytch's chest. "Breogh's blessing, healer. Thank you."

"He needs rest," Mendin added, turning to Flare. "A couple of days, at least."

"Pytch and Verdure are staying stationside with me, so that won't be a problem." Flare grabbed the datapad and slapped it against Mendin's chest. "Find a couple of sturdy earth sorcerers and get your patient to safety, then catch some rest yourself. Log me a report on every slimy detail the minute you wake."

"Um." Mendin blinked. "Where are you going?"

Ignoring the querulous question, Flare bent to press a comforting kiss to Verdure's cheek. "Okay?"

"Yeah." She nodded. "Thanks."

He brushed Pytch's now sweaty mane of hair back off his forehead. "Don't thank me yet. I haven't caught the asshole."

"But you will." Verdure nodded, turning to pin him with her brilliant green gaze. "I'll keep your schedule free and make sure everyone reports to their new posts."

"All right." Flare skated his gaze over the assembled sorcerers until he spotted someone he knew as more than a face in a crowd. "Carbon - I want a record of all servants currently on duty, particularly those in this area. Use whatever authority my name will get you to obtain it."

"Yes, First Flame."

"That's not my title anymore," Flare muttered, but the other man was already gone. Rolling his eyes, he gave Verdure a swift sideways hug and turned for the door. "I'll drop by later."

She didn't answer, and he walked off with Mendin shrilling in dissatisfaction behind him. The minute he made it back to his quarters, Flare punched in the call code he loathed most in the world.

"Yes?" Lesce's face appeared a millisecond after her irritated greeting. When she spotted Flare, she rolled her eyes. "Craddagh's Cauldron, what now?"

"Troops arrived."

"It's four in the morning, Flare."

He chewed the inside of his cheek, affecting a deliberately casual air. "Mendin's an interesting guy."

"Oh?" Plum coloured eyes flashed. "How nice of you to wake me up just to deliver that scintillating assessment."

"It's not like you to send someone so newly minted," he continued, rubbing at a kink in his neck. "Let me guess: hero complex?"

After a long sigh that said she understood he wasn't going to leave her alone until she played along, Lesce said, "What gave it away?"

"Oh, I don't know - maybe the fact that his name is *Mendin?*" Flare snorted. "Seriously, mending without a G? It's almost like choosing convalesce and then cropping the first five letters to make a whole new word - oh wait. You did that."

"Flare." Lesce ran both hands through her unbound hair, causing it to settle in faint waves around her shoulders. "It's not as easy for healers to find good names as it is for the other schools of magic. Mendin is young, but he's an excellent all-round healer with a specialty in digestive issues, circulation and toxins. I sent him to you because he needs solid, practical experience that he can't find here - he's high Class Two, borderline One, and has developed a tendency to prance around like he owns the place. Now, would you mind telling me what in the name of bloodied bandages you're doing calling me at this time of night to discuss facts you could've read in the file I sent you?"

Dropping into his single, hard-backed chair, Flare propped his boots on the tiny desk for no other reason than he knew it would piss her off. "How many other healers have the illustrious Mendin's specialties?"

"In general, or stationside?"

"Both."

The faintest flicker of awareness chased both sleep and temper out of her face and, one vertebrae at a time, Lesce straightened. "I have a few lower Class sorcerers with the individual talents but nobody as powerful nor with his particular collection of abilities in one body. Why?"

"Just trying to work out where best to distribute him; stupid name or not, Mendin's the highest Class healer you sent." Flare stretched languidly, his robe falling open to flash a healthy dose of chest and the thick rose gold chain of the Fire Elder. "It'd be a terrible shame if his oh-so-specific talents were wasted, don't you think?"

"Hmmm. Perhaps he'd benefit from someone experienced enough to give him responsibility whilst still keeping a firm hand on his ego," his sister replied, the corners of her eyes tightening. "Did you have someone in mind?"

"Pytch," Flare answered promptly. "He's my assistant anyway, and with Verdure on hand to watch his every move, I think Mendin will benefit greatly."

Lesce nodded slowly. "Be careful. He's got an attitude born of youth, talent and privilege."

"You know me, sis - I can handle anything thrown my way." Flare offered her a broad wink. "Shame there's nobody else, though."

"I'm sorry," she said, and in that moment, he knew she meant it. "The other healers are solid, but we don't have many high ranks to spare."

"I know." Flare clicked his tongue between his teeth, then shrugged and gave her a charming smile. "Don't worry, sis, I'll make sure to tease him mercilessly about following in your scandalous naming footsteps."

Lesce rolled her eyes, the brief moment of co-operation gone. "I'm cutting the connection now."

"Tell Salve I'll stroke him later."

Her eyes narrowed. "If you even think about my husband like that, I'll -"

"Too late," Flare sang, and terminated the call.

Silence fell. Whilst his lips curved in amusement at the shrieking he imagined Lesce was currently doing, Flare's mind chewed on the meatier issue - poison, and only one healer proficient in dealing with it. The gangly Mendin was also the only healer on station above a Class Four, meaning he'd be staying stationside. Luckily Flare had already decided that prior to the attack, or it'd be potentially suspicious to change the assignments. Small mercies.

His personal datapad beeped, and Flare tapped the screen to find a short message: *A technical glitch scrubbed servant rosters for the last three days. Kitchen says no orders were issued to deliver food to the cargo bays - Carbon.*

"Damn." He threw the device onto his desk, reaching up to tug at his hair. Not that he'd really expected the would-be murderers to make such an obvious mistake, but a sorcerer could hope, couldn't he? Now the only option was old fashioned investigation; yet another thing to add to his ever-growing list of things to get done.

A chime at the door had Flare out of his chair like a shot. Igniting one hand with a low word of power, he held it behind his back and palmed the door control.

"About time." Zaire strode inside without waiting for an invitation, his gait oddly uneven.

Flare made a point of giving the Ryllin an overt once over, noting the way his armour hung from his frame and dark shadows pooled under his eyes. "I might say the same. I've not seen you for three days."

Zaire raised a brow. "Offended?"

"Relieved." He removed his palm from the pressure plate, letting the door swish shut, and took his flaming hand out from behind his back. "I thought it was someone else."

Zaire watched him shake the flames out, then stepped in close. Surprise had Flare gripping the benchtop, but the Ryllin reached around him and tugged off the small maintenance panel beneath the door controls, revealing a host of wiring and whirring technology. Slender fingers settled against the exposed tech and a moment later, the skin of Zaire's hand simply... melted away. Rather than blood and muscle and bone beneath, a gleaming silver skeleton was already transforming, metallic fingers lengthening into cables and wires that dove into the panel with a mind of their own. Barely a hand's breath away, the deep indigo eyes which fascinated Flare against his will flickered with pinpricks of pale blue light, Zaire's pupils contracting until they were almost non-existent. If not for the steady rise and fall of his chest he might have been a statue, not even a hair wavering as his gaze focussed on a plane Flare knew he'd never have a hope of seeing, much less comprehending.

Torn between the captivating light show in Zaire's eyes and the fact that his hand was buried wrist-deep in the space station, Flare stayed where he was, reconsidering everything he knew about the other male.

Shrieking metal, seizing joints. Blood that looked like oil. A weight far greater than his body mass. Warnings from Eyrton about which arm to use in a handshake. Assailants dressed as servants looking for blood samples.

Zaire's lashes drifted shut and Flare's gaze narrowed on the place where his hand merged with the wall. One by one the wires retracted, reforming into that silvery skeleton he'd glimpsed earlier. Skin bloomed like moss and moments later, an elegant hand flicked the maintenance panel closed. The Ryllin's voice was low and cool as he spoke directly into Flare's ear. "It's safe to talk now."

Flare slid his hand down Zaire's arm, ignoring the other's flinch to entwine their fingers. "You're colder than usual."

"It's the machines." Zaire's voice bore a breathy edge. "You're so hot you're almost burning."

Yet he made no effort to pull away. Flare turned his head until carnelian eyes clashed with indigo, all trace of those flickering lights gone. "Does this mean you've come to share secrets?"

"Yes." Zaire's hand slid from his grasp as the other man stepped back. Reaching under his armour, he tugged out a slim plas-file and slapped it against Flare's chest. "I promised, after all."

"Indeed." Flare caught the file before it slid to the floor, sidling around the Ryllin who suddenly seemed larger than life. He had neither space or furniture for two, so he tucked his legs underneath him and settled on the floor, Zaire dropping down beside him a moment later.

The file contained a collection of hardcopy photographs. The first one was a body - or at least, what was left of a body. Most of a male torso, the bottom edge of the ribcage exposed, the severed spine glistening. One arm torn off at the shoulder, the other missing sections of flesh that exposed shattered bones beneath. The back of his skull was gone, a miraculously intact brain half hanging out, the man's face hidden by matted, bloody hair. The now familiar leather armour of Rylle clung with admirable desperation to what remained of the warrior, but it had been shredded in multiple places to reveal more flesh, more muscle, more bone. Gaping cavities yawned where organs should have been, the area surrounding the corpse a study in bodily fluids.

Flare examined the image with the impartiality which came from years of warfare, setting aside his emotional response with an ease that had ceased to frighten him decades ago. He ran a finger along the space where legs should have been, and sighed. "Warg."

"Yes."

The next image showed the same torso devoid of armour, floating in a tank of scarlet-tinted sapphire fluid. Long, dark hair concealed the face but there was no mistaking the shimmering silver finish to the protruding bones. Flare continued to turn each image, revealing more and more reconstruction, an impossible fusing of man and machine. He didn't need to see the final image but he looked anyway because he knew, in his heart of hearts, that it mattered. Then he glanced up at Zaire. "This is you."

"I was a silver-scrolled rogue - the best of our warriors. We were escorting the previous Ambassador to Galactic Station when we were ambushed by pirates." Indigo eyes shuttered, remembered pain tightening his features. "We held them off long enough for the captain to send out a distress call."

"How many survived?"

"None."

Flare jerked his chin at the images. "Why you?"

"Privilege." Blue-black lashes fell across pale cheeks. "My grandfather is one of the Oracle's Arms. My father is Lord of Rogues and my uncle - Eyrton's father - is at the forefront of a unique brand of extremely secret, highly experimental bio-technology."

"Making you the perfect test subject." Flare's unfeeling heart twinged but he was careful not to let it show as those indigo eyes popped open. "They put you back together again."

"No." Zaire shook his head. "There wasn't enough left for repairs - you saw it yourself. They built me anew."

"How?"

"I don't truly understand it, but my uncle found a way for the tech to become me. Or me, it. Either way, once the fusion was made, what remained of my body was consumed for fuel and regenerated as a completely different creature - though I look exactly the same. I'm not an android, nor am I an entirely biological being. The metal and wires are me, and the flesh and blood are also me. My thoughts are mine; my feelings, memories, desires, loves and hates. Nothing has changed. And yet I'm stronger than I ever was, faster, with sharper senses and so on. I can integrate with machines and access a higher, colder consciousness that is not, and has never been, in any way an organic construct." Zaire stared down at his hands, mouth tight. "This treatment, on top of returning me to life, was supposed to pave the way for a new world. The positive medical implications would be enormous."

Flare closed the file and tilted his head. "But?"

"Something went wrong." Zaire sighed, shoulders slumping. "The tech and I aren't fully integrated. Sometimes we work, other times we malfunction and I seize, or start to come apart at the seams - literally. One moment I'm braiding my hair, the next I'm punching holes in walls or crushing glasses without conscious thought."

"If you can't synchronise, the tech can't be offered to anyone else," Flare mused, tapping his chin. "But that's not stopping someone from trying to steal it - presumably for the almost superhuman benefits."

"Exactly."

"How is that related to the warg?"

"We haven't worked that part out yet. How are *you* related to the warg?" Dark eyes travelled the breadth of Flare's chest and back up again. "You don't look like you've been ravaged lately."

"Much to my disappointment, I've not been ravaged in years."

"Again with the sex." Zaire snorted. "Your reputation precedes you, Ambassador. Do you think of anything else?"

"You'd be surprised." Especially if the Ryllin learnt exactly how long he'd abstained. Flare flicked a glance downward. "Does yours still work?"

Blue tinted the skin at Zaire's temples and he spoke through gritted teeth. "I don't know. It's too dangerous to find out."

A shiver tracked down Flare's spine. He suppressed it with military ruthlessness. "Makes sense, I guess. I suppose you want my secrets now?"

"You promised." Relief lifted several years from Zaire's face and he accepted the slim file from Flare with shaking hands. "What are the warg to you?"

In clipped, professional tones, Flare told the story of Arcana's ascension, Fenris' appearance and the warg's invasion of Sorcen. Where once caution had stayed his hand, the knowledge that Zaire had willingly placed his life and his deepest secrets into Flare's lap had him explaining everything he knew about Taelon, right up to and including the strange arrival of Arcana's satchel in his room.

When he finished, Zaire gave him a long, considering look. "Are you in love with your sister?"

"*What?*" Flare's jaw dropped open in astonishment. "No!"

The Ryllin shrugged. "Just wondering. She's the only person I've ever seen you talk about without looking like you've just sucked on a bittlemon."

"She's my sister!" He cried, horrified. "I love her, yes - but I don't want to bone her! That's just - just -"

"All right," Zaire lifted both hands in a sign of peace. "I'm sorry. I was intrigued by the glimpse of life in your eyes, is all."

Flare slapped a hand, fingers spread, on the other man's partially exposed forearm. "I've got plenty of life. You complained about the heat already."

"Having a beating heart and being alive inside are two different things," Zaire said primly.

The statement struck too close to home, too close to the things he hadn't included in his tale. Flare withdrew his hand and bared his teeth. "Arcana happens to be the only person who's ever looked at me and seen something other than a tool to be used for either fucking or fighting. She's the only one who gives a damn if I think, or if I feel, beyond whether my fists or my cock or my magic is functioning at optimum levels. She's the only one who's never judged, belittled, coveted or salivated at me. The only one who gives of herself without asking for anything in return. I would die for her."

From the look on Zaire's face, Flare's words were far too real for both of them. They lay stark in the air, shimmering with sharp edges that neither were willing to touch. After a long moment, the rogue's face softened - not with pity but with a sad understanding. "It's not fun being one of a kind, is it?"

"No."

Zaire tilted his head to the side, indigo eyes narrowing. "Eyrton told me I was a fool to trust you."

"What do you think?" Flare ran a hand through his hair and shook it out, as though he could banish his uncharacteristic emotional outburst.

"I think Eyrton sees exactly what you show to everyone else." Zaire's indigo eyes sparked with challenge. "The image you choose to present."

"I have a lifetime's experience at it," Flare acknowledged. He stretched his arms behind him and leant backwards. "So, if you can literally melt into a machine, why do we need Krowley's DNA?"

"Because his personal files are encrypted with a DNA codex. I can break it, but only if the systems think I'm him - otherwise, the data disintegrates." Zaire flicked a look up at the clock. "I'm ready to hack, but when I mesh with the station on that level I'll be unaware of my external environment. I'm going to need backup."

"Not Eyrton?"

The Ryllin shook his head. "He can't be connected with this. If I get busted, we need to keep him clean or we lose all connection to the Alliance and the warg."

"Covert mission, huh?" Flare nodded when Zaire's lips thinned. "It's okay, I'm on one of those too - as you now know. A secret for a secret."

Zaire spat in his palm and offered it. "Swear."

"I already have." But he spat in his own palm and the two hands clapped together with wet finality. "Your skin's still cool."

"It'll always be cooler than most." Zaire shrugged, breaking the clasp to wipe his hand on the carpet. "I don't have the same insides."

There was something brittle in that admission, but Flare wasn't in the right place to address it. "When are we hacking, then?"

"After dark, if you're up for it."

"I am - but I need to make a quick stop first. Have you eaten dinner?"

Zaire blinked, surprised. "If you're about to offer me the station's pathetic excuse for cuisine -"

"Someone tried to poison me this morning," Flare cut him off. "I'm not eating anything I or someone I trust hasn't made themselves."

When the Ryllin stared in astonishment, Flare recounted the events of the day so far, ending with his conversation with Lesce.

"Another sister?"

"Don't worry, this one loathes me the way oil loathes water." Flare sighed. "Still, we're tied together by shared DNA and a love for Arcana. We make it work. Sort of. Not really."

Zaire barked a sharp laugh, the sound rusty from disuse. "So, you're inviting me to bomb in on the poor fool who was stupid enough to eat your poisoned lunch?"

"Something like that." Flare pushed to his feet and then offered a hand. "His wife makes an excellent curry."

Zaire eyed the extended hand with a shuttered expression. "I could crush your bones into powder before you so much as blink."

"Then I'd be the sexiest amputee ever to walk the halls of Alliance Station," Flare returned, shrugging. "I don't believe in fear."

"Someone's trying to kill you and you don't believe in fear? There *is* something wrong with you." Still, Zaire wrapped his fingers around Flare's wrist, his cool, smooth skin reminiscent of satin. When Flare tugged him upright without so much as a grunt, he raised a dark brow. "Those muscles aren't just for show."

"They were better before -" Flare cut off and shook his head. "Never mind. Stop looking at my muscles or I'll start getting ideas."

Zaire snorted, striding over to palm the door open. "You're always getting ideas."

"True." Flare followed him out into the hall. "You gave yourself a key, huh?"

"You're programmed into our quarters, too," Zaire responded, surprising him. Again, a single brow rose. "Well? I don't know where we're going, you know."

Partners, Flare recalled, feeling unaccountably vulnerable. He cleared his throat, pasted on his best naughty grin and straightened his robes - a black velvet with burnt orange underlay that brought out his eyes. "Allow me to escort you, then."

When Verdure opened the door five minutes later, her face blanked with shock - but Flare simply caught her in his arms and strode into the quarters she shared with Pytch, nostrils crinkling as he went. "Fire and brimstone, that smells good."

"I hope so." Rather than struggle, Verdure wrapped her legs around his waist and used the leverage to peer over his shoulder. "And you are?"

"Zaire, deputy Ambassador for Rylle." The rogue swept a jerky bow Flare now understood had nothing to do with his icy demeanour.

"Verdure, Class Two nature sorcerer." She smacked Flare's shoulder. "Put me down, you heathen, or the curry will spoil."

He slithered her down his body with a bedroom smile. "Now, that would be a crime."

"Stop. It." Verdure prodded him in the chest. "No games while Pytch is sick."

Flare flicked a glance at Zaire. "I don't suppose you'd care to make a little pit stop?"

"I'm not going to spring a leak," came the waspish reply, but the Ryllin was already disappearing into the bathroom.

"What in the name of - you know what? I don't want to know." Shaking her head, Verdure turned to the stove.

Flare chuckled and made his way into the apartment's single bedroom, where Pytch lay sleeping on the bed, pale hair spread across the pillow and the sheets tangled around his naked waist. Zaire joined him a moment later. "He doesn't look stupid."

"Neither do you, yet I've seen proof otherwise."

Zaire merely raised a brow, not breaking away from his inspection of Pytch. "You've slept with the woman?"

"Not for years." Flare shrugged, then grinned as Zaire blinked rapidly. "What? Weren't expecting honesty?"

The Ryllin raised a slender hand and pinched the bridge of his nose. "No, I - you're just so familiar with her."

"Flare's like that with everyone," Verdure chuckled, squeezing her head between them and wrapping one arm around Flare's waist for balance. "It's part of his charm. Pytch and I were lucky enough to garner his attention for a whole night, once. Well over ten years ago, now." Her face softened as she looked down at her husband. "It was our wedding anniversary."

"So it was." Flare's gorge rose as he struggled against memories that strangled and cut. Rather than let Verdure see how deeply he bled, he affected a wounded look. "And they didn't even call me in the morning."

"Oh, please." Verdure prodded him in the leg. "You made us pancakes, you fat liar."

"You remember!" He fluttered his lashes dramatically. "I'm astounded."

Zaire made a gagging noise in the back of his throat. "We're clear, by the way - in case this act is for the camera's benefit."

Flare immediately straightened, easing into the room so that Verdure was forced to let him go. "How's he doing?"

"Mendin says he just needs sleep - but he's returning to do a full check first thing in the morning." Verdure's eyes narrowed. "I'm going to handle both mine and Pytch's duties so that you can concentrate on catching the bastard."

"Keep an eye on the healer, too," Flare muttered, leaning forward to press the back of his hand to Pytch's forehead. "Lesce says he's getting a little big for his britches."

"Your not-stupid friend looks pretty good for having been poisoned," Zaire noted.

Flare nodded. "Mendin was able to draw out the toxin. When he comes back tomorrow, he'll give Pytch a zap of energy and speed things up."

"Mendin," Zaire said slowly. "As in mending, but without the g?"

Verdure snorted. "Yeah."

"Sorcen naming conventions are pretty unique," Flare explained, weaving a set of runes that shimmered orange in the air above the bed. "Parents name their baby, then when that baby matures, imprints into a school of magic and becomes an adult, they choose a new name for themselves. Second names are reflective of the school you imprint into and become the primary identifier, whilst the birth name becomes the follow up."

"So Veritax isn't your surname?"

He shook his head. "It's my birth name."

"It sounds like a brand of laxative." Zaire wrinkled his nose. "So… Flare and Pytch for fire. Verdure… some sort of plant magic?"

"Nature," Verdure supplied, watching as Flare finished his spell and settled it into her husband's sheets. "We have Fire, Water, Earth, Nature and Healing." Dark green eyes flicked towards Flare. "I assume there's a reason we're discussing this."

Flare stepped back from the bed, gave Pytch a final once over, then ushered them both out of the room. "Zaire's my partner now; we're chasing warg together. It'll work to our advantage if he has a basic idea of Sorcen culture."

"Do you think the poisoning has something to do with your new assignment to find the missing ships?" Verdure asked, her brow furrowing.

"Maybe." Flare propped his hands on his hips. "It could also be someone who wants me well away from the topic of the warg, or a Councillor who thinks I need taking down a peg."

"All of the above are viable - Galactic Station is a viper's nest, and you went ahead and stirred it up." Zaire folded his large frame into one of the seats around the small dining table. "So why isn't the boy's name Bandage or Stitch or something?"

Flare sighed, sinking into a chair of his own. "In recent years, particularly among healers, it's become a bit of a trend to find a relatable word and then... doctor it. My younger sister is the most notable recent example."

"Lesce?" Zaire tried the name with multiple pronunciations and then shook his head. "Nope. Can't work out the root word."

"Convalesce," Flare supplied.

Zaire's brow creased with a frown. "But you don't pronounce it 'Less'. You say it 'Lesk.' So she not only dropped letters, but changed the sound?"

"Yeah. It made huge waves at the time, being a Class One sorcerer and choosing such a non-traditional name - but then, for all she pretends otherwise, Lesce's no stranger to scandal. She married and had children far younger than most sorcerers do." Flare shrugged. "Out of all of us, she's always been the one who knew exactly what she wanted, and does whatever it takes to get it."

"Looks like she set a trend." Zaire nodded, then wrinkled his face again. "But... Mendin?"

"I know." Flare passed a hand over his face. "He'll probably regret it in a few years."

Verdure thumped a bowl of curry and rice on the table in front of each of them, her face creased into a scowl. "You both sound like crotchety old men. Put something constructive in your mouths and leave the poor healer alone."

"You're only saying that because he saved Pytch's life," Flare retorted.

A narrow shard of wood, reminiscent of a knitting needle but far more deadly, thumped into the table by his hand. He grinned at Zaire's surprise. "Verdure's a combat nature sorcerer; these arrows are her specialty. Should've done two, V - I could've used them like cutlery."

A second splinter embedded itself by the first. Laughing, Flare tugged both projectiles free of the table, arranged them just so in his fingers, and began to eat.

TWENTY
ARCANA

Arcana woke in soft shade, her body cradled against hard warmth and her nose filled with a scent she thought she'd dreamt.

"Fenris." Her lashes flew upward, her heart thumping out of time. "You're real."

Shame and regret twisted his elegant features. "I am real."

Cushioned by the lingering cobwebs of sleep, she simply lay and stared up at him. His face was narrower than it should be due to lack of food and his hair hung matted and clumped in his eyes and across the top of his shoulders, enhancing an already ethereal appearance with a kind of wild, stark beauty that made him look remarkably like his fey mother. Bruises and scrapes marred skin wrapped so tightly over his bones she could count them and his jade eyes carried a haunted quality that hadn't been present before - but he was there, solid and safe and real. "You came back."

"I'm sorry," he whispered. "I never meant to leave. I wasn't myself."

Wrenching grief squeezed Arcana's eyes shut again. "I -"

"No." Fenris' slender finger laid warm against her lips. "Do not dare apologise to me."

"I should say the same." She spoke around his finger, her hands tracing the breadth of a scarred chest pinched with starvation. "Caelum told me you were drugged. Chained. Beaten."

"And very nearly raped." Fenris moved his finger to her chin, tilting her head up so that his burning gaze locked with her own. The glamour whispered at her senses, so frighteningly weak that if not for her own reaching energy, Arcana doubted she'd have felt it at all. In the safe, warm silence between them he spoke, delivering a soft, blow by blow description of all that had befallen him since they tumbled into the portal. Arcana stroked his hair while she listened, teasing out tangles with her fingers until the gentle curls she loved so dearly began to show themselves once again. Her heart was aching by the end of the tale but when she drew a breath, Fenris shook his head. "Though it has been both difficult and cathartic to voice my trials, none of the details matter when it comes to what lies between us; I should never have fled from you. My only defence is that the meetha altered my thought patterns until I was no longer sure of reality. Even once I fled, I… it's like a terrible dream. I only vaguely recall wandering the desert, desperately hungry and thirsty, lost and alone and aching."

"You came back."

"Yes." A slow nod. "As soon as I came to my senses."

She considered his relaxed posture. "You must have eaten something, or you wouldn't be sitting here now."

"I ate - in a fashion." Fenris screwed up his face, the expression so at odds with his usually reserved demeanour that Arcana couldn't help but crack a smile. "Instinct appears to have taken over. I woke up elbow deep in a wild jinra."

"Literally?"

He hesitated, then sighed and gave another nod. "Literally."

"You think I'm bothered by that." She tilted her head. "If gorging on that jinra brought you back to me, I'm grateful you found it."

A great breath rushed out of him, and Fenris rested his head back against the wall. "I do not deserve you."

"Funny, I often feel the same about you." Rubbing a gritty hand over her face, Arcana winced at the scratches she found. "Where are we?"

Slowly, Fenris tilted his body, revealing the rest of the room. Arcana was cradled mostly in his lap, her head in the crook of one elbow and their legs stretched out in soft sand. The curved walls around her were smooth, dark wood, the ceiling tapering to an almost-point in the approximate centre. Light filtered in from a fold in the wall that appeared so fluid she was sure it was organic, sheltering them from the desert's intense heat whilst providing just enough light to comfortably see by. When she turned back to Fenris with a frown, he raised a single brow. "You really don't know."

"Know what?" She struggled to sit; he supported her back. "Are we prisoners? Did I sleep through a relocation?"

"No, and no." Capturing her fingers in his longer ones, Fenris spread her palm against the wall. "We're inside a tree."

"Inside a tree?" She dug her fingertips into the wood. "You're not making sense."

"While I was gone," Fenris elaborated, "You poured your magic into the earth. According to Caelum, you worked until you broke, then you worked again. Whilst my heart sunders at the thought that I pushed you to such lengths, the benefit is that you transformed this ridiculous excuse for a water soak into a true oasis."

Threads of memory tugged at her mind. "I made the pool of water bigger."

"It is now big enough to wade in," Fenris confirmed. "You also grew a tight ring of foliage around the banks, of which two trees are large and hollow enough to use as - well, as houses."

Another tug. "And food."

"Yes." He drew a large, sunset-coloured fruit from behind him and pressed it into her hands. "Some of the trees bear fruits which I have never seen, but the other males knew were safe to eat." Fenris' face softened and he rubbed his cheek against hers. "I wish you hadn't worked yourself into delusion, but I'm astonished at the result. How did you know what to grow?"

Arcana stared at the fruit in her hands, then up at Fenris. "I don't know. I don't remember deciding to grow anything." She frowned. "Maybe it's like the grumpy cactus."

"What?"

"There was a cactus... I infused it with my emotions when I was angry, and it attacked Caelum." Arcana shrugged. "If I channelled my magic here with sanctuary in mind, maybe... maybe the plants grew accordingly."

Fenris stared, slack-jawed, for a long moment, then shook his head. "I cannot even begin to fathom such a thing, but I suppose it doesn't really matter." His face tightened. "You created food, water, and safety; that's the important thing."

"I can see your mind working, you know." Arcana shifted in his lap so that they faced one another, and scowled. "Stop blaming yourself for running."

"I cannot." He cupped her jaw with one hand, silver gathering in the corners of his eyes. "I hurt you."

Silence fell, in which Arcana was wildly aware of the thump of her heart, the soft caress of the warm gloom, and the flickering fire in his eyes. It was a soft moment, the sort of thing she'd longed for in his absence, but rather than relax, she felt her temper stir. "You did hurt me, but it wasn't because you ran, Fenris. Okay, that's not entirely true - I did almost lose it, at first. I thought you'd rejected me."

Fenris flinched, but the expression on his face said he felt the words well deserved.

"But Caelum's smarter than he likes to let on," Arcana continued, catching his hand as it fell from her jaw. "He caught me with that sharp tongue of his, and made me see the truth. I hurt because *you* hurt. Your sorrow is mine; your pain and trauma are mine. You live inside me, deeper than anyone has ever gone before." She laid his hand against her heart. "I never wanted this - I was too afraid - but it happened nonetheless. What your absence broke, your return repaired."

Fenris shuddered, a single tear tracing the length of his hollowed cheek. When he spoke, his velvet voice was a rasp of emotion. "Time, then, for me to offer a truth of my own."

"Fenris-"

"Please; I should have told you this long ago." He stared, waiting, until she nodded. "The Weaver once told me that there was a warp and a weft for everyone in the weave."

"I remember you saying something like that to Flare."

"Indeed, I did." Fenris' eyes flickered, jade fire leaping. "What I did not realise, at the time, was that I had met mine."

Arcana gasped. "You think -"

"I *know*," he interrupted gently. "I have been irrevocably drawn to you since the moment we met. In your parent's front yard, on a frozen, foggy morning, I realised that no matter my duties to the Weaver, I could not easily walk away. When your brother warned me off, I knew his words made sense but I could not deny the compulsion to get under your skin - because you were already under mine. I suspected something more following Mirokke's death, when that altered place between layers of the weave whispered prophetic nothings in my ear, and I realised the truth when my parents witnessed the close call we had in their cave, though at the time I was not ready to admit it, not even to myself." Fenris exhaled slowly, his malnourished body trembling. "We are fated, you and I. Your blood and mine are meant to run together."

"Run together?"

"When the fey mate, it is done by biting and sealed in blood." His lips quirked in a rueful smile. "It seems, given my uncanny desire to bite you when I abhor it for all others, that I am more fey than I thought."

Reality tilted and Arcana clutched at his shoulders for balance. "I... but... on the ship, when you bit me..."

"I started, albeit unwittingly, the bonding process between us. Though I did not recognise the sensations until much later, by taking your blood I bound myself to you, lighting a fire deep in my gut which causes physical discomfort when we are far away from one another."

"Great Gods of Sorcen," Arcana breathed. "It *hurts* you to be apart from me? What about while I've been healing, and you were in the Pit?"

Fenris inclined his head ever so slowly, dark curls tumbling around his face. "Yes. I felt it, then, for the weeks of your absence, a dagger in my gut reminding me over and over of my own mistakes."

"No, Fenris." Arcana shook her head. "You can't beat yourself up over something you were unaware of, and that bite was consensual - so any blame should be equally shared." She glared up at him, refusing to feel guilt for something so intimate and precious that had occurred between them. "Is there a way we can fix the separation pain? It's bad enough dragging Caelum around on a psychic leash without thinking that rule now applies to you, too."

"It can be fixed," he acknowledged, "with a completion of the mating ritual."

Horror and agony swirled, her mind stretching to understand even as it denied the implication. "But... didn't we just say..."

"That there is too much magic in your blood? Yes." Heartbreak hitched in his tone. "For all we are two shattered pieces of a whole, to complete the ritual would risk smashing the block my mother put on my powers and kill us both."

Even as her soul danced at the knowledge that Fenris was hers in a way nobody else would ever be, part of Arcana cracked and wept. In halting words, she told him of her experience in the portal, the way her body had been altered and the many things she had learnt. She felt him flinch when she revealed that the Weaver had severed his blood bond, felt his fingers tighten in fury as she described all that had happened since she woke in Hiraptha.

When she was done, Arcana spread her hand over Fenris' heart, blinking through the tears in her eyes. "I'm sorry she broke your blood oath. I know what it meant to you."

"It was necessary." His voice was hoarse, agony in his eyes. "It also explains why I cannot feel anyone nearby, or why Taelon has not swept down from the heavens to slaughter us."

"It also negates our hope of rescue," Arcana murmured, wishing she had more comfort to offer. "As far as Caelum and I see it, our only hope of getting out of here is teaching him to jump."

"So it would seem." Fenris rubbed at his face, then at his heart, his long fingers twining with hers when she would have retracted her hand. "Do not grieve for me, Arcana. Though I am technically no longer the Overlord of my people, nor even, in truth, a Warden or a Guardian, the core of my soul has not changed. I am still timeless, and should I need, I have a host of other inane titles I could utilise."

"That's not the reason I'm sad," she said, swallowing around the lump in her throat. "It's that, with what she did... the changes she made..."

"The risk of my bite causing irreparable damage has increased." He nodded, his face drawn. "It is a risk we cannot take."

"And so, in demanding we stand for her and for the rest of the weave, the Weaver steals our ability to choose each other." Arcana squeezed her eyes shut, tried to bite back the words, but the aching, lonely part of her heart which had been walled off for so long spoke anyway. "I'm nobody's tool, and she's trying to make me one."

"I will never let that happen," Fenris growled, flashing fang in an uncharacteristic display of temper. "No matter where the weave takes us, whether our blood runs together or not, I am yours." Rage softened to tenderness and he lowered his head, feathering his lips across her own. "I am in love with you, Arcana. I will love you until the stars stop burning and the suns rend holes in the sky. I will love you until the oceans disappear, until the rocks crumble to dust and the last flame flickers into ash."

Wonder blossomed like a flower after drought and Arcana dropped her fruit to weave her hands into Fenris' hair, teasing the stiffened locks out with her fingers. "I don't have your way with words but you've owned my heart since the first time you made it skip a beat. When I burnt up inside the Weaver's portal, the only thing I could think was that I was an idiot for not having told you sooner. I love you so much it hurts."

Fenris dragged her close and kissed her, lips urgent and demanding. Arcana clung to his withered body, tangling her tongue with his even as she arched into his chest, unable to form a coherent thought beyond the warmth of the man who loved her.

"You're trembling."

"It's your fault." Swallowing hard, she caught his gaze with hers, knowing she might be asking the impossible. "I... I want you to love me."

He nipped at her mouth. "I just told you I do."

"No, I mean that I want you to make love *to* me." Arcana slid her hands over his chest, across the flat expanse of his stomach and down to his hips. His breath hitched and she froze. "I'm sorry. I should never -"

"No." Fenris caught her wrist, the movement so fast she barely saw it. His breathing came ragged as he lowered her hand to press it to his crotch, where something long and hard was coming to life. "Your touch could never hurt me. It's just that... well... I'm weakened, and I likely smell terrible. You've not eaten in days and as much as this tree is shelter, the floor is covered in sand. How can I take you like this, in such a place?" Frustration etched his features, and he pried the forgotten piece of fruit from between them and pressed it to Arcana's lips. "I should be forcing this down your throat, rather than my tongue."

The sudden urge to laugh bubbled up and Arcana let it, tugging free of his grip to take hold of the fruit and sink her teeth deep into the flesh. The flavour was sweet but not overly so, the juice carrying a tart edge that tingled against her tongue as she chewed and swallowed.

"One," she said, holding up a juice-stained finger. "We're both weak. I'm not asking for wild monkey acrobatics. I just want to be with you. Two," another finger, "You smell like sweat and earth and Fenris, and that suits me just fine. Three," she raised another finger and watched his eyes narrow ever so slightly, "If I eat this piece of fruit like a good sorceress and take care of the sand issue, will you perhaps reconsider?"

"You should be resting," he answered, but his voice trembled and the hard length against her thigh betrayed him. "Your magic -"

Arcana jammed her fruit into Fenris' mouth, cutting off his words. While his jade eyes blazed in indignation, she flattened her hands in the sand beside them and closed her eyes, reaching for the magic that lurked inside her. She *was* still weak, there was no escaping that fact; but for what she had planned, she didn't need much power. Spreading her senses into the oasis, she drew a tiny trickle of water towards her and then switched to nature magic, marvelling at the ease of the transition even as she visualised what she wanted. Fenris shifted in surprise beneath her and Arcana's lips quirked but she didn't open her eyes until she was done, looking down in satisfaction at a thick carpet of springy, mosslike undergrowth about the size of a bed, which now cushioned them from the sand underneath.

"Better?" She asked, rescuing the fruit - after smearing the juice all over his lips - and taking another large bite. Spreading one hand on Fenris' chest, she kissed him, savouring his heat and the tartness of the fruit juice. "I sure think so."

Fenris frowned down at her, but there was no disguising the blaze of amusement in his burning eyes. "Whatever will I do with you?"

"I can think of something." Arcana took another bite of fruit and then, as his eyes latched onto the motion with predatory focus, ate with relish until her impromptu meal was nothing more than a wrinkled pit. Tossing it over her shoulder, she reached for Fenris with sticky hands, laughing when he snared her wrists. "No?"

"Arcana," he tried, his voice a deep, insistent rumble that set heat pooling low in her belly. "I - we - you deserve better than this."

"Better than you? I don't think so." She shook her head. "I don't care about whatever it is that's making you worry, Fenris. I just know I love you, and I need you. Right now." Arcana blinked, reminding herself of the horrific ordeal he'd been through only days earlier. "If you want to."

"Weaver's grace, I want to." A rueful smile twisted his lips, his gaze dipping to where his erection pressed into her leg. "Surely you can tell."

"Well, then?"

Fenris searched her face, his expression softening in such a way that Arcana knew she'd won, even before he spoke. "Yes. For you, it will always be yes."

"Good." Arcana tugged at his grip and he let go, stomach rippling as she slid her hands around his waist and undid the tie on his singular item of clothing. "Never again," she whispered, throwing it aside. "You are free."

Fenris shivered, his lashes lowering to half-mast and his voice dropping an octave to echo in her very bones. "None of that matters so long as I'm with you."

"It matters." The long, thin scar that stretched from chest to hip beckoned and Arcana pressed her lips to the topmost corner. "I want to hear you say it."

His breath hitched. "I am free."

"Never again," she insisted, kissing her way down the sensitive flesh.

"Weaver's grace," he moaned, burying his hands in her hair. "Never again."

Arcana reached the steel of his abdomen, withered from hunger but no less perfect, and looked up from under her lashes. "You want me to stop, you say so."

Fenris shook his head, his eyes living flame. "I never want you to stop." His hands slid out of her hair to fumble with the lacings on her top.

"Given that I'm weak enough that biting you is as low a threat as it's ever likely to be, I do, however, want you naked."

"Thank all the gods for that." Hope and something far, far warmer curled low in her core as Arcana resumed her lazy exploration of the scar which fascinated her endlessly. "I'm not keeping these clothes - tear them off."

His hands flexed against her skin and the leather gave way. Fenris discarded the scraps to cup her breasts in reverent hands, a low growl rumbling in his chest. A heartbeat later Arcana was on her back on the soft moss, his mouth hot and hard and demanding on her own. She wound her arms around his neck as he lowered his weight, settling against her in a breathtaking combination of warm skin and erotic intent. When stars began to spark in Arcana's eyes, he tore his lips away to blaze a path down her neck and across her collarbone, slithering over her body to take one aching breast into his mouth.

Arcana groaned as his teeth scraped across her flesh, his tongue swirling across the sensitive nub of her nipple. She wound her fingers into his hair, unable to do more than hang on as Fenris tore her skirt away, swiftly followed by her underwear. One hand trailed down the back of her leg, nudging her knees apart to make space for his narrow hips. He nipped gently at the underside of her breast and drew back, raising up on one elbow until their gazes locked. "Are you certain?"

"Are you?"

"I have never been more certain of anything in my life." He grinned as the glamour rose around them, soft and shivering in a way Arcana had never felt before. She brushed against that fledgling energy with her own broken power, two mammoth creatures hobbled by circumstance, and felt Fenris' inhalation through every place their bodies touched.

With their essences wrapped around one another, she reached between them to caress his shaft, running her palm across the sensitive head and stroking the full length of him, revelling in the growl that vibrated through his chest. Once, twice, and then she couldn't wait any longer, wrapping her legs around his hips and shifting her body until he nudged her softest, most sensitive place.

"Now," she whispered. "Together."

Fenris laid his forehead against hers, chest heaving as he shifted his hips, stretching and inching his way inside her with infinite care. Arcana clutched at his shoulders as her body worked to accommodate his length, his girth - all at once too much and not enough, their bodies merging with a perfection that was overwhelming. After what seemed a golden eternity

Fenris was buried to the hilt and he paused, staring down as though to make sure she was real.

"I love you," Arcana whispered.

"As I love you." He lowered his head, lips soft against hers, hips moving in a slow, gentle rhythm.

Arcana rose to meet him, enchanted by the extraordinary feeling of his body inside her own. Fenris rumbled deep in his chest, his strokes long and deliberate, their lovemaking a gentle, tender thing that she treasured even as she needed more. Digging her fingers into his hips, she tugged - and he obliged her desperate hands by stroking swiftly in and out of her body, ever faster, ever deeper. The sensation curled and rolled around Arcana until she lost all conscious thought, buried in the fire they created, the exquisite pleasure that mounted and mounted.

She cried out and surrendered, exploding in a shower of ecstasy unlike anything she'd ever experienced. Fenris joined her a moment later, his body emptying into hers with such ferocity that all she could do was cling to him, her hips bucking uncontrollably and her nails digging into his back as wave after wave of pleasure cascaded over them both. He collapsed on top of her, muttering against the crook of her neck in the lilting language of the fey. Arcana didn't trust her voice so she kissed his temple instead, locking trembling arms around his waist when he tried to withdraw.

"I don't want to crush you," Fenris murmured, raising his head.

She stared into his eyes, watching the flames flicker and twist, savouring the feather and velvet slide of his glamour across her senses. "You're not heavy."

"I never thought starvation would have such a benefit." Fenris snorted a laugh, softening his words with a long, leisurely kiss which left her tingling all over. "Though, I will admit I still regret being too weak to love you properly. Are you all right?"

"Are you kidding me?" Her hands wandered lazily across his back, smoothing knotted muscles and revelling in the silken texture of his skin. "This is the most okay I've been in weeks." She dredged a cheeky grin, and offered his own words back to him. "Surely you can tell?"

Fenris' face softened. "I might have had an inkling."

"Then quit asking stupid questions." Arcana wriggled her hips and earnt herself a noise somewhere between a groan and a growl.

"You need to let me rest, or it will come off," Fenris admonished, unable to hide his smile. Captivated, Arcana shifted one hand to trace the outline of his lips. Not even pretending to misunderstand, he let the smile widen. "I missed yours, too."

"Good."

He slid gently out of her body and she groaned, feeling instantly incomplete. Fenris brushed his lips to hers, dropping to his side on the moss and gathering her close. "I'm sorry, but I have limited energy as it is. I cannot maintain that position much longer."

"Still think we should have rested?"

"And miss making love to you?" Astonishment twisted his features. "Not in this lifetime. My chivalry only goes so far, I'm afraid."

"At least now we know you can curb your urge to bite." She smiled as she curled into his chest, a yawn fighting for freedom. "How long can we stay here?"

"I'd like to say forever, but a more accurate response would probably be: however long you think Caelum will allow before he loses his patience."

Arcana spread her senses out, locating the deerken's warm, reassuring presence not far away. "I'm not ready."

"Neither am I." He sighed, his arms tightening - though not with the same strength he'd exhibited earlier. "It would be nice not to feel the biting edge of exhaustion all the time."

"When did you last eat?"

"Caelum brought me some fruit not long before you woke - I ate some, and saved the rest for you." Fenris yawned, displaying fangs all the more impressive for his gaunt figure. "It's not the diet my body needs, but it will do for now."

"You should hunt."

That swiftly, he turned to stone. "I won't leave you again."

"Fenris -"

"*No.*" Nightmares haunted his voice, his body trembling where it pressed against hers.

Broken all over again by the stark vulnerability in his eyes, Arcana wound her arm about his waist and pulled him close, blinking back tears as he burrowed against her as though she were his suit of armour. They lay like that for some time, her fingers tracing idle patterns on the skin of his back while he hid in the darkness created by their bodies, his face pressed into her neck and his soft breath warm on her chest. Eventually Fenris' tension drained and his breathing settled into the rhythm of sleep. Though Arcana knew there was much to be done, she tucked him closer and allowed her own lashes to drift downwards. The last conscious thought she had was one of sparkling wonder: he needed her. He loved her.

At last.

When she woke with a start, Fenris had drawn back just far enough that his burning gaze locked instantly with her own. The glamour was sluggish to respond, the whisper of a kiss across her mind. She took in his wan expression and frowned. "Are you all right?"

"I... yes." A long, slow exhalation. "It was but a dream."

A hard lump formed in her gut as she imagined what nightmares might stalk him, what he and the other men of Hiraptha had endured.

"We will do better," she promised him. "I will not keep slaves."

Fenris sighed. "You are a goddess, but even I cannot see how that transformation will be possible. I fear Gryde's hope is but mist beneath the sun - beautiful, but insubstantial."

"Gryde." Arcana's mouth tightened. "I should like to have a discussion with this so-called friend of yours."

"He is a product of his culture," Fenris said gently.

"He would've seen you raped!"

Her Guardian sighed, a shiver rolling over his wasted body. "As much as I hate to say this aloud, he thought he was helping me."

"Which is why," Arcana growled, "I won't keep these men as slaves. They're not beasts to be broken and trained - they're people." She pointed at the remains of her leather outfit. "People who get turned into *clothes* when they're no longer seen as useful."

Again, his face softened. "Wherever you go, I will be your blade. Whatever that means, wherever it takes us, I am yours."

"But you don't believe?"

"I wouldn't say that." Fenris took a deep breath, his expression thoughtful. "I have learnt never to underestimate you. Something that seems impossible becomes a malleable concept in your hands. So, like any good worshipper, I choose to have faith in my goddess."

"I'm not a goddess."

A sweet, warm kiss that held his heart. "You are *my* goddess."

Arcana studied the planes of his face, the way his ribs stuck out through skin stretched tight from malnutrition, the haunting jut of his hipbones. He'd suffered for her. He'd suffered for the Weaver, for the Timeless Kingdom, for his people, for a universe that likely had little idea he even drew breath, and he'd done it all without complaint. He was brave beyond measure, a warrior the likes of which she'd never before known, and he thought *she* was the goddess? The thought made her smile, her heart confetti inside her chest. "Well then, as your goddess, I have a gift for you."

"A gift?" Fenris blinked, the only outward sign of his surprise. "For me?"

"Yes." Rolling to the side, Arcana flattened one hand against the sandy floor. Magic trickled from her fingers, her lips moving as she whispered yet another spell the Elders had forced her to memorise and that she'd never expected to need. The sand began to bubble like water about to overboil the pot, ripples expanding outward until a section large enough for a person to lie on bucked and writhed. Tiny puffs of sand shot up in the air, driven by magic and pressure as Arcana manipulated the earth, summoning that which she'd hidden.

"The greatsword," Fenris whispered. Arcana fell back against his chest, her breath coming in gasps and a faint sheen of sweat coating her naked body. Above her, Fenris' eyes were glued to the leather scabbard and the hilt protruding from within. "How?"

"Caelum picked this pathetic excuse for an oasis because he knew the harpies left the greatsword behind," she panted. "We found it buried in the sand while you were still unconscious but it's too heavy for me to lift, so I hid it. I was going to give it to you when you woke, but..."

"I ran," he finished for her, his nod brief. "I understand. It's probably better I didn't have a weapon like that when I was out of my mind."

Arcana nodded. "Your leather pouch is there, too. My satchel never made it out of the portal, but there might be something in your bag you can wear."

"Perhaps," he agreed, his eyes flitting to the far wall, where his loincloth lay discarded among the ruins of Arcana's leather clothing. "I remember putting some emergency supplies inside, but the exact contents are lost in the fog of my mind. It is amazing what hunger and a raging allergy to aphrodisiac herbs can do to your cognitive function."

Though Fenris' tone was light, fury twisted Arcana's gut. "Never again."

"No." He stretched across her, filling her lungs with the scent of cinnamon and evergreens after dark. Long, elegant fingers, scarred from years of combat, closed around the greatsword's hilt as Fenris dragged the blade closer with a grunt of effort. Angling the greatsword just so, he drew it enough that she could see the alien characters carved down the flat of the blade. "This is an obscure elvish dialect long faded from use, but when I came into possession of the greatsword, the Weaver translated it for me. It says Iluk'hir, Heart's Blade."

"Iluk'hir?"

"The Elvish word for Starlight." Fenris ran his fingers over the characters and gave her the sort of intense look which had once struck her dumb with fear. "Starlight, Heart's Blade."

Arcana's breath caught as words he'd once spoken to her took flight on the winds of her memory. *Out here, in the night, you are made of shadows and starlight.*

"Fenris -"

"She knew," he murmured, sliding the blade back into its scabbard. "Such is the intricacy of the weave, the inexplicable paradox of all times, all realities, all layers. The Weaver put this blade in my hands knowing that, one day, it would be yours. That I would be yours."

"And you think that excuses the liberties she's taken?" Arcana shook her head. "The whole idea seems impossible."

"Our favourite word." Fenris' lips curved, turned serious again just as fast. "For the fey, mating is forever. The shining threads of the weave run through us, your warp to my weft, your light to my shadow. We cannot complete the ritual, but that doesn't change the fact that I love you more than my own breath." He shifted closer, the heat of his body leeching into hers, and drew both Arcana and the greatsword into the circle of his embrace. "Without the blood oath, I am no longer bound to the Weaver's service; should you command it, I would walk away from everything else and never once look back."

Tears blurred Arcana's vision. "Don't say that. No matter how angry I am, the Weaver needs us."

"I need you." Stark, unforgiving truth. Then, a twitch of a smile. "And my sword. I've really, *really* missed my sword."

Laughter bubbled in Arcana's chest and she let it out, filling the inside of their hideaway with the slightly hysterical sound of her mirth. "Given it's currently pressed against my back, I can't say I didn't notice."

"I am fortunate it's enchanted to be weightless in my hands, or I'd be spending weeks merely looking at it." He rained kisses over her face, licking up her tears and nipping at her jaw. "So? What would my goddess have of me?"

"This, right here, is what I've both feared and craved for some time now," she admitted, "but something tells me you were talking in a broader sense."

"I was." A hot breath on her neck, the scrape of teeth over her pulse. "I am not, however, foolish enough to complain when the woman of my dreams says such lovely things."

Melting into him, Arcana gave a fluttering sigh. "If you keep that up, I won't be able to think."

"Tempting, isn't it?" After a final nip, Fenris raised his head. "Go on."

"First off, we need clothes. I'm not putting that leather back on, even if it means wearing leaves off the trees," Arcana declared. "Then, we need to go outside and meet the men who are now our responsibility. I don't even know their names, much less their skills and temperaments."

"They may not open up to you immediately."

"I can't even speak the language, so I'm not expecting them to. I'm trusting you and Caelum to help me out, being as you're both male and therefore likely to seem safer." Arcana chewed the inside of her cheek. "The Empress said she would return in five days. By my reckoning, it's been three, perhaps four. I want us to present a united front when she returns, and to have this oasis appear more like a haven than somewhere we scrambled to in an effort not to die."

"You wish to integrate into the society?"

"No, I want us in a position of strength - but for now, that means playing along." She crooked a brow. "Neither of us are well enough to be razing cities and destroying empires right now."

"No," he conceded, and there was no hiding the disappointment in his face. "You are right."

Rage burnt in her gut and she twisted both hands in Fenris' hair. "I won't let them hurt you again."

"I believe you."

She wished she had the words to bring back the man whose silver tongue charmed governments and whose blade freed innocents, but Arcana knew in her deepest heart it would take time. Until then, if he needed her to be his strength, she would. Loosening her hold, she flicked a look at the leather pouch that hung from the greatsword's scabbard. "First up; clothes."

"Clothes." Fenris fought his way to a kneeling position and drew the pouch into his lap, brow furrowing as he tugged it open and began to rummage inside. "I'm still getting the hang of this unusual magic."

"It helps if you visualise what you're digging for."

Jade eyes narrowed in concentration, and a moment later Fenris made a triumphant sound and dragged out a pair of loose black training pants. "I thought I had these in here."

"Underwear?"

"I don't wear it." He waved the question off with an absent hand, oblivious to Arcana's dropped jaw as he shoved upright to tug the pants on. They hung dangerously low on his hips, but a swift tug on the draw-string prevented them from falling off completely. Fenris caught her sigh of disappointment and flashed a grin. "I'm half starved; it's not that impressive."

She shook her head, levering up to trace the lines that ran from his skeletal hips into his pants. "You're breathtaking no matter what - and these do strange things to my insides."

Fenris watched the progress of her finger, his cheeks darkening with a blush. "Having you touch me does strange things to *my* insides." His pants twitched, and the blush deepened. "And my outsides."

"Burke calls these paradise lines, you know." Arcana curled her fingers over the curve of his hip and leant in to press a hot, wet kiss to his exposed skin. "I never really understood why until now."

"Arcana," he sounded pained. "This is the first time I've worn real clothing in weeks and not thirty seconds in, you're making me wish to undress."

She chuckled and moved back. "Sorry."

"I suppose I can forgive you." Fenris crouched so they were eye level, his grin wicked. "In fact, if I weren't worried we might die from exertion, I'd already be naked and inside of you all over again."

Now it was Arcana's turn to blush. "Stop it."

"I shall do no such thing - if I have to suffer sexual frustration due to malnutrition, you shall join me." He dropped a kiss on the top of her head and returned to rummaging in the satchel. "Here. I'm afraid this is the best I can do."

Arcana stared down at the offering in his hand. Soft scarlet cotton, the edges trimmed in gold. "Our scarf."

"I know I promised to give it back to you on Corrin's Run, but I forgot." Fenris shrugged. "It's not clothing, but -"

"No, it'll work." Arcana accepted the scarf and shook it out, staring down at the long red rectangle. "These are meant to be worn more like shawls, folded and shaped to suit, so they're huge. Could you tear it? About two thirds down?"

"Here?" Without waiting for her answer, Fenris gripped the fabric firmly and flexed. It tore with a silken sound and he looked over the two pieces with a questioning glance. "What of underwear?"

Arcana curled her lip. "I guess I have to go without. Even if you hadn't torn the old ones, they're made of people skin."

"Hmmm." Brow furrowing, he again dove into his pouch. "What about this?"

"Oh." Arcana accepted a wide, soft linen bandage from him, chewed her lower lip between her teeth. "Maybe. Help me?"

Working together, they managed to wrap the bandage in such a way that by the time Fenris knotted and tucked in the ends, it was a close enough approximation to underwear that Arcana breathed a sigh of relief. Taking up the larger length of torn scarf, she folded it in half diagonally, wrapped the fabric around her waist and tied a knot at one hip. The makeshift skirt covered her modesty well enough, with the long side falling to her knees and the shorter side ending at the top of her thigh.

"Clever." Fenris nodded appreciatively. "I like it."

"I've done that before; it's the rest I'm not sure about." Arcana frowned, taking the remaining length of cloth and bunching it in her fists. She found the halfway point and set it between her shoulder blades, then bought the two ends around the front of her chest, crossing them over her breasts. Fenris moved behind her and accepted the long ends, twisting them together into a cord behind her head and then tying them onto the back piece.

"How is it?" He asked, his hands warm on her shoulders as he nudged her around to face him.

"I feel quite exposed," Arcana admitted, plucking nervously at the fabric over her breasts, "But it's better than wearing people."

"I assure you everything is covered." Fenris winked as he inspected her makeshift outfit. "I'm going to put this in my top five favourite things I've ever seen you wear."

Arcana snorted. "If this is in the top five, I'd hate to know what number one is."

"Nothing."

"What?"

"Number one is nothing. Naked," he clarified, stepping in to shape her waist with his hands. "That is my favourite thing to see you wear."

She went into his arms, feeling all the more human for wearing clothing that was her own choice, and laid her head over his thundering heart. "Are you going to be this saucy for eternity?"

"Weaver's grace, I hope so. Your blush is magnificent."

Arcana chuckled and prodded Fenris in the stomach. "Don't forget I can twist you into a pretzel whenever I feel like it."

"Oh, I've dreamt about it," he muttered, his breath tickling the shell of her ear. "One day, I want you back in the training arena of the *Wandering Sorceress*, and when I catch you this time, no amount of cold water will keep you safe."

Arcana succumbed to his need, tipping her head back for a desperate clash of lips, tongues and teeth. When he broke away, they both laboured for breath. "Stupid impending death."

"Indeed." Looking both amused and superbly male, Fenris released her to swing the greatsword's harness over his head. Once the blade was settled into its customary position across his back, he sighed with relief. "I never thought to be so comforted by such a normal thing."

Arcana twined her fingers through his. "Never again."

"Never again," He agreed, tucking her against his side. "Now, shall we face reality together? Something tells me Caelum is waiting."

TWENTY-ONE
FLARE

The double doors of Galactic Station's library slid open with the barest hiss of well-oiled gears. Book stacks spread in every direction, traditional tomes mingling with plas-files, holo consoles and their data crystals, and even the odd shelf full of crumbling scrolls. While Flare's research told him there was a staff of librarians, all he saw as Zaire led him through the night-dim rows was the occasional cleaning bot.

The Ryllin had said little during the remainder of their dinner with Verdure, and even less once they'd returned to the silence of the halls. Now, he stalked ahead of Flare with what would've been deadly grace, but for the odd jerkiness in his stride that had been present all afternoon. Flare studied the other male's figure as they walked, intrigued by the truth of Zaire's cyborg body. Or was it? A cyborg begged the idea of a man mechanically enhanced, but the male limping along in front of him, with his narrow hips, muscular frame and sour countenance didn't have mechanical parts - he had biomechanical parts, and Flare had never understood the difference until now. If Zaire was cut, he bled. His thoughts were his own, his body felt - and yet, upon a whim, the silver-scrolled rogue could melt flesh and bone and integrate with the very machines he didn't seem to be a part of.

Silver-scrolled rogue. Flare shook his head, covering the motion by trailing his fingers along the edge of a nearby shelf as they walked. He'd spent his last few days on Sorcen absorbing as much information as he could about the races who made up the Galactic Alliance - and Rylle had no higher calibre of warrior, no greater honour to bestow, than that of a silver-scrolled rogue. Added to the pressure of being the son of nobility and living proof of a technology which was so cutting edge it defied definition, it was no wonder Zaire was so sour all the time.

As though in accord with his thoughts, Zaire's shoulders hunched in on themselves and he came to a sudden stop. If Flare hadn't been unconsciously staring at the other man's leather-armoured shoulders, he'd have cannoned straight into him. As it was, he stepped close and flattened a palm over the rogue's lower back, a silent signal he was there and aware. He felt nothing through the leather, no shifting of muscle nor hint of body heat, but Zaire stiffened as though he'd been zapped. Expecting a scathing look at the very least, Flare was surprised when the Ryllin held up a long-fingered hand and flashed out several crisp, clear signals.

The language of the rogues was a little different from that which Flare used with his own men on Sorcen, but it didn't take long to decipher the message; there was someone up ahead. Leaning more heavily into his companion's weight, Flare poked his head beneath Zaire's raised arm and chanced a glance around the corner. The rogue was now solid as a block of concrete, rejection coming off his body in waves, but Flare ignored him to focus instead on the first sign of life they'd seen since entering. A librarian, he presumed, wearing long, loose pants and an ankle length jacket whose sleeves trailed along the floor behind him in an impractical fashion. In his hand, he had a datapad and a stylus, his body bent almost double as he scanned the shelves and then paused to make the occasional note.

Flare scanned the surrounds and saw that they'd almost reached the library's back wall, which was broken up regularly by dimly lit doors. The signs overhead declared them to be communal meeting or research rooms and he knew in an instant that this private section of a public space was where Zaire was leading him. If they walked through now, however, the librarian would instantly spot them, and potentially ask questions they didn't want to answer.

Leaning more heavily against Zaire and trusting the reluctant rogue to take his weight, Flare wriggled both arms forward and began tracing runes in the air, mouthing a spell with little more than an exhalation. A tiny flicker of light popped into being by the librarian's face. The man, his patrician features now revealed in the sudden glow, straightened in surprise. The light extinguished immediately and another appeared, a few steps away. A throaty exclamation of surprise escaped the librarian's lips as this light, too, blinked out, only for another to appear at the far edge of the stack. Movements cautious, the man tucked his datapad into a pouch at his belt and took a step towards the glow. It dipped as though shy and winked out - only to return just around the corner. Following the will 'o wisp, the librarian ducked around the shelf and out of sight.

Zaire needed no further invitation; he twisted a hand into the collar of Flare's robe and dragged him out into the aisle. With no other option if he wanted to keep his feet, Flare clutched at the rogue's waist for balance, his eyes trained on the spell as he continued to carefully lure the librarian in the opposite direction. He was barely aware of reaching one of those many doors, or of it swishing open, until Zaire yanked him through into the pitch-black room beyond. It was only when the door clicked shut, cutting his line of sight to the library beyond, that he released his magic and slumped.

On cue, the grip on the back of his robe was released and he flopped to the floor in a flurry of black velvet - a position that would have looked ridiculous except that the room was darker than the inside of his mind. Rearranging his clothes so they were no longer tangled in his arms or over his face, Flare snapped his fingers and a flame burst to life above his palm.

The room was a box of a thing, lined with shelves so heavily stacked with books and plas-files it was a wonder they remained upright. A single desk dominated the tiny available space, with a holo console in the centre and a lone chair on the opposite side. Zaire sat in the chair, eyes closed and head tipped back as though searching for absolution.

"You okay?" Flare kept his voice low but it still seemed to vibrate through the space and Zaire jumped, lashes flying up.

"Oracle's whispers," the rogue muttered, his glaring eyes so dark as to be almost black. "Do you always sound like that?"

Flare blinked. "Like what?"

"Forget it." Zaire passed a hand over his face and even in the flickering orange glow of the flame, Flare could see it was pale.

"Are you sure you're up to this?" He pushed to his feet, daring a few steps closer to the desk.

Zaire's face set like granite. "No choice. I've taken enough time off as it is - the longer we wait, the less chance of finding those ships."

"What's the matter?" Flare raised a brow when the rogue's jaw tensed. "Don't even bother trying to lie to me, little Ryllin."

A snarl, but that icy expression fractured ever so slightly. "Leg's not working properly. Synchronisation issue."

"How often does that happen?" Flare thought back to the ambush in the hallways, where Zaire's entire body had locked up but Eyrton had later pronounced it as an elbow issue. Something clicked in his mind. "It shorts you out."

"Only the new parts; the parts that aren't mine." His jaw set. "The problem starts small and builds until eventually I can't control anything I wasn't born with - and sometimes, not even that."

Flare thought back to the graphic pictures he'd seen earlier in the day. "Doesn't leave you with much."

Indigo eyes narrowed. "No."

"Why does it happen?"

"Nobody knows." Zaire barked a sub-vocal laugh, the sound whispering over Flare's skin and leaving a trail of goosebumps behind. "The joys of being an experiment."

"Hmm." Flattening one hand on the desk, Flare smoothed his opposite palm over the rogue's forehead. Zaire tried to flinch away, but his reclined position in the unforgiving chair prevented it. "No fever, but you're colder than usual."

"Don't. Touch. Me."

"Why not?" He retracted his hand, but it was a bare inch. "We're in this together. I can't have you locking up on me when there's work to do, and I'm trained in basic first aid. All soldiers are."

He wasn't sure which of his words got through - though if he had to guess, it'd be the soldier line - but Zaire's clenched jaw relaxed, and he nodded. Flare returned his palm to the other's forehead and then, a moment later, shifted it to his throat, feeling for his pulse with two fingers. It was sluggish, proof in point that something wasn't right, and the skin stretched over it was colder still.

"Well?" Zaire hissed, the muscles of his neck shifting beneath Flare's touch.

"I'm guessing, but you feel like you've been dabbling in too much ice magic." He chewed his lip a moment. "When the body gets too cold, it can't function. It seizes."

The flicker of an eyelash was all the reaction he got. "I'm not cold."

"You are." Making the sort of snap decision which had shot him through the army's ranks in record time, Flare began tugging at the buckles holding Zaire's leather armour in place. When the rogue made a paltry attempt to slap his hands away, his movements clumsy and weak, Flare bared his teeth. "Stop it. Let me work."

"Clothes on," Zaire panted, still trying to fight.

Flare slipped the last buckle free and, muscles bunching, yanked the armour off with brute force, catching Zaire as his body slid involuntarily sideways. "Forget your modesty, you idiot. There's little I haven't seen in my life, but I don't need you naked."

The rogue tried to answer but his jaw had already locked shut, his body shuddering with tension. Perching on the edge of the desk, Flare spread both hands over Zaire's chest, feeling the chill of his skin even through the navy thermal - a garment he now suspected had more than one purpose - and began to chant under his breath. For the second time in minutes his rumbling voice filled the room, an intimacy created by the looming shelves, the pressing shadows and the tiny, flickering flame that cast shadows over both their faces. The spell grew beneath his palms, runes spreading like wildfire over the navy fabric and sinking almost immediately to the flesh beneath.

Zaire bucked the moment the spell hit his skin and Flare pushed more of his weight into his palms, caging the rogue's legs between his own. "Dammit, Z, trust me."

Something wild flashed in those indigo eyes but the Ryllin settled, making no further protest as heat spread through his body; an amplified version of the same spell Flare had sunk into Pytch's sheets only a couple hours previous. Magic poured out in a steady stream and Flare kept one eye on his internal tank whilst simultaneously monitoring Zaire's temperature and their surroundings, every inch of his extensive training and experience enabling him to play medic and guard at the same time. After some minutes, the rogue's breathing became markedly easier, and his locked muscles began to relax. Flare continued pumping him full of heat, even when those slender hands circled his wrists and gave a warning tug.

"I'm fine."

"A little more," Flare insisted, curling his fingers slightly so that the tips dug into Zaire's pectorals. "I want to make sure."

"You're melting me."

He snorted, deliberately derisive. "I've been trying all week, and it hasn't worked yet. Don't disappoint me by surrendering now."

Zaire's eyes narrowed and he sat up with a fluid motion unlike anything Flare had yet seen from him. "You use sex as a defence mechanism everywhere you go, don't you?"

"What?"

"How many people see the real you?" Zaire continued, blue-black hair shimmering as he tilted his head to one side. "Are *any* of your responses real?"

Flare stepped back, waving his hands to extend the warming spell into the air, bringing the room's temperature to just this side of uncomfortably warm with a solid shove of power. His magic tank depleted a good quarter, and just as quickly began filling back up again. By the time he shot a warning glance over his shoulder, it was full. "You sound like Lesce. Not a compliment, in case you're wondering."

"I'm not interested in your affection," Zaire returned, rubbing a fist over his heart, "Not when I don't know if it's real."

"I have feelings," Flare defended, even as he wondered why he did it. "And contrary to the entire fucking universe's opinion, I've been celibate for months."

Zaire raised an eyebrow. "You really mean that."

"Of course I do!" He kicked the desk, suddenly and unaccountably furious. "It's all well and good to question my motives via what you know of my public file - the reality is very different."

Zaire's face didn't change. "Also truth. Huh."

Flare forced himself to take a step back, digging his hands into his hair and closing his eyes in order to concentrate on his breathing. One in, one out. One in, one out. When he dared another look, Zaire hadn't so much as blinked. Needing some sort of outlet - anything - Flare spat a word of power and several more flamelets blinked to life, turning the room from haunting to candlelit. The steady drain on his power wasn't enough to overcome the regeneration, meaning he could set a seal on the spell and let it cycle in his subconscious without fear of accidental burnout. That done, he turned back to Zaire and said, as calmly as he could, "You're a walking lie detector now?"

"Like everything else, it doesn't always work." As though broken from his own spell, the Ryllin spun the chair to face the desk and activated the holo console. "You were right about the heat. Thanks."

"Welcome." Not entirely sure what had just happened and even less interested in examining it, Flare stalked to his side and propped himself against the desk. "What now?"

"I disabled the monitoring systems when we came through the door," Zaire said, laying one hand over the console. As he spoke, his flesh began to melt, revealing silver bones that were already reshaping into wires. "Now, we hack Krowley and see what he's hiding."

"You're sure he's hiding something?" Flare asked, watching those long wires slide through cracks in the console and pull tight.

Zaire's gaze unfocussed, cobalt lights beginning to flicker in the depths of his indigo eyes. "I found redactions in the mission files we were given, sealed on his authority, but he denied it when asked face to face."

"Good. As long as we're not taking unnecessary risks." Flare decided to ignore Zaire's uncomplimentary snort and instead crossed his arms over his chest. "What exactly do you need from me?"

"I told you already - watch my back. I need to go deep into the system and I won't be aware of my surroundings." The rogue's tone was already distant, with a distinctly metallic edge to it. "If something happens and you need to pull me out, slap me as hard as you can."

Flare opened his mouth to answer, but his companion's eyes blazed with cobalt light, pupils shrinking until they were almost invisible. Zaire went still one muscle at a time, a fascinating wave of motionlessness that swept from his wrist up and over the rest of his body. Flare clicked his jaw shut, not needing any further confirmation - the Ryllin had gone where he couldn't follow.

He paced the confines of the small room, taking a few moments to peer through the closed drapes and into the rest of the library. The stacks were silent, the librarian nowhere to be seen and the vast depths of the room swallowed in the shadows the night-glow lighting nurtured. Flare let the curtain fall back into place and moved instead to the shelves, tugging out a book at random and carrying it to the desk.

Zaire took up half the space and the only chair, so Flare stood at the desk's narrow end, using the available surface to flip the book open while simultaneously keeping both his charge and the locked door in his peripheral vision. "Knitting patterns? Not my style."

After several more trips to and from the shelves, he came across a book that described the artistic pursuit of etching designs into wood with a burning tool. Fascinated, Flare kept digging until he'd unearthed several more tomes on the subject and then set about educating himself, mentally altering the instructions for the burning tool to suit a fire sorcerer with an enthusiastic index finger. Artisans weren't uncommon on Sorcen, with all schools of magic producing several - and Flare had seen many impeccable examples of work in Sorca City's colourful markets that he now realised had likely been done with the magical equivalent of this very technique. Having been enlisted into the military the same day he'd imprinted in a fiery blaze of glory, he'd never had the chance to explore much in the way of a creative pursuit.

Reading, however, was something he enjoyed, and study even more so. There was no requirement for him to know every single fire spell that ever existed off by heart - particularly the ones written in ancient Sorcen, the complex language of twisting runes and swirling characters that had become obsolete when his people had switched to the simpler, more efficient Universal Galactic. Once Arcana had bonded with Caelum, her magic mutating exponentially, he'd spent hours in her underground cell, chatting and poring over old scrolls or flipping ancient spellbooks until Flare knew not only every fire spell there was, but a good deal of other schools' incantations as well. The intention had been to spend time with his sister, to keep her personality afloat while she struggled to come to terms with the changes to her body and her power, but Flare had learnt ways to twist his own power, spells from other schools that could be altered to suit a fire sorcerer with an active imagination. His magic level didn't change in those months, but his power grew enormously - a distinction the Council of Elders had been far too foolish to comprehend.

Since then, he'd made it his purpose never to shy away from learning something new. So it was that with nothing but the flickering light of his own flames to keep him company, Flare began to apply the concepts in the book to the steel surface of the desk in front of him. Once he'd worked out the level of power needed to etch the metal with a black line rather than melt it, his finger swept across the shiny surface with ease, replicating the designs in the book before branching out into his own swirling patterns. He was no artist - not like Arcana, with her journal full of thoughts and sketches that looked ready to leap from the page - but he was no creative slouch, either, years of drawing runes and casting spells lending him an instinctive eye for line and curve that produced pleasing results.

He was almost out of available space when Zaire began to stir, the fingers of his free hand curling on the surface of the desk. The rogue groaned, shaking his head as if to clear it as a shudder wracked his body. Flare moved to his side and, after pressing a hand against skin gone ice cold all over again, began to mutter a fresh round of warming spells. The angle of Zaire's body made it difficult to reach his chest so Flare clamped down on one shoulder instead, pouring heat into the Ryllin as quickly as he dared.

Sweat began to bead on Zaire's brow before he managed to turn his head and look up, the cobalt glitter in his eyes fading back to indigo as the wiring hanging out of his wrist retracted and formed back into a hand. "Still melting me."

"Good." A smile curled Flare's lips, broad and genuine enough to surprise them both. Blinking through the shock of his body acting without his permission, Flare said, "Welcome back, handsome."

"Fuck off." Zaire's frown cut the odd moment, exactly as Flare knew it would. The rogue jerked out from under his hand, made to stand, and froze. "What in the Oracle's name have you been doing?"

"Art."

"You do art?" Zaire shook his head. "Of course you do art. Forget I said anything."

Raising a brow but not bothering to push further, Flare laid a hand against his companion's brow. "You've thawed a little. How did you go?"

"You never ask if I've secured the room before you flop out leading questions," Zaire muttered, slapping his hand away.

"Because I know you're not stupid," Flare responded. "Grumpy, but not stupid."

Zaire snarled wordlessly at him, then closed his eyes and drew a deep breath. "Coming back to my body is an unsettling process - I feel more like a machine after I've interfaced my consciousness with a system. It gives me the shits."

"Hah!" Flare braced his hip against the side of the desk. "So?"

"I got the files. There were multiple levels of encryption, so I didn't have a chance to read anything; just copied them for later. The DNA locks were only the outer layer of Krowley's protections." Zaire's frown was sharp. "Lucky you got both his blood and his sweat on that rag you called a robe."

Flare offered a lopsided grin. "You're welcome. You never did explain how the sample worked, by the way."

"No, I didn't." Indigo and carnelian clashed, then Zaire grunted and shrugged. "I was able to analyse the genetic code and synthesise the readings when I was inside the system just now. If anyone picks up the hack, it'll appear it was done from the outside."

"Clever." Flare filed away the new information about his companion's capabilities, then turned to begin clearing the open books he'd scattered on the desk. "I'll just stick these back in the shelf and -"

Zaire's grip on his arm, hard enough to bruise. "Someone's coming."

"Oh?" Flare spread out his senses, muttering a word of power under his breath. "I count three heat signatures heading toward us."

There was no mistaking the purposeful path of the newcomers and whatever senses Zaire was using to track them were obviously good enough that he knew it, too, because he simply nodded. There wasn't time to leave, voices filtering in through the thin door even as Flare's mind raced.

"- was the strangest light, and now it's coming from under the door." A high pitched, almost nasal voice that Flare was willing to bet his favourite shoes belonged to the librarian.

"Stand aside." A velvety female purr. "Weapons ready."

Zaire had a dagger in his hand that fast, but Flare shook his head. If they fought, it'd be immediately suspicious. He cast his eyes over the dimly lit room, the discarded leather armour and strewn books, the way heat curled through the air - and knew what he had to do.

There was a click on the other side of the door, a steady beeping that announced a manual override of whatever locking sequence Zaire had used. Spinning on his heel, Flare snatched the rogue's dagger away and thunked it point down into one of the books. Before his companion could protest, he fisted both hands in Zaire's blue thermal and shoved him back into the shelves. Wood splintered and books rained down, glancing off the taller male's shoulders to thud unceremoniously on the floor at their feet.

Shouts echoed outside the door as Zaire gripped the shelf behind him for balance. "What -"

Maintaining his grip on the Ryllin's shirt with one hand, Flare yanked free the leather tie securing Zaire's hair and curled his fist in the blue-sheened mass, muscles bunching as he yanked the other male's head down. It was too fast, too hard, but his body knew how to mould, how to soften, how to lure - and Zaire was already responding, even in his shock.

Flare sealed his lips over Zaire's just as the door swished open, liquid soft hair brushing his face and the scent of impending rain filling his lungs. Someone gasped; someone laughed. Someone coughed and stuttered an apology. The door swished shut.

None of it mattered.

Fire whispered through Flare's veins, a crackling roar of sensual heat that made the details of their successful escape irrelevant. For the first time in months, his body woke - and it wanted Zaire with a fury that was frightening.

Flare pulled away from the kiss that wasn't, desperately seeking composure, and froze when arms like steel bands slammed their bodies back together. He looked up into indigo eyes gone wide and where before he'd seen scorn and bitterness, he was astounded to see a flickering, erotic heat. When Zaire spoke, his voice was a rasp. "Again."

Swallowing heavily, his heart a racehorse in his chest, Flare tilted his head up in silent invitation. Zaire bent to meet him, their lips pressing together in a questioning manner. Cool silk, burning velvet, they brushed once, twice - and then Zaire groaned and slammed his mouth down hard, the kiss raw and demanding. Flare's blood roared in his veins as tongues tangled and hands tore at clothing; he barely had half a thought to spare to set a warding spell on the door. Not as effective as Zaire's methods, but anyone who touched it would find themselves with a serious burn.

"I hate you," Zaire growled, yanking Flare's outer robe off and throwing it aside. "Oracle's voice but I hate you."

Flare's laugh was low and edged as he tugged the rogue's blue thermal over his head and spread his hands across Zaire's chest, drinking in the smooth expanse of pale skin tinted with glacier blue. "You going to show me how much?"

"Shut up." Another hard kiss and Flare's underrobe was gone, followed quickly by both their boots and finally Zaire's pants, their mouths battling for supremacy the entire time.

Gasping, Flare wrenched back. Indigo and carnelian clashed, fire and ice in their gazes. "Make me."

When Zaire tackled him to the floor with a growl, he didn't even bother pretending to fight.

TWENTY-TWO
ARCANA

ARCANA'S JAW DROPPED AS SHE STARED AT THE VIBRANT GREEN OASIS SPREAD out before her. What once had been a dirty puddle was now a pool at least ten paces wide, shimmering with crystal water that held the faintest tint of blue. A softly sanded beach gave way to a ring of trees with squat, bulbous trunks and a cluster of fronded foliage on top, each one boasting a network of gnarled roots that faded into thick greenery beyond. Arcana's senses told her the jungle only extended another ten paces in each direction - but what had sprouted looked as though it had been there for generations.

"Incredible." She turned to look up at Fenris, his fingers trembling as they linked tightly with hers. "This isn't... I never expected... how is this possible?"

He shook his head, face enraptured as he drank the oasis in. "Magic."

"You've not had the tour?"

"I have not left your side since I returned."

Something tightened in her chest and she squeezed his fingers until those burning jade eyes turned her way. "Never again."

He nodded, but any response he might have made disappeared as Caelum stepped out of the trees, his antlers a glorious display of thick green foliage and fruit the colour of sunset. The slaves followed behind like a cluster of ducklings, some of them with their hands resting against his fur and the rest sticking close, bodies gaunt and faces nervous as they carried armloads of the same sunset-coloured fruit to the edge of the oasis and carefully set them on the ground.

"Arcana!" Caelum bounded over the pool with the enthusiasm of a fawn, leaving Arcana no option but to throw her arms around his neck lest he tackle her to the ground. "You're here."

Burying her face in his fur, she filled her lungs with the scent of burnt sugar. "I'm sorry."

"Don't be sorry." Laughter echoed in his voice, and she pulled back to see him winking broadly at Fenris. "You were busy."

Colour flagged the Guardian's cheeks, his hands clenching and unclenching by his sides. "Er…"

"Relax." The deerken reached out to nuzzle Fenris with his soft nose. "It's about bloody time - and I promise I didn't peep."

Reassured by his wit, Arcana went on tiptoe to kiss Caelum's jaw. "You might have learnt something."

"Nooooooo." Caelum pranced backward and shook his head, causing fruit and foliage to quiver dangerously. "I got enough of an education from Burke and Phase. I'm a virgin, remember? No traumatising the innocents."

Fenris gave a loud snort, then looked surprised to have made such a sound. Arcana grinned, slipping an arm around his alarmingly thin waist. "You can say it. Go on."

The answer was slow, as though her Guardian had forgotten what it meant to joke. "I doubt Caelum was ever innocent."

"You wound me." The deerken fluttered long, curling lashes. "Now, why don't you come and meet the kids?"

Maintaining her position against Fenris' side, Arcana followed Caelum around the edge of the oasis pool to where her group of harpies huddled miserably together, eyes wide and skin caked with grime. "You could've bathed them."

"They won't," Fenris answered quietly. "Not without your permission. Water is for the women."

Arcana's jaw dropped in astonishment and her temper rose when Caelum only nodded. "That's what they said."

"If I may?" Fenris glanced down at Arcana for confirmation, then spoke softly to the slaves. The language of Hiraptha flowed smoothly from his tongue, the clicks and twitters tinted with his distinct velvet rumble. After a long silence, one of the men with heavy whipping scars spoke, his hoarse voice a testament to the damage his body bore.

"They want to know if you're going to kill them," Caelum said, "because they haven't done any chores."

"If I -" Arcana cut off, forcing her expression to remain calm. "Of course not."

Fenris was speaking quicker now, his voice taking on the persuasive tone she'd seen him use to charm the Council of Elders. He gestured at his throat, abraded but otherwise free of a collar, then at theirs. They flinched and gasped as a single unit, and the man who'd spoken earlier spread his arms defensively in front of his brethren.

"They need your reassurance," Fenris murmured. "They don't believe you want to free them."

"Will you translate for me?"

"Yes."

Arcana took a deep breath and lifted her chin. "I don't keep slaves. I won't force you to stay here, but if you do, I swear I will protect you to the best of my ability."

Fenris repeated her words, paused, then linked his fingers through hers and drew them to his lips. He kissed her knuckles to another chorus of gasps. "They're not convinced."

"I can see that." She flicked a glance up at him. "You have the greater influence here; show them you're my equal by doing something they're not allowed to do."

The Guardian hesitated, his expression thoughtful. "Men are not allowed to bear arms, on pain of death. Do you trust me?"

"Of course."

Fenris released her hand to draw the greatsword in a fluid motion that had to burn his withered muscles, but he didn't so much as flicker an eyelash. The blade swished around Arcana's head in a flurry of shining silver, before it thunked back into the scabbard without clipping a single hair on her head. Fenris' chest laboured, the pulse in his neck kicking hard, but he kept his chin up and spine straight, spitting a few hard words that earnt another chorus of gasps. Arcana wished she knew what he was saying - particularly because Caelum looked amused. Again, the harpy with the scars replied, a distinct request in both his face and voice.

"Did it work?" Arcana asked.

"Partially. They're now asking for a demonstration of the other main thing males are not allowed to do."

"Dare I ask?"

Fenris' lip twitched and his bony arms shot out, almost too fast to see, to drag Arcana into his embrace. One hand splayed possessively across her backside, the other buried in her hair and tilted her head back - and then his lips were on hers, crushing and raw. Arcana relaxed into the hold, her hands fluttering up to settle against his chest as she sighed into his mouth.

After a long, drugging minute he broke the kiss on a growl, both of them struggling for air. Cupping her face, Fenris spoke slowly and clearly in Hirapthan, his expression tender and his words drawing noises of disbelief from the assembled slaves. Arcana turned the bold declaration over in her mind and, her tongue stumbling over the odd sounds, carefully repeated it back to him.

One of the slaves fainted.

"I hope I just said what I think I said," she murmured.

Fenris hummed softly, jade eyes intense as he watched the slaves gently slap their brother awake. When the harpy was blinking around him in bleary astonishment, the Guardian turned back to her. "I love you."

"Is that what we said, or what you're saying now?'

"Both."

Her heart melted all over again and she raised a hand to trace the sharp line of his jaw, very much aware that every movement was being weighed and judged by their terrified audience. "It feels like justice that the first words I ever say in that barbaric tongue are ones of tenderness. Will you ask them to stay?"

He spoke without breaking eye contact. The slaves conferred quietly among themselves - though judging by the twitch to Fenris' lips and the flickering of Caelum's ears, their privacy was a farce - before the scarred male faced Arcana and spoke again.

"We have nowhere else to go," Caelum translated. "The choice is an illusion."

Arcana turned in Fenris' arms to face them. "There is always a choice. Stay here and be free, work together as equals, or go back to the life you've known."

Fenris repeated her words. The slave snorted and replied.

"They will kill us," Caelum said.

Arcana shrugged. "It's still a choice, and one you are all free to make."

Another whispered conversation. Then, "We will stay, mistress."

"Arcana," she said, pointing at herself. "I'm nobody's mistress. What's your name?"

"He says you can call him whatever you want," Caelum answered.

"That wasn't what I asked." Arcana chewed her lip a moment, then laid a gentle hand on her Guardian's arm. "This is Fenris. His name, given him at birth. I'm sure you have one too."

The whipped male drew himself up and swallowed heavily. "Arax."

"Arax," Arcana repeated, treasuring the courage it must have taken to share that simple truth. "May I set you free?"

Arax glanced back at Caelum, who twittered her words to him. His hands clenched to fists but he nodded, crossing the sand to offer her his chain. Arcana reached instead for the collar at his throat and called her magic, shearing the metal in two with a word of power. The collar fell to the ground with a clatter and Arax reached up in amazement to feel the chafed skin around his neck.

"He doesn't know what to do," Fenris murmured. "He's putting on a face, but I smell fear."

Conscious of the fragility of the moment, Arcana smiled at him and offered her arm. "Welcome, Arax."

The harpy startled back a step, confusion twisting his features. Fenris clicked and twittered at him and after a heavy swallow, Arax accepted the forearm grip, pulse racing beneath his pockmarked skin. When he motioned her to follow him towards the other men, she did, Fenris a reassuring warmth at her side.

"Brok," Arax said, gesturing to the man who'd fainted. Arcana recognised him immediately as the harpy whose former mistress had brutalised him with her metal-tipped whip during their confrontation in the Gauntlet.

"Brok," Arcana repeated, touching a hand to his shoulder. The harpy flinched away, whimpering. "I'd like to take your collar off. Would that be okay?"

She waited while Fenris translated, while Brok gave the barest of nods, then laid her hand against the metal collar and watched in satisfaction as it separated and fell to the ground.

"Leiran," said a younger man suddenly, offering his arm.

"Hello, Leiran." Arcana clasped his forearm with a smile, then motioned to his neck. He tipped his head back and she dismantled his collar with a touch. The harpy turned it over in his hands for a long moment before drawing back his skinny arm and heaving it into the trees with a fierce expression that warmed her heart no end.

One by one the men presented themselves, their faces reflecting differing stages of suspicion, gratitude and awe. The last, an elderly man who declared himself Jora, kept his soft grip on Arcana's forearm, twittering and whistling.

"He says he's a tailor," Caelum said, his ears flickering in surprise.

Arcana looked down at the harpy's loose pants and spied a patchwork of colours and fabric beneath the layer of grime. "You do fine work, Jora."

"He wants to know why you're not wearing leather," Fenris added.

A silence settled as the slaves - ex-slaves, she reminded herself - waited expectantly. Arcana's lip peeled back from her teeth and when she spoke, her voice was a growl. "I won't wear people. People are not clothes. You are *not clothes.*"

Fenris translated, his quiet voice carrying her passion. Jora's weathered face wreathed in a smile and he patted her shoulder, twittering quietly. Beside her, Fenris drew a sharp breath. "He says it would be his honour to make something better for you, if we can get the fabric."

"Why does that sound important?"

"Because the women would never lower themselves to wear cloth; it's for males only." Fenris' lips pressed into a thin line. "If you do that, you declare them your equal in a public forum."

Arcana took both of Jora's hands in hers. "It would be an honour to wear your creations."

The tailor nodded and a murmur went through the men, with several turning to Fenris and firing out a rapid chain of questions. Whilst the Guardian answered, Arcana sidled up to Caelum and slid her arms around his neck. "Thank you for taking care of them."

The deerken's posture went stiff for a moment, then he relaxed with a sigh. "There wasn't much choice."

"I'm sorry."

"I already told you to forget it."

"How can I, when you make a face like that?" She played her fingers through the slightly thicker fur on his chest. "Will you forgive me?"

"For losing your mind and almost killing yourself, and thereby me, after Fenris abandoned you to flee into the desert in a drug-addled craze while we had no food, water, shelter or protection?" He nipped her ear, a sharp reprimand. "I suppose I could forgive you. Besides, heartache aside, you still took care of us."

"I could never abandon you, even when I shattered," Arcana whispered. "My magic has grown again, too."

"That's one way to put it."

"What is it? I know that tone." Arcana stepped back, following his line of sight into the trees. "What did I do?"

"I'm not sure." Caelum tugged free, drifting towards the treeline, and Arcana followed.

Fenris appeared at her side less than a step later. "Wait for me."

"You don't have to come. I know you're tired -" she cut off at the look on his face and reached to twine their fingers together. "All right."

The whisper of sand announced the other males following as Caelum crossed the beach to the pile of fruit that had been collected earlier. "These all grew when you spread your magic through the earth."

"And?" Fenris bent to palm one of the fruits, testing the ripeness with his grip before lifting it to his nose for a sniff. "It seems somehow familiar."

"I thought so, too, but it's not the actual fruit that struck me. These," Caelum nudged at the sunset fruit, "Grow in that quarter. There are some sort of berries in that quarter," a flick of his head, "citrus in that quarter," another flick, "and what appears to be some sort of potato in the final quarter."

Arcana blinked. "Like a planned garden."

"Yes."

"But I didn't plan anything - I don't even know what these are," she protested, pointing at the fruit in Fenris' hand. "I just shoved magic into the ground."

"I know. There are also trees tall enough to be cut down and used for building, vines that would make excellent rope, and some sort of flower covered in a floss I will bet my left antler makes either fabric or thread." Caelum's ears flickered. "You might have altered some of the trees for shelter with magic, but even without it…"

"It's like someone plotted this out, but never got around to finishing it." Arcana stared down at the sand beneath her feet, spreading her senses underground. "I thought it was weird there was so much water down there."

"To protect it from the twin suns," Fenris murmured. He shook his head, features slack with astonishment. "Someone was terraforming this hunk of rock."

Arcana spread her fingers over the trunk of the nearest tree and let her magic seep into the ground, expanding her senses beyond the boundaries of their tiny jungle. "There are more seeds. I can feel them… they're asleep." Stepping back from the tree, she moved to crouch at the water's edge and swirled her hand in the shallows. Energy flowed up her arm as swiftly as if Arcana had immersed herself in the pool, and she switched her focus from the seeds themselves to the underground water table. Her body groaned a protest but whatever barriers she'd broken during her grief-inspired frenzy negated the need for symbols or spells, drawing a thin ribbon of moisture close enough to touch the ring of dormant seeds. They immediately began to sprout beneath the ground, cracking their shells and straining for the surface. "They're growing. There's so many."

"The pool of water is enlarging." Fenris' hand was gentle at her elbow, guiding her a step backwards. "I'd gather the inner ring of trees were planned to allow for exactly the correct amount of water to fertilise this grove and support whoever intended to live here."

Arcana estimated the seeds she could feel and eyed the rapidly disappearing beach. "You're right. If I pull up enough water to fill the pool, the resulting moisture will spread far enough to nourish the remaining plant life."

"Do it," Caelum urged. "We've only got two days until the Empress returns."

She bit her lip, spreading one hand over the pain developing in her side. "If I do it now, I'll end up unconscious again."

"Then we wait." Fenris' hand splayed atop hers, his fingers warm. "A few hours' head start isn't worth damaging yourself for."

Caelum grunted in agreement. "I think the wood that could be used for building would make excellent firewood, too. If we hunt some meat, collect some wood and start a fire… everyone gets a proper meal."

"An excellent idea." Fenris passed a hand over his face. "My last meal is most definitely wearing off."

"The sooner we hunt, the better, then," Arcana murmured.

Caelum snorted. "Because you're both totally up to that task right now. Do me a favour and keep your blood sugars up, and I'll be right back."

After twittering a short set of instructions to the harpies milling off to one side, Caelum disappeared into the trees.

"Well, that puts us in our place, doesn't it?" Arcana chuckled. "Would you like fruit, fruit, or fruit?"

"Ugh." Fenris made a face. "More fruit."

"Come on, now, don't be like that." Arcana scooped up one of the sunset coloured fruits and bit into it, well aware she had his sudden and undivided attention. "It's sweet."

Fenris watched as she sidled closer and, when she pressed the fruit to his lips, bit. "I don't like sweet things."

"Liar." Arcana took another mouthful and this time, when Fenris stooped to accept her offering, she brushed a kiss to his mouth instead. "If you want me naked later, you'll eat, Guardian."

"Is that so?" He wrapped an arm around her waist and jerked their bodies together, eyes flickering with heat - but shared the rest of the fruit, and a second piece, without further protest. When Arcana discarded the final stone, Fenris dipped his head to claim her lips, the kiss raw and deep.

"Ow!" Arcana flinched as something bounced off her head and fell to the ground. "Is that a *spoon*?"

Fenris reached up to his head as the spoon kitten appeared with a barely audible pop. The ex-slaves squeaked in distress, backing away with wide eyes as Fenris, holding the orange-furred creature by the scruff of the neck, waved a long finger in her adorable face. "No, Lyra. That's inappropriate."

Bubbles of light fizzed in Arcana's heart as the kitten batted at Fenris' hands with her paws. "She found us."

"Given she was able to trace me from the Timeless Kingdom to Hiraptha city, following us a little further out into the desert should be no great surprise," Fenris said, amusement heavy in his tone. He gave the tiny creature a little shake. "I have no idea why you've taken a dislike to Arcana, but *I* like her. You will not pepper her with spoons whenever you feel like it."

"She's bonded to you," Arcana said quietly. "There's a chance my proximity makes her feel threatened."

"Then she must learn to share." The spoon kitten winked out, then reappeared on Fenris' shoulder, wedging herself between the greatsword's hilt and the slender column of his throat. Her long tail wrapped several times around his neck and she hissed at Arcana, her giant blue eyes filled with temper. Fenris immediately poked her nose. "I said *no*, Lyra."

Arcana's heart softened further as the kitten purred and rubbed at his quivering finger. "She's not the least bit scared of you."

"Neither are you," Fenris murmured, the whispering remnants of the glamour wrapping them in an intimate cocoon. "Perhaps I should throw you both in the lake and see who emerges victorious."

"Oh?" A smile twitched her lips. "Kinky."

The Guardian blinked. "You sound like Flare."

"Flare." Arcana sighed, turned her face up to the mercilessly blue sky. "I hope he's okay. Who knows what Taelon's up to in our absence?"

"Flare is the smartest, most dangerous male I've ever met. He'll be fine until we get back."

"I dunno... the last message we had from him, he was seriously struggling." Arcana dropped her head to Fenris' chest, ignoring Lyra's warning hiss to breathe deep of his evergreen and cinnamon scent.

Her Guardian's hands smoothed up and down her spine, his touch soothing for all his body shook with fragility. "We will figure this out, one way or another."

"I know."

"But do you believe?"

Arcana was saved from answering by the crashing and muttering behind them that announced Caelum's return. His antlers had morphed from fruit-laden velvet to coffee-black blades and several large, shorn-off branches were skewered on their points. In his teeth - his herbivorous teeth - he carried a bundle of sandy fur.

"Is that… a rabbit?" Arcana stared at the gangly creature in surprise.

Caelum spat the dazed animal on the ground. It had a rabbit's pointed ears, large eyes and soft nose, but the hind legs were too long, the body too big, as though someone had merged a rabbit and a wallaby into a whole new creature.

"Dinner," the deerken announced.

Arcana's stomach immediately rebelled but Fenris stepped forward and broke the creature's neck with a practised movement. "Thank you for your sacrifice, little one."

"Great Gods of Sorcen," Arcana murmured, pressing one hand to her mouth. "I can't believe you just did that."

Fenris cocked a brow. "You've seen me cut warg in half."

"Yes, but… he was so cute." She fought the sudden urge to blush as his other brow rose. "Warg are not cute."

"Neither are they delicious, nutritious, or taking shelter in the nearby bushes," Caelum announced, shaking the branches onto the ground with a thud. He looked up at the gaping group of ex-slaves and spoke in a rapid burst of clicks and whistles. One of them answered. "Verga knows how to cook."

The harpies came slowly forward, their eyes locked as one on Lyra, who was now purring where she lay against Fenris' skin. After Caelum spent several minutes offering reassuring tweets and clicks, Verga, a mid-sized male with a slender frame and black hair with tawny flecks in it, accepted the almost-rabbit from Fenris with a nod. He hefted it and, in a voice like shifting sand, said, "Bwalja."

"Bwalja," Arcana repeated, and was gratified with the barest hint of a nod.

Fenris reached into the leather pouch at his back to pull out a hunting knife, offering it to Verga with a velvety twitter. The harpy's jaw dropped but he accepted the knife with a gentle inclination of his head and squatted to begin skinning the bwalja.

"If we are to cook, we will need a fire." Fenris drew the greatsword and reached for a branch. "This will be a good start."

"You're going to use the greatsword to chop wood?" Caelum demanded.

The Guardian shrugged. "Normally, that would be a terrible way to abuse a sword - after all, that is why axes were created - but we have no axe, and in my hands the greatsword will never blunt or break, so I think in this case the sword gods will excuse us."

Caelum snorted. Fenris grinned and turned to his task, whitened knuckles the only sign of strain as he began to chop branches into more manageable lengths.

"They're not as broken as I remember," Arcana murmured, watching as Arax began to build the fire.

"I did my best," Caelum returned, muscled shoulders rippling in the deerken equivalent of a shrug. One of the other males drifted close and after a soft conversation, he collected his fellows and led them into the jungle. Catching Arcana's raised brow, Caelum shrugged again. "They're nervous without a task. I sent them for kindling."

"They trust you," Arcana said, pride filling her heart.

Caelum humphed a laugh. "Don't worry, you're still useful - we need bowls, cutlery, a cooking pot, cups and jugs for water; the list goes on. Provided your body can handle the magical strain, of course."

"I'll just have to go slowly." Arcana chewed on her lip, mind churning. "We're going to need more branches."

"I can handle that." The deerken nudged one of the smaller, unclaimed pieces of wood her way. "Start with this, and I'll bring more. The harpies will feel better for seeing me wandering nearby, anyway."

"Okay - but I can't make a cooking pot out of wood. It'll burn."

Caelum's ear flickered. "Could you melt some sand into glass, once the fire's going? Or maybe we can get a shallow rock to reform?"

"I can try." Arcana settled herself cross legged in the sand as the other harpies returned, their arms stacked with smaller sticks and fallen leaves. Leiran, his features barely those of an adult and his frame the most emaciated, held a long, narrow stick and a flat piece of bark, which he promptly set on the ground by Fenris. The Guardian spoke softly, and with a hesitant smile, the younger male nodded and began the arduous process of making a spark. Arcana looked up to find Caelum still watching her, his face soft. "What?"

"I'm just glad you're both alive, awake, and together." His eyes flicked up to where Fenris was working, his dusty teal skin sheened with sweat, Lyra clinging to his neck. "Do us all a favour and don't make any spoons."

Arcana laughed, and it felt good. Everyone froze, the ex-slaves with varying expressions of uncertainty and Fenris with his face creased into a slow, warm smile.

"Forks might be the better choice," he agreed. As though sensing the tone of the conversation, Lyra gave an indignant yowl and the Guardian pursed his lips. "Maybe one spoon?"

Hope fanned to life inside her, and Arcana flashed a cheeky wink. "Only if she behaves. I'm a finite resource right now, you know."

"Indeed." Fenris turned to Lyra, his expression stern in the face of enormous eyes and a tiny pink nose. "Well? Will you be a good girl?"

Lyra drew her lips back from her tiny, kittenish teeth and hissed.

Everyone, including the harpies, laughed - and Arcana thought it was one of the sweetest sounds she'd ever heard.

TWENTY-THREE
FLARE

Flare came to with a heart thumping steadily in his ear and the sweeping planes of Zaire's bare chest spread out beneath him. The rogue's fingers were tangled in his hair, Flare's arm and leg thrown over his lover's in a masculine sprawl that spanned age, race and species. The walls around him were those of his own quarters, and when Flare cast his mind back over the night before, he had the vaguest memory of making a rumpled dash for whoever's quarters were closest after they'd finished trashing the library's meeting room.

Zaire's breathing changed tempo and a moment later his voice rumbled beneath Flare's jaw. "What time is it?"

"I have no idea."

"Get up and check."

"You get up and check."

Neither of them moved.

After several minutes of silence, Zaire's fingers began to stroke the tangles from Flare's hair. "Do you regret it?"

"What?" Flare lifted his head, propping his chin on one arm. "Of course not."

The rogue relaxed visibly. "You're telling the truth."

"I often do."

"It's just -" a hitched breath, an arrhythmic thump of the heart. "On Rylle, my sexual orientation isn't widely accepted."

Flare's eyes went wide. "Really?"

"Yes. We have a ratio of one male to every two females in the population; perhaps less. If you're male, it's anticipated that you'll do your breeding duty no matter what." Zaire bit his lower lip. "It never used to be so strict, but there was an incident that left our people at a disadvantage. Many of those left on Rylle are either sick, too old or too young."

"The warg."

After a long pause, Zaire nodded. "Yes. It was while my father was still a child, but yes. If not for the Oracle's vision, we'd have never survived."

"And those remaining are expected to rebuild the race?" Flare cleared his throat. "Can you even father children anymore?"

"Unknown - but the last time I was on Rylle, it was made clear that I was expected to try."

"No wonder you avoid the place." Flare dug his fingertips into his lover's pectoral muscle, was rewarded with a throaty grumble. "That's an unfair amount of pressure."

Zaire's laugh was harsh and all too familiar. "Someone like you, concerned with unfair?"

"You know very little about me," Flare reminded. "I've been used by my government plenty."

The Ryllin grunted at that, but made no further effort to push. "I reviewed Krowley's data while we slept."

'Slept' was an interesting way to put it; more like passed out after several hours' worth of energetic lovemaking that had seemed equal parts passion and battle. Groaning, Flare stretched as best he could in the cramped confines of the room. "I'm going to have bruises."

"You already do." Zaire's free hand spread over Flare's thigh, where the perfect imprint of his fingertips was clearly visible. "Sorry."

Flare caught that hand and flattened it against his skin. "Don't fucking apologise to me, you stupid bastard." A pause, two heated gazes clashing. "I liked it."

"You really are crazy." But the rogue relaxed a little further, his body softening in invitation. "I could've killed you."

"Damned if that doesn't make me hot," Flare muttered, then grinned as Zaire's temples darkened with a blush. "What? Clearly we're both self-destructive right now. Hey - at least you know your equipment works."

"Yeah."

Enjoying the deepening blush, Flare added, "And it works well."

"Stop it," Zaire hissed, though his abdomen was beginning to tighten beneath Flare's stroking fingers. "What we did was stupid and dangerous."

"So you don't want to do it again?"

A quick blink. "I didn't say that."

The honesty roused Flare's sense of humour and he fell back with a laugh, dragging Zaire with him until they were curled up face to face, each one's head pillowed on the other's hand. "Tell me what was in Krowley's files."

"I can do better than that." Reaching behind him, Zaire fished out a datapad, melted two of his fingers into wires and inserted them into the device's data port. Pinpricks of cobalt appeared in his irises and the datapad flickered, blanked momentarily, and then began to play a recording.

"It's some sort of security footage," Flare murmured, watching as multiple Ryllin in blue and silver uniforms moved around the bridge of a starship. The routine seemed fairly commonplace, officers at their stations and a liaison in animal skins standing by the captain's chair. Flare squinted at the words in the top corner of the recording, ran the serial number against his mental databank. "This is from one of the ships that disappeared."

"The flagship," Zaire confirmed, his voice echoing with a metallic overtone. "Keep watching."

Lights started flickering across consoles and though Flare was unfamiliar with the ship's makeup, it didn't take a genius to recognise them as warning lights. They spread from station to station, a rolling wave of amber and red that sent crew members scurrying and had the captain out of his chair, gesticulating wildly as he issued orders.

A contingent of guards in Alliance aubergine and gold hustled into view, led by three officers whose uniforms were accented with thick piping and embroidery. "Who are they?"

"The Chancellor's personal guard - or some of them." As Zaire spoke, the Ryllin frigate shuddered, the running lights flickering ominously. Several crewmen staggered and the panel controlling the bridge's main door exploded in a shower of sparks. The door itself jerked violently open and warg poured in, descending on the crew in a hail of teeth, claws and unholy bloodlust. The screen went dark.

"That's it?"

"Yes." Zaire's gaze flickered and the recording reappeared, the footage zooming backwards. "Watch this part again."

Flare stared at the screen as the door panel exploded and the warg poured in. "Go back ten seconds."

"You see it?"

"That guy." Flare's finger tapped one of the Chancellor's guards. "Can you slow it down?"

The footage obligingly crawled forwards. Right before the door panel exploded, the guard in question slapped a hand over his hip in a gesture that appeared innocent - unless you were a well trained warrior with an eye for body language. "He shot the door panel," Flare murmured. "No wonder Krowley wanted to keep this under wraps."

"Question is: Did Krowley keep it hidden because he thinks the Chancellor's shady, or because he's hiding his own incriminating evidence?" Zaire's eyes flickered and the recording sped forward to the moment the warg shoved through the door. "Look at that guy in the bottom left."

Flare frowned at the figure in question. "He's wearing Krowley's animal skin uniform, but... is that *smoke* coming out of his loincloth?"

"I can't tell for sure. Possible." The image expanded until the barbarian took up most of the screen, but the footage had become so pixelated it was impossible to make out clear details. "I tried cleaning the recording up, but it lost a lot of quality in the transmission. If I had to hazard a guess, I'd say the upload wasn't completed before the drives were wiped."

"Wiped?" Flare stared at his lover in astonishment. "Warg don't wipe drives - those ships are scattered space flotsam by now."

"I'm not so sure about that." Zaire's eyes flickered again, cobalt pinpricks of light that winked on and off like stars. The datapad cleared, then displayed a file full of shorthand notes and date codes.

Flare skimmed the contents, lips moving silently as he catalogued the new information. "One of the tracking beacons sent back a range of co-ordinates timed well after the attack. The ship was moving."

"Not only that," Zaire added, tapping the screen with his thumb, "But it suddenly cuts off about twelve hours later - as though someone realised the error and did a second, more thorough sweep."

"Which warg don't do."

"No."

Flare rolled onto his back and stared up at the ceiling, brain working overtime. "This has Taelon written all over it."

"I thought you'd say that." Zaire withdrew his fingers from the datapad's interface and set it aside. The moment the wires retracted and his flesh was back in place, he splayed his hand palm down on Flare's chest, seeking life and warmth. "Why go to all this trouble, though? Why not just announce yourself and continue spreading the warg through the galaxy like the plague he is?"

"I have a couple of theories, based on what Arcana told me and what

I've observed myself. First of all, Taelon seems to be co-ordinating and controlling the warg, but only to a point. I'm willing to bet my left nut that whatever he's using to keep them in line works on the upper echelon, but leaves most of the soldier types slave to their insatiable bloodlust. That means his only option as an invading force is to slaughter everyone."

"And?"

Flare shrugged. "If what Fenris says is correct - and I have no doubt it is - Taelon doesn't *want* to kill everyone. He wants to corral the universe under his control and present us to the Weaver tied up with a pretty, warg-shaped bow. Prior to this point, the Guardians, Wardens and deerken have been our hidden caretakers. Taelon wants to prove to the Weaver he's got what it takes to do it better so she'll agree to let him be her new consort."

"Meaning," Zaire drawled, "If he can take the Galactic Alliance by treachery, he doesn't have to slaughter everyone."

"Yes. Treachery or terrorism - either would work."

Zaire propped himself on one elbow, eyes hungry as they tracked down Flare's body and back again. "Given the lengths he's going to, disappearing ships and trying to poison you, I'd say treachery."

"Targeting me makes sense - I've been anti-warg since the minute I touched down." Flare let his fingers wander the breadth of Zaire's ribcage, pausing to palm his hip bone. "Which makes me wonder if Chancellor Kaiora is aware of what's going on."

The rogue let out a breath, his erection twitching against Flare's thigh. "Surely if she was, she'd just hand the Alliance over?"

"Maybe." Flare caught the Ryllin's leg and hauled his body on top, framing the other male's face in his hands. "Maybe not. Kaiora might be in charge, but even I know surrendering the Alliance to someone else's control requires a majority vote. She's more likely to get that by appearing innocent."

"I hate it when you're right." Zaire lowered his head to nip at Flare's bottom lip. "So much."

"Perhaps you should demonstrate just how much," Flare murmured.

Indigo eyes, impossibly close, impossibly large. "Perhaps."

When they surfaced an hour or so later, it was to the chiming of an incoming call on Flare's wall console. He debated ignoring it but, noting the chime for an urgent call, rolled out of bed and answered.

"Great Gods of Sorcen," Verdure cried, holding up a hand to block the holocam. "Put some clothes on!"

Flare propped both hands on his hips. "You've seen my chest before, V."

"I know that tousled look," the nature sorcerer snapped. "I know what you've been doing!"

"Checking the plumbing?" Flare returned waspishly. After a short silence, he added, "I'd have ignored you, given my *tousled look*, but the call code was urgent."

"Oh. Yes. Well, it is." Clearly reluctant, Verdure dropped her hand. "There's been more poisonings."

Zaire appeared at Flare's side an instant later, his voice cracking out like a whip. "Who? Where?"

"Er…" Verdure's eyes went wide as she looked from one bare-chested male to the other, then she gave herself a shake and referred to the datapad in her hand. "Six poisonings in total. Four servants, two actual Ambassadors. One Ambassador and two servants are dead, the others critical. I sent Mendin to do what he could."

Flare tapped a finger against his chin for a long moment. "Send me the relevant file."

"Yes, sir."

"How's Pytch?"

Verdure cast a glance over her shoulder. "Up and about, but still wobbly. I wouldn't recommend active duty until tomorrow."

"I wasn't about to suggest it." He sucked his teeth a long moment, eyeing the slender lines of Zaire's body as the other male disappeared into the bedroom and returned with his datapad. "Got it?"

"Yeah."

"All right. V - call in two of the stationside team to sit with Pytch, and meet me at my quarters in half an hour."

"Yes, First Flame."

Flare frowned. "That's not my title any more."

Verdure's smile was far too wide, given the circumstances. "It is today."

"Brat." As soon as she disappeared, Flare turned to Zaire with a raised brow. "I thought you were worried about your image?"

Zaire snorted. "Is she going to tell?"

"Of course not."

"Then it doesn't matter." Cobalt sparked in his eyes as he interfaced with the datapad and then sagged in relief. "Not Eyrton."

"Good, but I want comprehensive details of who, where and how while we shower," Flare instructed, tugging Zaire into the bathroom.

The rogue blinked. "We're showering together now?"

"I only gave Verdure thirty minutes," Flare reminded, tapping the datapad until Zaire withdrew his probe and set it down. "If we want to be ready in time, it'll have to be together."

Blue tinged Zaire's temples. "I've never done that before."

"Shared a shower?"

"No."

Flare's grin was wild and wicked. "Allow me to educate you."

Thirty-five steamy minutes later, Flare strode out into the corridor to find Verdure lounging against the wall outside. "You're late."

"Pfft." He waved a dismissive hand. "You could've come in and made yourself a drink."

"My access was disabled," Verdure snapped, her eyes narrowed.

Flare turned to Zaire, who shrugged as he buckled up the last of the straps on his leather armour. "I had to be sure we were secure."

"Fair enough." Giving Verdure an enigmatic smile for the sake of the cameras in the corridor, Flare set off in the direction of the higher ranked quarters. Two thirds of the way there, he swept into a service hall and picked up his pace, keeping his shoulders square and gait purposeful.

"First Flame?" Verdure's query was soft and uncertain as she almost jogged to keep up. "We need to -"

"Not long now," Flare interrupted, giving her a smile over one shoulder that sat somewhere between carefree and arrogant. "Try to keep up, my dear."

The nature sorcerer frowned but fell silent. Zaire kept easy pace alongside, thumbs jammed through the weapons belt which held his twin daggers. His head was down, hair a waterfall that protected his face from passers-by, but Flare was under no illusion as to his watch-fulness.

"What?" Cold, hard, as indifferent as the night they'd met.

"What, what?"

"You're staring." A slash of indigo. "It's fucking rude."

"You're walking easier than yesterday."

Zaire's step faltered for the barest moment. "Maybe."

"Definitely," Flare insisted. "Weight off your shoulders, perhaps?"

"I hate you."

"I know."

Verdure was still shaking her head when they reached the humid, over-grown jungle deep in the bowels of the station. Flare slapped his hand to the scanner, grinning as the opening door allowed steam to billow into the corridor.

"The oxygen garden?" Verdure asked, stepping slowly inside. Her head flicked back and forth, eyes unfocussed. Flare felt the tingle of magic over his skin, knew she was communing with the greenery. "Incredible."

"I need you to find me something, V." He gave her a heavy look. "Something unique."

Comprehension dawned in those bottle green eyes and Verdure snapped to attention. "At once, First Flame."

"Still not my title."

"Of course not, sir." Another unrepentant grin, a crisp salute, and she was gone.

"Brat," Flare muttered again.

"What should she have called you?" Zaire asked, curiosity marking his face.

"Fire Elder." Flare sauntered through the doorway and turned his face up to the canopy, breathing deep of the hot, heavy air. "First Flame is my old title. Someone else does that job now."

"The difference being?"

"The Fire Elder sits on the Council of Elders. Stuffy bunch of backwards assholes who can't navigate their way out of a paper bag and drove me to drink in less than two weeks of being forced into the position." Closing his eyes, he took another deep, cleansing breath, feeling the tingle of magic - fire magic - building beneath his skin. "The First Flame leads the military. Takes care of his soldiers, the people, the planet, and most importantly, is allowed his own fucking privacy. For the most part."

"Bitter."

"So are you, assknuckle." Cracking an eye, he flashed a look over one shoulder. "You coming or what?"

Zaire remained firmly on the threshold. "I can't go in there."

"What, will you rust?" Flare raised a challenging brow. "I'll help you polish your equipment until it shines."

The rogue's mouth pressed into a thin line and Flare wondered whether Zaire was trying not to laugh, or not to punch him. Either prospect was delightful. Still, those indigo eyes flickered about the room, the Ryllin's feet glued to the spot. His chest rose and fell too quickly, as though he couldn't get enough air. Flare was no fool - he knew anxiety when he saw it. Raising a hand to his now sodden hair, he pushed it off his face, came away with a handful of water, and flicked the moisture at Zaire.

"Hey!" The Ryllin jerked back as droplets splattered across his face and neck. "Fuck you."

"Now?" Flare asked, his voice deliberately lazy. "You wouldn't dare, Ambassador."

Zaire grunted, jaw set. After a long moment, he took one deliberate, measured step inside the doorway. Moisture already clung to his skin, to his armour, the humidity so intense it boiled out through the still open doorway. The door slid shut behind him, causing the rogue's chest to work double time, the whites of his eyes glittering around the deep indigo irises Flare was so drawn to. "Oracle's voice, but I hate you."

Flare stepped closer, muttered under his breath, and tossed out a spell. Water sizzled and popped, the mist around them evaporating to leave a bubble of hot, dry air which blocked out all sound. "Is it the water or the temperature?"

"I can't breathe in here," Zaire managed, his voice a tortured rasp. "I drowned in my own blood once."

"I can help, but it'll likely give away our predilection for each other's nocturnal company. The choice is yours." Flare held out a hand.
"Trust me?"

"No." But that long fingered hand slipped into his, clenched so tight bones ground together. "Never."

"Hah." Ignoring the pain, Flare whispered a new spell, releasing the air bubble so that he could channel his magic better. Orange runes sparked in the mist around them, hissing and spitting where the humidity touched, bought to life by Flare's trailing index finger. The runes sank into his robes the moment they were formed, sending waves of heat rippling over his skin - and over Zaire, who hissed in surprise as the water clinging to his body began to evaporate in a puff of steam. Flare gave him a meaningful look. "The spell takes constant concentration; I can only keep it active by locking it to myself. We stay in contact, you stay dry. You let go...."

"I get it." Zaire's breathing was already steadier, his back straighter. "I'm ready."

With a nod, Flare tugged him deeper into the jungle, walking without any real direction. After a good thirty minutes, a tunnel began to form in the greenery to his left. Flare ducked inside, conscious that it wouldn't last long - and sure enough, the vegetation began to spring back into shape as soon as he passed by. By mutual agreement, both men picked up their pace.

Verdure waited in a small, well manicured clearing populated by ankle high herbs with narrow, spiny looking leaves. Gathering his robes in his free hand, Flare crouched at the edge of the small garden - with the plants in neat rows, it could be nothing else - and peered at the innocent seeming foliage. "How sure are you, V?"

"The magical signature is exactly the same as what I detected in your food." Verdure pointed at the garden as she spoke. "From what I can tell, as little as a single leaf would do the trick - permanently."

"Potent, then."

"Yes. Should I...?" She wiggled her fingers.

"No." Flare craned his head, making certain that whatever cameras or listening devices were in the area had a good view of his face, a clear sample of his voice. "I want no doubt that it was me."

"You need your hand." Zaire's rumble close beside him.

"For a minute." Flare chanced a look into the Ryllin's stony face. "You can do it."

"Fuck you, of course I can," he hissed, releasing Flare's fingers as though burnt. "I'm not an invalid."

Painful feeling rushed back into Flare's hand and he bit his tongue a moment, breathing through the rush of sensation. When Zaire's eyes dropped to the bruises already purpling his skin, Flare spoke through gritted teeth. "Don't. Take a step back and let me work."

Without bothering to wait for Zaire to obey, he dropped to one knee and flattened both hands against the earth. Fire-orange runes crawled across the back of his knuckles as Flare began to chant, his words measured and the flow of magic steady, draining his tank almost to halfway before smoke began to rise from the tips of the nearest leaves. By the time the last of the herbs wilted, the now-delicate husks no more than formed ash, his magic sat at less than a quarter full - a level he advised his warriors never to drop to unless their lives depended on it. Flare gauged his options, spoke a harsh word and sent a large shockwave outwards, the force and heat more than enough to disable any technology in the imme-diate area. With his tank now containing only fumes, Flare cut the magic off and sat back. Wiping muddy palms on his thighs, he closed his eyes and savoured the heady lightness that accompanied such a large energy release - even though his body already drew in more to replace it. When he cracked an eye a minute later, his tank was already half full. By the time they left the jungle, it'd be overflowing.

"Well?" Flare opened both eyes and levelled them unerringly on Verdure.

The nature sorcerer nodded. "All dead."

"Good." He watched until the last few tendrils of smoke dissolved into the humid air, then stood. "I took out any cameras too - but not before they got a lovely shot of my face."

Zaire held up a hand when Flare made to walk off, his brow pinched. "None of those plants actually caught fire."

"No." Flare ran his eyes over the rogue, noted his building anxiety levels, and snapped out a terse command. The spell he'd used earlier licked over his skin, settling into his bones. Holding out a hand to Zaire, he continued, "I burnt them from the inside out."

When the Ryllin simply stared, Verdure stepped in. "Flare is Sorcen's penultimate fire sorcerer; he can do things nobody else can. It's better not to question."

"I'm not one of his slack-jawed fanatics." Zaire's return was as cool as the fingers he twined with Flare's. "If we're working together, I need to understand how his power works."

Flare held his breath a moment, considering, then shrugged. "Stick."

"Yes, sir." Verdure waved her hand, spoke a few low words, and the nearest tree bent over to deposit a scraggly branch in her palm. A moment later, the leaves sheared off and Flare held a reasonable pointer in his grip.

"Sorcery is based on three things," he said, using his boot to smooth over a section of dirt. "First off, a sorcerer's natural ability to withstand magic."

"Withstand it?" Zaire drew closer, watching as Flare used the tip of the stick to draw a crude human figure. "I thought you used it."

"Yes and no. Think of the glazing on pottery; it keeps the moisture out, but if it cracks under pressure and water gets in, the vessel crumbles." Flare flicked the stick through his drawing, disfiguring the image. "A sorcerer's classification - their strength - is based on how well they can withstand, and therefore wield, their magic."

"Second thing is the tank," Verdure supplied, coming to stand on Flare's other side.

"Yes. Fuel tank," Flare clarified, drawing a rectangle in the dirt and making measurement lines up one side. "How much magic you can hold at any one time."

"And the third?" Zaire watched as the stick moved again, etching a complex set of equations in the dirt.

"Regeneration; how quickly the tank refills." Flare drew an arrow back to the tank, and then another to the wobbly person. "These things affect all types of sorcerers, but there are no hard and fast rules. I've known lower class sorcerers with immense storage tanks they have no hope of ever emptying, and higher class sorcerers with such a slow regen they empty their power out in one or two spells."

"Surely there's some sort of average," Zaire said.

"Yes." He nodded, erased the images, and began to draw again. "Basic magical lore says that the higher your classification, the bigger your tank and the smoother your regen. In theory."

Zaire paused, thinking. "So as the top dog, you have the biggest tank and the best regen."

"No."

"No?" The rogue looked surprised. "Admitting a weakness?"

Flare snorted, not even bothering to pull on the facade of charm he used for most everyone else. "I only have one weakness, and it's no secret. However, that's not the point of this - you wanted to know how my magic works, didn't you?"

"Yes."

"Right." He began to make markings on his new illustrations. "My ability to withstand magic is off the chart. So much so that the energy infiltrates my body on a permanent basis, meaning I have to regularly slough off the excess or risk accidentally setting things on fire."

Verdure stifled a gasp and he flicked her a hard glance. She stiffened to attention. "The secret is safe, First Flame."

"I know." Flare took a long breath, and then admitted to Zaire's questioning look, "No, that's not normal. It's very abnormal, in fact. My storage tank is on the larger side of average, nothing special; but my regen is one of the fastest on Sorcen. Coupled with the fact that my body can contain more than its fair share of magic, I have the ability to burn an extreme amount of power quickly, and replace it just as fast. In a combat situation, if I use the right spells, I can literally cast forever and not make so much as a dent in my reservoir."

"Considering you're also razor sharp, that makes you a formidable opponent," Zaire mused. He frowned. "Your siblings are also strong?"

"Lesce is Class One, but in a different way. Her tank is enormous, her regen middle of the road. Her capacity to withstand magic is below average, meaning she needs to be careful how she exerts herself, but healing's different to the other schools so it's not a big deal."

"And the other?"

"Arcana is an enigma. She was a Class Five water sorceress at first, with drearily below average everything." Flare smiled in recollection. "She decorated cakes for a living."

Zaire blinked. "I thought you said she was off saving the universe."

"Once she bonded Caelum and ascended, her magic surpassed the realms of Sorcen's understanding." Flare drew a decisive line through his diagrams. "Her limits can't be measured by such rudimentary means."

"Huh." The rogue stared down at the dirt, his face impassive. "Why don't you own the planet, then? Between the three of you?"

Flare shuddered at the thought. "Lesce is the only one of us with political motivation - and that, only because she thinks we're all her patients to be cared for."

"Yet you commanded the military and are now an Elder."

"Not by choice," Verdure broke in quietly. "I happen to know for a fact he'd be happier in the ranks."

"Yeah." Flare nodded, keeping a tight lid on that old wound. "And our government messed Arcana up so badly she ran away. Believe me, the last thing she wants is to be in charge."

Zaire caught his tone, but whether deliberately or by accident, he misinterpreted it. "I'll bet the rumour mill thinks differently."

"Oh, yes," Verdure nodded. "There's been conspiracy theories out for years, but they've gotten worse since Flare took a seat on the Council of Elders."

"I'm not surprised." Flare offered a smile somewhere between rueful and amused. "Has the public stopped attaching me to Gravella?"

Searching his face for the truth but being unable to discover it, Verdure gave a reluctant nod. "The polls say your official grieving period is over."

"Meaning?" When she fidgeted, Flare frowned in a way he knew she hated. "V."

She sighed. "There might be the odd insinuation that your relationship with Gravella - don't growl at me like that - was a way to get a voice on the Council."

"And now that she's dead, I've jumped in directly," Flare muttered, then shook his head. "I've got better things to do."

"Like fuck everyone?" Zaire asked, his expression innocent.

Flare growled, bunching his fist in the neck of Zaire's soft undershirt. "Last I heard, you weren't complaining, little Ryllin."

Zaire's chest rose and fell, far too fast. "I didn't throw me into a bookshelf."

"I didn't ask for it again and again," Flare hissed, dragging the rogue down until they were nose to nose.

"I hate you."

"Not as much as I hate myself."

Silence fell, and they both blinked in surprise, close enough to share breath. Zaire's hands closed on his hips, unaccountably gentle. "Flare."

"Don't." Struggling to repair the inadvertent breach in his armour, he tried to step back. Zaire kept him in place with his augmented strength, not so much as an eyelash flickering with effort. Growling, Flare slammed both clenched fists into the other male's chest. "I can't do this right now."

"Too bad." Zaire slid one hand around to his lower back and tugged their pelvises into alignment, spine curving as he tempered his height to match. When he spoke, it was against Flare's lips. "What do you need?"

"My sister." It was out before he could stop it, torn through the tiny chink in walls he'd built around his heart long ago. "I need my sister."

For a long moment, he thought the rogue would snarl and swear, pick a fight like he always did. Instead, Zaire's lips brushed across Flare's in a sweet, hot promise. "The Alliance has the reach to find her."

"Maybe." He had to believe; he *had* to. "Yes."

"All right." Another almost-kiss. "Let's go see the Chancellor - we get her on side, we get access to the Alliance's resources. If you think you can charm her enough, that is."

Of course he could. Even broken and bewildered, he could charm the stars out of the sky. Closing his eyes against a sudden surge of fatigue, Flare let his forehead rest against Zaire's. "Why bother? You hate me."

Long fingers clenched against his spine, hard enough to leave another bruise - but when Zaire sealed their lips, the kiss was gentle, almost longing. "Not as much as I hate myself."

TWENTY-FOUR
ARCANA

The morning of the Empress' visit dawned as swift and hot as every
other day in Hiraptha, the endless vista of piercing blue sky broken only
by the sprawling canopy overhead. Arcana stood quietly in the shade of
one of the fruit trees, the smooth bark reassuring against her spine as she
watched Fenris picking berries from a bush nearby. His dusky teal hands
were stained purple with juice, dark curls hanging into his eyes in a way
that the Guardian found irritating, and Arcana incredibly appealing.

"This should feed us," he said, straightening with a ripple of muscle
that sent butterflies winging in Arcana's stomach. The past two days had
been kind to him; proper food and rest had brought colour to his face and
the light in his burning eyes was noticeably brighter. His body was still far
too thin, his training pants held up by a belt that did nothing to disguise
the sharp angles of his hipbones, but he no longer walked the fine line
between the living and the dead. Seeing her appraisal of his body, Fenris
raised an eyebrow. "What is it?"

"Nothing." Arcana crossed to stand before him, running her fingers
lightly over the scar that cleft his chest in two. "Just admiring the scenery."

His cheeks darkened. "You did that only an hour ago."

"If you think," Arcana teased, stealing a berry from his loose grip, "that
I can't appreciate the view just because some of it's hidden, you're sadly
mistaken."

Fenris blinked, then gave her the wicked, bedroom smile he saved for
her alone. They'd been run off their feet during the daylight hours,

ensuring their small settlement had what amenities it could and learning about the harpies whose lives were now in their care. Never had Arcana felt so stretched; between pushing her recovering magic to its limit, memorising what few Hirapthan words she could from Fenris while they laboured alongside the other males and trying to snatch both food and sleep wherever possible, she was beyond exhausted. When night fell, however, and Caelum coaxed the harpies to curl up beside him in their tree, neither she nor Fenris found the will to spend those two precious hours resting. Those soft minutes were all they had alone, time they spent whispering and loving and learning the depth and breadth of each other's hearts.

"You look sad." Fenris tucked a strand of hair behind her ear and bent to brush his lips to hers. "Why?"

Arcana took a deep breath, her chest aching. "What if we never get out of here? What if this is all there is, forever?"

He was quiet a long moment, the glamour rising warm and gentle around them as he searched the depths of her gaze. "I have learnt that 'forever' is a relative term. Sooner or later, everything changes; we will either find our way off this blasted half-world, or Taelon's warg will sweep far enough through the galaxy that he comes upon us by accident."

"That could take years."

"Centuries," Fenris agreed. "None of it matters as long as we are together."

Arcana smoothed her hand over his heart. "I see you rubbing your chest when you think I'm not looking. You miss the blood bond."

"Of course I do." Tumbling the berries into one of the wide wooden bowls Arcana had shaped for just such a purpose, Fenris fixed his gaze on the canopy above, his jaw a brutal line. "I have been bonded to the Weaver for the majority of my life. I love my people; I loved my duty. It would be an astronomical lie to say it hasn't left a hole inside me." He pursed his lips. "In addition to that, with the blood bond severed, my people - my parents - will think I am dead, and it pains me to think of their grief."

Arcana stood on tiptoe, stretching to cup his face. "I can't see Flare giving up on us, any more than I can see your mother accepting the truth of your death without proof. After all, she didn't last time, did she?"

Fenris shook his head slightly, but there was no stopping the curve of his lips. "And you wonder why I fell in love with you."

"Lay it on any thicker and my head will explode," Arcana chuckled, dropping her hands and lifting the basket. "Now come on, or Leiran will die of starvation."

Of all the ex-slaves, Leiran had proven the trickiest to nurture. One minute he seemed reckless, saying and doing things that would've seen him dead under the rules of slavery, and the next he retreated so far inside himself he seemed catatonic. It'd taken almost a full day before Jora explained that the young harpy had been his former mistress' taster, the only food he ever ate from her table - to ensure it wasn't poisoned. He was so terrified of food he refused to eat, succumbing only when, in desperation, Arcana had eaten a spoonful of his stew first to prove it was safe. After watching wide-eyed, he'd dared a few mouthfuls and then stopped, his stomach so shrivelled it could take no more.

"Breakfast," Fenris announced in Hirapthan as they made their way across the sand to the fire pit.

While the other men began to fetch bowls, Arcana called a stream of water from the oasis pool and washed the berries twice over. Verga, who had taken to the food preparation with unparalleled enthusiasm, added several slices of citrus to the bowl of berries along with a hefty dose of sweet, syrupy jam he'd made the previous day while Arax pulled a fresh loaf of damper from the coals of the fire and began tearing it into steaming sections. Arcana accepted the first section with a smile, smeared it with the fruit concoction, bit into it, and then turned to offer it to Leiran.

The young harpy swallowed, scrambling backwards as though the rustic bread were a naked blade. "No."

"Leiran," she murmured, crouching by his side and ignoring the instinctive flinch her actions caused. Taking his hand, she set the bread into his palm. "Please."

He twittered rapidly, the words beyond her comprehension, lungs working like a bellows. Fenris arrived at that moment, holding a second piece of bread with jam-coated fruit. "He still doesn't trust you."

Swallowing the instinctive hurt that came with the announcement, Arcana nodded slowly. "Would you talk to him?"

"Of course." Switching to Hirapthan, Fenris spoke softly with Leiran, his free hand massaging Arcana's shoulder with rhythmic strokes. The younger harpy replied, his face pale as he motioned at the bread he'd been given, then at the almost identical piece Fenris held in his hand. "He believes your kindness is a trick, that because he ate from your hand yesterday, today you will punish him with sickness."

"Oh, Leiran." Arcana's heart wrenched. "I just want to help."

"They are preconditioned to distrust women - it will take time," Fenris replied, then crouched beside her and motioned to his bread. Taking a healthy bite, he brushed the rest over Arcana's lips until she blushed and opened her mouth, allowing him to feed her. Leiran watched the exchange wide eyed and, once the chunk of bread was gone, finally took a tentative nibble of his own breakfast.

"Yes." Arcana smiled as wide as she dared. "Good."

A horn sounded, loud enough to ripple the water in the pool and send a shiver through the trees. Leiran dropped his breakfast into the sand with a terrified squeak, his hands going to his collarless throat.

"I'd say the Empress is here," Caelum drawled.

"Yes." Fenris' expression remained calm but his jaw set so tight that tendons stood out in his neck. "Our time is up."

The horn rolled out again, invasive and with a distinct note of demand that set Arcana's teeth on edge. The harpy males flinched away from it, even the older, more experienced Jora unable to contain his instinctive reaction.

Arcana stood and dusted her hands on her thighs. "Caelum, get the harpies inside their tree and tell them to stay put. I want you visible, but guarding the door. She doesn't get to see them, no matter what."

"Got it." The deerken turned towards the men, herding them upright with body and voice. By the time they were safely ensconced inside their treehouse, Caelum's velvety antlers had hardened into shimmering blades.

"Get the greatsword," Arcana murmured, laying a hand on Fenris' arm.

"Males are not permitted to bear arms."

"*Fenris.*" She slapped him hard in the chest, drawing his gaze at last. "Get. The. Greatsword."

For a long moment they simply stared at each other, and then the Empress' horn ululated through the oasis for the third time. Fenris disappeared and by the time the demanding sound died, he was back, buckling the greatsword's scabbard into place across his chest. "This used to fit better."

"It will again." Arcana reached out and twined their fingers together. "Are you okay?"

"No, but I am mending." He drew the greatsword with his free hand, the silken sound of silversteel on leather whispering through the silence. "Your magic?"

"Enough."

"Good." Fenris set the greatsword point down in the sand and smiled wide enough to show fangs. "Open the door."

Tightening her grip on his fingers, Arcana raised her other arm, palm out, and began to chant. The ancient Sorcen resonated deep in her chest, soft green runes forming in the air around her outstretched hand. One by one the trees and bushes began to bend and curl, forming a tunnel trunk by trunk, frond by frond. By the time the corridor was complete Arcana was gasping, her grasp on Fenris the only thing keeping her upright. Dredging at the last of her now reluctant power, she locked the spell into a perpetual loop and sagged against her Guardian.

"The last time I witnessed that spell, it was done with such ease - I fear I've never truly considered the full breadth of your usual powers until now," Fenris murmured, sliding his arm around her waist to better provide support.

"Me either," Arcana managed, forcing her legs straight and her shoulders back. "I've never been in a position like this before."

"That makes two of us."

They stood in silence as a silhouette appeared at the far end of the tunnel. In another life, Arcana would've been fascinated by the way downy hair and soft feathers shifted in the wind - now, as she watched the harpy warrior thump her spear into the sand, she only felt tired. Tired of questioning, tired of pushing, tired of fighting, tired of hurting. That fatigue ate into her very bones as the breeze caught the hangings on the harpy's spear, setting beads and feathered cords waving lazily. Feathers that she now knew came from Hirapthan men, plucked so they'd have no chance at the flight their women took as a sacred right. Anger stirred, sparking her battered temper and filling the hole her magic had created as it soaked into the jungle. These women had hurt their men; moreover, they'd hurt Fenris, the man who'd become such an integral part of her life that she struggled to remember what things had been like before the velvet rumble of his voice had begun invading her dreams. And what had she been doing while these men - her man - had been suffering? Bouncing aimlessly from one obstacle to the next, flipping from frying pan to fire, as Caelum liked to say, without taking the time to gather her frayed edges into some semblance of order and find a solid place to set her feet. Choices, she'd once told Fenris - life wasn't about what happened to you, but what you chose to do with it. Here, now, it was time for her to choose.

"Tempered," Arcana whispered.

"What?" Fenris didn't move, his gaze firmly locked on the harpy at the opposite end of the tunnel. "I don't understand."

"You once put me back together when I was a shattered ruin; now it's my turn." She squeezed his fingers. "We went through the fire like any good blade, and now we're tempered. A few nicks, maybe, but stronger than we started."

"Tempered," he repeated softly. As the harpy silhouette was joined by another, and another, and yet another, Fenris rolled his shoulders and lifted his chin. That swiftly, the half-starved slave was gone and in his place stood a warrior who'd fought and bested opponents of incalculable strength. "Thank you."

"You're welcome." Arcana shot him a glance from beneath her lashes. "Together?"

"Together."

The Empress and her entourage progressed down the tunnel at a stately pace that was just shy of infuriating, a conglomerate of softly twittering shadows who continually craned their heads at the dense jungle around them. The first few harpies to step into the light were warriors, each dressed in matching leather armour in shades of white, turquoise and gold to match the coloured feathers and beads on their spears. Geometric designs had been painted over their faces in the same shades, their raptorlike expressions forbidding and their yellow eyes sharp.

The centremost harpy of the trio cast her eyes over Fenris and Arcana but made no comment save to raise a hand and snap her fingers. Her companions stepped aside to reveal a pair of identical male slaves bearing an ornate wooden chest between them, their muscular bodies painted a shimmering, metallic gold and their pure white manes braided into a single, elaborate tail which reached almost to their knees. Each one wore billowing pants as white as their hair, the fabric so sheer it drew attention to what it should have concealed. Golden collars ringed their throats, from which hung delicate chains that dangled from the loose grip of the richly dressed handmaiden behind them. After a whispered conversation with the head guard, the handmaiden made her way to the guard on her left, the two males ghosting along behind without so much as the flicker of an eyelash.

Lifting her chin, the head guard trilled out a short speech in Hirapthan and the assembled harpies all dropped to one knee in the sand. The Empress stepped into the clearing, her slim figure draped in swathes of leather that had been bleached a pure white and decorated with strings of turquoise beads. Gold winked from every available surface, culminating in a glittering crown set with turquoise stones and hung with so many strands of beads it almost completely disguised her long, downy hair. Two handmaidens trailed in her wake, their own finery nothing in comparison to the shocking wealth of their ruler.

The Protector of Hiraptha raised an eyebrow at Arcana, who returned the expression and gestured to the ruler's headdress. "That looks heavy, your Imperial Grace."

Empress Hisha'maniketh blinked, her stately progress arrested while those around her gasped. The guards tightened their white-knuckled grips on their spears but the Empress laughed, a deep, rolling sound of genuine amusement.

"From the moment my women found you wandering the desert, you have intrigued me, Arcana." The Empress waved a jewelled hand and her entourage rose to their feet in a whisper of beads and feathers. "Now you amuse me. How novel."

Arcana inclined her head the slightest fraction. "I live to serve, your Imperial Grace."

"Hah!" The Empress jerked her chin, setting a plethora of beads clacking together. A final group of guards stepped from the trees, two familiar women among them.

"Mirran." Arcana smiled at the wise woman, now with a string of amber and black beads plaited into her downy mane over her left temple. "My congratulations on your promotion."

Mirran inclined her head but said nothing as Beera shoved her way to the Empress' side. Her face was dark with fury and she jabbed a finger at Arcana with enough force to set the many beaded necklaces around her neck clattering wildly. "You dare speak to my Empress with such casual abandon? I will see the flesh flayed from your bones!"

"Beera, wisest of my women." Empress Hisha laid an indulgent hand on her companion's arm. "Be at peace. She doesn't yet understand our ways."

"As evidenced by the insult of an unbound male in your presence," Beera hissed, her eyes glittering with malice as she swept a look over Fenris, silent and proud by Arcana's side. "Carrying a weapon, no less. Such an insult is punishable by death."

"Oh?" Arcana tilted her head to one side. "Perhaps you should consider the impact of insulting me by having chained men in *my* presence, wise woman."

Beera spluttered outrageously but the Empress merely laughed again, the musical sound at complete odds with everything else about her. "Well met, my unusual friend."

Arcana raised an eyebrow. "I wasn't aware we were close, your Imperial Grace, having only met once before."

"I own the world. People are my friend if I say they are my friend." The Empress waved a hand at their surroundings. "Did you do all of this?"

"I did, your Imperial Grace."

The Empress shook her head, the tiniest of smiles tugging the corner of her lips. "I must admit, I am impressed. It's not often I underestimate someone the way I have underestimated you. Tell me, Arcana, will you be after my empire next?"

"No, your Imperial Grace." Arcana spread her hands in a gesture of peace. "I wish only to live life on my own terms."

"Is that so?" Empress Hisha examined her perfectly manicured nails, the jewels on her many rings flickering in the light. "And if I refuse to agree with those terms?"

"Then we have a problem," Arcana murmured, "which I'll be forced to solve."

"Careful now, my newest sister." The Empress raised a single, warning finger. "In your own holdings, you are the mistress and make the rules. Coupled with the understanding that you are still unfamiliar with our customs, I shall allow the many insults you've cast to stand - but my indulgence will not last forever."

Arcana inclined her head ever so slightly. "In that, we are in agreement."

"Your Imperial Grace," Beera breathed, her face a mixture of astonishment and apoplexy. "This is sacrilege."

"The Goddess works in mysterious ways, Beera." Empress Hisha turned a benevolent smile on her wise woman. "Trust me, won't you?"

"Always, my Empress." Beera bowed until her nose was level with her knees, but the stiff tension in her shoulders gave lie to the deference.

"As I was saying," the Empress said cheerfully, "you may make your own rules in your own holding, but in the greater community you will be expected to follow our laws - particularly when visiting the Palace."

"You make it sound as if that will be often," Arcana said.

"Of course! We are friends, are we not?" The Empress' smile was full of teeth. "Besides, the Goddess has requested to meet you at your earliest convenience. An honour I'm certain you'd not decline."

Arcana exchanged a glance with Fenris and nodded. "It would be our pleasure, your Imperial Grace."

"Excellent! I'll send a messenger with the details." The Empress clapped her hands together twice, and her two identical male slaves stepped forward. They deposited their ornate chest at the Empress' feet, bowed so low their faces brushed the sand, and retreated without so much as a squeak. "In accordance with the laws of Hiraptha, this chest contains welcoming gifts from the kingdom. The amount of water you've claimed

accords you a great deal of power - enough to put you in the upper eche-
lons of my nobility. With that in mind, you are granted free access to any
and all parts of the city, save my private chambers. You have also earnt the
ability to contract a personal wise woman. For the time being, I will gift
you Mirran, as she is yet to secure a contract for herself. I will cover her
fees for a week as is custom, and after that, should you choose to keep her,
you must negotiate the continuing sum yourself... in addition to what you
already owe, of course."

Arcana blinked, her surprise only mitigated by the open shock she saw
on Mirran's face. "I'm sure that's not -"

"I insist." The Empress' voice was silk over steel. "It would be unwise
to spurn such gifts."

"Of course, your Imperial Grace." Arcana inclined her head. "I meant
no offence; only that I had no wish to put the wise woman out."

"It is her duty to serve where I will it." Empress Hisha turned slightly,
not looking at Mirran so much as acknowledging the other's existence.
"Isn't that right, newest of my wise women?"

"Yes, most gracious one." Mirran curtseyed so low her legs wobbled,
her pulse beating a rapid tattoo in her throat. "Is the honour to serve as
Empress wishes."

"Indeed. Perhaps, as you advise Arcana, she can improve your
working knowledge of the Goddess' sacred tongue," the Empress mused,
her face creasing with indulgent amusement.

Mirran squeaked and bobbed a second curtsey, colour flagging her
cheeks. Irritated by the way the Empress' smile widened, Arcana took a
half step forward and offered the wise woman a short, sharp bow. "The
honour is mine. Mirran's advice during my convalescence was
impeccable."

"Oh?" Empress Hisha's smile faded like mist in the sun. "I look
forward to hearing how well she does this time around, then."

Arcana held out a hand and Mirran, her face pale, shuffled forward to
take it. "Welcome aboard."

"Thank you, mistress."

"Arcana."

Mirran nodded but remained silent, casting a cursory glance in Fenris'
direction before taking up a place on Arcana's other side. The Empress
watched every movement with the sharp eyes of a predator, her talons
flexing in the soft sand. When the silence drew out to uncomfortable
lengths without breaking, she turned her attention to the oasis, her movements marked by the soft clatter of beads. "Where are your males?"

"Resting," Arcana replied. "We have worked hard these last few days."

"I have no doubt." The Empress made her way to the oasis pool, stopping just short of the gently lapping water. "I would see them."

"No."

Gasps went up through the entourage, the harpies not needing to understand the words to know Fenris' flat reply had been a refusal. Beera hissed, long and low, pointing a trembling finger at the Guardian. "You will not speak."

"Why not?" Fenris turned his face in her direction, though Arcana knew without doubt he still watched the Empress, whose lips were creased in the softest of smiles. "I have followed your customs without protest these last weeks, while you cared for Arcana - as was the bargain made with the wise woman who found us at this very spot. Now that Arcana is well, that bargain no longer stands."

"Bargain?" Beera squawked, her feathers spreading in echo of her fury. "*Bargain*? Those are our laws!"

"Not my laws," Fenris returned equably.

"Empress," Beera growled, her body stiff with tension. "This insult to your honour cannot stand."

Empress Hisha remained silent, her eyes on the oasis pool. After almost a minute, she raised one hand as though to signal for silence - and Fenris snatched an arrow out of the air directly in front of his face. Arcana's heart lurched in her chest as he moved again, snatching a second arrow from the space in front of his chest. Without changing expression or making a sound, the Guardian drew back his arm and threw... and the air split on a pained squawk.

"See, wisest of my women?" Empress Hisha said, her smile still firmly in place. "Violence is not always the answer."

Arcana swallowed her laugh at the hypocrisy of that statement; Beera bowed her head. "He cannot always be watching, your Imperial Grace."

"I highly doubt that."

"His very breath is an insult to your person."

The Empress blinked, a slow lowering of lashes. "You were the one who suggested I should claim him for my own bed, his mistress be damned, did you not?"

"Of course, but that was before he began to -" Beera cut off, her face paling as Fenris lifted the greatsword from where it had rested point down in the sand.

"You sought to break our bargain?" His voice was deadly velvet, raising goosebumps on Arcana's arms. Muscles bunched under dusty teal

skin as Fenris shifted his stance in such a way that all six of the Empress'
guards brandished their spears.

"You are male." Beera swallowed, her reply wavering with uncertainty.
"There was never a bargain; only the will of Hiraptha."

"*I* am the will of Hiraptha," Empress Hisha said quietly, still not
turning from her gentle examination of the clear oasis pool. "You would
do well to remember it."

"I -" Beera stopped, then dropped to her knees and pressed her forehead into the sand. "I beg your forgiveness, your Imperial Grace. I sought
only to protect."

"*I* am the Empress," the Empress continued, turning at last to fix a
steely gaze on her subject. "*I* am the Protector of all Hiraptha."

"Yes, your Imperial Grace. Always, your Imperial Grace."

Empress Hisha tilted her head to one side, lips pursed as she took in
Beera's shaking form. After a long moment, she turned to Fenris. "I kept
your bargain, male, did I not?"

"Fenris," Arcana said quietly. "His name is Fenris."

"Fenris." The Empress tested the word, rolled it over her tongue like a
fine wine. "You may kill my wise woman, if you like, for her
indiscretions."

Beera whimpered; the oasis remained silent and still. After a long
moment, Fenris said, "I will not spill blood indiscriminately in the place
which has become our home."

Empress Hisha smiled again, and for the first time, it held a hint of
warmth. "Do you hear that, wisest of my women? Mercy - from a male."

Beera said nothing but her cheek and necks darkened, hands clenching
into fists in an ill-fated attempt to hide her bone-deep fury. Empress Hisha
deigned not to notice, chuckling to herself for a few moments before snapping her fingers at the men kneeling on the sand. They rose in unison to
flank her, followed swiftly by the guards. After inclining her head in
elegant farewell, the Empress of Hiraptha turned and walked away.

"Are they going to leave Beera here?" Arcana muttered.

Fenris' muscles rippled as he shrugged. "Perhaps she intends you to
decide."

"Ugh," Arcana wrinkled her nose as she watched the Empress' proces-
sion beat a stately retreat. "I hope not."

Half-way down the tunnel, Empress Hisha paused and looked back.
With a broad wink at Arcana, she called, "Come along, wisest of my
women. There'll be time for grovelling later, after I soak my talons."

"Yes, your Imperial Grace." Beera shot upright with an undignified flap of her wings and chased after her Empress as though she might catch fire.

Arcana waited until the entire group was back out in the desert, then closed her eyes and called her magic to dismantle the spell, ignoring the sharp wave of pain which came with the sudden spurt of power - not much, but enough to shatter the holding pattern and send the jungle slapping back into place.

When she opened her eyes, the sandy floor of the oasis bit into her knees and her fingers were tight around Fenris' forearm. He was down beside her, his free hand gripping her shoulder in quiet support. The glamour whispered warm and velvety across her skin as their eyes met, his face creased in concern. "How bad?"

"I'll live." The words were raw, as though she'd been screaming. "Did I -"

"No," he murmured, dark teal curls whispering over his forehead as he shook his head. "But I can smell your pain."

In complete contrast to the churning nausea in her gut, Arcana's smile was bright and wide. "You can?"

"Of course I -" Fenris cut off, looking stunned. "I can smell your pain. My senses are starting to return."

"The glamour is stronger, too. Nowhere near full," she added, seeing the question in his face, "but gaining."

Long lashes drifted shut for a fraction of a moment. "It would have been better to stay dead."

"It was never dead," Arcana replied, forcing herself to loosen her white-knuckled grip on his arm. "Just resting."

"It is a curse."

"It's part of you, and I like it." When his face softened - so subtly that she'd have missed it if she wasn't so finely tuned to Fenris' expressions after so many months together - Arcana knew she'd won the round. "We'll get through this."

"I hope so." Fenris helped her upright, hauling her against his chest when her legs immediately buckled. "Caelum!"

"You rang?" The deerken's head poked around the curve of the harpies' tree, his cheeky grin fading as Fenris swung Arcana into his arms. "Oh. Don't worry, she's just tired."

"Rest, then," Fenris declared. He looked up, taking in the few male harpies who'd dared to peek out of the tree. "The Empress is gone, the oasis is safe - we all deserve some time to recuperate."

One of the males spoke; Arcana identified Arax's husky tone. She tried to translate but her brain refused to co-operate, her eyelids drifting closed. She heard Caelum's quiet answer, his voice fading into the background as Fenris walked them into their hollowed out tree.

"What -"

"Hush," her Guardian murmured, settling her into the sand and curling his lean body protectively around hers. "Later."

"No. Now."

Laughter vibrated through his frame. "Arax wanted to know where Mirran's intending to sleep. Caelum was promising him you'd grow more trees into houses when we left."

"Oh." She tried to open her eyes and struggle upright, but his warm hand on her breastbone held her down. "I can do it."

"No, you can't," Fenris murmured, his lips soft on her cheek. "The last few days have been overwhelming and you're exhausted."

"The Empress won't leave us alone," she said, making no protest when he tangled his legs with hers. "Beera wants our blood."

"Instinct tells me the Empress will reserve her final judgement until we meet her Goddess."

Arcana considered that, replaying the invitation over in her mind. "Do you think she's real?"

"She'll be real in some representation or other - but as for a living, thinking deity?" His deep velvet voice was thick with skepticism. "I don't see how."

"I suppose we'll find out soon enough."

"Not," Fenris returned dryly, "If you don't recover your strength."

"Bully."

"Someone has to be, the way you insist on pushing yourself." One of his strong hands stroked hair off her face, his next words little more than a rumble of midnight feathers. "We need you to be strong, Arcana. Those arrows today were a statement, a test - it will not be the first one."

"Fine." Arcana relaxed into his embrace, her cheek pressed against his scarred chest. "What happened to the second arrow?"

"I still have it. We'll examine it… after your nap."

"Stay with me?"

"Always."

Smiling into the safe space between them, Arcana set the uncertain future aside and let the steady thump of his heart carry her into sleep.

TWENTY-FIVE
FLARE

Chancellor Kaiora's quarters were well protected behind several doors, six of her personal guard and, last but not least, a woman with the lower half of a spider whose entire body was covered in bright purple fur and whose mouth seemed drawn into a permanent pout.

"No," she said, stormy grey eyes focussed determinedly on the console in front of her, "I will not allow you in unannounced. The Chancellor is very busy, and there are currently no gaps in her appointment schedule. Come back next week."

Flare exchanged a look with Zaire. "Does the Chancellor normally have a full appointment book after dinner?"

The woman's willowy arms fluttered for a moment and at long last she looked up from her console. "I beg your pardon?"

"It's night-time," Flare said, reaching out to tap the timepiece on a desk piled so high with hardcopy files it was lucky to be still standing. "Does she normally take business meetings with her nightcap?"

"Oh." A frown, her eyes following the line of Flare's arm up his shoulder and, finally, to his face. The fur on her cheeks ruffled in an unseen breeze, her many legs clicking rapidly against the floor in an astonishing display of what was either a rare form of arachnid tap dancing, or nerves. Deciding on the latter, Flare offered her a megawatt grin with a mild bedroom edge. The poor female's facial fur stood straight up on end, causing her to cover both cheeks with her hands. "*Oh.*"

"Are you all right, Miss…?" Flare leant forward, allowing his smile to fade into an expression of concern. The fur on her arm was soft and slinky, each hair straining towards his light touch. "May I get you a glass of water?"

"Naavah," she said faintly, her eyes glued to his fingers. "Yes, I think - no!" Snatching her arm back as though burned, Naavah took a deep, shuddering breath. "Why are you here?"

Flare spread his hands in a gesture of peace, his smile lopsided. "I know what was used to poison the Ambassadors and their attendants. I think the Chancellor, whatever she's doing, would like to know too."

Smoothing down the fur where his fingers had been, Naavah bent to examine something on her console, her pout sharpening into a moue. Wondering what, exactly, the other woman saw, Flare waited with outward patience while Naavah snatched several files seemingly at random, turned in place with a clattering of her many, claw-tipped legs, and shot away in a confusion of purple fur and cream fabric.

"She won't let us in," Zaire breathed, his lips against Flare's ear.

"Yes, she will." Flare lounged against Naavah's desk, but didn't attempt to circumnavigate it. "Wait and see."

The arachnid returned on the heels of his statement, devoid of her files. "This way."

The corridor was short, the door at the end unassuming. Naavah rapped twice and it slid open to reveal Chancellor Kaiora wrapped in a fluffy pink robe, her striking amber hair tumbling around her shoulders in loose waves and the soft grey skin of her face covered in black mud.

"Thank you, Naavah," she said, clasping her fingers in front of her with considerable dignity. "Gentlemen?"

Swallowing his laughter, Flare accorded the Chancellor a bow and crossed the threshold, Zaire hard on his heels. His host exchanged quick words with the spider by the door and then, that quickly, the three of them were alone.

"I apologise profusely for intruding upon your personal time, Chancellor," Flare said, turning to offer his most blinding smile.

"Save it, sorcerer," Kaiora grunted, all four of her golden eyes narrowing. "I've got less than ten minutes before this mud mask needs to be washed off - talk."

Zaire fished the plastic bag containing the herb sample out of his leathers and passed it to the Chancellor. "This is the poison."

"That?" Kaiora's nose crinkled, causing the drying mud on her face to crack. "Are you sure?"

"I have a Class Two nature sorcerer on staff," Flare said quietly, moving to the Chancellor's sideboard and lifting a carafe. Popping the crystal stopper free, he sniffed. "Brandy?"

She inclined her head. "Apple."

Setting out three glasses and pouring two fingers' worth of apple brandy into each, Flare jerked his chin at the files Naavah had left on the Chancellor's coffee table. "Are they the victims' records?"

"Yes." Kaiora accepted her brandy without looking away from the unassuming sample in her other hand. "I cannot, for the life of me, find a connection between them."

"May I look?" Zaire asked, accepting his own glass of brandy. His face was blank as Flare clinked their glasses together, but the Ryllin neverthe-less sipped afterwards. "I might see something you missed."

Chancellor Kaiora lifted her gaze at last, her brow furrowed as she glanced between the two of them. When a discreet chime echoed through the living room, she sighed. "That's my timer. Naavah!"

"Chancellor?" The door slid open to admit the arachnid at once.

"I'm going to shower. Keep my two guests company whilst they look through the files, won't you?"

Naavah inclined her head. "Yes, Chancellor."

Kaiora slugged her brandy back in one go and set the empty glass on the sideboard, along with the herb sample. "I'll be out in fifteen minutes; that's how long you have to look."

"Of course." Flare flourished a bow, watching from the corners of his eyes as the Chancellor turned away to hide her twitching lips. "Enjoy your well-earned break."

"I'd enjoy it better if I was alone," Kaiora muttered, and disappeared through a door on the opposite wall.

When Flare straightened, it was to see Zaire already seated on a chaise, the pile of files in his lap. He began flicking through them with astonishing speed, cobalt sparks flickering in the depths of his indigo eyes. Flare picked up the rogue's discarded brandy and poured it into his own glass, sipping while Naavah watched. When he caught her eye, the fur on her face rippled as though in a breeze and she dropped her gaze. "My apolo-gies, Ambassador. It is rude to stare."

"Don't worry - I'm used to it." Flare waved the words away and offered a disarming smile. "What are your people called?"

She startled, her many legs clicking on the tiled entryway. "My people? We have no real name, but… the official Alliance records list us as the Arachnaida. It is as good a name as any."

"I take it there's not many of you around," Flare said, bracing his body in a relaxed position against the sideboard.

"No." Naavah hesitated, her stormy grey eyes drinking in his deliberately non-threatening posture, and then confessed in a whisper, "As far as we know, I am the only one."

Flare's fingers clenched tight around his glass and he set it down lest he break it by accident. "I'm sorry. I know what it's like to be alone."

Purple fur rippled as she frowned. "You? Alone?"

"Don't believe me?" He smiled, a sharp, dark smile that didn't belong in the presence of one as obviously skittish as this female. Softening the impact with a shrug, Flare turned his gaze to Zaire, well aware the rogue was listening even if his attention seemed elsewhere. "Camouflage comes in many forms."

Naavah fell silent, dropping her eyes to her hands - which were clenched to fists. "Yes."

"With that in mind, perhaps - do you smell smoke?" Flare shoved off the sideboard, following his nose down the hall to a closed door. He palmed it open to reveal a large bedroom, the bed a canopied four poster which Kaiora's four-foot body would be well and truly lost in.

"There," Zaire said from beside him, pointing at a door in the east wall. Smoke curled out from beneath in thick, lazy tendrils.

Flare slapped his hand over the palm controls - no response. "Naavah, override the door."

"I cannot," Naavah appeared in the doorway behind them, frowning at the datapad in her hand. "It's malfunctioning."

"I can -" Zaire began.

"No time." Bunching his robes in his fists, Flare flowed through a series of well-practiced movements and kicked the door with a foot that burst into flame as it connected. The fire itself wasn't necessary so much as the magic behind it; magic that tripled the force of his natural kick.

The door shuddered and bent, creating a gap where it joined the wall. Zaire wrapped his hands around the lip, grunting with effort as he yanked it open in a display of impossible strength. Smoke poured out in earnest, followed quickly by crackling flames tinged with the faintest hint of green. Flare yanked the Ryllin close, turning his back to the fireball which shot out of the newly opened doorway. Flames crawled over his back and legs but Zaire was protected, stumbling back against the bed as the enormous wave of heat struck with an almost physical force.

"Are you all right?" Flare asked, extinguishing his clothing with a snap of his fingers. As soon as Zaire nodded, he turned and dove into the inferno.

Someone screamed behind him - Naavah, judging by the higher pitch - but Flare had no time to comfort her. Instinct told him the Chancellor was in here somewhere and if she still lived, every second would be vital. Fire licked at his robes all over again, crawling over his skin and into his hair, but Flare was fireproof, felt nothing but a mild warmth. He tasted the smoke and detected the taint of chemicals, the source of which no doubt gave the flames their faintly green tinge. Squinting into the billowing shadows, he navigated the bathroom mostly by feel until a slumped shadow in the shower cubicle caught his attention. Identifying Chancellor Kaiora behind the superheated glass, he rushed forward, weaving his fingers and chanting under his breath. His flame shield shimmered into existence between the shower and the rest of the room, holding the flames at bay as he pulled the shower door open. A quick check revealed Kaiora's pulse to be faint but steady. Hauling the tiny woman into his arms, Flare went to shield her face in his robes only to realise they hung in melted strips from his skin.

Melted? Flare considered the green tint to the flames again and frowned. While it was common for his clothing to be burnt off in an all-consuming blaze, having fabric melt was so far from the realms of normality that it rang instant alarm bells. Tugging the washcloth from the dormant showerhead, he threw it over his shield and into the blaze. It melted into a puddle of unnatural slag on the floor, and seconds later dissolved entirely.

No natural fire behaves like that.

Cradling Kaiora in one arm, Flare shucked the sticky remains of his robes and kicked them into the far corner of the shower. If he couldn't take the Chancellor through the flames, that left no other option than to plumb the depths of his power and remove the threat entirely.

Lesce is going to kill me for this. He set his feet and began a new chant, his free hand tracing shimmering runes in the air. Power hummed in the confined space, Flare's flame shield flickering in silent warning as he diverted energy from one task to another. Trusting the meagre barrier of the shower door to keep them safe, he deactivated the shield entirely and clenched his hand around the shimmering orange runes. The spell activated with a muffled clap, and Flare ceased his chant to inhale as deeply as his lungs allowed. Sparks flickered at the edge of his vision but the flames in the room began to waver and shrink, their power pouring in through his clenched fist and punching directly into his veins. A gap opened in front of him; Flare opened the shower door and stepped into it. The clear space widened as he walked, one hand clenched in a white knuckled grip around the Chancellor, the other beginning to glow with an orange light. Every slow inch forward saw the fire abate further, until by the time he returned to the living quarters, not so much as a whiff of smoke remained.

"Take her," Flare managed, shoving Kaiora into Naavah's waiting arms. His throat ached, his voice squeaky with tension and as Zaire stood, he thrust out a warning arm. "Don't touch me. I need to siphon it off."

"The fire -" Naavah began, leaping back as Flare raced past her. "Where are you going? The flames are gone!"

Flare sprinted to the kitchen, pulled open the large, man-sized freezer, and began yanking drawers out with reckless abandon. Power continued to build inside him in a furious frenzy and he knew he was going too slow, his single hand too shaky to get a good grip, his muscles stiff with tension.

"Move." Zaire shouldered him aside and completed the task in less than a minute. Flare climbed inside the freezer as soon as it was empty, hunching his shoulders and tucking up his knees to make sure he fit.

Looking into Zaire's indigo gaze, his own vision compromised by flickering flames, he said, "Shut and barricade the door. Don't open it until I say so, no matter what you hear."

The door shut with a slam.

Flare unclenched his hand, setting free the overload of power his body was struggling to contain. It poured out of him in a roar, fire and furious force, slamming against the sides of the insulated freezer and instantly melting what little ice clung to the inner walls. The water evaporated before it had a chance to drip or trickle, filling the air with an instant's steam before that, too, was scalded to nothing. The discharge was simultaneously instant and infinite, tearing Flare into a thousand shining, faceted pieces before shoving him back together with painful finality.

He slumped against the interior of the now pitch-dark box, ignoring the way his skin hissed as it contacted the superheated metal. After a moment's scattered thought, he rested his head against the door. "Zaire."

The freezer was wrenched open and Flare tumbled unceremoniously onto the floor. He groaned as he hit the tiles, pressing his skin against the cool surface. Fingers touched his shoulder, drew back with a hiss. "Oracle's voice!"

"Don't touch," he muttered. "I'm hot."

"Bit late for that," Zaire grunted, hunkering down beside him. "You all right?"

"I'll be fine. Kaiora?"

"Naavah's begun first aid, but she also sent an alert to the medical team." Zaire's leather armour creaked and Flare imagined him shrugging. "I called for your Sorcen healer, too."

"Smart." Flare coughed, the motion reminding his body it wasn't nearly recovered enough for the sort of strain he'd just put it under. "The fire was chemical in nature. Whatever accelerant was used made the flames acidic - Kaiora was meant to die a quick death, her body disappearing without a trace."

"Lucky you were there to do… whatever it is that you did." A glass of water clinked onto the tiles in front of him. "You sound like hell, though."

Flare stared at the glass of water for a long minute before he dredged up the strength to raise his head and take a sip. "If you swallowed an entire fire, you'd sound like shit, too."

"You *swallowed* it?" Zaire's indigo eyes raked him from end to end. "I don't understand."

"It's tricky to explain." Finishing the glass of water, Flare shoved up to a sitting position and recalled he was naked, bar for the black streaks of soot that marred his bronze skin. "Huh. Awkward."

"I've seen it already."

It was true and in any case, Flare supposed, nudity was the least of his concerns. Running a hand over his face, he said, "Sorcerers who can put out fire don't slap it down; they drink it into themselves. The secret isn't power level but the ability to cope with overwhelming amounts of energy - so no, before you ask, it's not a common ability."

"Your off-the-chart capability to withstand magic," Zaire guessed. "That's how you manage it."

"Yes, and I'll thank you to keep that to yourself, if you don't mind." Flare glared until his companion nodded. "The spell keeps the extra energy contained but the bigger the fire I extinguish, the harder it is to hold. If I don't expel the power within a certain time frame, it finds its own way out."

Zaire looked over Flare's head to the ruined freezer. "Explosively."

"Yeah." Flare coughed again, his breath tinged with smoke. "If the fire ingested is larger than the sorcerer's scope of power… things don't end well."

"You sound as though you speak from experience."

Memories surged; melted limbs and missing faces. Flare squashed them back into the box from whence they came and rolled to his knees.

"I've never had to worry, I'm fireproof. It's everyone else who'd have disintegrated when I went off like a bomb."

"Hence the freezer."

"Yeah. Hence the freezer."

Pounding boots cut off any reply Zaire might have made and moments later, the Chancellor's quarters were full of medical and security staff. After undergoing the mandatory checks and attaining a clean bill of health - and a pair of cargo pants he donned with a grimace - Flare was allowed into the Chancellor's study, whose futon had been temporarily converted to a sickbed while the forensics team overhauled Kaiora's bedroom and what remained of her ensuite.

"Chancellor." Flare inclined his head, meeting all four of her golden eyes in turn. "You wanted to see me?"

Kaiora lay propped against several cushions, her face streaked with grime and her amber hair matted and singed. Her gaze roved over his naked chest, stopped at the waistband of his pants. "Stars abound, you have actual legs."

"Of course I do." He glanced down at the pants and shook one of the legs in question. "I don't understand the fascination with this sort of clothing, but I can wear it if I have to - and the doctors wouldn't let me in here naked."

"No, I'd imagine not." The Chancellor's lips twitched for a fraction of a second before she sobered. "I owe you my life, Ambassador."

"Flare."

"Flare." All four of her eyes closed. "It appears station security is compromised. I'm calling an emergency meeting of the Galactic Council first thing tomorrow morning, where I intend to induct you as my new security chief."

"First thing tomorrow morning?" Flare looked up at the doctors, turning invariably to Mendin. "Will she be well enough?"

"If she attends in the mobility chair," Mendin allowed, "it might be possible. The Chancellor inhaled a lot of smoke."

"Hmm." Flare looked back at Kaiora. "You really should rest a little longer."

"We can't afford to wait," the Chancellor insisted. "Four people are dead."

Zaire cleared his throat. "I thought it was only three."

"Another Ambassador passed barely an hour ago," one of the doctors said. "He had a compromised immune system from a pre-existing condition, and we weren't able to combat the damage done by the poison fast enough."

"See?" Kaiora grabbed Flare's wrist, hissed at the heat in his skin and let go. Though her body was weak from the recent ordeal, her face was fierce. "We cannot afford to wait."

"Say I agree." Flare dropped into a crouch beside the futon so they were at eye level. "Why me? I've been here little more than a week."

"And in that week you've rattled the Council, created chaos at the ball, seduced half the space station, taken on a major assignment, bolstered our martial forces by almost a quarter, evaded death twice that I'm aware of, had sex in the library - which, by the way, has the librarians in an absolute tizz - arranged for the damage said sex caused to be repaired, garnered the silent but solid support of at least five star systems purely because they saw your name on the Ambassadorial list, unearthed a mysterious poison and saved me from the jaws of a flesh-eating fire without sustaining any apparent damage." The Councillor drew in a wheezing breath, a trembling hand pressed to her chest. "Have I missed anything?"

"I also pissed off my younger sister on at least two occasions, and am currently wearing pants for the first time in twenty-four years."

Chancellor Kaiora barked a sharp laugh. "I forget your true age. You act so young."

"My people live for an average of three centuries," Flare returned. "Seventy-five is still considered whippersnapper material."

"Indeed." Golden amusement turned serious. "So? Will you take on the role?"

"How do you know you can trust me? I just blew up inside your freezer."

"You just -" the Chancellor blinked, two eyes at a time, then shook her head. "You're trying to charm me away from my point, Ambassador, and it's not working. Although I wish you'd cover your chest."

Flare looked down at said chest, his bronze skin streaked with soot and dusted with crisp orange hairs. He was still a little thin but muscles rippled beneath the surface, each clearly delineated, all the way down to where the cursedly-uncomfortable cargo pants rode dangerously low on his narrow hips. Spreading his fingers over his sternum in a deliberately provocative movement, Flare looked up from beneath his lashes. "What's wrong with my chest?"

"It's a weapon." Shivering from the effect of his bedroom voice, Kaiora jabbed a shaking finger in his direction. "Stop. Avoiding. My. Question."

"If I do this, I want full access to Alliance resources and full authority to make decisions, answering to nobody save yourself." Flare sat back on his heels, head tilted to one side. "I'll also need full control of the military arm of the Alliance… and for you to call me Flare on a permanent basis."

Chancellor Kaiora pursed her lips, her lower eyes narrowing as she stared into his face. Flare didn't need to wonder what she saw; he wore a laughingly arrogant expression, his carnelian eyes glittering with just the right amount of challenge. After a long minute, Kaiora held out a hand. "Naavah."

"Yes, Chancellor." The arachnid handed over a slim datapad and a thin hardcopy file.

Kaiora tapped at the datapad for some moments, a furrow of concentration between her brows. When she lowered it face down on her blanket-covered chest, her expression was guarded. "It's done - with one caveat."

"Oh?"

"You betray the Alliance, and Naavah will eat you." A four-eyed blink. "Literally."

Flare's laughter was full-bellied and real. "Oh, Chancellor - I have no desire to impeach you. Trust me, in charge is not a place I like to be. I'm here for the good of Sorcen."

"The good of Sorcen?" Kaiora quirked a brow. "There's more to it than that, Ambassador."

"Flare, remember? You promised."

"Only if you call me Kaiora."

He inclined his head, amusement still curving his lips. "All right, Kaiora, I'll come clean at least this much - my ulterior motives are personal and I swear upon my life, not in contradiction to the Alliance's wellbeing. In fact, fulfilling my personal quest will be to the benefit of everyone."

"I see." Kaiora's eyes dropped, caressing the line of his arm and halting where the fire-orange runes of his loyalty oath to Arcana were clearly visible. The design was glowing with an overflow of power after his explosion in the fridge, a soft pulsation that kept time with Flare's heartbeat. "Odd that I believe you."

"Does this mean Naavah's not making me into breakfast after all?" A deliberately disarming smile. "I'm disappointed."

"I highly doubt that," Kaiora replied. "Now get out of my sight, before I lick that ridiculous chest of yours from top to bottom."

Shocked silence fell, in which Flare allowed his smile to widen. "It would be my pleasure to fulfil your request, Kaiora."

"I don't know why I said that," the Chancellor muttered, both hands over her face. "I really don't."

Flare stood and gave Mendin a hard look. "Allow her to schedule the Council meeting, but keep me updated on her condition. If she's not up to it, we reschedule."

"Yes, Fire Elder."

"Naavah - stay by Kaiora's side until I can arrange a guard roster," Flare added, turning to the female hovering by the end of the bed. "Kill anyone who breathes wrong."

Fur rippled over Naavah's torso in a long wave. "Yes, Ambassador - or do I say Security Chief now?"

"Flare!" He waved his hands helplessly overhead. "I'm nobody special. Just Flare."

Zaire snorted a laugh. "And I'm the fairy godmother of cotton candy."

"Fuck you," Flare growled.

"Here?" Zaire cut the medical team a considering glance. "People are looking."

Twisting his neck until it cracked, Flare stood toe to toe with the silver scrolled rogue and lowered his voice to the midnight register. "That's never bothered me in the slightest."

Zaire's indigo eyes flashed and he stormed from the room - but not before Flare caught the sensual shiver which shimmied through his lithe frame. With the rogue gone, Flare was left with the Chancellor's narrowed gaze fixed firmly on his face. He smiled at thirty percent power with a hint of wicked and gave her the flourishing bow he'd shamelessly stolen from Fenris.

"Charming," Kaiora murmured, handing him the thin file she'd been tapping her fingertips against. "And dangerous."

"Rest well, Kaiora." Flare tossed her a quick salute, tucked the file under his arm and strode out.

He received several odd - and lingering - looks on the way back to his quarters, but kept his head down and walk purposeful. By the time he stashed the file for later, showered the soot away and found a fresh set of robes, the tension clawing at his gut had soothed somewhat. When Flare finished applying his smoky makeup and swept into his tiny living area to find Zaire leaning against the bench wearing a pair of tight blue leggings, black combat boots and nothing else, he'd reclaimed his former equilibrium enough to raise an eyebrow in question.

"Would you have done it?" Zaire asked, crossing blue-tinted arms over his slender chest.

"Done what?"

"Slept with the Chancellor."

Flare blinked. "Are you serious?"

"Curious."

"The answer is no."

"Huh." The rogue sucked on his teeth a moment. "We're not exclusive, though."

"I know." Flare strode to the other man and, ignoring the crossed arms pressing into his sternum, dropped a hot, wet kiss on Zaire's shoulder. "I wouldn't have done it because I didn't want to do it."

"Not even for the good of your people?" Skepticism in his voice, cool distance in his body. "What if it had been the price for the access we know full well will help you find your sister?"

"Some prices are too steep to pay," Flare answered, frowning when his voice was more ragged than he intended.

"Explain."

Looking up from beneath his lashes, Flare caught the teeth-gritting vulnerability in Zaire's expression and sighed, letting loose the leash he kept on the truth. "I was a soldier before I was an adult. For those of us with more destructive magical abilities, it's often the only way to keep ourselves and the ones we care about safe. For whatever the reason, I was blessed - cursed - with the ability to read body language like you read books. I shot through my basic, intermediate and advanced training in record time, quickly became an unparalleled warrior both physically and magically. I'd killed more people than I'd had birthdays within two months of entering the army."

"I didn't realise your planet had so many wars."

"There are always bad people," Flare replied, "and for the most part that's all it was - but there were a couple wars, yes. Neighbouring planets seeking aid, internal rebellion, that sort of thing. Every time I killed, every moment I used my ability to read body language to get under someone's guard, I…"

"You lost a piece of yourself." Zaire shifted, his arms uncrossing to slide around Flare's waist. "I understand."

Given the political climate the Ryllin had been born into, Flare knew the sentiment was legitimate. "I began to search for a light to battle the dark. It didn't take long to realise that whilst violence turns inward, love reaches outwards - and with all I knew about my own body, it didn't take long to make it work to my advantage. No strings, no relationships, just a mutual sharing to take the rough edges off that deep blackness inside me."

"What changed?"

"I realised, over the years, that whenever there was a political guest around, I'd be invited to sit next to them at the formal banquet. Not unusual, given my rank." Flare's smile was sour and full of teeth. "We'd invariably end up in bed, they'd leave with a smile - and the difficult trade agreement was smoothed out, or Sorcen had a new ally, or that territory across the ocean decided against their uprising."

Muscle turned to steel beneath his hands as Zaire stiffened. "They were using you."

"Like their personal whore." Flare nodded. "I told myself it didn't matter, as long as all parties involved enjoyed themselves, but… it did. The thing I'd been saving for myself, the thing that was meant to spread light, was being subverted."

"You stopped?"

"No." He sighed, battled against the need to protect his heart, lost. "I was lonely. One sister was off gallivanting around the universe being broken in her own way and the other couldn't stand the sight of me, even then. So I kept going, living my hollow life and hating myself a little more each day, because I didn't know how to stop. Eventually - after Gravella betrayed what little trust I'd given her, after Arcana met Fenris and I saw in them an echo of what I'd never have - something broke, and I couldn't do it anymore. Even the thought of bedding someone made me want to vomit."

"You never fell in love, not even once?"

"I don't seem to have the capacity." Flare rubbed one hand over his heart and frowned. "There's only emptiness inside."

Instead of pushing and sniping and picking a fight, Zaire smoothed Flare's hair back from his face and bent until their foreheads touched. "I see you."

"There's nothing to see." Flare swallowed heavily. He hated this part; he'd always hated this part. "I can't give you what I don't have."

"I'm not asking for it." Zaire pressed a tender kiss to the corner of his mouth. "I'm not in much better emotional shape than you - we're each other's crutch, for now, but in a real relationship? We'd tear each other apart. This is what it is, and I won't ask you for exclusivity, or marriage, or whatever you're worried I'll ask for. I just want your company while we both try not to bust apart at the seams."

Flare considered that, remained quiescent while Zaire stroked a hand up and down his spine and pressed fluttering kisses along the seam of his lips. "Then why ask about Kaiora?"

"Because I could tell it was fake. You went out of your way to make her all hot and bothered, but it wasn't real." The rogue's fingers tightened. "*This*, whatever it is, is real."

"Yes." Flare sealed his lips to Zaire's and allowed his eyes to drift closed, taking solace in the cool strength of the other male's embrace. "Even if you hate me, this is real."

"I'll *always* hate you," Zaire whispered, and it was a dark, wicked promise that did interesting things to Flare's insides. "And you'll always hate me. Hot, kinky, dirty, sweaty hatred."

Flare groaned, his hands fisted in the Ryllin's hair and his body insistent against the other's abdomen. "Deal."

"I do have one more question."

Pulling back before he shredded both their clothes, Flare forced himself to take a deep, shuddering breath. "Sure. I've already told you everything I've never told anyone else."

"Will you explain your sexual orientation to me? I know it's a highly personal thing, but I'd like to understand."

"Oh." Flare furrowed his brow. "Well, I… I guess it's about the person. Everyone has something about them that's fascinating, something worth exploring. With each new sexual experience, I learnt to appreciate the different facets of gender, age, race, species - there's so many aspects to a single individual that you can't ever double up." He paused, shrugged. "I don't know how to explain it. I want to peel people open and see their secrets."

Zaire's lip curled. "So do serial killers."

"Eh." Flare shrugged again, but this time he smiled. "We've all got our issues. Now that you've stripped me completely bare, is there something you wanted with your partially naked visit?"

A searing look from indigo eyes. "I thought we'd go to Macadre, see if we can learn anything new - and before you ask *again*, my shirt was wet. It's in the drying unit."

"Ah." Pressing a final kiss to the hollow of Zaire's throat, Flare stepped back. "I also need to look through that file Kaiora gave me."

"This one?" Zaire picked it up off the desk, where he'd presumably dropped it after ferreting through the contents. "Just guidelines for your new position - not that you're likely to follow them."

"You know, in some cultures, it's rude to search someone's room."

The rogue gave a loud snort. "Shouldn't leave interesting things half hanging out of your sister's bag then, should you?"

"Whatever." Flare pursed his lips, not even bothering to pretend to be irritated. "Well then, if I'm not boning up on rules I'm likely to ignore, what are the chances you can create a secure holo connection? I need to make a couple of calls while we wait."

"Sure, because I have nothing better to do with my time than overhear your booty calls."

Flare narrowed his eyes and waved an admonitory finger. "Now now, no cracking jokes. I'm the funny member of this partnership."

Not bothering to dignify that declaration with a response, Zaire strode into Flare's bedroom, kicked off his boots and climbed onto the bed. After he'd rearranged the pillows against the headboard and reclined comfortably, he laid his hand against the console embedded in the wall and closed his eyes. The skin of his fingertips melted away, silver bones visible for only a second before they moulded into wires and plunged into the data port beneath Zaire's palm. Less than a minute later, dark lashes lifted to reveal indigo eyes sparking with cobalt lights. Lifting his free arm in welcome, Zaire said, "If you want to make the calls, you'll have to come over here."

It was a lie and they both knew it, but Flare climbed onto the bed beside his lover nonetheless, lining up their bodies and pillowing his head in the crook of Zaire's shoulder. After sliding his arm around Flare's ribs and under his robe to lie against his skin, the rogue hummed a single tone under his breath and the console screen popped off the wall, angling on its' flexible arm so they could both watch comfortably.

"You don't mind being in the call?" Flare asked. "Your lack of clothes is going to make our relationship pretty obvious."

"I think it's a little late to worry about that now."

"Suit yourself." Shrugging one shoulder, Flare reached for the screen and tapped the call sequence he hated most.

Lesce answered almost immediately. "About time."

"I love you, too, sis," Flare drawled, adopting the derisive tone he saved for Lesce alone. "No, really, don't say it back - I can feel the affection pouring out of you."

Plum eyes narrowed. "Who's that?"

"This is Zaire, Ambassador to Rylle and the reason this holo connection is secure."

"You're sleeping with him." Lesce's expression was less than impressed as she examined Zaire from the safety of her Tower office, the impressive black robes of the Healing Elder hanging elegantly from her frame.

"Do you have a problem with that?" Zaire asked, his tone frosty.

Flare hissed and jabbed his lover in the ribs. "That's my line."

"Too bad."

"She's my sister!"

"And I'll talk to her if I want."

"Shut up."

"Make me."

"Craddagh's Cauldron, Flare," Lesce interrupted, her face pained. "Of all the things you could've done, you went and got yourself a bicker-bonk?"

"A…" Flare repeated the word in his head, couldn't stop his grin. "A *bicker-bonk*?"

Zaire's chest vibrated underneath him, laughter echoing in the metallic undertones of his voice. "Does that make you the bicker-bonk*ee*, or the bicker-bonk*er*?"

"Maybe we're both the bicker-bonkers," Flare mused, watching as his sister's face began to turn purple. "Seeing as there's no real dominant in the partnership."

"Hmm… but I spend most of my time on -" Zaire cut off as Lesce screamed, loud and shrill and enraged.

"Enough!" She spluttered when the noise ceased. "Both of you, enough! I swear by all the seven gods, Flare, I will throttle you when I see you next!"

Flare snickered. "You can't even throw anything at me, because I'm here and you're there."

"What do you want?"

Switching to business mode, he gave his sister a concise run-down of all the goings on since his arrival on Alliance Station. Though her pulse throbbed in her temple, she listened in silence, nodding as he stopped to interject personal observations and assumptions. "I've got one other call to make after this, then Z and I are going to see what other information we can dig up."

"All right." A sharp nod, the black diamonds in her Healing Elder's circlet glittering in the light. "Excluding the fact that Flare demonstrated a top-secret ability that I thought he'd agreed to keep under wraps, do either of you believe this situation proves the Chancellor's innocence?"

"Hard to say," Zaire replied. "On one hand, we could assume so. On the other, it may have been a ploy to merely make her seem innocent."

Lesce's brow creased neatly, her expression studious. "That's a pretty big risk, if what Flare said about the fire's flesh eating capabilities is correct."

"I know. My gut says Kaiora had nothing to do with this attack, at the very least, but... we can't afford to let our guard down just yet." Flare grimaced. "I'm moving her down on the suspect list, but we need more information."

"My thoughts exactly." Another regal nod, his sister's eyes hard. "And what of Arcana?"

"Working on it."

Plum eyes shifted to Zaire. "You. Screw this up and I'll show you what happens when healers get angry."

"My people are relying on me as much as yours are relying on Flare," was Zaire's cool response.

"That's not what I was talking about." For a fraction of a second, Lesce's face softened - then her customary scowl was back in place. "Call me as soon as there's more news."

The connection went dead.

Flare flopped back against Zaire, his breath leaving in a rush. "At least it was relatively painless."

"Hmmm." The rogue's arm tightened around his body. "You realise she's worried about you?"

"What?" Flare tried to sit, gave up when Zaire's arm refused to budge. "Are you insane?"

"The fighting, the baiting... even the screaming," Zaire said slowly, his voice contemplative. "It's a front. She's trying to draw you out, keep your wounds clean and your rage pure."

Flare frowned. "Like lancing a boil?"

"Fuck you're gross, you know that?" The rogue shuddered. "Yes, like lancing a boil. Ugh."

"I think you're imagining it," Flare muttered. "Lesce hates me."

"Then why did she just warn me not to break your heart?"

Something prickly and uncomfortable happened in the vicinity of Flare's chest and he cleared his throat. "I don't know what you mean."

"Liar." Zaire chuckled deep in his chest, his lips warm on Flare's temple. "You might not want to admit it but she's looking after you, in her own way. Now come on, bicker-bonk, make the next call before I get bored."

"Bicker-bonk." Flare snickered, allowing Zaire to lighten the mood, and reached out to tap in another code - one he hadn't used in a long, long time.

"Who is this?" The female's voice was harsh, the visual deliberately obscured. "Do you have any idea who you've -"

"It's Flare," he interrupted. "If you take that damned tea towel off the camera, you'll see."

Whispering in the background, then a male voice. "Identity confirmed."

"I know that, you blithering idiot! I'd recognise Flare's voice anywhere." Another set of whispers, then the cloth was torn away. "What do you want, sexy legs?"

Zaire snorted. Flare elbowed him in the ribs. "I'm calling in a marker."

TWENTY-SIX
ARCANA

THE FIRST THING ARCANA DID WHEN SHE WOKE WAS TO SEND HER MAGIC INTO the sandy earth, accelerating the growth of another three trees until their hollowed centres developed. Though she didn't move, content to remain curled against Fenris' heat, the Guardian's hand began to trace the curve of her spine barely five minutes into her work. When she opened her eyes, it was to find his burning jade ones staring back at her.

"Hi," She said, tilting her head to kiss his jaw.

He shifted at the last minute and their lips met instead. "Good afternoon."

"How long was I out?"

"A few hours." The corners of Fenris' eyes crinkled. "Caelum's already broken up two fights between Mirran and the rest of the harpies."

"What?" Arcana sat up in a rush, would've collapsed if Fenris hadn't caught her. "Whoa."

"Are you all right?"

"I think so." Closing her eyes, she sent her senses inwards. "My magic's recovered hugely while we slept - I think that's the cause."

"Hmm." Fenris brushed her hair back from her face with one hand whilst supporting her shoulders with the other. "Indulge me and define 'hugely.'"

"Well over fifty per cent of my normal capacity." Arcana opened her eyes and smiled, unable to contain her excitement. "I can feel a barrier at the bottom of my tank, but it's flimsy. One solid push and I'll be -"

"No," Fenris said quickly, his face blanching. "Your body wouldn't have left the barrier in place if you were ready. Don't overload your senses faster than necessary."

Arcana sighed, her shoulders drooping. "I guess."

"Look at you," Fenris chuckled. "The Arcana I met several months ago would not be acting so terribly put out."

She narrowed her eyes and poked him in the leg. "The Arcana you met several months ago never spent a night without any magic at all, either."

"Not even as a child?"

"Well, yes," she allowed, "but that doesn't count. I didn't know what I was missing."

Fenris chuckled again and rolled to his feet, hauling her up against his chest with strong hands, a wicked grin and a searing kiss. When Arcana's head stopped spinning and her legs proved able to hold her weight, they went in search of lunch - more fresh fruits and vegetables - and then opened the wooden chest Empress Hisha had left behind. It contained a pile of soft, silken fabrics in a variety of colours, a selection of woven rugs, some broad, short candles with multiple wicks, three tooled leather water skins and a length of leather cord with a carved ivory figurine suspended upon it.

"Is that meant to be the Goddess?" Fenris wondered, his long fingers delicate on the miniature harpy woman's wings.

"I don't know." Arcana looked up to see Caelum step out of the trees, five of their nine harpies trailing along behind him. Raising her hand in greeting, she repeated her question.

Mirran stepped out in front, feathers fanning as she twisted her hands together. "Is Empress."

"The Empress gave me a pendant of herself?" Arcana took the necklace from Fenris and examined the ivory closely. A moment later, her stomach churned. "Is this made from male harpy bones?"

"Of course." Mirran frowned at Arcana's obvious horror. "Is normal to repurpose males. Bones for jewellery, arrow tips, hair combs - many things. Light, easy to carve."

Arcana hissed out a breath through clenched teeth. "They're *people*, Mirran."

The wise woman scratched at her downy mane. "So honoured Caelum says." Looking even more perplexed, she shot a glance in the direction of the glowering males on the deerken's opposite side. "Males is agreeing."

"The fights?" Arcana asked, turning her attention to Caelum.

His tail swished back and forth. "Mirran's discovered these lovely friends of ours have a backbone. Particularly Jora, Arax and Leiran."

Arcana and Fenris exchanged a glance. The first two names were no surprise, but Leiran? So far he'd been little more than a quivering, starving mess. Deciding to leave that for now, Arcana looked over the four males in attendance. "Where's Arax?"

"Helping Brok exercise now that his whipping scars are healing in earnest. From what I can understand, they may be brothers. The other males are sketchy on the details." Caelum's ears flickered. "They had an interested audience, so we came back on our own."

"Are they safe?"

"Inside the treeline," Caelum confirmed, "and I can hear them."

"As can I," Fenris added.

Arcana nodded and turned to Jora, holding up the ivory pendant. "How do you honour your dead?"

Before Fenris could begin to translate, the older harpy limped forward. "Once upon a time they were burnt, their ashes set free upon the winds."

Silence, every single eye focussed on the harpy's terracotta face.

"You speak my language," Arcana said finally.

Jora inclined his head. "Some of us do; a well kept secret."

"In that case, I believe I've met a friend of yours." Fenris moved forward to clasp one of Jora's hands in his own. "Father to all males."

Joy lit the older harpy's yellow eyes. "He is our beating heart."

"How?" Mirran whispered, looking so scandalised Arcana worried she might faint. "How is possible?"

"Your gender is not as omnipotent as you'd like to believe," said Jora, the corners of his lips quirking in an amusement that had to have been a lifetime in the making. Raptor eyes trained on Arcana. "I'm trusting you with our most precious secret. Should the Empress find out…"

A test, then. Arcana smiled and inclined her head. "She won't."

"The wise woman may tell her."

Arcana looked at Mirran. "Well? Will you betray our confidence?"

The female blanched, her feathers rippling in shock. "I - no."

"Swear it," Jora demanded, "On your oath as a wise woman."

Mirran's face turned deadly pale but she stammered a promise, falling silent only when Jora nodded in satisfaction. He pointed at the necklace in Arcana's hand. "Considering our meagre cooking fire will not burn hot enough, I'd suggest temporary burial."

"I can make the fire hot enough, and give him more dignity than the ashes beneath the cookpot." Arcana stroked her thumb over all that remained of someone who'd once lived and breathed, perhaps had hopes and dreams of his own. "If you'd like to perform a ceremony?"

Jora nodded. "At sunset."

"At sunset," Arcana agreed - and then, because it seemed the right thing to do, she set the ivory carving into Jora's palm and closed his fingers around it. "Hold him safe until then."

"Thank you." To her surprise, Jora kissed the pendant and then tied it around his neck. "He will be with his brothers until the last."

"Your diction's as formal as Fenris,'" Caelum murmured, looking from Guardian to harpy and back again. "Coincidence?"

"It's the way we're taught." Jora shrugged. "I don't use the language often enough to have picked up all the appropriate shortenings."

The deerken's eyes narrowed on Fenris. "What's your excuse, then?"

"Universal Galactic is also not my first language. I learnt it in the Weaver's court, and it came with attendant formality." Fenris tilted his head to the side, soft curls whispering across his forehead. "I may be wrong, but I believe my exposure to both you and Arcana has considerably dulled the edge of that formality."

Caelum snorted. "Not when you spout lines like that."

Arcana reached up to stroke the deerken's furred jaw. "You're tired."

"Yeah." A flicker of his ears. "And not exactly the mother hen type."

"Unfortunately not all of my brothers are brave," Jora said, his face sad. "Many are still awaiting the order for death."

"And you're not?" Arcana asked.

Jora shrugged. "Should you lose us, we will be executed for having existed outside the laws of Hiraptha. If I am already dead, one way or the other, why should I feel fear?"

"I swear on my life that I will never abandon you like that," Arcana whispered, her hands clenched so tight that her nails dug into her palms.

"A week ago, I would have laughed at those words. Now?" Jora glanced pointedly around at the trees, grown with her magic alone. "For the first time in my life, I am betting against the power of our rulers and placing my faith elsewhere."

Arcana blinked back a sudden wash of tears, looking over the other three males in attendance to see if they agreed. Whilst Leiran met her gaze, his chin lifted defiantly, the other two still flinched away. "How can I win their trust?"

"Don't let them down." Jora shrugged. "Prove you are different not just by word, but by action."

Arcana couldn't help but grin at that, releasing Jora's hand to scoop a length of soft, pale blue fabric from the wooden trunk. "You're a tailor, right?"

"Yes." He eyed the fabric. "You wish clothes?"

"Not just for me - for all of us. Is there enough?"

Jora moved forward to peer into the chest, his weathered hands sorting through the pile. "No. If you want one garment per person, I'll need at least this much again - and thread, basic supplies."

Leiran inched forward and placed his lips to Jora's ear. His skin was a soft, pale peach, his downy mane a speckled black and grey that someone had untangled, leaving it to fall gently over his shoulders and down his back. He was fragile, malnourished - but in that moment, Arcana realised that with time and care, he'd be astoundingly beautiful.

"Leiran is right," Jora said at last, patting the younger harpy on the arm. "You need to go to the market."

Mirran shifted uneasily from one talon to the other. "Unwise."

Arcana frowned. "Why?" Both harpies began to speak, and she held up a hand for silence - then pointed to Jora. "You first."

"Market is the best place to get the supplies we need, and for you to absorb a greater understanding of Hiraptha's culture." Jora spread his hands. "If the Empress truly intends to invite you to the palace, you'll find yourself among the court. Better to go in armed with knowledge than totally blind."

"All good points." Arcana switched her focus to Mirran. "Now you."

"Makes many supplies at market," Mirran allowed, "but also much dangers. Newly named, many challenges. Breaking rules, draw attention." She hesitated, drew herself up as if in preparation for a blow. "Also, males must be bound at market. Penalty is death."

Arcana chewed the inside of her cheek for a long few moments. "We're already breaking rules and drawing attention - if the Empress truly intends us to visit the Palace, we'd better be as prepared as possible. Am I right in assuming physical appearance will be important in the court?"

"Yes." Mirran and Jora spoke in unison, then exchanged a startled glance.

"Then we go to market," Arcana decided, smothering her smile behind one hand.

Jora cleared his throat. "You should take an escort, a guide."

"I will go," Fenris said immediately.

"Respect, but bad idea," Mirran shook her head. "Better to stay, to guard the home. Challenges may come here while Arcana is distracted at market."

Leiran stepped forward, watching Fenris and Arcana through narrowed eyes. He spoke in a high-pitched trill, his clicks and squawks far more lilting and lyrical than those of his counterparts. Fenris answered, followed by Jora and then, with some hesitation, Mirran.

"Leiran has volunteered to accompany you," Fenris said at last, his brow etched with a frown. "I will stay behind with Mirran and the rest of the men to ensure the oasis is safe in your absence."

Arcana reached up to cup his cheek. "Are you okay with that?"

"No, but it makes the most sense." His body vibrated beneath her touch, the only outward sign of distress. "I cannot hide behind you forever."

The ache in Arcana's heart must have shown on her face, because Fenris turned his head to kiss the inside of her wrist - and then, when she shivered, to scrape his fangs across flesh he'd once bitten. Buoyed by the flash of his past, more confident self, she smiled. "If you're sure."

"I am."

"When does the market open?" Arcana asked, letting her hand slide down the column of Fenris' throat and over his scarred chest.

Leiran waved a hand and chittered.

"It's open now," Caelum translated. "The sooner we go, the better."

"Now, then," Arcana agreed. "If that suits you?"

Leiran waited while Fenris translated and then nodded, dropping to his knees and sweeping his downy mane aside. He pointed to his neck, still chafed from when he had last worn his slave collar, and spoke.

"He says you'll need to chain him again, as per the laws," Caelum said.

Arcana went down on her knees in front of the harpy, tipping up his chin with gentle fingers. She waited until his raptor eyes met hers, then she said, "No."

Leiran blinked and twittered.

"He says that if he walks unbound in the markets he will be killed," Fenris translated.

"I'm aware of that - but I won't chain you. If you are bound to me, then I am bound to you." Arcana pushed herself upright and trudged to the edge of the jungle, where several vines draped from the trees. Selecting one at random, she used her magic to shear it off and returned to kneel in front of Leiran, laying the length between them. "Watch."

Summoning her magic, Arcana closed her eyes and laid both hands over the vine. The plant twitched and hissed as it reshaped in response to her touch, becoming a length of braided cord with a spiralling bracelet at either end. She slid her hand through one of the bracelets, then offered the other to Leiran. He took the bracelet from her and slid his hand through, flexed his fingers, then chittered quietly.

"He asks how you intend to secure it," Caelum chuckled.

"I don't. Wearing it will be his choice." Arcana glanced at Mirran. "Will it suffice?"

"I..." The wise woman's feathers fanned, then settled. "Yes."

Leiran looked slowly from Mirran to Arcana and back again. After a long moment, he opened his mouth and a strange collection of syllables tumbled out. Frowning, he tried again. "Yes."

"Yes!" Arcana laughed, taking his frail hand in hers and squeezing gently. The younger man looked surprised and then blushed, carefully prying his fingers free from her grip. "Let's go to the market."

Leiran waited for the translation and then nodded agreement. Arcana stood, balanced herself against Fenris' chest and rose on tiptoe to kiss his cheek. He turned his face inwards at the last moment, catching her lips with his own, his fingers digging into the base of her jaw. "I'm giving you three hours, then I'll tear Hiraptha apart until I find you."

"Noted." Arcana swung onto Caelum's back and extended an arm to Leiran, pulling him up behind her. "Tell him to hold on tight."

Caelum spoke and moments later two thin, trembling arms encircled her waist. She glanced back at Leiran to see his face pale but his expression determined. When she raised a questioning eyebrow, he nodded. "Yes."

"Wait." Mirran stepped forward, three large, filled water skins in her hands. "Will need for payment."

Caelum stood patiently whilst Fenris settled the skins over his shoulders then, after a final nudge at the Guardian, trotted into the trees. Swallowing against the urge to look back, Arcana focussed instead on using her magic to part the foliage, the job far easier than it had been the day before. When they were out in the desert, she turned to close the tunnel and saw Fenris watching them, tension writ in every line of his body. "How can I leave him, Caelum? He was hurt so badly."

"You have to - at least for now. Take comfort from the fact that he's trusting you to come back."

Arcana raised a hand and Fenris did the same, his burning eyes holding hers until the trees snapped back into their former places. "We'll be fine."

"Of course we will," Caelum snorted, moving steadily away from the oasis. "You're only going to the market, for Sorcen's sake!"

Stifling a laugh, Arcana leant over the deerken's neck, dragging Leiran down with her. Caelum leapt forward as soon as their weight shifted, the ground whizzing past beneath his hooves. Leiran stiffened, his arms tightening convulsively and his face turning into Arcana's back to hide from the wind generated by their passing.

The desert sped by in a blur. Caelum slowed as he reached the outskirts of Hiraptha city and twittered at Leiran, who answered in kind. "The market's not far from here."

Arcana straightened as Caelum traversed the streets, Leiran's musical voice guiding his way. The city seemed deserted until they rounded a corner and entered a marketplace overflowing with tented stalls and would-be shoppers. Hirapthans leapt aside as Caelum approached, dragging their slaves out of the way by their chains and staring wide-eyed.

"They're surprised, but it won't be long before they overcome it. Be on your guard," Caelum warned.

"I'm watching."

Caelum and Leiran exchanged quiet words and the deerken stopped beside a tent on the outer edge of the market. "Leiran says this stall sells fruits different to what we have at the oasis."

Arcana slid to the ground and helped Leiran down beside her. The male fastened his eyes firmly on his talons, wrapping shaking hands around the cord which joined him to Arcana as though it were his lifeline. Bending a little so she could see his face, she murmured, "Yes?"

"Yes." It was the barest thread of sound, but it was there. Swallowing heavily, his tone firmed and he dared a look at her from under his lashes. "Yes."

Nodding, Arcana turned to the stall. The fruit vendor had a long table in front of her tent, piled high with a selection of fruits. A Hirapthan woman lounged on a couch inside the tent, her eyes closed. A man chained to a post by the bench watched out of wide eyes as they approached.

"What do we want?" Arcana asked, looking at Leiran. She waited patiently while Caelum relayed her question, while Leiran inspected the produce without actually touching it. After a few moments the harpy male turned to Caelum and spoke quietly into his ear.

Caelum indicated a selection of fruits with his nose. "These."

"Can he negotiate a price for me?" Arcana asked.

Leiran went pale as Caelum spoke, but straightened his spine and chittered to the man chained beside the bench. The slave looked from Leiran to Arcana and responded, flicking a nervous glance at the woman sleeping behind him.

Caelum snorted. "Apparently the men aren't supposed to speak with each other. They're afraid of being punished, but it's obvious you don't know the language. The woman is asleep, so the man is hoping that you'll pay and leave quickly."

"I'll pay very quickly if the price is fair," Arcana answered. Caelum repeated her words and the slave nodded. He eyed Leiran and gave a figure, waving a vague hand at the stall.

"One skin of water for all that we need." Caelum sounded amused. "From what I can tell, that's a very good price - he just wants us to go away."

"All right." Arcana drew down one of the skins from between Caelum's shoulders and offered it to the male. He indicated a contraption beside him, a large funnel that emptied into a jug underneath.

Leiran looked up at Caelum, who bent his head and listened while the other twittered in his ear. "Apparently a 'skin' is a form of measurement. You have to pour the water into the funnel to prove it's clear and safe, and stop when the jug is full. A full jug is the equivalent of a skin."

"Okay." Arcana unstoppered the skin and poured her water into the funnel. The jug filled quickly and she looked up at the man for confirmation. He nodded, taking the jug and pouring it into a large, darkened barrel behind him, returning the empty vessel to the stand. "Can you ask Leiran to help me select the fruit?"

Leiran blinked in surprise and then nodded, moving closer to the bench. Still being careful not to touch, he pointed at pieces of fruit and the male on the other side packed them swiftly into a bag made from roughly woven string. The exchange took place in silence, with the slave throwing nervous glances in the direction of his sleeping owner. He pressed the filled bag into Arcana's arms and bowed his head, chittering softly. She smiled. "Thank you."

While Caelum passed on her words, Arcana tied the handles of the string bag to the water skins, redistributing the burden carefully over the deerken's shoulders. Leiran positioned himself between Arcana and Caelum as they moved away, his knuckles white where he gripped the bracelet at his wrist.

"Is he okay?" Arcana asked, looking down at the man hovering by her elbow.

Caelum spoke, waited while the harpy answered. "He says the market is a place that makes him uncomfortable."

"Interesting that he volunteered, then."

"He's testing you." Caelum's ears flickered. "I overheard the men discussing the truth of your words last night, while it was dark. Leiran thinks he's the most expendable of the lot, so I'm pretty sure that's why he volunteered - if he lives, you're legitimate. If he dies, the rest of the group haven't lost one of their stronger members."

"Great Gods of Sorcen, Caelum," Arcana whispered, anger curling in her veins. "How can people do this to each other?"

The deerken snuffled at her hair, his words gentle. "Prove him wrong. Give him - all of them - a reason to live."

"I think you're attributing me with more power than I actually have," Arcana muttered, rubbing at her forehead. "Can you ask if there's some-where we can buy plants over produce? I can add to the oasis that way, make us more self sustaining."

Caelum gave her a knowing look, but turned to their harpy companion without protest. "Leiran says it's uncommon, but there are a few stalls - they'll be more difficult to deal with than the fruit vendor, though, as they're almost exclusively for the rich."

"Aren't we rich?"

"Yes, but..." Caelum trailed off as Leiran spoke again. "They won't allow him to deal on your behalf."

"Ah. Well, we'll have to see about that, won't we?" Arcana smiled down at Leiran and nodded encouragingly. The harpy shrugged and directed Caelum to a stall filled with saplings in makeshift fabric pots.

"Herbs," Caelum announced. "Both eating and medicinal."

"Do you know what each one is for?" Arcana asked, looking down at Leiran. He fidgeted for a moment, then gestured at the saplings and spoke in a low voice.

"Food on the left. These three on the right are the most common for healing and can be traded with wise women for their services, or used, if you know how," Caelum said.

"Can we afford one of each?" Arcana asked. Leiran gave her a long look, then glanced up at the store owner. Before he had a chance to open his mouth, she squawked raucously at them.

"She says she won't sell to the likes of you, wingless wonder," Caelum said cheerfully.

"Are there other vendors?" Arcana asked, keeping her face blank. Leiran shook his head when Caelum asked, and the woman behind the counter smiled vindictively. "Well then, she'll have to sell to us. Is Leiran the problem?"

"From what I can pick out of her swearing, you and Leiran are equally the problem. Leiran says that a fair price for the saplings would be half a skin of water per plant," Caelum added.

Ignoring the woman's screeching, Arcana reached behind her and unstoppered one of her skins. She waved a hand and a long tail of water rose from the neck, arcing in a clean line over her head and into the woman's collection jug. The Hirapthan's grating screech cut short as she stared at the water - and when it became apparent the torrent was unlikely to cease, she shouted at her two slaves for a new jug, then another. When eight full jugs of clear water sat on the sand, Arcana ceased the flow and waited. The woman blinked at the jugs and then narrowed her eyes at Arcana's seemingly bottomless water skins, twittering out a few grudging words.

"She wants to know what you want," Caelum said.

"One of everything," Arcana said, gesturing at the bench.

Caelum conveyed the request and the harpy woman snapped out a response, gesturing at Leiran. Caelum's tail swished, his tone heavy with irritation. "She says he's too weak to carry everything; it will have to be delivered later."

Leiran's fingers were warm on Arcana's wrist, his face set with determination as he met her gaze and twittered softly. His words cut off as the Hirapthan female shrieked in rage and darted out of the tent, hand raised.

Arcana caught the woman's wrist and she drew up with a startled squeak. "Caelum?"

"Leiran is touching you, making eye contact. He's breaking the rules," the deerken replied softly. "She was going to punish him."

Arcana looked from the enraged female to Leiran, his hand steady and his eyes clear - and knew that here, now, was where the male had chosen to test her mettle. Bending down close to the female harpy, imbuing her tone with as much disapproval as she was able, she said, "No."

The woman squawked and yanked on her arm. Caelum's breath hitched. "She's calling you a traitor."

"Tell her I look after the people I care about," Arcana growled. Caelum repeated the words and the woman stiffened, looking down at Leiran's hand and back up again. When she tugged her arm again Arcana let go, watching her stomp back into her tent while she spouted abuse at the top of her lungs. "What is she saying?"

"She won't sell to you. You forfeit your water for breaking the laws of Hiraptha."

"Really?" Arcana waved a hand and her water lifted out of the jugs, shining clear globes that hung in the air. She turned to the crowd, who watched in tense silence. "Who here is willing to take my water in return for dealing respectfully with Leiran? I'm looking for plants, cloth and tailoring supplies."

Instead of repeating her words, Caelum bent to whisper in Leiran's ear. The male's eyes widened but he lifted his head and spoke in a loud, clear voice which carried easily across the watching crowd. The Hirapthan woman in the stall came rushing back out of her tent, gesturing at the water and shouting loudly.

"She's challenged you to combat for insulting her," Caelum translated. "And, apparently, robbing her - which is an interesting interpretation of events."

"Tell her I accept." Arcana turned to the furious harpy and smiled. "If I win, I take everything in your tent. If you win, you get all the water I have."

Caelum announced the terms and the Hirapthan woman shouted acceptance, fumbling in her belt for a wicked, curved knife. She leapt forward and Arcana flicked a finger, sending one of the water globes to knock the knife from the Hirapthan's grip. Another flick and the globe exploded, glittering in the sunlight before it reformed around the woman's head so that her face was completely submerged.

The crowd watched in silence as the harpy female kicked and flailed to no avail. Her struggles grew steadily weaker, until her eyes lolled back in her head and she slumped into limp unconsciousness. Arcana waved the water away, drawing it from the other woman's lungs in the process. The Hirapthan came to with a start, turning onto her stomach to vomit noisily on the ground.

"Do you yield?" Arcana asked. Caelum whispered in Leiran's ear and he translated the words in his clear, musical voice. The woman nodded, throwing herself on the ground at Arcana's feet and babbling incoherently.

"She's begging for her life," Caelum said.

Arcana made a face. "Her life isn't mine to take. She asked for combat and got it. I'm no killer."

"I have to tell her *something*."

"All right." Arcana paused, running her eyes over the market stall. "I'll let her keep the water which I used to fight her with - but remind her that everything else inside her tent is now mine, in accordance with the challenge."

A lengthy transition of messages passed from Caelum to Leiran and then down to the woman on the ground. The woman looked surprised, the crowd gasped.

"She says thank you." Caelum sounded amused. "Everything is yours."

Arcana waved a hand and returned the water she'd used in combat to the harpy's jug, the remainder filling her own skins so that they bulged and stretched. "Ask Leiran to give us a hand, would you?"

"We can't possibly carry all that."

"Yes we can." Arcana abandoned the water magic and summoned the earth through her bare feet, splintering the post inside the tent and causing the two slaves chained to it to jump back in fright. "We've just acquired some extra help."

"Everything inside the tent. Oh, you're good," Caelum chuckled.

Leaving the deerken to explain the matter to Leiran and the rest of their audience, Arcana gathered the men's chains and used her magic to secure them to the bracelet on her wrist. She'd have liked to free them immediately but decided not to push the crowd, turning her attention instead to the market stall. She caressed the leaves of a sapling on the bench, spreading her energy through the baby plants to ensure they were all healthy. Once satisfied, Arcana fashioned one of the tent's hangings into a large sack, lifted the first plant pot - and paused as someone touched her arm. She glanced back to see Leiran, his expression light with approval.

"Yes," he said.

Arcana grinned, set the sapling down and squeezed his shoulder. "Yes."

He smiled and began to help her, holding the sides of the sack so that she could load the young plants inside. When it was full, she made a new sack and they began again. Twenty minutes later, the tent was empty save for the single jug of water Arcana had promised to leave behind, and Caelum and the two new men were overloaded with bulging sacks.

A harpy stepped out of the crowd, waiting while Arcana finished her final preparations. She inclined her head in greeting, then looked at Leiran and spoke. He answered with confidence, spine straight and shoulders back, then glanced up at Arcana.

"She's offering to sell you some fruit and vegetable trees... and some sort of animal, I think. She also knows a tailoring vendor who will likely deal with us," Caelum said.

Arcana looked down at Leiran. "Yes." He turned back to speak to the woman, beckoned to Arcana and set off after the Hirapthan. Grinning at the imperious tug on their connected wrists, Arcana followed. "Think he trusts me now?"

"Definitely." Caelum's voice held laughter as he kept steady pace alongside, the two new slaves trotting nervously behind. "I still can't believe that worked."

"Which part?"

"All of it," he admitted. "We might get out of this alive after all."

Arcana smiled, leaning over to kiss his nose. "Such an optimist."

Leiran stopped in front of a large tent that had been patched together from several smaller ones. He spoke briefly with the female who'd invited him to follow, then looked at Arcana.

"He wants to know what you need," Caelum translated.

Arcana held out a hand and Leiran took it, allowing her to draw him closer so they could speak out of the female's earshot. "I don't know anything about the best plants or animals for us to grow, own, or eat. Do you?"

Caelum lowered his head to repeat her words in Leiran's ear.

"Yes," the harpy answered, his musical voice curling around the word with pride. He looked up at Caelum and chittered.

"Apparently this vendor has a good reputation. She sells an excellent variety of goods and is well known for supplying the Palace," Caelum said.

"I want to set up the oasis so that we can sustain ourselves completely, rather than being dependent on the city." Arcana thought over what they already had and shrugged. "Buy whatever you think we need."

Arcana watched Leiran's face change as Caelum relayed her message. After a long moment, he swallowed and spoke again.

"He says he'll do his best, but we won't be able to carry it all," Caelum said. "Particularly if you still want to get fabric and supplies for Jora."

Arcana frowned. "Fair enough. Tell him I'll pay extra to have the goods delivered."

Leiran nodded as Caelum translated, then turned back to the woman at the stall. She listened carefully to his quiet words, then looked at Arcana and spoke a few quick sentences before returning to negotiate with Leiran.

Caelum snorted a laugh. "She said that considering you just eliminated one of her major competitors, she'll deliver the goods for free."

"I'm not sure if I'm amused or embarrassed," Arcana chuckled.

"Does it matter?"

"No," Arcana replied, looping an arm around his neck and watching Leiran speak. "No, it doesn't matter at all."

TWENTY-SEVEN
FLARE

"More dead ends," Flare grumbled, leaning back in his shiny new office chair and covering his face with both hands. "Tell me again why I agreed to this?"

"Because you're an idiot," Zaire sniped, slapping a hardcopy file down on the desk. "Here's the latest medical report on Kaiora."

Flare sighed. The last two days had passed in a blur, his body running on fumes made up of sleep deprivation and adrenaline. His mind was a constantly whirring machine, unable to let him rest even in the few moments Zaire insisted he take for himself. Shoving his hands up off his face and into his hair, he tugged the fire orange strands for a moment before sitting up and flipping the medical report open.

It contained nothing new. Shortly after her attack, the Chancellor's vitals had taken a dive. Mendin, thankfully still on scene, had identified a poison likely inhaled during the course of the firebombing and had immediately worked to mitigate it. Flare, barely finished writing his preliminary suspect list, had received a panicked call from Naavah and Galactic Station had promptly gone to hell.

"At least she's awake," Flare muttered, scanning the contents of the report and then closing the file. "If Mendin hadn't been there, we might not be so lucky."

Zaire's nod was sharp. "His specialty with poisons isn't widely known, I take it."

"Not really." Flare shrugged. "A healer's a healer in the eyes of the general population."

"You know what they say about assumptions."

"In this case, I'm glad." He drummed his fingers on the desk, eyeing the slim datapad Olivie had given him as part of his new position. Zaire had spent a good twenty minutes ensuring the device was secure and it now held the notes Flare had taken over the last two days as he'd interviewed every single Ambassador that was part of the Alliance, trying to ferret out who might want their Chancellor dead. But... "Either they're all innocent, or they're all guilty."

"Yeah." Zaire shoved a plate of flatbreads topped with bright orange meat in front of Flare, taking one for himself. "Any hits on your other search?"

"No." Flare bit fiercely into a wrap, hiding disappointment behind the ferocity of his movements. "All data on the warg is linked to specific Alliance incursions. Nothing to hint at what happened to Arcana or where she might be."

"What about the lead you tapped the other day?"

"Nothing yet." Swallowing the last of his wrap, Flare slapped the light which had begun to flash on his desk panel. "Flare."

"Chief." Naavah's voice, sounding as weary as Flare felt. "The Chancellor asked me to inform you that she has rescheduled the Council meeting for three hours past station-rise tomorrow morning."

"She's barely out of bed!"

"The medics have given her a clean bill of health, though they recommend further rest." A thread of steel entered the Arachnaida's voice. "I will ensure she returns to bed as soon as the meeting concludes."

Flare growled in the back of his throat, the sound escaping his normally impeccable control and causing Zaire to prod him in the shoulder in silent warning. He took a deep breath, forced his frustrations back in their box. "Thank you, Naavah. I'll arrange security."

"See you tomorrow," she replied, and cut the connection.

Zaire hitched one half of his sculpted behind onto the desk and waited in silence while Flare contacted Pytch and issued a string of orders. When the comm was at last silent, the Ryllin tilted sideways until he was sprawled lazily across the length of the desk, head propped on one hand and indigo eyes at Flare's face height. "We have twelve hours to kill, it seems."

Taking the invitation of his lover's upturned face, Flare tangled his hands in Zaire's silky hair and kissed him hot and wet and deep. "Want me to make you scream?"

"Big words," Zaire drawled - but his voice was too husky to carry it off. "I thought we might go to Macadre, seeing as we never made it the other night."

"Why?"

A sleek black brow shot skyward. "Because it's more interesting than your cock?"

"That's not what you said last night… or this morning."

"Hah!" The Ryllin gave a derisive snort. "Your ego is more puffed up than Krowley's." When Flare said nothing, the rogue's stiff expression slid into a grin. "Way I see it, we've done all our official interviews, right? So people are more likely to relax and wag their tongues in a social setting if they think the pressure's off."

"Meaning that if we *have* missed anything, it might turn up there." Despite the warning wrench in his gut, Flare nodded. "All right, but I have a couple things I need to do first."

"Such as?"

"One; prove that my cock is more interesting than you give it credit for. Two; shower and change." He offered his best bedroom smile. "In that order."

Zaire slapped a hand over the desk panel and the office door locked with an audible snick. Heat glittered in the depths of his indigo eyes as he lunged off the desk, tackling Flare to the floor in a move that rolled them across the carpet in a flurry of leathers and robes. "Deal."

Two hours and a sizzling shower later, Flare strode through the doors of Macadre with Zaire at his side. He'd donned the same black velvet robe as the previous time he'd visited the club - only on this occasion, he'd eschewed the underrobe, revealing an amount of chest that bordered on scandalous. His makeup was smokier, his orange hair swept out and up with a hair product that tipped the ends in black. The effect was dark, dangerous and - according to the rogue stalking along beside him - unfairly sexy.

Zaire, in an uncharacteristic effort to look approachable, wore navy leather pants, black boots, and a royal blue shirt with baggy sleeves that were cuffed at the wrist. Unable to abandon his armour completely, a matching navy leather waistcoat completed the outfit, fastened down one side with a series of shining silver buckles that matched those on his boots. Twin daggers, their scabbards covered in the iconic curlicues that marked him as a silver-scrolled rogue, hung from a weapons belt that perched precariously low on his hips. The effect was slick, dangerous and - not that Flare would admit it aloud - unfairly sexy.

Too bad the seduction of Zaire wasn't the reason they were here.

Once more ignoring the dance floor for the more intimate mezzanine, Flare wrapped layer after layer of armour around his heart until, by the time he reached the top step, he'd buried his doubts and was firmly back in his bad boy persona. Quirking his lips into a smirk that was seventy percent supercilious arrogance and thirty percent dark promise, Flare tugged Zaire closer with a firm grip on his leather waistcoat. "You want to make a spectacle, or fade out?"

"Fade." The rogue's indigo eyes were black in the dim lighting, his cheekbones razor sharp. "If we look too attached, nobody will approach you."

Flare loosed a throaty laugh laced with a healthy dose of darkness, his soul already quaking at the thought of what was to come. "You really don't know how this works, do you?"

"If we call too much attention to me, I won't be able to overhear anything," Zaire hissed, the curtain of his hair providing a cocoon of intimacy. "Don't blow my cover just to be a fuckwit."

"Fine." Flare released him with a naughty wink. "I'll see you later, then."

Shaking his head, Zaire melted into the crowd as if heading to the bar for a drink - and was invisible in moments. Not bothering to search when he knew full well he'd never spot the Ryllin, Flare sauntered to the mezzanine's banister and leant against it, posture casual and eyes sharp. The dancers below gyrated with reckless abandon, the music woven by Macadre's live band so popular that the club was filled to overflowing on a nightly basis.

"Fascinating, aren't they?"

Turning to the tall drink of a woman who'd arrived beside him, Flare ran a deliberately provocative eye over her almost-sheer white gown and smiled his best shark smile. "Deja vu, Priestess."

"Indeed." Lysse's laugh was bright and tinkling, her long, flower-tipped lashes lowered in coy delight as she waved a woodgrain arm down at the dancers below. "Do you wish to join them? I still dream of the last time we moved together."

As though on cue, a waiter appeared by Flare's side, a lone tumbler of clear liquid on his tray. "Water, Chief?"

"Just Flare," he replied, accepting the glass with a nod.

The waiter beamed, bowed, and backed off. Lysse's full lips pursed as she watched him go. "Do you often ask servants to call you by name?"

"I don't believe in servants," Flare answered, making no attempt to hide his irritation. "Just people."

Lysse's laugh was soft and throaty. "Do you honestly expect me to believe a man of such power believes all are created equal? How novel."

Rather than answer, Flare balanced his glass on one palm and began muttering under his breath. His skin immediately began to heat, setting the water aboil. When it threatened to overflow the tumbler, Flare sealed his free hand over the top of the glass so that the bubbles caressed his flesh. After years' worth of use the spell came easy - so easy one wouldn't guess how many late nights and scalded eyebrows had gone into perfecting it - and in less than a minute the water had turned a deep amber. As the bubbles began to subside, Flare lifted his hand from the top of the glass, drew a couple of runes in the air and ushered their shimmering forms into the liquid. Each one created a very real ripple and by the time the contents of the glass had settled, Flare was left with a healthy measure of thick, smooth firewhiskey.

Habit made him want to toss it back in one go, but instead, he sipped. "Passable."

"Incredible," Lysse murmured, edging closer so that their shoulders touched. She leant over, ostensibly to better see the contents of Flare's glass, but he knew better; the position put her face close enough that they shared breath. "So much power."

It was a parlour trick, but no point in saying that aloud. Deliberately wafting the firewhiskey under her nose, Flare took another sip. He drew the motion out, watching her over the rim of his glass as she drew ever closer. When he at last lowered the tumbler, their noses brushed. "Do you like power, Priestess?"

"Lysse."

"Lysse," he repeated, his voice a dark velvet thrum. "I find it interesting that a woman such as yourself is merely a joint Ambassador rather than taking on the entire duty."

A secret smile, her cheeks darkening with pleasure. Dipping her head so her fern-frond hair slid becomingly across her brow, Lysse pressed into the hard lines of his body. "My planet has two peoples on it - mine, and Krowley's. It seemed only fair to have a representative of each."

"It doesn't create infighting?"

"I believe," Lysse whispered, "in learning to co-operate, even when heathens are involved."

Flare remained still; let her tilt her head, let her lean in to press her lips to his in a featherlight caress. Nausea churned in his gut and his heart slammed against his ribs in a frenzy of panic but he held firm, the corner of one lip quirking in a smirk just this side of assholeville. When Lysse's lashes drifted open, revealing the new-grass green of her eyes, he rumbled, "Co-operation with figures of authority has never been my strength."

A blink, as her mind worked through the comment. "Oh?"

"Yeah." Flare set his lips against the shell of her ear, the texture like smoothest paper. "I blame my inner heathen."

Then, while she shivered with ill-concealed desire, he turned and walked away.

Over the next two and a half hours, Flare made more firewhiskey than he thought he'd have needed. Most of it was for himself; keeping his supercilious smirk in place while others rubbed their hands, faces and - in one unusual case - feet all over him was an exercise in effort. He covered his disgust by working magic, handing firewhiskey to the hopeful males, females and in-betweens who were more than willing to bare their souls in exchange for the chance to roll in his scent. By the time he made his way to the bottom of the mezzanine stairs where Zaire awaited, Flare's heart was a trapped bird in his chest.

The plan had been to leave immediately, but Zaire took one look at Flare and hauled him into the deeper shadows beneath the stairs. "What the fuck have you done to yourself?"

"I'm fine," Flare muttered. "Not even drunk."

"That's not what I mean and you fucking well know it," the rogue hissed. "You look like shit, Flare."

Hearing his name on the other male's lips was a balm. "Say that again."

"You look like -"

"No. The other."

Zaire's eyes darkened. "Flare."

He shuddered, his soul swimming for the surface. "Again."

"Flare?" The voice - not Zaire's - had him glancing out of the relative safety of the shadows to a tall, willowy woman who appeared entirely made of branches. The lights from the dance floor made her almost-sheer gown invisible, displaying every slender curve of her waiflike body.

"Lysse." It came out a hiss, but she must not have heard the tone, for she ducked enough to see into the alcove. "What do you want?"

She blinked in the face of his bad manners, her expression set into such innocent confusion he knew at once it was fake. "I was hoping to have a word with you in private."

Flare clenched his teeth at the way she said 'in private,' with honey dripping from every syllable and sex all-but oozing from her pores. "No."

Zaire's hand slapped him in the bare chest and it took a good three seconds for Flare to realise he'd started forward with clenched fists, was now being restrained. Lysse, however, pursed her lips in consternation. "Was I interrupting something?"

No. Yes. No. Yes. Great Gods of Sorcen, he was fucked up.

"Priestess," Zaire began, his voice stiff with temper. "I think you should leave. Flare -"

That did it. The sound of his name on the lips of someone who actually said it with weight, with emotion, with a deep, dark fury that matched the one inside him. Flare grabbed the front of Zaire's leather waistcoat and hauled him close, taking his lips in a kiss that was violent in its desperation.

The Ryllin squeaked - actually squeaked - in surprise as Flare spun them both, slamming Zaire against the wall so he didn't have to look at the club any longer. Music thumped through Flare's veins in time to his heart and after a long, shocked moment Zaire went soft, allowed himself to be kissed with a wrath unlike anything Flare had ever felt.

The crackle between them was fiercer than ever and Flare clung to it, clung to the man whose scars matched his own, whose wounds ran so deep that he'd recognised a kindred spirit. Zaire's fingers twisted in his hair and yanked, breaking the kiss. "Stop."

"I don't want to."

"Yes, you do," Zaire ground out. "You're better than this."

"I'm not," he confessed, because the past few hours had proven it. "I will never be."

"*No*," Zaire snarled, lips curling back from his teeth in the most emotive expression Flare had yet seen him make. "You're fucking whipping yourself in front of me and I won't have it. The Priestess is gone - so stop, or I walk away. Right. Now."

Flare teetered on the edge of the abyss, filled with the knowledge that if he wanted, he could tumble them both into a blackness which would forever bind them together - and forever ruin them.

He stopped.

Zaire must have felt the fight go out of him, because the Ryllin pulled him close, wrapping both arms around his body in an embrace that was strength and comfort rather than sex and heat. "I hate you so much right now."

"Not as much as I hate myself," Flare muttered. Zaire's chest jerked beneath him and then they were laughing, a wicked, curling laugh which was full of bitterness and mutual understanding. "We are so fucked up."

"Broken," Zaire agreed, pulling back just far enough to search Flare's face. "And one of us, I might add, stinks like liquor and everyone else's sweat. I recommend a shower as soon as possible."

"Great Gods of Sorcen, yes." Flare took a deep breath and dragged what remained of his swagger back into place. "Let's get out of here."

"I hate seeing that look in your eye," Zaire murmured, but he let go, following when Flare led him around the edge of the dance floor and out into the street.

The relative quiet was a balm and they walked in silence, close enough their arms brushed with every other step. Zaire didn't ask any questions and Flare didn't volunteer any answers, their footsteps swallowed by the station's artificial night cycle. Nevertheless, Flare was aware of every breath his companion took, every move he made - so when Zaire's spine stiffened and his step faltered, he was immediately looking around them for the threat.

It came as no surprise when a group of silent figures in servant's uniforms stepped from the shadows.

The tunnel was narrow, three servants ahead and three behind. Hoods and scarves hid their faces, uniforms baggy enough that it was impossible to catch any distinctive features. Flare set his back to Zaire's, each of them facing a group, and waited.

Without breaking the eerie silence, the servants pressed in. Flare spoke a single word of power, conjuring a fireball in the cradle of his palm. He threw, watched it strike the chest of his central opponent and spread over the linen uniform with ravenous hunger. The man screamed as he burned, the spell making the flames cling and crawl, consuming his body and invading orifices until, in a matter of moments, the scream cut short.

Flare ducked a ham-sized fist, clenched his own fists in such a way that they burst into flame, and slammed a heavy punch into his enemy's gut. The servant doubled over, slapping frantically at the flames igniting over his clothing as Flare turned toward the third attacker. This one went down immediately, Flare's elbow striking a scarf-covered face at point-blank range and shattering bones like matchsticks.

He turned back to find his first opponent running in with arms wide and shoulder lowered. Flare accepted the tackle, gathering his legs to his chest even as he fell. Twisting his flaming hands in the man's uniform, he rolled and flipped them both, slamming the thug spine-first into the floor and knocking him unconscious with a ringing blow to the side of the head.

The sound of seizing metal drew his attention and Flare looked up in time to see Zaire thrust a scrolled dagger into the chest of his opponent. They fell together, the attacker limp and the rogue toppling like a tree, the impact softened by the weight of the servant underneath. One of the other would-be assailants slouched against the wall, blood oozing sluggishly from the slash across her throat. The final servant remained frozen in the corridor behind Zaire, a syringe poking out of one sleeve. Flare extinguished the flames ringing his fists, patted out the ones spreading over the chest of his unconscious assailant, and gained his feet.

"If you surrender now, I won't hurt you," he promised, holding out a hand in invitation.

Silence.

"I'm going to help my friend now." Flare began to close the distance to Zaire, one hand still up and the other hidden behind the curve of his robes. "Please don't run."

The servant squeaked, dropped the syringe, and ran.

Flare finished his final rune, slapped both hands together and pushed outward. Fire scythed from his joined palms, striking the servant mid-thigh and severing their legs with a hiss. A high pitched, feminine scream reverberated in Flare's ears as she toppled, the wounds cauterised before the servant hit the ground.

"I told you not to run," he growled, kneeling by Zaire to check the man's pulse. Ascertaining his heart was beating - arrhythmic but strong - Flare rolled his lover over and looked into wide, staring eyes. "Hold on. Let me question our friend, then I'll get you out of here."

Yanking Zaire's dagger out of the corpse which had become a temporary mattress, Flare made his way swiftly towards the fallen woman. Choosing to abandon her legs, she'd begun to drag herself away on her elbows, but stopped when Flare stepped in front of her in a swish of blood-soaked velvet.

"Stay back," she panted, her Universal Galactic thickly accented.

"I don't want to hurt you," Flare told her, crouching in an effort to make himself less intimidating - although, honestly, the dagger probably didn't help. "I just need to know why you're after my friend."

She babbled incoherently, the sleeves of her servant's uniform dropping back to reveal tentacles instead of arms. Flare threw himself aside as the ends of those tentacles split open, revealing two mouths full of barbed teeth which snapped in the air where his face had been only moments earlier. He rolled to his knees but she was on him, one of those mouths sinking all of their teeth into the forearm he thrust up for just that purpose. Grunting through the pain, Flare shoved Zaire's dagger into the cavity of her draping hood and, just to make sure she was truly dead, incinerated her head with a snap of his fingers.

The body crumpled at once, the neck a cauterised stump. Evaluating the power remaining in his tank, Flare ratcheted the output down and aimed a repeat of the spell at his own arm, incinerating the tentacle whose mouth - and teeth - were still burrowed deep in his flesh. When his magic cut out, all that remained were two perfectly semicircular sets of teeth-marks, each oozing blood and a green-tinted fluid.

Shaking his arm to settle the tattered remnants of his sleeve into place, Flare retrieved the silver dagger and made his way back to Zaire. At some point the Ryllin had passed out, eyelids drooping and face relaxing into an expression far more youthful than he appeared while animated. Ensuring both daggers were returned to their scabbards, Flare scooped the taller male up in his arms. Staggering the first few steps, he got them both moving, teeth gritted as he traversed the night-dark corridors of the station before arriving at a now familiar door. With no hands free, he kicked it, the platform boots he'd chosen for Macadre causing a satisfying thump.

"What in the - shit," Eyrton growled, temper bleeding into concern as Flare shoved into the living area. Zaire's cousin looked decidedly mussed, skin flushed and lean hips wrapped in a sheet. "Get him to his room. I'll be with you as soon as I see my guest out."

Flare grunted a response, pain - both inside and out - stealing his words. He stumbled through Zaire's door and flopped them both onto the bed, the rogue still cradled in his arms. His lungs had begun to burn, sweat beading on his brow and trickling down the back of his neck. Relaxing against the stiff lines of his lover, Flare dropped his face onto Zaire's shoulder and let his eyes drift closed.

Rough hands shook him awake a few minutes later, Eyrton's concerned expression joined by another fuzzy one that Flare vaguely identified as Mendin. Damn healer was everywhere, he reflected, and tried to sit up - only to discover his limbs completely unresponsive and his body a useless weight.

A cool hand spread over his brow and Mendin frowned. Warmth tingled at the point of contact, rippling through his body in a wave of effervescence that bordered on ticklish. After a cursory sweep of his system the magic concentrated on his bitten forearm, Mendin's other hand shoving the ruined sleeve up to assess the physical damage.

"What in the Oracle's name did that?" Eyrton asked, his eyes, so similar in colouring to Zaire's and yet so incredibly different, flicking between Flare and the rogue on the bed beside him.

"I don't know," Mendin muttered, "But it's a paralytic venom that would eventually have shut down his entire nervous system."

Eyrton shook his head, silver streaked hair tumbling over his bare shoulders and emphasising a muscular but scarred chest. "Your Fire Elder sure knows how to party."

"My Fire Elder is the epitome of selflessness, and in this case, he saved your cousin's life," Mendin snapped, anger lending his magic an edge that had Flare hissing between clenched teeth. Eyebrows shot upward and the healer immediately tempered his mood. "Sorry."

"Fine," Flare managed. Then, fighting with all his strength, added, "Chotharin."

"*Chotharin?*" Mendin and Eyrton echoed in unison. While the healer blinked and choked, the Ryllin Ambassador shook his head. "You should be dead."

Flare counted slowly to twenty, swivelling his eyes to a position where he could watch them both and still see Zaire in the periphery. "Fire."

"What?"

"He means," Mendin clarified, "That the unusually high content of fire magic present in his blood negates a large amount of poisons and lessens the effects of others. It's the only reason he was able to get back here alive."

"Oracle save me," Eyrton murmured, shaking his head. He prepped a pressure injector and jammed it into Zaire's forearm. "That's one monster of a risk."

"Bit the arm," Flare managed, watching as Zaire's body twitched, then relaxed. "Takes longer to reach the more important things."

Mendin produced a towelette from somewhere about his person and wiped at Flare's forearm. "Healed. You'll feel like shit for a few hours, though."

"Fine," Flare breathed, rolling his head so that it fit better against Zaire's shoulder. "Z?"

"Just a seizure." Eyrton sighed, brow furrowed as he checked his cousin's pulse. "Total lock up."

Mendin frowned at the cryptic comment. "Want me to check him?"

"I don't know." Eyrton hesitated, looking at Flare for guidance. "I'm not sure how your magic works."

"I swear on my oath as a healer to keep any secrets I sense," Mendin said quietly.

Eyrton tugged at his hair a moment, then nodded. "Do it."

Placing his palms flat against Zaire's leather-clad chest, Mendin closed his eyes. After a few moments, they popped open. "Great Gods of Sorcen!"

"Is he all right?" Eyrton asked, already reaching for the first aid kit.

"I..." Mendin trailed off, gaze unfocussed as his magic flowed through Zaire's body. "He's... wow."

"He's fine," Flare chuckled.

Mendin drew his hands back with a nod. "I can't explain what I felt just then, but whatever shot you gave Zaire has relaxed his muscles and put him into a restorative sleep. No internal ruptures or seizure damage."

"Not a word, Mendin," Flare said firmly. "Not a single word."

"Of course not." The healing sorcerer's face stiffened with affront. "I swore."

Eyrton clapped the healer on the shoulder and, after a few murmured words, Mendin left. Perching on the edge of the bed, his chest bare but his legs clothed in soft navy training pants, the older rogue said, "Talk."

Flare talked. He kept the excursion to Macadre as clinical as possible, but noted Eyrton's brows twitch a couple of times nonetheless. When Flare began to recount the ambush in detail, however, Eyrton listened with narrow eyed intensity.

"Still after his blood," the rogue muttered, pushing a hand into his unbound hair. "Oracle knows how they've found out."

"Whoever's behind this is thorough. All it'd take was a scan in passing, a word or an accidental display of strength and they'd know Z was different," Flare pointed out.

Eyrton said nothing, brow furrowed. After a long minute, he rose and began to unbuckle Zaire's leather waistcoat. "We were careful when we came to Galactic Station. Managed almost a year without issue."

"What changed?" Flare shifted to allow the leather waistcoat to be peeled off and dumped on the floor, followed by Zaire's loose shirt.

Pausing at his cousin's boots, Eyrton shrugged. "I don't know. The only thing I can think of is that Z stepped into the spotlight when he took on the search for those missing ships. Up until then, I did most of the public stuff while he shadowed."

"The ships," Flare breathed. One boot hit the floor, followed by another. "They were Ryllin medical frigates."

Eyrton froze. "You think someone hacked the ship's medical database?"

"It makes sense." Flare lowered his hands to the sash on his robe, but his fingers didn't work properly. Eyrton took over the task without prompting, unravelling the heavy velvet with capable ease. "There's definitely a spy in the Alliance, though their motivations are unclear. I'm certain they hijacked the ships and are behind the poisonings and the attack on Kaiora. It's not much of a stretch that, if the attacks on Z started *after* the ships disappeared, whoever it is was able to access the data on his unique condition and is responsible for the attempts to steal his blood."

"Huh. You might actually have a point there." Eyrton helped Flare sit up, pushing ruined velvet off his bare shoulders. "Oracle's voice, are you naked under this?"

"Of course," Flare snapped. "Are you suddenly a blushing virgin?"

"No, I just..." Eyrton cleared his throat, tilted his head in Zaire's direction. "You two, well, um."

"We're fucking each other blind," Flare agreed, watching in fascination as the other Ryllin did, indeed, blush like a virgin. "Still not sure what that has to do with seeing me naked."

Gathering himself with effort, Eyrton finished removing Flare's robe, tugged off his boots and socks, and tossed everything in the corner with Zaire's clothes. Unabashed by his nudity, Flare scrabbled at the bedcovers and, with Eyrton's assistance, managed to get both himself and Zaire under the blankets.

"If someone hacked Z's records, they wouldn't find evidence of the original warg attack or the ensuing bio-mech experiment. Those details are kept by my father, in his private lab." Dropping onto the side of the bed, Eyrton stared down at his palms. "However, all ships *are* linked to Rylle's overall medical database, and even though Zaire's private records aren't on there, his public ones would look suspicious to anyone with a discerning eye."

"How so?"

The Ryllin hesitated, then shrugged. "Zaire is a decade older than I am."

"What?" Flare blinked, examining Eyrton's face, his body - scarred with evidence of a warrior's life - his silvering hair. Zaire, meanwhile, maintained the flush of youth, his hair blue-black and silky, his musculature slender but strong and free of scarring. Realisation dawned. "The cyborg fusion."

"Yes. He not only ceased to age when it was done, he actually regressed. The government tried to keep it quiet, but there are likely photos out there from before the attack, where he looks far more his age."

"Which is?"

"He's sixty-four to my fifty-one," Eyrton answered. "Average lifespan of my people is around a hundred and twenty."

Flare considered, then nodded. "He looks about thirty."

"Thereabouts - but then, so do you, and I know you're seventy-five."

"My people carry magic in their veins," Flare shrugged. "We live a lot longer."

"So will Z."

"How long?"

Eyrton rolled one shoulder in a shrug. "Possibly double his natural life span, possibly triple... possibly forever. He's one of a kind, completely experimental."

"Damn," Flare muttered. "No wonder he's so bitter - he's likely to outlive everyone he's ever cared about."

"Among other things," Eyrton agreed. "It's possible that whoever set out to collect Z's blood had no idea about his other skills, but instead sought the secret to his youth - although if they've been paying attention, they'll have realised there's more to it than that by now."

"Likely." Flare yawned widely, burrowing closer to the unconscious rogue in question. "Eyrton?"

"Yeah?" The Ryllin paused half-way to the bedroom door, glancing back over his shoulder.

"Z's suffered enough. Don't let me break his heart."

Surprise flitted across the warrior's face before it softened. "Maybe he'll break yours, sorcerer."

"I don't have one," Flare admitted, his lashes drifting closed and the chill of Zaire's skin comforting beneath his cheek. "That's what worries me."

TWENTY-EIGHT
FENRIS

Fenris examined the gaunt face of the man reflected in the flat of the greatsword's blade and wondered what had become of the Guardian who once wore the same skin. Since setting foot on this wretched world, ejected from the portal realm like so much inter-dimensional flotsam, he'd done nothing but misstep. Time and time again, opportunity had presented itself and he, secure in his own blind arrogance, had allowed those moments to pass merrily by.

No more.

He might be stripped of his blood oath, his connection to his people and his duty a raw wound inside of him, but he was finished being the victim. No longer would he sit and wait and wonder while the universe fell apart around him, innocents crushed beneath the boot of evil. If all he could do was lend his blade to Arcana, he would do it. He would fight until there was no more breath left in his body, no more blood for his useless heart to pump through his veins. He would stand before whatever threatened her and he would -

"Mrow!"

Sighing, Fenris raised a hand to the soft weight that had appeared on top of his head, and caught the cheeky creature by the scruff of her neck. "No, Lyra."

"Mrowmm." The spoon kitten stared out at him from behind stunningly large blue eyes, unabashed by his stern expression and the merciless heat of Hiraptha's twin suns. "Mrrrrrow?"

"Yes, you *have* interrupted a spectacular brooding session." Fenris placed her on the ground, in the shadows created by his body, and shook a stern finger beneath her nose. "How am I supposed to sulk if you keep appearing atop my head and ruining the mood?"

Lyra blinked and disappeared. Shaking his head, Fenris made to gain his feet - and paused when a warm, comforting weight reappeared around his neck. "Mrow."

"*Lyra*."

"Row?"

"If you will not let me examine my internal thought processes, then I shall resume strengthening my body," he warned, imbuing his tone with the strict edge he'd once used on new Guardians. "If you are determined to stay locked around my throat, you had best be prepared for the consequences."

A small silence, then the dry rasp of a little pink tongue against his neck. "Mrooowwww."

"Very well, then. Don't say you were unwarned." Wondering - not for the first time - how he'd managed to secure the unusual creature's affection, Fenris pushed to his feet and gave the greatsword an experimental twirl. His muscles still burned, but nowhere near as badly as before he'd paused for a break.

After a deep breath to reclaim his centre, Fenris began to move through one sword form after another. Sweat trickled down his back, the glare off the desert sands in which he'd chosen to train a constant source of discomfort that had him squinting more often than not - yet he refused to seek the solace of the shade. He needed to get stronger, to return his body to optimum health. The urgency beat at him with every passing moment, but he forced himself to go slowly, to work in strict increments. He'd spent many weeks trembling with exhaustion and had no desire to return to such a state should it be avoidable.

Lyra stayed in place while he spun and danced, the greatsword catching the sunlight so that it flashed beacon-bright. Ordinarily such a display would have bothered him greatly, but considering the Empress already knew where they were camped, Fenris concluded a little extra light show would do no harm. Particularly considering he'd selected the slice of desert furthest from Hiraptha City, the lush vegetation of Arcana's oasis providing a shield from all except the most determined of eyes - and if the Empress chose to send more sentries to overfly the territory, he'd remove them without compunction.

A susurration of sand drew his attention and Fenris paused to look over one shoulder. Jora waited at the treeline, leaning against one of the trunks whose bark sheeted off in thin, paperlike layers. Returning the greatsword to its' scabbard with a flourishing thump, Fenris dusted his palms on his training trousers and moved into the shade by the harpy's side. "Good afternoon."

"And to you," Jora replied. He eyed the sweat running in rivulets down Fenris' chest. "I didn't mean to interrupt."

"You have not," Fenris assured him. "I was due for another break." They stood in silence for three whole minutes, staring out at the desert while Lyra purred loudly and licked sweat from his neck. "Did you have a purpose to this visit, or do you wish only my company?"

The tailor kicked at the sand beneath his bare talons. "I have a purpose. I wondered how long you and Arcana were planning to stay."

"Stay?" He didn't normally consider himself dense, but on this occasion, Fenris' brow drew into a frown. "Where would we go?"

"Home." Jora waved a vague hand out into the distance. "It's no secret that you're not from Hiraptha."

Still frowning, Fenris lowered himself to a seated position in the sand, motioning Jora to do the same. "We have no current way of returning to our home. This is our home now."

"For how long?"

"Jora, my friend, I would ask you to speak plainly - I do not understand what you are trying to tell me."

"You forget that I speak the Goddess' tongue, and while I do not comprehend the meaning of words such as 'jump' in the context you've used them, I am smart enough to comprehend your intent." The other male lifted his hands, turned them back and forth in front of his face as though to see inside. "When you go, we will be put to death. Our skins tanned for clothing, our manes spun into binding for arrows and our bones carved into jewellery. I have lived a long life, for a male, and do not fear death - but the others, they're young. They deserve better."

"Arcana swore to protect you," Fenris began, blood boiling at the thought of such a grisly fate. "She would never allow -"

"When she leaves," Jora interrupted quietly, "Who will stop it?"

Fenris opened his mouth to respond, snapped it shut. Considered. "Weaver's grace."

"Will Arcana take us with her? Will *you* take us with you?" Jora tilted his head to the side in that avian way the harpies had. "Is there a place at your home for men who were once slaves?"

"Yes," he replied at once. "The trouble will be, as it is now, the transportation." When Jora said nothing, Fenris' brow furrowed again. "What else?"

"Leiran told me, this morning before he left, that his feathers have begun to grow back."

"Is that not a good thing?"

The harpy shrugged. "Hirapthan law demands all males be plucked before their feathers are large enough to render them capable of flight. Any male flouting this law is to be executed on sight."

"Disfigurement or death." Fenris looked down at the heavy scarring on Jora's arms and tried to imagine how he would feel without a limb. "Have you ever flown?"

"No."

"I do not make the habit of speaking for others, but I can say with certainty that Arcana will not force your feathers to be plucked," Fenris said. He sat suddenly straighter. "You already know that."

"Yes." Jora's lips quirked, haunted by the spectre of a smile. "It is why I came to see you - if she, and you, truly mean to defend us, then the choice must be made now."

One eyebrow shot up of its own accord. "You just stated the execution order would come upon our leaving."

"Not," Jora murmured, "if we're seen with flight-worthy feathers. In that, the order will be immediate and without exception."

"I see."

They sat in silence for another few minutes before Jora clapped him companionably on the shoulder, rose, and left. After a few moments, Fenris' nose caught the shifting breeze and crinkled. "There is no sense lingering in the trees, wise woman. I can smell you."

"Your nose is sharp," Mirran acknowledged, moving to take Jora's place. Speaking in Hirapthan, her voice was smooth and cultured. "I was looking for Arcana. She hasn't returned yet?"

"You would have seen her if she had," Fenris replied, jerking a thumb over his shoulder. "Anything from the market will go straight to the settlement."

The wise woman linked her arms over her bent knees and examined the sand beneath her. "I was not at the settlement. The males make me uncomfortable, and I them. I feel... conflicted."

"I was under the impression your belief in the laws of Hiraptha were absolute," Fenris said. He measured her profile, noted the tension in her jaw. "Is your vow of silence as a wise woman not enough to protect you?"

Instead of answering, the harpy smiled. "Do you know how I became a wise woman?"

"You know that I do not."

"Not really - if the males can carry on an entire society under our noses, then anything is possible." Her voice was dry, her face sad. "All Hirapthans are born fatherless, but I was unique in also having no mother."

"Males are killed after fathering children?"

Mirran frowned. "Of course not."

"You just said Hirapthans are all born fatherless."

"Yes, of course." Realisation dawned and she waved an impatient hand. "Males are not considered Hirapthan. Female chicks are kept by their mothers, males are sent to the Pit to be processed into the training programs."

"At *birth*?"

"Yes, at birth," Mirran growled. "No mother wishes to acknowledge the shame of hatching a male, and will have the evidence sent away as swiftly as possible. It is one of the many duties a wise woman fulfils. Now, do you want to hear the story, or not?"

Reigning in his rage, Fenris spoke through gritted teeth. "I am listening."

"I was hatched without a mother. There was some debate about whether I should be allowed to live, but Beera, the wisest of the women, took me into her keeping to be trained in her image." Mirran pursed her lips, gaze distant as she pierced the veil of her memories. "Once I was grown, it was explained that the reason for my orphan status was because my mother had broken our laws. She fled the city with my father, attempted to live with him as an equal in the desert. They were caught, of course, my father executed on the spot. My mother was to be sacrificed to the Brokkarra but when her eggs were discovered, she was made to incubate them before the sentence was carried out."

"Yet you say you never met her?"

"No." Mirran's face pinched. "She was sacrificed before I finished cracking through the shell of my egg. Sometimes, though, in my dreams, I imagine I can hear her screaming for me."

Fenris considered the wise woman's revelations and reached a startling conclusion. "You're sympathetic to Arcana."

"Perhaps," Mirran murmured, her feathers flaring, "I'm merely tainted by the blood in my veins."

"No." Fenris clamped a hand on the female's shoulder, ignored her flinch. "You know the difference between right and wrong, Mirran. You know this world in which you live stole something precious from you. You *know*."

"The life Arcana describes... the love you share," Mirran whispered, her eyes shining wet. "If I'd been born in a different time and place, perhaps I'd have witnessed such a thing between those who created me."

"Love is not a crime," Fenris growled, his heart thundering with the need to right such colossal wrongs. "It is not only worth living for, but dying for. Without love, we are nothing."

Laughter echoed through the trees behind him, high and full and so familiar he ached. Mirran stood abruptly, dashing at her face. "She's back."

"Mirran - damn." Fenris sighed as the harpy launched skyward in a flurry of sand, disappearing from sight in a matter of moments.

Still draped around his neck, Lyra raised a sleepy head. "Mrow?"

"Yes, she fled. Come now, let us greet your favourite person." Using the tree beside him to support a body stiffening after too much exercise, Fenris clawed his way upright. "Weaver's grace. I haven't felt this awkward since my adolescence."

Rather than move to meet the woman whose hands cupped his heart, Fenris drew the greatsword from its' scabbard, dug it point-first into the sand and transferred his weight so that he leant against the hilt. The position soothed the ruffled edges of his soul, allowing him to regain some semblance of composure.

He didn't have to wait long, Caelum's burnt sugar scent preceding him out of the lush jungle less than a minute later. Fenris inspected each of his disproportionately long, slender legs and, noting them free of injury, spent the next few seconds examining his broad chest, powerful shoulders and muscular hindquarters. The deerken's face was set with what Fenris' nose confirmed as amusement, his ears swivelled eagerly forward as he bumped his soft nose against Fenris' cheek. Accepting the caress in the spirit with which it was given, Fenris ran his fingers across the silken silver fur at the base of Caelum's jaw and nodded in approval. "You are uninjured."

"Of course." The deerken's nostrils dilated as he huffed air into Fenris' face, the sensation startlingly intimate but not unwelcome. "What do you take me for, an amateur?"

"Never." Fenris offered a slight smile. "It helps to calm my anxiety to know for certain, however. Where is Arcana?"

Traces of her scent clung, as always, to the deerken's fur, and he knew he'd heard her laughter. She couldn't be far, given the elastic band effect hadn't kicked in, but - Caelum huffed again, the warm blast of air cutting through his galloping thoughts. "She just stopped to check one of the berry vines. It looked a little wilted."

"It's fine now." Arcana stepped out of the shadows, her scent the most decadent milk chocolate and her skin shimmering pearlescent in the sunlight. "Just needed a little nudge."

Fenris drank her in greedily, his voice trapped in his throat. Their time in Hiraptha had her hip bones pushing at her skin but the curves he craved were still present, ink-black hair hanging long and straight over her shoulders. Her eyes were almost too large for her face, wide and deep and blacker than the darkest night. Unable to help himself, Fenris locked his gaze to hers, felt the glamour roar to life deep inside, a beast craving release. The scarlet scarf she'd once lent him still clung to her body, emphasising breasts he itched to caress and offering teasing glimpses of her thighs. Weaver's grace, she was a gift; a precious, irreplaceable gift he both cherished and feared in equal measure. The cage of his chest was no match for his heart as it thundered inside him, finally free to acknowledge just how much he'd despised being left behind whilst she journeyed into possible danger.

"You're safe." Not the pretty words he wanted to offer, but ones from the depths of his soul nonetheless.

Smiling that crooked smile Fenris wanted to kiss into his own body, Arcana closed the distance between them. "I'm safe."

At the sound of her voice, the kitten around his neck hissed in warning. "Lyra, *no.*"

"It's all right." Smile widening, Arcana reached out her hand to the kitten, who promptly yowled in rage and disappeared. "We'll get there eventually."

Giving up any pretence of composure, Fenris wrapped both arms around her waist and buried his face in her midnight hair, inhaling the heady intoxication of her scent. "I worried for you."

"Fenris." The emotion - the affection - in her tone was far more than he'd ever thought to receive, and it brought moisture to his eyes. Burrowing deeper, he found the slender column of her neck and pressed his lips to her fluttering pulse. The tease of her blood ignited something primal inside him, erasing the lingering ache in his gut that her absence had caused and urging Fenris to bite with a ferocity that, if he wasn't used to it by now, would have knocked the air from his lungs. He wanted her. He *needed* her.

He could never have her.

Scraping his fangs over skin that shimmered with the inner glow of the moon, Fenris savoured her shiver and then drew back to examine her face. "Tell me everything."

She did, and he listened, absorbing each word for later recollection even as his mind sorted through the implications of her actions. Once she stopped, Fenris related the contents of his discussions with both Jora and Mirran, watching Arcana's face move through a range of fascinatingly emotive responses.

"Jora's right," she murmured at last, when he'd subsided into silence. "We need to make a decision."

Fenris twisted his fingers in the fabric of her skirt. "You never intended to leave them undefended, and neither did I."

"That's not what I mean." Pushing out of his embrace, she paced towards Caelum and back again. "We've been winging it until now, avoiding asking any pointy questions... but, Fenris, tell me true: why are we here?"

Fenris exchanged a look with Caelum, got a baffled ear-twitch in response. "The portal dimension opened a rift and spat us out?"

"No." Arcana made a slicing motion with one hand and out of the corner of his eye, Fenris saw a plant sprout from the sand. "I don't believe it's that simple. I *can't* believe it. We were spat out a rift, yes, but at random? Not a chance. The Weaver's been pulling our strings since long before I was even born - there's no way this was an accident. She sent us here, to this godsforsaken lump of partially terraformed rock with its backwards culture and suffering people, and she did it for a reason."

"To put us out of Taelon's reach," Caelum said immediately.

Arcana whirled on the deerken, jabbing her finger in his direction and causing a fruit tree behind him to blossom with fat orange flowers. "She cut Fenris' bond. We could be in Taelon's backyard and he wouldn't know we were there. Distance helps, yes, and I'm certain we're out in the middle of bloody nowhere, otherwise the Galactic Alliance would have colonised this useless excuse for a planet by now, but that's not everything. There's more we're not seeing - and I'll bet my favourite cheesecake it's got to do with these blasted harpies."

"You believe there are secrets here the Weaver wishes us to learn?" Fenris considered the notion, considered the conviction behind Arcana's passion. "So far, I've thought about only how we might leave, not that there might be a reason to stay."

Caelum lowered his head, scratching at one foreleg with his antlers.

After a long moment, he shook himself all over and sighed. "I hate to say this out loud, but I think Arcana's right."

"Of course I am." Kicking at the sand in a display of temper which spoke to Fenris' soul, Arcana resumed her pacing. "The first thing I'm going to do when we rescue the Weaver is punch her right in the middle of her stupid face. 'I dare not even think the answers to your questions, or Taelon might hear me.' Bullshit! She just gets her jollies from messing with us."

Fenris couldn't help it; he laughed. The sound bubbled up through his chest, wracking his body until he clung to the greatsword to remain upright, tears of mirth pouring down his cheeks.

"Oh look, the Guardian has a funny bone." Caelum's dry voice was only fuel for the fire, Fenris' laughter intensifying until his body ached.

When at last he got himself under control, Fenris raised his head to find Arcana watching him with her arms crossed and her lips quirked in reluctant amusement. "Well, I'm glad one of us thinks this is funny."

"No, I -" Fenris trailed off into a choking chortle, cleared his throat, and made an attempt to stand up straight. "It was simply that I cannot believe we've been here this long and not figured it all out, and now that we have, all you want to do is punch the Weaver. The being responsible for creating time, the universe, all of it... and you want to punch her in the *face*?"

Caelum's ears flickered. "Sounds like Arcana."

"Indeed." Fenris tried to maintain an impassive expression, failed, snorted a laugh and shoved a fist in his mouth to stop it getting worse. "I apologise."

Where his reasoning had failed, watching him attempt to speak around his knuckles at last drew Arcana's lips into a broad grin. "Great Gods of Sorcen, I love you."

"Huh?"

It was perhaps the most inelegant thing he'd ever uttered, but Arcana merely chuckled, tugging him down to her level so she could feather kisses across his jaw. "You heard me, Guardian. How can I keep up my perfectly enjoyable temper tantrum when you laugh like that? Adorable."

"I..." Blinking at Caelum for help which never came, Fenris frowned. "You're welcome?"

Her grin widened, and this time, her kisses found his mouth. Confusion morphed quickly to desire and Fenris bunched his hands in her hair, inhaling her smile as he demanded - and got - passion in place of playfulness. When Caelum cleared his throat, Fenris drew back, revelling in the sight of her flushed cheeks and swollen lips.

"Less pashing, more planning," the deerken drawled.

"Sorry." Arcana took a half step back and paused, looking around her in amazement. "What happened?"

She and Fenris stood in the middle of a perfect circle of flora, gently blooming saplings and softly waving grasses brushing Arcana's waist. Caelum raised an eyebrow. "Well, when Daddy gets all steamy with Mummy, she leaks energy and the plants grow."

"That's never happened before."

"Indeed." Scenting her embarrassment, Fenris assumed his best innocent expression. "Perhaps I am getting better at demonstrating my affection."

"Hah!" Arcana swatted him in the arm, laughter replacing her blush.

"More likely you're now strong enough to start showing off whatever changes the Weaver made," Caelum muttered, leaning down to nip at one of the plants. "Angry cactus notwithstanding."

"The Weaver," Arcana repeated, staring at the backs of her hands. "Do you ever wonder how much of your life is actually yours, Fenris?"

He shook his head. "No. I gave my life gladly to her cause; until she severed the blood bond, I have never questioned my purpose."

Arcana stilled, and he scented the pain which frissoned through her body. "Is that it, then? Am I just a replacement?"

"No!" Moving with the preternatural speed which was his birthright, Fenris knelt in front of her, reaching to cup her face. "*Never*. I felt for you long before she cut me loose, Arcana. You know that."

"But what about when we get out?" Arcana caught his gaze with hers, delicate features suffused with uncertainty. "We're isolated here, cocooned in our own little bubble - but you have a multitude of duties waiting for you that will only increase with the passage of time."

Never had Fenris resented those duties as he did in that moment. Hardening his voice so that she'd understand his conviction, he drew close enough that they shared breath. "I am yours, first and foremost. Whether or not we can complete the ritual which would join us is irrelevant - you are my mate, Arcana, my other half. There is nothing more important than you."

"Love and duty don't always coincide," she muttered - but the terrible ache was gone from her voice and she softened in his grip. "All right, I believe you. Moment of self-doubt over."

"Good." Fenris rose to his feet, stole a kiss and shook out stiff legs. "We need a plan."

"I won't abandon Jora and the others," Arcana said at once. "Even if Caelum learns to jump, I can't go without knowing they're safe."

Fenris nodded. "On that, we are in firm agreement."

"If we're meant to find something here, then my odds are on either the secret men's society having it, or the Empress having it," Caelum put in.

Arcana shot the deerken a sharp look. "Nothing in the dreambank?"

"I've got no access here - apart from my personal vault." The deerken's head tilted to one side. "I've been getting a lot of reading done, though."

"You and your psychic bookshelf! Let me guess, more of the fabulous Lord Whitehaven?" Arcana fluttered her lashes coquettishly.

Caelum snorted. "Considering you're currently living your own angsty romance, I'd not be throwing shade on my reading habits. There's more to a period romance novel than bodice-ripping and pistols at dawn, you know."

"Please," Fenris interrupted, stepping between them with his hands raised. "We can debate the merits of the dashing Luthier Whitehaven another time."

"You know his name," Arcana and Caelum said in unison.

"Ah. Well, I -"

"You know his name," Caelum repeated, unholy glee in every word. "You've read some of them!"

Aware his cheeks were heating, Fenris appealed to Arcana with both hands raised. "They really are quite thought provoking."

"Hah!" Caelum crowed, prancing back and forth. "Yes! I *win!*"

"Great Gods of Sorcen," Arcana muttered, rubbing at her face with one shimmering hand. "It's like I don't even know you, Guardian."

If he hadn't caught the laughter in her scent, Fenris might have thought her serious. Putting on his best mock scowl, he grumbled, "Can we return to the topic at hand, or shall I demonstrate how to rip a bodice correctly?"

Caelum snorted a laugh. "This is my favourite conversation ever. Ever, ever, *ever.*"

"I'd disagree, but I think this is the most normal I've felt since we set foot on this bloody planet," Arcana muttered, a mischievous smile peeping through her attempted disgruntlement. "All right, then. The Empress intimated she'd like to get to know us better; if we can spark some kind of friendship with her, we'll be better placed to advocate for our people. On top of that, the more time we spend at the Palace, the more chance we have of unearthing whatever it is we're here to unearth."

"Seems solid," Caelum agreed. "She's already curious about you anyway."

"We run a risk that she will not abide by your decisions regarding the males, however," Fenris reminded. "If that is the case, she will demand we submit or die."

Arcana tipped her face to the searing cerulean skies. "I didn't come all this way to die, Fenris - nor will I stand idly by while people are enslaved and mistreated."

Fenris traced the lines of her profile, emotion swelling so thick and huge inside him that, for a long moment, his words were stolen. He thought of Gryde, protecting those he cared about as best he could. He thought of the Father, and Clecke, hiding away in hope of a better life. He thought of the Weaver, who had risked everything to catapult them across the known universe to this place, these people. Most of all, he thought of Arcana, willing to face down an entire kingdom on her own for a handful of harpies she barely knew.

When she turned her head to pin him with her midnight stare, he smiled wide enough to show fang. "My blade is yours, now and always."

"Caelum?" Arcana cut the deerken a sidewards glance.

"I'm in." His tail flicked back and forth, the only outward sign of his excitement. "Long live the revolution."

TWENTY-NINE
ARCANA

Arcana finished winding her final spool of thread and set it into the woven basket at her feet. If the estimates Jora had given were correct - and she had no doubt they were - then the last two days' worth of efforts would be enough for him to finish the first round of clothing. She cocked her head as raised voices floated out of the jungle, identifying Mirran's strident tones and Leiran's more musical ones as they engaged in yet another argument over the best place to tether the animals that had been delivered from the market.

"Great Gods of Sorcen," she muttered, as the heated exchange rose into a series of unintelligible squawks. "I don't think they've stopped shouting at each other since we got back from the market."

"Headache?" Caelum's sleepy voice preceded his raised head, antlers coated in a soft layer of winding vines that mimicked the ones hanging above. "Or is that my brain, still rattling around inside my head after all that failed jump training?"

"Stop beating yourself up - nobody's expecting it to work first try." Arcana debated whether to go and break up the argument, but after a final stream of vitriol, the two harpies fell silent. "And I don't have a headache so much as pins and needles in my butt."

"I was going to suggest asking Fenris for a massage but I don't need to watch him grabbing your butt," Caelum muttered, shaking his head in disgust. "Ever since you two were reunited, he can't keep his hands to himself."

Arcana blushed, because it was true; when Fenris was near, more often than not he was touching her - and when he wasn't, he was watching her. "Slavery left deeper scars than he's willing to admit to."

"That, and he thinks you're the sexiest thing he ever laid eyes on."

"Go back to reading your bodice-rippers," Arcana growled, poking him with a bare toe, "Or I'll braid flowers into your fur."

The galaxies in his eyes swirled in lazy amusement. "You can't. It's so hot here I'm basically bald."

Arcana had a witty reply well and truly prepared, but swallowed it as the bracken crackled and a flustered looking Leiran appeared. He twittered at Caelum, waving his arms in such a way that she spotted the soft bumps on his skin where feathers were beginning to push through.

"He says Jora's asking for you. Apparently..." Caelum's brows lowered, and quite suddenly his long legs were scrambling to get him upright. "There's a message from the Empress."

"About time." Arcana stood, shaking her legs to ease their cramped ache. "I was starting to think we'd have to seek her out ourselves."

Caelum laughed, then repeated her words in Hirapthan when Leiran frowned. Arcana caught snatches of the ensuing conversation, the lessons she'd crammed in at every opportunity slowly starting to bear fruit. At first it had been just herself, Mirran, Fenris and Caelum - then Leiran had arrived, with Jora to help, and before long the other male harpies had begun to show an interest, learning Universal Galactic while Arcana learnt Hirapthan in return. Her constant mistakes had the males in stitches of laughter more often than not, the cooking fire becoming a cheerful place where they were at last beginning to relax.

When Arcana stepped into the cleared space around the oasis pool, however, there was only a sombre silence. Fenris stood alone by the water's edge, an arrow in one hand and a piece of parchment in the other. Arax and his brother, Brok, held guard positions by the hollow tree Jora had appropriated as his workshop, with several of the other harpies clustered nearby.

"What happened?" Arcana asked, crossing straight to Fenris and laying a hand on his arm. Tension hummed through his body, dusty teal skin corded with muscle that was developing almost as she watched. After revealing that their limited diet of fruit and bread was stalling his recovery, Arcana had attempted to convince Fenris to either go hunting in the dark of night and consume whatever blood he needed, or to take it from one of the animals she'd procured from the market for eggs and milk. Instead, he'd taken Arax and Brok out with him and taught them to hunt, making meat a staple in Verga's cookpot ever since. The difference in her Guardian had been immediate, his body beginning to fill out and his subtle musculature firming up. He was still a far cry from the healthy male she'd first ogled aboard the *Wandering Sorceress*, but he was no longer deathly thin and emaciated.

Now, he turned a set expression her way, jaw clenched so tight that a muscle twitched. It wasn't until Arcana smoothed her fingers over that jumping spot that he relented enough to say, "Mirran is gone."

"Gone?" Arcana frowned. "She was shouting at Leiran only a few minutes ago."

"You only missed her departure by moments." Fenris threw the arrow tip-first into the sand and thrust one hand into his hair. "There were two messages. One for you, inviting us to join the Empress this afternoon, and one for Mirran. She's been recalled to the Palace ahead of time to take up a new contract."

"Why?" Though she couldn't read the parchment, Arcana took it anyway - and balked when she realised it wasn't parchment at all, but a thin sheet of leather. "Great Gods of Sorcen, this is people skin."

"Yes."

Suffused with helpless rage, Arcana stormed over to the cooking fire, where even now Verga was preparing lunch. He looked up with a nervous smile at her approach, an expression that shifted quickly to alarm when Arcana bent down and thrust her arm elbow deep into the coals of the fire.

"It's all right," she told him, hoping her Hirapthan was correct. Magic flooded her veins and a moment later, the leather sheet in her other hand caught fire. Straightening to her full height, Arcana shook the embers off her skin and raised her voice, reciting the short Hirapthan plea for peace that Jora had taught her a few days previous.

Verga watched the leather burn with a satisfied expression. When it was done, he nodded. "Good."

"Yes," Arcana answered, aware he'd chosen the single, simple word for her benefit. Releasing the ashes to the soft morning breeze, she stomped back to Fenris. "I hope you memorised what it said."

"Fortunately for us, I did." Though his body was still tense, his lips twitched at the corners. "We're to attend the palace in two hours. The Goddess has summoned us."

"Has she, now." Arcana narrowed her eyes. "I've got questions for this so-called Goddess. And for the Empress, too - she's taken Mirran early and against the terms of our agreement."

"According to the missive Mirran received, it was urgent."

"Did she want to go?"

Fenris rolled one shoulder in a shrug. "I cannot say for certain. She stank heavily of fear, and allowed me to read the missive, but said only it was the duty of a wise woman to go where her Empress wills." The Guardian glanced over Arcana's shoulder, where the males were clustered around Arax and Brok. "They believe she will betray us, no matter her oath to Jora."

"Hey." Reaching again to cup his jaw, Arcana drew Fenris' gaze back to her own. The glamour rose around her, thick and warm with a thousand tickling feathers which, when she brushed her energy against them, wrapped her in an ethereal echo of Fenris' scent. "We've got this."

The Guardian dropped his forehead against hers with a sigh and Arcana ached all over again, feeling fear in every erratic thump of his heart. "Arcana, I -"

She cut Fenris off by the simple expedient of sealing their lips, shoving her tongue past his teeth to sweep inside his mouth. He groaned, a helpless sound of defeat, and locked his arms tight around her. As he gained in strength so too did his embrace but Arcana didn't complain, not even when her ribs creaked a desperate warning and Fenris' hands clenched so tightly in her clothes that the fabric made an ominous tearing sound. She poured her heart into her kiss, fingers gentle as she combed back the dark teal hair which tumbled over his forehead in lazy curls.

"I want you," she whispered, the sound breathless and for his ears alone. "Right now."

Fenris shuddered in her arms. "We can't."

"We can." Arcana didn't have to look, knew through her connection with Caelum that the deerken had corralled the males and was talking with them in a firm, quiet voice on the other side of the oasis. "There's always time for love."

Something which may have been a sob or perhaps even a growl caught in Fenris' chest - but he was scooping her into his arms, the landscape around them a blur as he plunged into the jungle. It felt like only a few steps, but when he slammed her spine-first into the moss-covered trunk of a tree and covered her mouth with his, Arcana couldn't hear the camp, couldn't smell the cooking fire.

Two swift tugs at the knot on her skirt and it fell away, followed quickly by her underwear. She lifted her legs without being asked, wrapping them around Fenris' hips as he shoved his pants down just enough to set his erection free. Arcana felt him hesitate and broke the kiss, looking up into his eyes. "Love me."

"I do." His eyes shone wet, his face stark with desperate hunger. "Weaver save me, I do."

"Now, Fenris. Love me *now*."

He sank into her body with one huge thrust, his body pinning her to the tree and his heart in his eyes. "I love you."

Wrapping her arms around his shoulders, Arcana held on as Fenris began to move, repeating his words with every desperate thrust of his hips. He was glorious muscle and pure, unbridled emotion, every movement of his body sending shivers of ecstasy straight into Arcana's blood. She'd never get enough of him, not if they lived millions of years.

Their lovemaking was sweaty and raw but when they fell, they fell together, bodies locked and souls alight. Arcana felt the scrape of teeth along the bared skin of her shoulder and twisted her fingers into his hair, needing Fenris' fangs inside her as his body was inside her. He didn't bite down, though, and a moment later the scrape became a kiss.

"You're meant to stop me," he muttered, the reprimand ruined by the lazy, sated masculinity that seeped from every pore.

"I know." Arcana tightened her legs around his hips and leant back against the tree, taking in every inch of his passion-flushed face. With the glamour a sensual caress across her senses, she spoke in a voice too husky to be her own. "And you know that I won't."

"Are we going to have this argument forever?" He growled without heat, running both hands up the sides of her ribs and back down again. "Biting you would mean the destruction of several galaxies, not to mention our own deaths."

Rather than voice the suspicion she'd begun to form deep inside, Arcana gave him a lazy smile. "Lucky you're so responsible, then."

"Speaking of responsible," he murmured, features twisting with guilt, "I am not sure we should have fled the oasis like that."

Arcana reached out her senses, caught the edge of Caelum's amusement and his frustrated affection. "Caelum's got them in hand."

"We have let too much fall on his shoulders."

"Fenris, he's fifty-two years old," she chuckled. "He has astonishingly broad shoulders and is more than capable of taking the weight." When Fenris didn't respond, she stretched up to press a kiss to his chin. "You're too used to doing everything yourself. We're a team now, remember?"

Fenris screwed up his face at that, but relaxed a moment later, his body long and lean where it draped against hers. "It is a habit proving hard to break."

Arcana held him close, ignoring reality for a few minutes longer while their hearts thumped in harmony and their bodies remained locked together. Eventually Fenris withdrew, stepping away from the tree and making sure she was steady on her feet before he fixed his clothing and bent to retrieve hers.

"The arrow," Arcana said as they made their way back to the pool. "Did someone try and shoot you again?"

Fenris took her hand and squeezed. "No. The missives were wrapped around the arrow and it had been fired into one of the trees bordering the desert."

"Probably didn't want to risk Fenris' temper," Caelum guessed, his head poking out from the canopy of a short, stout fruit tree. "It's gotta be humiliating when a guy clips your wings with your own arrow without bothering to use a bow."

Arcana eyed the juice stuck to his furry face and raised a brow. "Breaking for lunch?"

"Yeah; Verga made some sort of meaty something or other that isn't really my style. He's packed yours to go and Jora's waiting with clothes." Caelum gave both Arcana and Fenris a waspish once-over. "I'd suggest a wash before you change outfits."

A blush stole over Arcana's cheeks but it was eclipsed by the blindingly gorgeous - and quintessentially male - grin that Fenris turned her way. Detouring via the sheltered area of the oasis that was designated for washing, they scrubbed each other clean and returned to the cooking fire in damp clothing.

As Caelum had promised, Jora was waiting. The tailor inclined his head in greeting and handed Fenris a pair of loose, flowing trousers in a midnight blue fabric. "For you."

"Thank you." Fenris stripped off his old pants without so much as blinking, despite the fact that he wasn't wearing any underwear, and pulled on his new trousers. Elegant, cool and with plenty of room for him to move should he need to fight, they secured at the waist with a thick tie that, once secured, hung from one hip in a pleasing tumble. Paired with the greatsword's harness, the blade's hilt jutting over one shoulder and the scabbard angling out behind the opposite hip, Fenris looked both fearsome and striking.

Jora checked the fit with a practised air and nodded. "They will do."

"They are perfect," Fenris declared, taking the harpy's arm in a warrior's grip. "Thank you."

"You're welcome." Jora smiled through his surprise - but the expression faltered when he turned to Arcana. "I have never made anything like your dress before. I hope you like it."

"I'm sure I will," Arcana reassured him, accepting the bundle of dusky blue cloth he set in her hands. Not quite so brazen as Fenris, she retreated to their hollowed tree to change.

The dress, when she shook it out, stole her breath for long moments - and then Arcana was wriggling into it as fast as she could. The bodice was simple and flowing, with two long, scarf-like ties which went over her shoulders, crossed back under her breasts and then tied in the centre of her back to both create shape and provide support at the same time. The trailing edges of those thick ties tumbled down to blend with the skirt, a multilayered collection of fabric which bled from the dusky blue of the dress's bodice into the same midnight shade as Fenris' trousers. There was also, to Arcana's delight, matching underwear. It was no doubt an effort to utilise leftover scraps of fabric but she appreciated the gesture, feeling decidedly decadent to have a proper pair of underthings.

When she stepped out into the sunshine, Fenris' jaw all-but hit his chest. Jora descended on the dress with the air of a professional seeing one of his most daring creations brought to screaming life, and Arcana stood motionless while he checked her over, adjusting the ties and tugging the fabric so it sat better over her chest. At last, he stepped back and bit his lip. "Do you like it?"

"I love it!" She threw caution to the wind and wrapped the harpy in a tight hug. "Thank you, Jora."

Fenris muttered under his breath in fey, the lilting language so beautiful that tears pricked the corners of Arcana's eyes. Shaking his head, he ran reverent fingers down the blended colours in her skirt. "You look extraordinary."

"There's one more thing." Jora dug in the pockets of his patchwork pants and drew out two long, braided pieces of fabric. Containing Fenris' midnight blue, Arcana's dusky blue and a shade in between, they bore striking similarity to the plaited bracelet Fenris wore on his left wrist, only on a much larger scale. Jora turned his raptor-yellow eyes on Arcana. "It is customary for a male to wear a mistress' colours at court but I knew you wouldn't want any appearance of ownership. I thought perhaps this would work instead."

Without waiting for her answer, he wrapped one of the plaited lengths twice around Fenris' bicep and knotted it in place, then did the same for Arcana with the other length. If they hadn't already been a matched pair before, it was obvious now - each wearing the other's colour, with a middle ground shade that spoke of meeting half-way. Arcana smiled broadly. "Jora, you're a genius."

"Not really." Terracotta skin darkened in a blush and his scarred forearms flexed in a rolling motion reminiscent of the way Mirran flared her wings when embarrassed. Visibly gathering himself, Jora tugged at the trailing end of one braided cord. "I do not know what the reaction will be if Fenris goes to court unbound. This was all I could think to mitigate the chaos you're going to cause."

"Mirran said mating males don't necessarily need to be chained, as long as they're with their mistresses," Arcana pointed out. "Surely not even the Empress can twist the laws against me in that instance."

"Perhaps, perhaps not." Jora shrugged, then motioned at Fenris' neck, the chafing from his slave collar almost completely healed. "Chained or otherwise, they all wear collars. They all belong to their mistresses."

Arcana's eyes narrowed. "I don't own anyone. People are not possessions."

"I know." The harpy's eyes were filled with fierce approval. "That's why I thought you could wear matching colours instead."

"An excellent solution," Fenris approved. His eyes flickered out over the oasis, then back to Jora. "Will you be safe here in our absence?"

The harpy nodded once, his lips firming into a line. "We will set the traps you helped us build the moment you are beyond their reach, and we will remain on alert. Should danger come, we will follow the plan and then hide as ordered."

"Good." Bending down to press a kiss to his cheek, Arcana smiled brightly. "We'll be back as soon as we can."

After Jora wandered away looking dazed but otherwise pleased, Verga pressed a long, leaf-wrapped roll of seasoned meat and salad into her hands, followed by one twice the size for Fenris. The Guardian made a polite query in Hirapthan and laughed at the response, slapping Verga on the back before meeting Arcana at Caelum's side.

"Apparently I'm bulking up so quickly he feared a single serving would be inadequate," Fenris chuckled.

Arcana caught at one of Caelum's antlers and swung onto his back, careful not to jostle her own wrap as she did so. "I hope I don't end up having to put you on a diet."

"Unlikely." Lips curved in amusement, Fenris took her proffered arm and swung up behind her. "My metabolism is too swift for such a necessity."

"I almost hate to say this out loud, but I've missed having the two of you up there," Caelum said as he trotted towards the trees. "Sure beats being mother hen."

Arcana laughed as she called her magic and waved a hand, creating a tunnel through their dense jungle with little more than a thought. It had never been so easy, something that was both welcome and worrisome after several weeks with barely a trickle of power up her sleeve. Closing the tunnel behind them as she went, Arcana poured her emotions into the oasis, imbuing the outer rings of trees with her anger and her furious desire to defend those who lived inside it. By the time they stood in the desert, that outer ring of trees was blanketed in thorny vines and the undergrowth glared outwards with clawed branches and sinister looking flowers.

Caelum inspected the altered scenery, one black-tipped ear flickering. "I still like the angry cactus, but these are also cool."

"I'm glad you approve," Arcana chuckled, tugging on the charcoal ruff of fur that ran down the length of his spine. "Now, if you don't mind, we have an appointment to keep."

Caelum snorted but turned away, haunches bunching. Arcana leant over his neck as he picked up speed, Fenris plastered along her spine. The familiar position was somehow more intimate now they were lovers, his body curled around hers and his arm dropping to tighten over her hips rather than her waist. At just over seven feet tall, the Guardian had enough height to rest his chin on her shoulder and nuzzle against her neck - something he'd never done before but wasted no time doing now, while the desert blurred around them and the sun beat mercilessly overhead.

"You smell like paradise," he murmured, his lips tickling the shell of her ear. The subvocal tease was whipped away by the wind of their travel but Arcana heard it nonetheless, every hair on her body standing straight in rapturous attention. His fingers splayed across her hip bone as he shifted his body against hers. "I thought my cravings would lessen once we were together but the exact opposite has occurred."

Arcana shivered as his fangs grazed the flesh below her jaw. Tightening her grip on Caelum's neck, she turned her head just enough to nip at Fenris' nose. "Later."

A throaty rumble of a laugh, but he removed his fangs and settled in for what could only be described as a snuggle, eating his wrap as though it were the most normal thing in the universe to do while riding bareback on a deerken through an alien desert. Shaking her head, Arcana followed suit, finishing her own lunch as the sun-baked outline of Hiraptha's Palace solidified out of the heat haze.

Caelum slowed from his breakneck speed as they hit the streets, neatly dodging passers-by until he arrived at the far quieter path to the Palace's ornate front doors. The two harpies on guard came to stiff attention as they approached, leaning forward to tug the doors wide so that Caelum could enter unhindered.

Without a formal gathering of courtiers, the throne room of Hiraptha was even more cavernous than Arcana remembered. Great stone pillars broke up intricate brickwork and heavy tapestries adorned the walls, each one meticulously worked in shades of turquoise and gold. The goddess statue dominated the royal dais, her cupped hands empty of all but a few white cushions.

A pair of harpy women stood to one side, where a large hanging had been tied back to reveal a white and gold door. As Caelum moved up the aisle, they grabbed their spears and barred the doorway, brows drawn close in a frown.

"We're here to see the Empress," Arcana announced, not bothering to try and use her rusty Hirapthan. Caelum dutifully translated, coming to a halt at the top of the dais steps so that both she and Fenris could dismount.

Before the guards could answer, an older harpy stepped from the shadows behind the enormous goddess statue. She was dressed in dark leathers adorned in strings of rainbow beads, her skin a terracotta so dark it bordered on rust. A beaded golden headpiece nestled amongst the black down of her mane and every movement clinked with the sound of wealth. Sharp raptor's eyes swept over Fenris' clothing, then Arcana's, her top lip curling back in a sneer. When she spoke, her words were thick with a scorn that required no translation.

Fenris stiffened beside Arcana but remained silent as Caelum answered the woman in quiet, almost bored tones. The harpy gave an irritated squawk, but her reply was cut off as the white and gold door opened and Beera appeared.

"Ah," the wise woman said. "You're here."

"We are," Arcana agreed. After a suitably drawn out pause, she flicked a glance at the unfamiliar woman. "Who is this?"

Beera's eyes narrowed at the barely contained hostility, but she waved an introductory hand at her compatriot. "This is Flik'hithan, Matron of the Slaves. She rules the Pit and is responsible for ensuring all males are properly placed throughout Hiraptha."

Arcana didn't need the title, nor Flik'hithan's purse-lipped look of disapproval, to know the other female held a position of high regard within the court. Feathers, beads and carved ivory charms dripped from every available limb, accompanied by so much body paint that it was impossible to tell the true shade of her skin. Arrogance was stamped on each line of her weathered face, her body a symphony of self-entitlement. Forcing a bright smile onto her face, Arcana switched to Hirapthan. "Pleased to meet you."

Flik'hithan's eyes widened at the casual greeting, talons digging into the stone floor as Arcana looked her dead in the eye rather than bowing to acknowledge her superiority. The Slave Matron twittered at Beera, who shrugged and responded in short, sharp sentences. After a crisp silence, Flik'hithan drew herself up, turned and swept down the aisle towards the front door.

Beera waited until the other harpy was gone before returning her gaze to Arcana and stepping aside. "The Empress will see you now."

Following the wise woman's lead, the two guards relaxed their stances and retracted their weapons, making room for Arcana, Fenris and Caelum to pass into the Palace's inner sanctum.

Arcana half expected a corridor or a foyer, but instead, they stepped directly into a large, round chamber painted a blinding shade of white. Empress Hisha'maniketh reclined upon an enormous turquoise cushion in the exact centre of the room, eyes closed and legs dangling over the edge of what was less a chair and more a bowl. The unusual perch was supported by a thin pillar of white which rose from the floor much like the stem of a wineglass, and sprouted two thin, white chains from either side. At the end of each chain were the same identical slaves Arcana had seen at the oasis, their bared chests oiled to a sheen and their flowing white pants so sheer as to be invisible, showing off every inch of the bodies underneath.

Equally sickened and infuriated, Arcana turned her eye to the rest of the minimally furnished room. A scattering of white cushions dotted the floor, offering comfort to guests while still keeping the Empress on a very literal pedestal. A Hirapthan-sized statue of the goddess stood in one corner of the room, cupped hands outstretched as though to catch falling water, or accept an offering. The statue's nondescript features were serene, but Arcana was reminded of the cursed wall inside Iniron's temple and shivered. Fenris nudged her with an elbow, arched a brow and then very deliberately rubbed his own arms.

It was cold, Arcana realised. She looked around the room but there were no other features besides a doorway in the opposite wall. Where was the cool air coming from?

"My Empress." Beera spoke in smooth Universal Galactic, dropping to one knee before the Empress' chair. "Your guests are here."

The Empress lifted her lashes slowly, as though waking from a pleasant dream. Her raptor's eyes held deep amusement as they swept over first Arcana's attire, then Fenris', before settling at last on Beera. "Thank you, wisest of my women. Is there anything else, before you withdraw?"

"The Slave Matron wished to see you," Beera returned evenly. She glanced back at Arcana and cleared her throat. "Seeing as you were expecting guests, I turned her away."

The Empress sighed, but her act fooled nobody - it was obvious she'd been very much aware of what had happened out in the throne room. "She still sees herself as my mother, thinking to stick her beak in whenever she so chooses. You were right to send her out."

"Thank you, Empress." Beera stood, then hesitated. "She will likely return in a few hours."

"Eh." Empress Hisha waved a careless hand. "I'll see her if I feel like it. Even the Slave Matron must learn to wait for her Empress' dictate. Is that all?"

"Yes, Empress."

"Good. You may go." The wise woman looked like she wanted to protest, but instead she bowed low enough to scrape her forehead along the floor, then scrambled to her feet and retreated. When the door thumped firmly shut, Empress Hisha's face creased in a bright smile and she jumped down from her half-egg chair, turquoise and gold beads clacking. She crossed to take both of Arcana's hands in her own smaller ones, squeezing tight. "I'm so pleased you're here, at last!"

Thrown, Arcana worked hard to keep her voice even. "Are we late?"

"No, no." The Empress shook her head, downy mane flying about her face. "I've just been so *bored*."

Words bubbled in Arcana's throat, none of them appropriate for the situation. Just as the silence began to draw thin, Caelum lowered his head towards the Empress and she stroked her hands through his short fur with ill-disguised delight. With his eyes half-lidded, the deerken said, "I'm sad that you took Mirran before her time was up."

"Oh?" The Empress' hands stalled in their caresses. "I wouldn't think such an incredible beast as yourself would be interested in the career of a single wise woman."

Caelum's tail swished in annoyance, but his tone remained even. "Her contract was for a week, and we didn't have a chance to revise it."

"A situation arose." The Empress shrugged. "One of my elder wise women has become too old to keep up with the demands of her position and decided to retire. Mirran was the only other wise woman without a permanent contract."

"Where did she go?" Caelum asked. When the Empress frowned, he lowered his head and rubbed shamelessly at her shoulder. "I liked her. If I know where she is, I could visit."

An almost childlike delight sparked in the Empress' eyes and she cuddled Caelum's enormous head close. "Mirran was assigned to the Slave Matron. There are a team of three wise women who manage the Pit, the mating male compound and the repurposing enclosure. I can't say for certain where exactly she'll be doing her duties, but it's probably why the Slave Matron attempted to visit me just now." The Empress sighed and pressed a soft kiss to Caelum's furred brow. "My mother disliked Mirran from the moment she hatched, but that changes nothing. I had a spot to fill, and I filled it."

"And what about us?" Arcana asked, her voice returning in a rush of irritation.

"What about *you*?" The Empress raised a brow. "I am the Empress. No engagements are more important than the ones I decree."

"Even if it means breaking your own word?" Arcana crossed her arms over her chest. "That doesn't seem like a good ruling policy."

The Empress filled her cheeks with air, then abruptly laughed. "The more time I spend with you, the more I like you. Tell me, Arcana - are you this famously difficult where you come from?"

"I'm afraid so."

"I had a feeling." The Empress chuckled again. "Very well, I shall offer you an opportunity at recompense. When you next see Mirran, you may approach and ask her what post she prefers. If she wishes to return to your employ and you can negotiate a price for her services, I shall restructure my wise women to suit and release her to your care. Will that do?"

Arcana inclined her head. "Yes, thank you."

"I should warn you, though - positions like the one Mirran has been given are highly coveted. Were it not for our shortfall, she would wait years for such an opportunity, and may not want to give it up." The Empress gave Caelum a final pat and then stepped away, straightening her immaculate white leather skirt. "Now, enough business talk. Are you ready to meet the Goddess?"

"Yes, your Imperial Grace," Arcana replied.

"Hisha." The Empress grinned and winked. "When we are in private, I wish for you to call me Hisha."

"And what of Fenris?"

The Empress looked to Fenris and bit her lip. "It is treason to interact with a male as an equal. I find myself divided, however, for surely that would offend you?"

"It would," Arcana said firmly.

"Goddess?" The Empress turned to the statue in the corner. "Advise me."

"Analysis of the male Fenris shows him to be wild, raw and virile. Whilst the laws are clear, he is not of Hirapthan genetics. Thus, addressing him directly would be unusual but not treasonous." The statue's smooth, artificially cheerful female voice echoed slightly inside the chamber. "In this instance, I would recommend putting the dictates of custom aside, or you might risk the friendship you hope to build with the one known as Arcana."

Hisha nodded enthusiastically. "Your counsel makes sense. Male Fenris, it would please me immensely if you would also address me as Hisha whilst in private."

Fenris exchanged a loaded glance with Arcana, the burning jade of his fathomless eyes hiding the look from an Empress who suddenly seemed half her years. "It would be my honour, Hisha."

"Excellent!" Hisha clapped her hands, then made a sweeping gesture towards the statue. "In that case, I present to you the Goddess of Hiraptha. Goddess, this is Arcana, Fenris and the honoured beast Caelum."

The statue emitted a gentle, chimelike sound. "Welcome to Hiraptha, Arcana, Fenris, and honoured beast Caelum. I am the Goddess. It is a pleasure to make your acquaintance."

"The pleasure is ours," Fenris replied, his voice as smooth as the flourishing bow he executed. "We've been eagerly anticipating the opportunity to meet you."

Another chime. "Truth," the Goddess announced.

"The Goddess is the mentor, guardian and confidante not only of the Empress, but all of Hiraptha," Hisha said, feathers fanning proudly as she made an expansive gesture. "Her wisdom has guided us since the dawn of creation."

"I'll confess, this is the first time I've met a deity," Arcana said, clasping her hands in front of her. "Do you have a physical body, Goddess?"

"I interact with the citizens of Hiraptha through the Empress, and I convene with the Empress here, within the Palace. A living, breathing body would be redundant," the statue said.

Empress Hisha stepped forward, eyes alight with curiosity. "Do you have a Goddess where you come from?"

"In a way," Arcana said slowly. "I believe I've met some beings like your Goddess, though they're not called by that name."

"Truth," the Goddess declared, her affirmative chime tinkling through the chamber.

"And you, Fenris?" Hisha drew the syllables of Fenris' name out so they were a purr, her eyes taking a long, sultry trip down his body and back up again.

"I have met many who claim the title of God or Goddess, but few who were able to live up to such an exalted term," the Guardian replied. His shoulders tightened as Hisha's overtly hungry gaze returned to his face. "In my culture, it is considered rude to stare in such a manner."

Hisha blinked. "Goddess? Clarify."

"Your overt sexual attraction is making him uncomfortable," the Goddess replied. "Prior analysis of his genetic code, gleaned from the samples provided shortly after his arrival, leads to the assumption he is also able to scent your desire and hear your elevated heart rate."

Fenris' hands tightened to fists and Arcana immediately smoothed her fingers across the back of his knuckles. After a deep, steadying breath, the Guardian nodded. "Your Goddess is perceptive."

"Of course. She's the Goddess," Hisha muttered, frowning. Tapping one talon, she looked to Arcana. "Why shouldn't I appreciate him? He is male - pleasing us is his function."

Arcana made a supreme effort to strangle her hostile urges and spoke in what she hoped was a calm, measured tone. "Would you like to be ogled in such a way?"

Hisha's frown deepened. "I'm the Empress. It's a requirement for all males to respond on command."

"Truth," the Goddess chimed.

"I don't understand," Arcana admitted.

"I can show you." Hisha brightened at once, then turned and issued a swift command in Hirapthan, clicking her fingers in emphasis.

A discreet door set in the back wall slid open, and a male harpy sauntered in. He was well built, with a couple of old whipping scars across his shoulders that only served to increase his inherent sensuality. His tawny brown mane was braided in a long tail down his back and flecked with black and grey, his dark bronze skin oiled to a sheen. His collar was of beaten gold, set with turquoise and white stones which complemented the bright white loincloth clinging to his narrow hips.

Fenris stiffened, the movement so imperceptible Arcana fancied she'd have missed it if she didn't know her Guardian so well. Though the male harpy's face betrayed no hint of recognition, his raptor eyes trained demurely on the ground, Arcana would have bet her last cupcake that the two knew each other.

"This is my..." Hisha paused, lips moving as she tried and discarded several different words. "Head concubine. I call him Bir'yan, which translates loosely as 'favourite' in your tongue." Stepping closer, the Empress spread a proprietary hand over the male's chest. "Now, watch."

With her free hand, she caught hold of Bir'yan's loincloth and tugged it off his body in one swift movement, leaving the male completely naked. Sliding her hand up the sculpted planes of his chest, Hisha curled her fingers in his collar and yanked until he bent, putting their faces on a level. She twittered softly in his ear while he stared impassively at the floor, appearing not in the least discomfited to be nude in front of an audience.

The Empress stepped back, her face expectant, as Bir'yan straightened. Arcana could only watch in horrified fascination as the male's penis twitched, thickened, and became fully erect in a matter of moments. As moisture began to bead on the tip, Fenris made a choking sound and turned away, his body shaking and his eyes squeezed closed. "That's not adoration," he growled. "It is abuse."

"Abuse?" Hisha's expectant grin faded swiftly to confusion, then anger. "*Abuse?* What about this smacks of cruelty? He is dressed, fed, given a safe place to sleep, and a platform upon which to adore an Empress. How can that be abuse?"

Fenris swung back to face the Empress, top lip curling to reveal fang. "Did he ask to be stripped naked, fondled, drugged, violated? Do you even know his true name?"

"He's male." Hisha shrugged, confusion stalling her fury. "They do not have the capacity to understand a name, nor the ability to form opinions. If not for the mercy of Hiraptha, they would all starve in the desert without an intelligent thought between them."

Silence. A silence so terribly loaded, Arcana's skin crawled with it. At first, she didn't know what she was missing - until Fenris' feral expression stretched into a vicious grin. "Where is your Goddess and her truth now, your Imperial Grace?"

Hisha flinched at the malice he injected into her title, but drew herself up and turned to face the statue in the corner of the room. "Goddess. Verify the truth of my statement at once."

"I cannot," the statue replied. "I do not have permission."

"I am the Empress," Hisha snapped. "I give you permission."

"You do not have the authority to grant such permission," the Goddess said. "It can be granted only by her Imperial Grace Prynna'thekeyra, First Empress of all Hiraptha."

"I... what?" Shaking her head, Hisha looked more and more uncertain. "But I am the Empress."

"You are an Empress," the statue corrected. "You are not *the* Empress."

While the harpy stood gaping, Fenris strode across the room and snatched Bir'yan's loincloth from her hands. He wrapped it around the other male's hips with shaking fingers, lips against the harpy's ear as he spoke in a swift murmur. The slave didn't move, but his erection faded away as though it had never been.

"Goddess," Arcana said slowly, "Why are the men enslaved?"

"I do not have permission to answer that question."

"Were they free, once?"

"I do not have permission to answer that question."

"Were males and females on Hiraptha once equal? Were the laws ever different?"

"I do not have permission to answer those questions."

"Stop," Hisha held up a trembling hand, her face pale. "Goddess, how do I change your permissions to receive answers to these questions?"

"You cannot. Only the First Empress can provide proper clearance."

Hisha hissed out between her teeth, glorious white feathers fanning in frustration. Shoving a hand into her equally white mane, she spat a curse. "The First Empress has been dead for six generations, my Goddess. She cannot bestow such permissions!"

"Truth."

"And my word as Empress is not enough?" Hisha shook her head even as she spoke. "No, it isn't. One of the first lessons you ever taught me was that the First Empress is the mother of us all, the Empress of Empresses. Her authority is greater than mine, even in death."

"Truth."

Growling in a very un-Empresslike manner, Hisha stomped across the room and kicked the Goddess statue in a fit of temper. After a long moment, she turned back to face Arcana, shoulders set and expression determined. "From the moment you arrived upon Hiraptha, you have challenged everything I ever thought I believed. Now, today, I invite you here in friendship and you shake the very foundations of my existence."

"Is seeking the truth really such a damnable offence?" Fenris asked quietly.

Hisha's eyes blazed and she lifted her chin. "I cannot answer that without time to think upon today's events. In a week's time, I will be touring the city and communing with the people. Will you join me upon my journey, that we may discuss this further?"

"A week?" Arcana looked to Fenris, then to Caelum, found the answers in their eyes. "We'd be delighted."

"Good. I shall also arrange an audience with Mirran once the tour is concluded, to negotiate the terms of her future." With the barest flick of her fingers, Hisha threw herself into her egg chair and closed her eyes. "Dismissed."

Arcana hesitated a moment, then bowed low and left, her companions hard on her heels. It was only once they were safely into the desert, bent low over Caelum's neck, that she said, "Are we going to discuss the fact that the Goddess is a computer?"

"I'm too busy being traumatised by that slave's supernatural ability to conjure a hard-on at will," Caelum muttered.

Once again draped over her spine, his mouth close to both Caelum's ear as well as her own, Fenris loosed a low growl. "Gryde. His name is *Gryde*."

Gryde. The harpy who had been friend, protector and unwitting tormentor during Fenris' captivity. Arcana smoothed her hand over her Guardian's cheek, felt his arm tighten around her waist in response. "We'll get him out."

"He will not leave his people." Fenris' voice was filled with pain and the echo of nightmares. "Either the laws change, or he will stay and serve until his dying breath."

There was nothing to say to that, so Arcana watched the sand fly by beneath Caelum's hooves. The oasis was a welcome haven of greenery ahead, the thick trees providing a cover from the twin suns that Arcana suddenly craved with all her heart. Waving a hand to dispel the defensive magic, she sat up as Caelum slowed to a walk inside the thin foliage of the outermost edge, drawing a measure of peace from the broad branches and dangling vines.

"So," Caelum said, pausing beside a thickly gnarled trunk. "The Goddess is a computer, sworn to secrecy by a woman who's been dead approximately five hundred years. At some point this planet was partially terraformed, presumably by whoever installed the Goddess computer inside a facility with climate control and solar power, around which the Palace was built. Am I missing anything?"

Fenris swung his lithe frame onto an outstretched branch and tugged Arcana into his lap, arms wrapping tight around her ribs and chin resting on her shoulder. "No, I think you've summarised all our thoughts. The only thing I do not comprehend is why the project was abandoned and the harpies left to their own devices."

"We may never answer that question," Arcana murmured, leaning back into his embrace. "I'm more interested in what other technology the Goddess might have up her sleeve, and how we go about accessing it."

"There's one other thing." Caelum moved forward to place his head on her thighs, eyes drifting closed as both Arcana and Fenris scratched the space between his antlers. After a long, quiet moment, he said, "I heard singing while we were in there."

"Singing?" Arcana repeated, her fingers stalling their caress. When Caelum grunted a reprimand, she resumed her petting. "You mean real singing, or... *singing* singing?"

"The same song that led us to the icy ruin where we found Fenris," the deerken admitted. "Soft and distant, a siren crooning in my head. You were right, Arcana - the Weaver sent us here for a reason, and that reason lies buried in the depths of the Empress' Palace."

"So many questions," Fenris murmured, his chest rumbling against Arcana's spine. "And such little information from which to extrapolate answers."

She snorted. "Welcome to our life, Guardian. One thing I'm sure of, though."

"Oh?"

"Hisha is the key."

"She can't spill secrets she doesn't know," Caelum reminded, one eye opening to swirl lazily in her direction. "She was as shocked as we were."

"I know." Soft green leaves began to bloom on Caelum's antlers and Arcana reached up to stroke one. "Hisha's offering friendship; I say we take it. Worst case, we might make the lives of these harpies better by convincing her to relax her laws. Best case, we get further inside the Palace and find whatever it is we were sent here to find, like good little bloodhounds."

"I agree." Fenris' lips trembled as they pressed into Arcana's neck, his evergreen and cinnamon scent wrapping her in a comforting blanket of affection. "It appears there is much to be done."

"King of understatements, you are," Caelum muttered. "Truly, I don't know how we'd survive without you around to regale us with the obvious."

"Indeed." Fenris chuckled deep in his chest, then sighed and squeezed Arcana tight. "You realise Hisha may try to fight us."

"She might." Arcana twisted in his arms, reaching to cup his cheek in one hand as she pressed a tender kiss to his lips. "She'll lose."

Burning jade eyes blazed into hers. "I believe you."

"Together, then?"

"Always."

THIRTY
FLARE

Flare swept through the enormous double doors with a nod to the guards either side, his boots echoing through the empty council chambers and his robes swishing across the light-speckled floor. Zaire kept silent pace beside him, silver accented armour polished until it shone and head bowed so that his blue-black hair hid his face. As when Flare had first arrived on Galactic Station, Kaiora stood alone at the far window in her golden mermaid gown, staring out at the star-pierced vista of space. She turned in an elegant sweep of fabric to meet him, the fine lines at the corners of her eyes the only outward hint of discomfort.

"You should still be in bed," Flare growled, drawing to a halt at the edge of her trailing skirts. "Where's your security detail?"

The Chancellor pointed a pixie-like finger straight upward, where the barely visible outline of Naavah clung to the vaulted black ceiling.

"Inventive," Zaire grunted.

"Necessary," Kaiora corrected. "This allows me to maintain the illusion of strength without flouting our new Security Chief's tyrannical decree that I must be under guard at all times."

Flare's lip twitched, but he bit back his witty reply as one of the service doors whirred open and a slender woman walked in. Almost a head shorter than he, the newcomer wore the aubergine and gold uniform of Galactic Station and carried a datapad in one hand. Tawny brown hair had been drawn back into a crisp bun and her eyes, a curious shade of mustard, tilted up slightly at the corners. Her face was slim and pointed and when she spoke, her voice had a delicate trill to it. "Chancellor, if you've a moment?"

"Of course." Perceptibly straightening, Kaiora waved a hand at Flare. "This is the new Security Chief I was telling you about. Flare, this is my Station Manager."

"Prynna Brandburg," the woman said, offering a fine boned hand. "It's a pleasure to meet the famous Flare Veritax at long last."

"Flattery will get you everywhere," Flare returned, waggling his eyebrows in the ridiculous way that always made Arcana laugh. It worked now, too, Prynna's lips stretching into an easy smile. "Kaiora, you didn't tell me you were hiding treasure in the bowels of this floating wreck."

Kaiora snorted. "Shameless, as always."

"It's what makes me, me," Flare returned, flashing the Chancellor a lazy smile at seventy percent power. He saw her lashes flutter as she attempted to cover her reaction, and turned to Zaire. "Shall we give these ladies their privacy?"

The Ryllin had so far watched the exchange with an impassive expression, but now he nodded. "Yeah. I can see Olivie over there, prepping to let the rest of the Council in. If you want a word with him, now's the time."

"Chancellor, Station Manager, if you'll excuse me." Flare performed a frothy bow and turned away.

"If you ooze any more masculine charm, they'll melt," Zaire muttered, his body brushing Flare's as they crossed the cavernous room.

"Z -"

"Save it." The Ryllin's voice was little more than a hiss of expelled breath, but his indigo eyes glittered with heat. "You might fool everyone else on this blasted Station, including yourself, but I know when you're faking it. You owe me nothing, least of all an explanation."

Skin tight with unease, Flare nevertheless pasted the aforementioned fake smile to his face as they came within hearing range of Olivie. "Mister Harthax! I trust this morning sees you without a hangover."

The portly administrator's brows shot up. "No morning ever sees me with a hangover, Security Chief."

"Just Flare, Olivie, please," he groaned, rubbing a hand over his face. "Or, if you're determined to stand on ceremony, one of my Sorcen titles will do. I can't keep up with all the pomp this station bathes in daily."

"As you will, Fire Elder." Olivie inclined his head politely, but his eyes twinkled with mirth. "How can I help you?"

"Just checking the security roster, if that's all right with you." Flare held out his hand for Olivie's datapad and received it a moment later. He tapped the screen to bring up the diagram he and Zaire had worked out the day before and gave it a cursory once over. "All right. Where's Pytch?"

Olivie took the datapad back and tapped at it for a few moments. "Due any moment, sir. He and the security detail you arranged will be in place before we open the doors to the rest of the Ambassadors."

"Good man, Olivie." Flare clapped him on the shoulder, careful not to knock him off balance. "Am I speaking today, or is it just Kaiora?"

"According to the schedule, you'll be standing beside the Chancellor while she delivers her address - whether or not she requests your input at the time will be entirely up to her."

Flare nodded. "I guess that's as good as I can hope for, given the circumstances."

"You should know, Fire Elder, that your sudden appointment and subsequent interrogations have caused quite the stir," Olivie said, his voice quiet. "I'd expect questions at best, and outright challenge at worst as the meeting proceeds."

"Is that official, or scuttlebutt?" Flare asked. When the other man hesitated, he offered his best rogue's grin. "Olivie, I thought we were friends."

"We are barely acquaintances, Fire Elder." The administrator's words were officious, but the corners of his lips twitched ever so slightly.

Flare clapped both hands over his heart. "Barely acquaintances? Olivie, how could you say such a thing? Here I'd die for you, and you're brushing me off as some passing ship in the night? For shame."

Beside him, Zaire choked, turning the sound into a cough which he hid with his fist. Olivie's expression didn't change, but the faintest hint of pink dusted his cheeks. "It is my duty as the Chancellor's administrative aide to remind you that such fraternisations are discouraged, Fire Elder." He paused. "However, if it saves you drowning your sorrows in some sordid backstation establishment, then as your barest of acquaintances, I might let slip that the scuttlebutt is far more trustworthy than anything heard through my official channels."

"See that, Z? He does care." Flare sniffed loudly, wrapping an arm around Olivie's shoulders for a brotherly squeeze of the sort that made Lesce growl for an entire day.

Olivie shot him a long-suffering look. "I believe your associates are here, sir."

"Thanks." Raising a hand to Pytch and Verdure in greeting, he gave Olivie a broad wink and sauntered off.

"You really are insane, you know that?" Zaire muttered, catching up with barely two of his long-legged strides. "I've never seen Olivie blush before."

"That was barely a darkening of his cheeks," Flare scoffed. "Yours is much more satisfying."

The rogue's indigo eyes narrowed and he clenched one hand around the hilt of a dagger. "Come closer and say that again."

Flare coaxed a laugh, allowing it to echo inside the hollow cavity of his chest. He still felt raw after the previous night, his gut clenching in an effort to retain what little breakfast he'd managed to shove down his throat - but there was far more at stake than the gaping black hole where his soul should have been, so he plastered a dazzling smile on his face and exchanged firm forearm grips with both Pytch and Verdure.

"Everything ready?" Flare drenched his voice in confidence and kept his posture easy as the doors to the chamber opened and other Ambassadors began to file in.

Pytch clicked his heels together and thumped a fist to his heart. "Yes, First Flame."

"Not my title any more," Flare reminded him.

The bastard simply grinned wider, flicking pale blond hair back off his forehead with an irreverent twitch of his head. "Yes, First Flame."

Flare clenched his jaw as the two sorcerers moved into position at the back of the room, the rest of the Sorcen team already in place. Resisting the urge to run both hands through his hair, he turned towards the Chancellor and stopped as Zaire grabbed his wrist. "You're not ready for this."

"I'm fine." Flare stared up into intense indigo eyes, throttling his demons with unforgiving hands. "I was in worse shape when I first got here."

"What you did at the club last night... you can't do that again."

This wasn't the conversation he wanted to have, or where he wanted to have it, but he owed Zaire more than platitudes. The gaping wound inside him had sat dormant these last weeks, but after his trip to Macadre? Yeah, he could feel the backslide as much as his lover could. Flare blew out a swift breath and gave up the truth. "If I want Arcana back, I need to find those ships. And if I want the ships, I need to sort out this whole mess; poisoning, assassination attempts, the lot. Interviews and intimidation gave us nothing, so I had to try a different approach." He swallowed heavily, forcing the final words out even though they were sharp as razors. "Lesce told me to use every tool in my arsenal to find Arcana."

"Not that one." Zaire's grip tightened until the bones in Flare's wrist creaked and he knew he'd have bruises later. "Not any more."

Something hot and tight and deliciously dark curled through Flare's veins. "Jealous?"

"Impossible. I know for a fact how hot under the collar I can make you." Zaire yanked roughly, their chests colliding as though they were arguing. "I can't save you, Flare."

"Nobody can save me," he hissed, baring his teeth even as he basked in the soothing cool of the Ryllin's body.

"You're wrong. You can save yourself - you just have to believe it's worth the effort." With a final tug that managed to get both of their straining erections brushing against each other, Zaire released his arm and stomped away.

Flare stood alone, using every ounce of his will to regain control. Thank the gods for Zaire's tight leather armour and his own billowing robes, or the evidence of their ridiculous lust would be on display for all to see. After a moment to straighten his heavy scarlet overrobe and black linen underrobe, Flare set his shoulders and strode to Kaiora's side, where Zaire already waited. Dismissing Station Master Prynna with a regal nod, the Chancellor clapped her hands for attention.

"Thank you all for coming." Kaiora's voice rang deep and pure through the chamber, and if Flare hadn't witnessed her illness himself, he'd never have guessed how close she'd come to death. "I called this emergency meeting for a number of reasons. First, as you know, three days ago there was an attempt made upon my life. Through the quick thinking and exceptional skills of the people close by at the time, the attack was unsuccessful. However, when put side by side with the recent bout of poisonings and Ambassadorial deaths, there is no doubt that we have someone with ill intent in our midst."

"You want to find the saboteur? Look at the man beside you," Krowley growled, gaining his feet in an explosion of spotted animal hides. Jabbing a finger in Flare's direction, he bared his teeth. "None of this was an issue before he arrived on Galactic Station."

"Ambassador Flare Veritax is the man who saved my life, and I will thank you to remember that, Ambassador Krowley." Kaiora's voice was firm. "His actions are the only reason I stand here today, and were the driving force behind my decision to officially instate him as Galactic Station's new Security Chief."

A wave of murmurs followed her statement, but they fell quickly silent when Krowley barked a sharp laugh. "Can't you see, Chancellor? He's fooled you - and giving him this power has elevated Sorcen to levels of authority within the Alliance they'd not normally gain this early in their dealings. Everywhere I turn, I'm tripping over arm-waving, spell-spitting magicians, and you're really wondering where the danger is coming from?"

"Sorcerers," Flare said, raising his voice so it cut cleanly through the chatter following Krowley's statement. "The correct word is sorcerers. And as you know, I've been more than generous in offering Sorcen's assistance to the Alliance. Even now, our earth sorcerers are working alongside your mechanics to convert the fleet's ion engines to our crystal ones. Our healers fight death and disease alongside your medics and our soldiers train on the daily with your own. We have given much to the Alliance, and in return, you give us suspicion? Such accusations are beneath your warrior's honour, Ambassador."

"You wish to challenge my honour?" Krowley snatched his ritual spear from where it rested beside his chair and slammed the butt of it against the floor. "You wish to meet your death at my hands?"

"Enough!" Kaiora laid a restraining hand on Flare's arm, though he hadn't moved a muscle while he spoke. She tilted her head up towards Krowley. "You yourself gave Ambassador Flare the task of finding the lost ships of both Rylle and Karrjhan. Why do such a thing if you believe him incapable?"

Flare donned a shark's smile, nasty and full of teeth. "It's a test - one I am expected to fail. I knew that when I took it on."

"Too bad you didn't put that meagre intelligence to work when it counted," Krowley sneered. "You might not have failed in so spectacular a fashion."

"Considering Ambassador Flare has only been on the case for a week, when you had almost a month before handing over the reins, I feel it's far too early to be flinging such accusations about," Kaiora snapped. "Now, if we may, I wish to bring this meeting back to the matter of the treachery upon our station." The Chancellor glared at Krowley until he growled and sat with a thump. "As your new Security Chief, Flare and his teams have the attendant authority to do whatever is necessary to ensure our collective safety. Part of that involves ferreting out the predators in our midst - and whilst I understand this may inconvenience some of you, I expect full co-operation with his investigations."

"What if Krowley's right? What if Ambassador Flare is the danger?" A feminine voice grated from the back corner.

"I'm not *the* danger but I am *a* danger," Flare said, turning his eyes in the direction of the voice. As gasps went up in a chorus through the chamber, he gently removed Kaiora's hand from his arm and strode to stand directly before his audience. "I have fought in Sorcen's military for fifty-seven years. I've killed more people than you've had orgasms, and I've ferreted out traitors, spies, criminals, and a couple of lost kittens." A smattering of nervous laughter echoed his words, but Flare kept his face set and his voice hard as he slid his gaze across the assembled Ambassadors. "There is more at stake here than your petty political rivalries. More at stake than your endless orations about grain supplies, or your invitation to one of planet Grr'hiklakkan's mind-bending dinner parties. I've spent my career fighting for the lives of those who cannot fight for themselves and I'm not about to be dissuaded now because you'd all prefer to stick your heads up your own backsides. I will hunt the traitor among you, whether you like it or not, and I will deliver justice, whether you like it or not." Flare spread both arms in dark invitation. "Anyone who disagrees is welcome to do so now."

Silence fell, thick and true, as the room held its' collective breath.

"Cowards," Krowley shouted, when nobody moved. "Frightened of a man in a *dress*. I will show you what a weakling he is! Ambassador Flare Veritax, I challenge your might, your authority, and your honour."

"If you didn't, I'd have been disappointed," Flare responded, kicking the corners of his lips up in a taunting smile. "I'm right here, Krowley. Come and get me."

Krowley's ceremonial spear was flying through the air before Flare had finished speaking. With three swift movements and a single word of power, he created a thin barrier of fire between himself and the projectile. When the spear hit, the shaft and decorations caught instantly alight. The iron tip wedged itself in the flame shield and turned first red, then orange, then searing white as the heat from Flare's magic seeped into every atom. Reaching up with a casual air, he plucked it free and let the shield go.

"Cheap shot, Ambassador," Flare drawled, tossing the superheated metal up and down in one hand. "Would you like this back? It is yours, after all."

Krowley blanched, then clenched his fists, but his answer was stolen by the sudden blare of klaxons.

"Proximity alert," a panicked male voice echoed through the room. "Repeat, proximity alert. Unidentified ships on the radar, coming in ho -"

A howl cut the voice off, followed by a truncated scream, and the comm went silent. Flare barely had a moment to register three ungainly looking battle cruisers out the window, their hulls painted a combination of black and sickly green, before the air around him began to shimmer as if in a heat haze and a creature appeared less than ten steps away. Though it stood on two legs and wore the dirty remnants of a pair of jeans, it was anything but human. Its body was covered in fur and the head closely resembled that of a wolf, though the ears were too large, the snout a little squashed and the eyes a dull, flat amber. The roar that burst from its lips wasn't lupine, either, more the sound one would expect from a slavering monster.

"Warg!" Flare bellowed. Drawing back his arm, he flung the iron spear-tip, watching it spin end over end to thunk into the creature's chest with a searing hiss. The warg howled and fell, but the air still shimmered as more and more of the creatures, each as deadly and unwashed as the first, popped into existence around the chamber. "Everyone out!"

Screams punctuated the announcement, interspersed by the howling of the warg and the swift whistle of claws slicing the air. Flare ducked and spun, conjuring a melon-sized fireball in each palm and releasing them into the faces of the two nearest warg. One crumpled lifelessly to the ground, half of his skull missing, while the other stumbled, smoke rising from singed facial fur. Flare clenched his fists to ignite them and slammed a flaming punch into the creature's gut. The warg bent over with a grunt, and Flare wasted no time incinerating the beast's face with a fireball the size of his head.

"Duck!" Long shards of wood, akin to arrows and yet not, shot towards him and Flare ducked. The beast Verdure had skewered toppled, his body glancing off Flare's so that he was forced to roll aside or be crushed.

Strong hands yanked him upright and Zaire peered into his face. "Okay?"

"Yeah." Flare looked around the rogue to see Pytch and Verdure in a defensive formation in front of Chancellor Kaiora. After a second to ascertain they were uninjured, Flare wove a set of runes in the air, chanted a couplet under his breath and slammed his palm into the floor. Orange lines of fire spread out from the point of impact like rays from the sun, splitting at their furthest point to join in a rough circle. A thin, superheated wall rose from the circle, curving overhead to create a bubble of safety. Locking the spell in place with a single word, Flare rose and turned to Kaiora. "Why is everyone still here?"

The Chancellor's grey skin was pale but her face showed no fear. "The last communique I received through my earpiece was to announce that someone has hacked the Station controls. We're locked in."

"And all weapons, bar the few of us who have ceremonial ones, are outside," Zaire snapped, flashing his twin silver daggers in emphasis. "Stupidest rule ever - they're sitting ducks out there."

"It wouldn't matter anyway," Flare murmured, his eyes roving over what was quickly becoming a one-sided battle. "The warg are killing machines; a few blasters and the odd extra sword won't make that much difference."

"Your faith in our abilities is doing wonders for my confidence, Security Chief." Kaiora flinched as a warg threw itself bodily into Flare's shield, only to recoil with flames licking over matted black fur. "What do we do?"

"Give me a minute," Flare muttered, fingers flexing while his mind whirred. "Where's Naavah?"

"I don't know," Kaiora snapped. "I neglected to have her tagged like a runaway pet."

Flare snorted and turned to Zaire, who watched the battle with a tight jaw. "Can you unlock the doors?"

"If you can get me to a wall panel... maybe." The Ryllin frowned. "It'll take time, though, and I'll probably seize afterwards - maintaining sync with my body is harder after an interface."

"I'll guard your back and I won't let you seize," Flare promised. When Zaire gave a reluctant nod, he turned to Pytch. "Can you take over the bubble spell?"

The Class Two fire sorcerer ran assessing eyes over their shield. "If I reduce the size by a third, I can hold it for five minutes - but after that, I'll be bone dry."

"All right. Here's the plan; I hold the bubble as long as I can, at which point, Pytch will take over. Verdure, since we don't know Naavah's location, stay here and make sure Kaiora is protected at all times. Do not leave her side until the warg are dead, or we're all safe. Got it?" Receiving their affirmatives, he looked to Zaire. "You're with me."

"All right." The Ryllin swallowed heavily, regripping his daggers. "What about the bubble? Won't it -"

"It's keyed to me, so as long as we're in contact, you'll be fine."

Tension stiffened Zaire's shoulders, but he nodded. "Okay."

"Let's go, then." Clapping a hand around Zaire's wrist, Flare dragged him through the bubble.

Warg immediately sprang in their direction and Flare released his lover to fight, the rogue standing at his shoulder as they ducked and spun and carved their way into the enemy. It was the first time he'd seen Zaire in full swing and if he hadn't been fighting for his own life, Flare would've caught his breath at the sight. Backed by the powerhouse strength of his cyborg DNA, Zaire's daggers sliced limbs clean off, his kicks shattered bones and his body moved with liquid grace. Flare felt almost awkward alongside him, watching the rogue's back and dispatching warg with as little magic as possible. His magic tank was already below half full and maintaining the bubble was a steady draw that prevented regeneration, but he wasn't the youngest sorcerer to claim the title of First Flame for nothing - he'd fight to his final breath, and then he'd fight some more.

After minutes that felt like hours, they reached a comm unit set into the wall beside the floor length window. Zaire wasted no time putting his daggers away and spreading one palm across the screen, skin melting and bones turning to wires with astonishing speed. He looked down at Flare as cobalt sparks flared to life in the depths of his indigo eyes and when he spoke, his voice carried a metallic edge. "Kaiora was right; someone's hacked the system."

"How long do you need?"

"To free the Station? Hours. To open the door?" Zaire paused, one eyelid twitching. "Three minutes."

"Do it." Flare turned his back to the Ryllin and set his feet, clenching both fists to ignite them.

Three warg closed in, moving in growling synchronicity as they spread to pin him down. Flare watched them closely, waiting for one to break formation - and blinked as a familiar, silver scrolled dagger buried itself hilt deep in the eye socket of the central warg.

The creature crumpled with a gurgle, Flare yanking the dagger free before the warg hit the ground. Fire spread from his fingers to douse the blade, making it glow white hot - and when he whipped it around his body in a one-handed slash, the dagger cut through the nearest warg as though it were made of silk. The beast clutched at the wound that stretched from groin to chin but it was too late; blood and organs spilled free as the warg slumped to the ground.

A growl echoed behind him, far too close for comfort. Flare gasped out a spell as he spun around, claws raking his shoulder - but the warg who'd been about to rip his face off stopped with a jerk, dull amber eyes wide with surprise. Flare had the barest moment to note two long, blood coated spider's legs protruding from the creature's chest before it was flung aside to reveal Naavah, the Arachnaida's purple fur slicked flat and her torso splattered with blood.

"Sorry I'm late," she said, flicking the remains of an internal organ from the tip of one razor-sharp leg. "Are you well, Security Chief?"

"I'll live." Flare tore the shredded remains of his sleeve away and rolled his injured shoulder, cataloguing the damage as superficial. "Where were you?"

"I saw you protecting the Chancellor so I went searching for a way out, but found none." Naavah took up a position beside him while Zaire worked. "Now our Ambassadors are dying."

Flare cast his gaze over the room, grinding his teeth in frustration. The sorcerers he'd put in place fought bravely alongside the handful of Alliance soldiers who'd been stationed by the door, several nursing nasty injuries and some already dead. Eyrton and Krowley stood guard over a huddled group of Ambassadors half way up the tiered seating, the former with both daggers out and the latter wielding a broken chair leg like a club. Another group cowered in the opposite corner, two of Flare's sorcerers and a lone Illtaxxian cassilisk standing before them. The alien had discarded her clothing, exposing an impressive obsidian exoskeleton and the long blades which grew on the outside of each arm. A scattering of severed warg parts on the ground at her feet stood testament to her skill but where one warg fell, two more stepped in to take their comrade's place and Flare had no doubt that, despite rumours otherwise, no cassilisk's strength would last forever against the mindless bloodlust of the warg.

Further around again, on the far side of the full-length window to Flare and Zaire, Olivie huddled behind a wrecked display cabinet with the tentacled Ambassador Vashkeena from Ykkron Nine. Neither were armed and though the warg had yet to see them, it would only be a matter of time.

Flare clenched his fingers tighter around the dagger in his hand. "Z?"

"They're fighting me. I'm struggling to gain traction," the Ryllin ground out.

"Shit." Blowing out a soft breath, Flare looked up at Naavah's blood-stained face. "Warg don't back down. We have to kill them all."

"We're outnumbered three to one - and that's assuming those Ambassadors with weapons can stop defending their colleagues long enough to assist us." Her voice betrayed no hint of concern, not even when a warg sprang out of the melee to rush them. Naavah slashed with her front legs, raking deep gashes in the warg's chest. It stumbled back with a roar and made to come forward again - only to convulse and drop to the floor. The wounds Naavah had inflicted began to bubble with a caustic green fluid and before Flare had so much as blinked, the warg fell still.

"Great gods of Sorcen," Flare muttered.

Naavah's fur rippled in embarrassment. "I am quite venomous."

"I can see that." Still, if they launched themselves into the fray, it meant leaving Zaire unguarded - and Naavah, for all her undeniable deadliness, was one against a horde. "It still won't be enough."

"We can't just let them die." Zaire's voice, thick with the metal of the space station. "No point trying to open the fucking door if nobody will live to see it."

Flare nodded, and made the call his heart demanded. "Z, disengage."

A metallic groan echoed behind him and a few seconds later, Zaire staggered to his side. Flare shook the flame out of his left hand, sucked the heat from the silver scrolled dagger in his palm, and handed the weapon back. The rogue took it, his fingers slow to curl around the hilt and the tendons standing out in his neck. His skin was frigid to the touch, indigo eyes glittering with both desperation and determination.

"He is unwell," Naavah said quietly, dispatching a pair of warg with two of her venom-tipped spider legs. "He cannot fight."

"Buy me a minute?"

She stepped in front of them, setting all eight of her legs and flattening her fur against her body. "I will try."

"Thanks." Spinning the frozen Ryllin around, Flare shook the flames off his other fist and bunched both hands in Zaire's hair. "Stop fighting yourself. Let go."

"I... can't."

Flare growled, dragging the other male's stiff body closer. "You will *not* seize up on me. The moment you do, Eyrton's dead."

"It's the nanos." Zaire gasped for air, each word more difficult than the last. "I can't... I'm not... They aren't..."

"They are *you*," Flare snapped. "This is your body now, Z. You're fused into one singular entity."

Tears sheened the rogue's eyes and he tried desperately to shake his head, his skin beginning to turn a glacial blue. "No."

"Yes," Flare growled, and kissed him. It wasn't a nice kiss - it was filled with fury, desperation, a warrior's killer instinct, and every ounce of heat and screaming life that Flare could muster, along with a good dose of fire magic he couldn't afford to lose.

Seconds they didn't have crept by, but one body part at a time, the rogue responded, until at last he shoved Flare away. "Fuck you."

"Later." Flare grinned, then turned to Naavah, who was casually tossing aside her fifth warg carcass. "Ready?"

Rather than move, the Arachnaida swept an assessing glance over them both. "Why did you do that? He is not your mate, and you are not his."

"Just because we're not in this forever doesn't mean we want to watch the other one die," Zaire growled, resettling his daggers in his fists. "Haven't you ever kissed someone just to stop the empty howling inside of you?"

Naavah blinked. "I've never kissed anyone at all."

"It's never too late to start." Flare chuckled in spite of the situation, lifting his robes to step over the pile of warg corpses at their feet. "Come on, let's see if we can save some lives before the warg steal our own."

They fought, and it was dirty and bloody and horrific - and Flare hadn't felt so gloriously alive in months. He rationed out what little was left of his magic and made it count, while on either side of him, Zaire and Naavah stabbed and sliced and tore into their enemy. The bubble he maintained around Kaiora and his friends flickered and Flare let it go, knowing Pytch would weave a new spell and hold it for as long as he could. It wouldn't be enough, but they'd fight until the very last moment. Every warg they took down was one less to hunt his sister, one less to spread through the universe in an unstoppable tide.

"What's that?" Zaire's voice, heavy with strain, spoke almost directly in Flare's ear. He ducked a swiping claw, shot a thin jet of flame straight up into the base of the warg's chin, kicked the body aside and turned.

The air in the centre of the room had begun to shimmer as if in a heat haze.

"Fuck." Flare drew the tatters of his magic to him, sorting through spells in his head. "It's a teleporter displacement field."

Zaire swore, even as he rammed his dagger into the eye of a warg and dodged the snapping teeth of another. "More of them? Eyrton's barely hanging on. We're not going to make it."

"Firius' balls we aren't," Flare growled. "You give up on me now and I swear I will kill you in the afterlife."

The warg shuffled backwards as four figures shimmered into solidity in their midst. The first was absurdly tall and wore a black monk's robe complete with drawn-up hood. Beside the robed figure stood a woman with skin so blindingly hot pink it would've been difficult to look at her, were it not for the black combat pants and tank she wore to tone the colour down. Her legs ended in cloven hooves instead of feet, and two gnarled black horns emerged from her tight white curls. On the female's other side stood a burly male of middling height, his features elegant, his skin a soft shade of lavender and his short, tumbled hair a deep shade of violet which matched his eyes. In front of the three unknown warriors stood a stocky, grey-skinned woman with four arms, two of which were set on her hips while the other two clutched the biggest plasma rifle Flare had ever seen. Sharp blue eyes were framed by unfairly long lashes, high cheekbones accentuated by the bone frill that fanned out from the top of her skull, topped with an array of small horns as though it were a crown. The slits of her nostrils flared wide as she took in the scene and then, without batting so much as an eyelash, fired the plasma rifle into the nearest warg at point blank range.

The creature fell with a wet plopping sound, and the woman met Flare's eyes over the smoking corpse. "Hello, Flare. Sorry we're late."

"Burke." His voice croaked with relief and he couldn't help but grin. "Welcome to the party."

She inclined her head and clicked her tongue against the roof of her mouth. "Kill them all."

The room erupted as Burke's companions drew a variety of weapons from about their bodies and descended on the warg with breathtaking skill. Burke let loose with her rifle over and over, blasting through the howling beasts with reckless abandon. Flare corralled his regenerating magic and went to meet her, drawing level with the Curator of Corrin's Run as a bright explosion lit the window behind him.

Howls went up room-wide as one of the warg's three battle cruisers exploded, debris spiralling outward to pepper the sides of Galactic Station with devastating force. The floor lurched and Flare staggered, managing to keep his feet as he took in the three new ships outside, each one a mish-mash of parts and covered in a spray of virulent yellow alien characters. He looked back at Burke and grinned. "Have I told you I love you lately?"

"If only I believed it," she laughed, taking a nearby warg's head off with her rifle. "Looks like your station's shields are down."

Flare nodded, watching as the two remaining warg ships immediately began trading weapons fire with the vessels from Corrin's Run. "I hope you've got good people out there."

"Rito can handle it." Burke waved one of her free hands, her eyes tracking yet another target, and another, as she let loose with her plasma rifle over and over again. "I really like this rifle."

"It suits you," Flare agreed, slapping the heels of his palms together and shouting a word of power. Flames spiralled from his joined hands, blasting a warg sneaking up behind Zaire. The creature shrieked and stumbled sideways, setting two of his comrades alight. With a quickly traced rune and another few swift words, Flare encouraged the flames to spread, engulfing the three warg until they dropped to writhe on the floor. He caught Zaire's wide-eyed look and shrugged. "You're welcome."

A shout cut through the noise and Flare spun around to see first one, then another warg flicker and disappear. The teleports picked up speed and though he moved to try and catch the stragglers, within moments the invading creatures vanished and the room was oppressively still.

"They're gone!" Someone cried, and a ragged cheer erupted from the cowering groups of Ambassadors.

"Wait," Flare held up a hand for silence. "Something's not right."

In answer to his fears, the smaller of the two warg ships took shelter behind it's larger compatriot, exterior laser cannons swivelling to point at Galactic Station.

"They're going to blow us to pieces," Kaiora shouted. Flare looked over to see the Chancellor racing in his direction, Verdure and a pale faced Pytch by her side. "Engine room confirms the station's shields and engines are disabled. We're completely vulnerable."

"Sorcerers, to the window!" Flare shook the flames from his hands as he sprinted for the enormous sheet of plexiglass. Running feet echoed behind him and in moments, his pitifully small band of sorcerers had spread out in a line. "We hold this line, or we die trying. Clear?"

"Yes, First Flame," Pytch yelled, and was quickly echoed by the others.

"Earth sorcerers, Gangrin's Amalgam, Level Four." Flare watched as his trio of earth sorcerers began to move in unison, tracing runes and chanting the ritual words aloud. As the first volley of laser fire tore out of the warg battle cruiser, a shield of earth and stone took shape in the dark void of space outside the window. It took the laser fire with barely a jerk and though chips of rock shot free, they swiftly windmilled back into the construct as it grew.

"It's not going to be big enough," Zaire murmured, his hands landing on Flare's hips as he used his greater height to peer over one shoulder.

Flare leant into the other male's strength for a fraction of a moment. "Water sorcerers, Hathaya's Skin, Level Two."

More movement, this time to his right, as the four water sorcerers dipped and flowed and sang. Water began to spread across the earthen shield, turning to ice as it appeared. Laser fire plowed into the magical construct but as with the flying rock debris, the ice spiralled back in on itself, reinforcing what the earth sorcerers created and spreading the shield wider still, a thick barrier of ice whose magical reinforcement made it as strong as the rock.

"Status report," Flare demanded.

"Gangrin's Amalgam, four minutes," one of the earth sorcerers replied.

The higher class water sorcerer nodded with grim determination. "Hathaya's Skin, three and a half minutes."

"Dig deep," Flare commanded. "Give me five minutes, both of you."

"Yes, First Flame." Their voices were weary, but beneath that was a core of steely determination.

"Fire Sorcerers, front. Firian Cannon, Level One. Nature sorcerers, front. Lordlin's Pike, Level One. On my mark." Taking his own orders, Flare raised both hands and began tracing runes in the air, aware of Pytch and Verdure doing the same on either side. They chanted aloud, but as a Class One sorcerer, Flare had no need to say the entire spell, instead whispering a single word as he drew on the essence of the incantation. Spreading his fingers against the plexiglass, he drew a deep breath. "Aim for the cannons. Mark."

Maintaining fire in the vacuum of space required huge amounts of energy, but his people didn't falter. Flare's fireball streaked from the side of the Station alongside two others, followed by two long, sharp spears of wood large enough to batter down a door. Guided by their creators, the projectiles streamed up and over the shield, avoiding the punishing laser fire to slam into the side of the warg ship.

"Burke!" Flare called. "Give me some good news."

She was silent for a moment. "Rito says you've taken out a third of their weapon arrays."

He nodded. "Again, on my mark."

"Yes, First Flame."

Flare's hands wove and dipped once again, shadowed by his fellows. "Mark."

The second volley shot out, one of the fireballs significantly smaller than the rest. It wobbled through space and in a matter of moments, the laser fire coming from the warg ship changed trajectory to slam into it. A sorceress to Flare's right crumpled with a whimper, eyes closed and face pale.

Olivie rushed forward, placing stout fingers against her throat. "She's alive. Unconscious."

"Rito reports weapon arrays down to sixty percent," Burke said.

Verdure tugged on Flare's sleeve. "I've only got one more in me."

"Me too," Pytch murmured.

Flare grunted. "Shield status?"

"Two minutes," one of the earth sorcerers replied. As he spoke, a water sorcerer moaned and collapsed, his companions stiffening as they scrambled to take the strain of the magic.

"Thirty seconds," one of the remaining water sorcerers croaked.

"Damn. Pytch, with me." Flare spun from the window and strode to the nearest warg corpse. "Z, I need as many personal teleportation units as you can carry."

The rogue moved at once to comply, Naavah at his side. By the time Flare crouched beside the warg's body, his fingers flashing over the teleporter with practised ease, he had a pile of six devices at his feet. "Attach them to the body. Pytch, pick another warg and do as I do. Someone get this man some more teleporters."

Burke's three companions sprang into action, the lavender skinned male dragging a second warg to Flare's side while the other two began gathering devices from the remaining bodies.

"What are we doing?" Pytch asked as Flare reached over and began to program the main unit on the second corpse. Behind him, the water sorcerers began to sigh and slump, the change to the tone of the laser fire providing proof that the ice shield had failed.

"One minute," the earth sorcerer warned.

"Acknowledged." Flare wove his fingers in the air above his warg body. "Pytch, build Cochrane's Grenade, highest level you can. Infuse it into the teleporter with a five second timer but don't activate until I say so."

"I can't infuse," Pytch gasped, fingers already moving as he struggled to comply. "I never perfected the skill."

"You want to die?" Flare demanded. As the other male shook his head, he sank his spell into the main teleporter and moved to the next, which Zaire had shoved into the waistband of the dead warg's shorts. "Then do it."

"I -"

"Dammit, Pytch!" Flare finished the second and moved onto the third. "Repeat the words after me and copy my movements, or you're going to miss your mother's birthday in a couple weeks."

The fire sorcerer's breath whooshed out in a rush, but his trembling voice began to chant. Relief flooded Flare's system as the first spell sank into the plasteel and stayed put. He finished arming his own devices, tucking them safely into the dead warg's clothing, then moved to help Pytch with his final unit.

"Ten seconds," the earth sorcerer called.

"Not long now," Flare promised, flicking both the main teleporters on. A red light blinked once, twice, and then turned green. "Pytch, release your timers."

"Done."

Flare smacked his palms down on the button in the centre of each device. The warg bodies shimmered, and a moment later, disappeared. No sooner had they vanished than two of the earth sorcerers collapsed, their breath coming in gasps and their shield fracturing.

"First Flame!" The remaining sorcerer cried, his face white with strain. "I can't hold it!"

"Yes, you can. Just a few more seconds." Flare gained his feet, eyes trained on the window, counting down in his head. Exactly five seconds after he'd released the timer spells, fire sprouted from the side of the warg battle cruiser and it listed to one side. The laser fire stuttered, then cut out, followed closely by the ship's running lights. "Burke?"

"Rito reports the cruiser is dead in space," Burke announced, "and my people have almost breached the shields of the final ship. It's over."

A ragged cheer went up from the surviving Ambassadors but the sound cut short as the final earth sorcerer slumped into unconsciousness, his earth shield disintegrating into so much dust. Pushing aside the desire to join his comrades for a nap, Flare instead began dragging them away from the windows. "Anyone with medical know-how, front and centre!"

Several Ambassadors slipped from behind their protectors to comply. Naavah and Zaire began to arrange the sorcerers against one wall, while Burke's three companions helped Flare gather anyone else who needed medical attention.

The female with pink skin stopped Flare on her second trip, her smile luminous as she held out one hand. "Kella, Guardian to the Weaver."

"Flare, Fire Elder of - *what* did you say?" Flare's mouth dropped open even as he instinctively returned her forearm grip.

Kella grinned. "Yeah, you heard correctly. Even if Burke hadn't told me who you were, I'd have picked you as Arcana's brother in a flash. Damn, but she wasn't wrong about you."

"You've seen Arcana?" Just like that, his weariness dropped away. "When? Where?"

"Few months ago." Kella waved a vague hand. "She and Fenris and that crazy deerken Caelum busted us out of a bad situation with one of Taelon's lackeys, ditched us with Burke and then flew off into the sunset." She pointed at the figure in the monk's robe. "That's Llane." Her finger moved to the one with lavender skin. "And Goliath. They're Guardians, too."

"When we're done here, we need to talk," Flare commanded.

Kella laughed, the sound sweet and tinkling. "You're on."

"Incoming!" Burke's yell cut through the hubbub of conversation.

Flare shoved past Kella in time to see the final warg cruiser explode in a ball of fiery wrath, spraying enormous pieces of wreckage into space. The Corrin's Run ships absorbed the impact with their shields, but Galactic Station had no such luxury.

"Get away from the window!" Flare shouted. "Brace for impact!"

People moved in a rush to comply, scrambling backwards as fast as they could go. A large piece of plasteel slammed into the station and the floor tilted, throwing Flare to his knees. His eyes widened as a familiar portly figure slipped and fell, rolling towards the window even as part of the warg cruiser's bridge came hurtling on an intercept.

"Olivie," Flare cried, scrambling to his feet. "Get out of there!"

The administrative aide's face filled with panic as he scrabbled at the floor, the smooth surface so slick with blood and fluids that it was impossible to gain purchase. Trusting to the steep incline to give him speed, Flare threw himself across the room. He heard Zaire shout behind him, but his one and only thought was to get to Olivie before the inevitable collision. His arms wrapped around the portly man's waist and they slammed into the window together, the impact knocking the breath from Flare's lungs.

His lips were already moving, his body curling protectively over Olivie's as he yanked on his magic - now well over half full, thanks to the break in combat. The gargantuan chunk of twisted plasteel bore down on them with impossible speed, and though he knew he was going to be too slow, Flare covered Olivie's eyes with his free hand, tucked the male's head into the shelter of his chest, and put every ounce of his strength into the spell.

Whether or not the protective bubble worked, he couldn't say, because the melted remains of the warg's ship slammed into the window behind him and everything went black.

THIRTY-ONE
ZAIRE

ZAIRE REXALLIS DUGRONDE, FOURTH SON OF NOBLEHOUSE DUGRONDE, twice anointed silver scrolled rogue, carrier of the prototype bio-mech virus code named FauxLife and Galactic Ambassador for Rylle, stood in front of his uncle's state of the art medtank and fumed.

"You know, death staring the display isn't going to change what it says, cousin." Eyrton's slap on his back sounded like skin on wet plascrete, and Zaire didn't need to look up to notice his cousin's wince.

"He's still not awake. Four days, and he's still not awake."

"At least he's alive." Eyrton looked up at the man floating in the viscous sapphire fluid and shuddered. "How anyone could survive having the side of their head shorn off, only the Oracle knows."

Zaire grunted. Not only had Flare survived having a large section of his skull, including one ear, completely amputated, he'd powered a fire shield large enough to protect Olivie Harthax and seal the hole in the side of the space station while he was at it. All while being unconscious, his life's blood seeping onto the floor and his brain glistening in the mocking light of the flames which seemed to run in his very blood.

Still, Flare *would* have died if Zaire hadn't gone against everything he'd ever been told by his uncle and sliced open his own veins, dripping his mech-infected blood into the gaping wound in the side of the sorcerer's head while Eyrton hid them from prying eyes. Nobody had stopped Zaire when, the council chamber doors opening as if by magic, he'd scooped up his lover's body and raced for the medical bay, calling the Sorcen healers

"

even as he stripped what remained of Flare's robes off and tossed him in the medtank with desperate abandon. Without the medtank - kept on hand for Zaire, should he need it - the virus wouldn't have the right environment to properly fuse with Flare's cells and heal him. As it was, without the presence of Zaire's uncle Thorpe DuGronde, the Ryllin scientist who'd created the virus, all they could do was hope.

That, and summon the man to Galactic Station post-haste.

As though hearing his thoughts, Eyrton's fingers tightened on Zaire's shoulder. "He'll be here soon. Less than an hour now."

Zaire said nothing. There was, after all, nothing to say; Flare's wounds had healed and his ear had regrown within the first twenty-four hours and the Sorcen healers had pronounced him at full health shortly thereafter. It was the sorcerer's inability to regain consciousness that was the problem - the bio-mech virus had been created and calibrated specifically for Zaire and his Ryllin biology. Who knew if Flare's Sorcen insides would handle it the same? Who knew if the catastrophic injury had damaged his brain so severely that, no matter the virus' efforts, the man would never wake?

After standing by his side for another twenty minutes, Eyrton heaved a long sigh and left. Zaire stared into the deep, dark blue gel, tracing the limp male form within as he blinked tears from his eyes. "Fuck you, Flare."

How had the sorcerer gotten under his skin? Both a kaleidoscope of shattered glass, neither were healthy enough to be in a relationship with the other - yet he couldn't deny that since the moment Flare had plunked down beside him at that damned banquet, the howling demons inside Zaire had lifted their noses in interest. Scenting another who walked the fine line of darkness, fractures buried deep and light buried even deeper, his demons had wrenched and tugged at the leash, demanding to be acknowledged by one of their own kind; and he, fool that he was, had surrendered entirely to their need. Standing alone in front of the medtank, Zaire had nothing left to distract him from the fact that Flare, with his body, his burning spirit and that oracle-blessed voice that did things to his insides, had pulled Zaire back from the razor's edge upon which he'd been teetering and challenged him to live.

What a cosmic asshole.

The door swished open again and a moment later, the grey-skinned female from Corrin's Run appeared by his side. Ignoring him completely, she bent over the monitor displaying Flare's vitals, took a metal flask from her belt, uncapped it and took a long swig. When she was done, she slapped the flask into Zaire's hand and raised her face to the tank.

"Repairs on the station are nearly complete," she said in her gravelly voice. "Alongside those Guardians - who, by the way, are more useful than I'll ever let on - your sorcerers and the mechanics shared between the two crews, the shields will be up and running in the next forty-eight hours. Kaiora doesn't trust me, but she's signed a treaty between Corrin's Run and the Galactic Alliance and we're officially in this together. You did it, Flare. We're hunting the warg."

The woman looked down at her feet for a moment, the gauze wrappings dangling from her bone frill drifting in the faint breeze from the air conditioning. When she looked up, she bared her teeth.

"We're not doing this without you, though. I hope you know that. You will wake up, and you will fight this fight. I did not fly halfway across the galaxy to watch you die, and I sure as all the hells am not going to be the one who tells Arcana we vented your body out the hatch with full military honours." Taking a steadying breath, she jabbed a finger in the tank's direction. "I don't care what you got hit with, soldier, this isn't the time to rest. You wake up, you get up, and you help me grind Taelon's bones to dust. Got it?"

Silence. The monitor didn't change, and Flare's body didn't so much as twitch. The woman sighed, then turned away, resettling the enormous plasma rifle she kept permanently strapped to her back. Her footsteps crossed to the door, which swished open.

"Keep the flask, Zaire. I'll come back to refill it for you tomorrow."

"I don't need it."

She snorted. "Don't drink from it, then; but just so you know, the firewhiskey inside is a batch Flare made himself when I last saw him."

Zaire remained motionless as the door swished shut and her footsteps receded. A minute later, the datapad on the desk in front of him pinged, announcing his uncle's arrival. Before long, they'd know if Flare was going to wake - or worse, if Zaire had killed him with the blood he'd so desperately dripped onto the surface of his brain.

"I hate you, Flare." Unscrewing the flask, Zaire took a long swig and then barked a bitter laugh. "But not as much as I hate myself."

~ THE END ~

Thanks for reading!

Can't wait for the next instalment?

Keep up to date with all the latest shenanigans at:

www.sliceofsammy.com

ACKNOWLEDGMENTS

For Flare, the casual cameo with a charming smile and a sharp tongue who took over my heart and demanded so much more.

IF YOU LOVED THIS ONE...

Please leave a review!

Reviews really help authors; it directs our books into the right kind of
hands, which in turn allows me to keep writing more books for you to
enjoy.

So, if you had a blast reading this story, I'd be ever so grateful if you left a
review wherever you can.

Thank you!
♥

ALSO BY SAMANTHA STORMFURY

Prince of Storms. Lady of Shadows.

God of Chaos.

Bound in eternal servitude to the Atlantean royal family, dark fairy Liria Atlannon spends her days bending to the whims of her mistress. When Atlantis' youngest Princess announces her betrothal to the great Pharaoh Taos of Egypt, Liria has no choice but to follow her Princess across the sea to a kingdom - and a life - unlike anything she has known before.

As Commander of the Pharoah's honour guard, it is Prince Raiden Horushood's duty to defend his brother at all costs. He's never met a foe he couldn't conquer - until Set the Anarchist, god of war and chaos, attempts to steal the Pharaoh's fiancee from her own welcome banquet. While Raiden rages helplessly in the thrall of Set's magic, Liria, the softly spoken handmaiden who spends most of her time staring at the floor, not only turns Set away but injures him in the process.

With the threat of an unpredictable god hanging overhead, Raiden begs Liria to join the Pharoah's honour guard. Though Liria aches to become part of something greater, self preservation dictates she stay away from the vital, strong, and irritatingly handsome Prince Raiden. For if the warrior angel gets too close, he'll discover that the biggest threat to Merged Egypt is not Set at all – it is Liria Atlannon, damned by the magic which shackles her soul, steals her free will and shapes her actions… until all that remains is a shadow.

———

Read on for a sneak preview of Chapter One!

HEARTH AND HOME

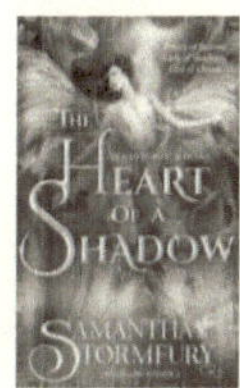

Liria Atlannon looked around at the cool marble pillars of Princess Ione's quarters and knew she wouldn't miss it for even a moment. There was something to be said for the elegance of gold-shot marble which glowed in the light of the noonday sun, and perhaps even something to be said for the open, breezy architecture and gauzy drapes in Atlantean aqua - but for her, the paradise island of Atlantis had only ever been a prison.

Moving quietly to the edge of the balcony, Liria set delicate hands on the railing and cast her gaze out over the cheery city which glittered in the sun, shimmering marble and deep gold sandstone broken up by swathes of cloth in all the shades of the ocean. Beyond that, the azure sea lapped lazily at a pristine shore of pale sand that sparkled with hints of silver silica. A pair of Atlantean Dreadnaughts bobbed offshore, one with her steel decks unfurled like a silvered ocean lily, and the other curled in tight upon itself in preparation for an underwater journey.

"Beautiful, and yet I don't see that I will miss it."

Liria lowered her head as the Princess Ione came up beside her, lest the other woman see the way her face set into an involuntary grimace. The motion shifted her focus to her fingers, gripping tight to the balcony rail. Her skin had begun to turn the mottled blue-grey of a storm-tossed sky, her emotions slipping their leash and causing the truth of her nature to creep through. Drawing deep of the salt-laden air, Liria forced her face into smooth lines and exerted just enough power to shift her skin back to the blemish-free cream her mistress preferred.

"You won't miss it?" she asked, her voice carefully modulated to be soft and submissive. "Surely Atlantis is in your bones, your highness."

Princess Ione tossed her head. She was beautiful - exquisite, even, with long black hair that hung in perfect curls midway down her back, softly tanned skin and deep, dark blue eyes - yet there was a glitter in her gaze, an edge to her cultured smile that spoke of bitter hunger.

"No," Ione said, her lip curling. "I am meant for greater things than to be the fifth child of the ruling family of Atlantis. I am meant to be a queen."

"And so you will be," Liria answered, bowing slightly from the waist. "Your marriage to the Pharaoh of Egypt will ensure such."

An arranged marriage sounded like the worst kind of torture to Liria, but Princess Ione had been the driving force behind the entire affair. In fact, Liria's eavesdropping around the palace had her safe in the certainty that the King and Queen of Atlantis had only acquiesced to keep Ione happy; no-one had actually expected Pharaoh Taos to accept.

"Yes. Soon, I will be Queen of Egypt," Ione breathed, spreading her arms wide and tipping her head back to stare at the sky. "Soon, I will witness the technological marvel of Egypt's great airships, and view their crystal-topped pyramids with my own eyes. I shall rule over the country which stands at the forefront of science and magic, sip wine with the most powerful of gods and be bathed in the adoring praise of my subjects – while Atlantis will become but a faded memory, a pale imitation to be laughed at and forgotten." The Princess clasped her hands at the base of her throat, gleaming midnight eyes locking on Liria's face. "Are you ready, my shadow, to follow me on this path to greatness?"

It wasn't like she had any other choice, but Liria knew better than to say such things aloud. Instead, she bowed deeply, locking her gaze on the embroidered hem of Ione's gown. "Of course, your highness."

Princess Ione ran her slender fingers across the shimmering surface of Liria's wings, the sensation akin to hot knives slashing her wide open. Her breath caught in her throat, the urge to protest becoming the very thing that ensured her silence as the magical chains which bound her to her mistress snapped into full effect.

"Such flawless mystery in you, Liria. The subtlety of twilight, of hidden, magical things. You are well suited to accompany a jewel such as I." Another caress of Ione's fingers, her movements flicking away the long layers of trailing gauze that served to shield Liria's wings from view. "I wonder if Pharaoh Taos' wings are as magnificent as yours?"

"He's of the blood of Horus, your highness, and thus carries the wings of the falcon - whereas I am but a lowly fairy. I'm sure my wings are as nothing in comparison to the strong, feathered pinions of the angels."

"Hmmm. I suppose we shall see, soon enough." Ione tapped Liria's spine, silent permission for her to straighten. "I've heard the angels can even carry passengers, should the need arise."

So had Liria, but she didn't say as such, lest the Princess ask where she'd come across the knowledge. Instead, she adjusted the many layers of gauze which hung from her shoulders so that they once more protected her wings from casual view and said, "Perhaps, once you are wed, you can convince the Pharaoh to take you flying."

"Oh, yes." Ione clasped her hands to her full breasts, dark blue eyes shining. She blinked a few moments later, a crease forming between her brows. "And you will follow us, my shadow, will you not?"

Liria inclined her head again, glad of the way her hair swung forward to hide her face. "Such is my duty, your highness."

Want to find out what happens next?

Grab your copy here:

https://sliceofsammy.com

LOVE A FREE BOOK?

LEARN TO LET GO... OR BURN.

Dating Noah Acheson has always been gentle, predictable and above all, safe – but when the softly spoken foxkin breaks the rules of their carefully crafted relationship, Deanna cuts him off, retreating to her private sanctuary deep in the Australian bush.

Stinging from Deanna's rejection, Noah returns from a brief stint fighting fires in New South Wales to face an infinitely more vicious fire front in Victoria. Though his broken heart still very much belongs to Deanna Schellponte, he's determined not to chase her – until the wind changes, turning the fires towards pack land, and Deanna is reported missing.

With fire raging all around, Noah races into the bush to find the wolfkin he loves. To survive, Deanna and Noah must confront not only the fury of Mother Nature… but the ghost whose memory tore them apart.

Get your FREE copy here:

https://sliceofsammy.com/contact

OTHER TALES BY SAMANTHA STORMFURY

Sorcery and Stardust

A sweeping science fiction series following the adventures of Arcana, Fenris, Caelum and Flare as they work to save time and space from the bestial warg and their vicious leader.

The Kin Chronicles

A paranormal romance series featuring the Kin, a race of people who can shift into animals and live alongside humanity in an alternate contemporary reality.

The Merged Worlds

A fantasy and paranormal romance series that starts in a time before our written history, when gods roamed the Earth, technology was crazily advanced and humanity shared their space with angels, vampires, fairies and a host of other magical creatures.

A Perfectly Paranormal Anthologies

A collection of paranormal romance anthologies in conjunction with several other wonderful authors.

To find out more about any of these, visit my website:

www.sliceofsammy.com

WANT TO KEEP IN TOUCH?

I love to hear from, and hang out with, like minded people (yes, that's you!) and expand my tribe. Whilst I'm most active in my newsletter, you can also find me in other places from time to time! If you've already joined my mailing list and are still looking for more, then check out the following:

BLOG - www.sliceofsammy.com/blog

INSTAGRAM - @sliceofsammy

Or send me an email at -

samwrites@sliceofsammy.com

I love hearing from readers and authors alike!

See you there ^_^

Love,
    Sammy
    XOXO

ABOUT THE AUTHOR

Hi, I'm Sam!

I've been writing my whole life, scribbling stories on anything close to hand – from the shopping list to napkins to post-it notes.

I grew up reading fantasy of the likes of Anne McCaffrey, Terry Pratchett, and their peers. I'm also a lifelong vampire fan, along with all things spooky. In my late teens I was introduced to paranormal romance and discovered a whole new layer of storytelling with a bit of a spicy edge! Taking what I learnt from all of the above, I devoted myself to creating full-bodied characters, meaty plots, epic adventure, and a little bit of naughty sauce on the side.

I completed a Diploma of Professional Writing and Editing after high school and spent the next several years in my writing cave, working on a novel that is now in a drawer somewhere, followed by a couple of others who shared the same fate. (What can I say? I'm a recovering perfectionist.)

I came close to debuting my novel career in 2009, then ended up pregnant and took some time off to have kids. I debuted for real in 2019 with *Sorcery and Stardust* and won ARRA's Favourite Debut Romance Author for 2019, which was extremely cool!

I write speculative fiction that is a fusion of multiple sub-genres and therefore doesn't fit particularly well into any of them, but after many years and a lot of angst, I'm okay with that. I love all my characters and their stories for different reasons, but have a soft spot for an excellent villain and a tortured protagonist.

I had an attack of the Real Life in the early 2020s which resulted in a long hiatus, followed by a gradual rebuild into the Samantha Stormfury you know today. I learnt that sometimes, there is nothing you can do but hold on, even if it feels like there's nothing left to hold onto - and in doing so, I had a strength I never realised I was capable of.

I believe in unicorns, dragons, and true love. I'm passionate about great writing, interesting characters, chai tea - and, until the stars burn out of the sky, holding on for happily ever afters.